ALSO BY DAWN TURNER

Three Girls from Bronzeville

An Eighth of August

Only Twice I've Wished for Heaven

MAJESTIC HILLS

a novel

BY

DAWN TURNER

SCRIBNER
New York Amsterdam/Antwerp London
Toronto Sydney/Melbourne New Delhi

Scribner
An Imprint of Simon & Schuster, LLC
1230 Avenue of the Americas
New York, NY 10020

First Scribner hardcover edition August 2026

Interior design by Julia Jacintho

Manufactured in the United States of America

10 9 8 7 6 5 4 3 2 1

Library of Congress Control Number: Number has been applied for.

ISBN 978-1-6680-4931-0
ISBN 978-1-6680-4933-4 (ebook)

for my mom

"THE PLACE IN WHICH I'LL FIT WILL NOT EXIST UNTIL I MAKE IT."

James Baldwin

PROLOGUE

new pointe, illinois

forty miles southeast of chicago

just before dawn

They stand nearly naked in their U-shaped driveway. A veil of dust covers her dark skin, making her lithe frame shimmer. Her hair is, as her aunt once put it, so short you could smell her brains. Now, a crown of foliage and insulation fluff sits atop her head. She is dressed in nothing but her husband's oversize Morehouse T-shirt. He is what old folks used to call a "redbone": light caramel coloring and green eyes. Blood oozes from a gash over his right brow and drips onto his undershirt. An awful bruise, the kind that leaves a stain even when healed, is forming on his right shoulder. He removes his glasses and wipes them on his boxers. When he looks at his watch, praying for a weather or emergency alert, he sees only that the screen has shattered. The air feels charged, suffused with electric particles that make the hair on their arms stand up straight. And yet humidity reigns. Behind them is their once-grand house. Amid the debris is their once-shiny bronze plate inscribed *THE BLAQUES*. Strobes of lightning illuminate their front yard, now filled with their neighbors' belongings: a white beekeepers jumpsuit swings from a tree branch; a dressmaker's dummy lies supine in a drainage ditch; the splintered remains of a red canoe sit wedged between two trees; a rifle sprouts from the ground, its barrel pointing up to God. She recalls water sloshing in the toilet, just minutes before. He remembers a high-pitched hum, like from a tuning fork. Now, sirens blare in the distance. When an explosion shakes the ground, they duck. Hot air swooshes around them, and their bare feet sink into the softened earth. They breathe in a tangy, ferrous smell. One by one, towering trees begin to topple and jackknife, half drowned in mist.

He reaches for her hand.

She reaches for his.

They begin to run.

CHAPTER ONE

a year ago

The morning was bitter cold as Langdon waited on a South Side Metro train platform, transfixed by an electronic advertisement. He examined the screen the way one might study a painting in an art gallery, losing himself in its composition, its depth of colors. This, though, was only a real estate ad—pixels, not possibilities. Josephine had already made it perfectly clear that she was not leaving the city. Langdon wiped snow off the screen. He wasn't sure why he found the image of this suburban subdivision—with its stately homes and sprawling wooded lots—so arresting. For a while, he'd been scouring real estate listings and squirreling away printouts in his hospital locker, the stacks mounting like a looming promise. Now, as he basked in the glow of the screen, he wondered if he was merely reacting to a slew of dispiriting nights in the emergency department. And an insatiable need to end a shift stretched out on a blanket in his very own backyard, where he could leave the world behind. A month ago, he'd turned thirty-four, and he felt both anchored and adrift.

As the 5:45 a.m. train pulled in, Langdon snatched a trifold brochure from an adjacent kiosk and boarded. He sat near the doorway, leaning his head against the window. His glasses fogging, he stared at the embossed Harmony Realty business card stapled to the brochure.

The commute north to Roosevelt Road was brief, as was the walk to the glass-encased tower where he and Josephine lived on the twentieth floor. He'd moved into her condo when they married four years ago. Though it was one of the more modest units, it was her pride and joy. Inside, he hooked his keys by the door and flung his book bag on the bench. As he entered their bedroom, he heard a telltale buzzing emanating from the bathroom. He chuckled and tapped on the door.

"Blaque, you doing what I think you're doing?" His T-shirt and briefs, which Josephine had slept in, lay in a jumble on the floor. As he always did, he tossed them into the hamper.

"Maybe . . ." she sang.

He opened the door. Through the steam, he saw his naked wife standing in front of the toilet, straddling it, using his beard trimmer. Coiled wisps of hair, as fine as pencil shavings, dotted the water. She hit the Off button.

"I use that on my face," he said, stroking the bushy hair on his chin. "And my head."

"You're pretty bald, baby," she said. "And your face is familiar with this terrain."

He walked up behind her and kissed the nape of her teeny-weeny Afro. Her ass was slightly darker than the rest of her body, her legs so long that when he drove their car after she used it, he had to adjust the seat forward a notch. Her height was in her legs, his in his torso.

Josephine swung around to face him, and they held each other's gaze before they held each other, his palms pressing against her spine, her cheek brushing against his beard.

"Just floating this . . ." He leaned back, looking at her sheepishly.

"No, not this again." She groaned but drew him closer.

"Hear me out, Josey. What do you think about moving to the country and not another part of the city or the burbs? Exurbia." He waved his hand in front of him like a pitchman and caught his reflection in the mirror.

"*Ex-who-bia?*" She looked indignant. "When? Seventy years from now when I'm a hundred and eight and you're a hundred and four?"

Their four-year age difference had bothered her early on, but he'd never minded.

He'd broached the topic of leaving the city a few times. And now, as he had before, he stressed that leaving didn't mean fleeing. There was a distinction. He was neither running away from the city nor jonesing for the perfect suburban zip code. He was under no delusion that perfection existed.

"It's called Majestic Hills." He hurried to his coat and returned with the slick advertisement. As he gestured with it, a chill fanned from its pages. "Wooded lots, about three acres each, some narrow, like bowling lanes. It's in New Pointe, population fifty-five hundred. About forty miles southeast of us."

He heard himself proselytizing, as if the brochure had been seared into his memory, absorbed in his sinew.

"There's even a cute little clubhouse that sits on a pond shaped like a kidney."

Josephine mimed throwing up as she slipped into her underwear. "Lang, I thought we'd settled this. What's going on?"

"I love this city, but I'm just tired of the noise." He hesitated. "The sirens all day and night—at work, at home. The roar of motorcycles on Lake Shore Drive. City workers jackhammering. Car alarms."

Tired wasn't the half of it. "Fed up," "exasperated," and "desperate" rang truer. But he didn't want to worry her, because she worried about everything.

Instead, he reminded her how she'd marveled at his large childhood Evanston home, how she'd swooned over the backyard that once held a doghouse; the massive oak that once held a hideout; the perfectly imperfect place that, because of his younger brother's death, had absorbed more than its share of heartache. She'd never lived in a house. She'd grown up in a rented two-flat and lived in apartments since.

"I totally understand," she replied. "The building sent out an email recently about caulking windows to help with the noise. I'll get some quotes. Easy-peasy."

His shoulders slumped. She rested her hands on them.

"We can't move. Wouldn't you miss our friends and family? The lakefront. The fireworks at Navy Pier. Not to mention Millennium Park, the planetarium, the Field Museum. All outside our windows."

"But if we wanted any of that, it's a short drive back into the city from Majestic Hills."

"Forty miles ain't short." She sniffed his deodorant stick and slid it under her armpits. "And living in the woods is not a selling point. Makes me think of Unite the Right maniacs with their tiki torches and replacement theories, and Minutemen with their bunkers of AK-whatevers." She daubed lotion on her throat. "And lynchings."

Lynchings? The word felt traitorous. Like playing the race card against a fellow soldier. "Really, Josey?" His cheeks burned red when he was upset. "Girl, we're probably already living among Unite the Right lite."

"What do we need with a house that big?" She picked up the brochure. "A, I'm not interested in being the only Black family on the block. And B, I know what you're thinking: you want to get me out there and knock me up."

Before they married, she'd told him that she wasn't sure she wanted children. The first time he'd visited the condo, he gasped when he read a framed William Blake quote on her nightstand: "Sooner murder an infant in its cradle than nurse unacted desires." He knew the quote was more about one's passions and ambitions than about babies. Still, he felt forewarned.

"And," she continued, "I don't want to be pregnant with a bunch of ashy little ones, marooned out in the low country with no friends or family willing to drive out to visit us. Absolutely not." She nuzzled her nose into his neck. "Dream other dreams, husband."

From the bathroom, Langdon watched Josephine pull the bedroom's blackout curtains together. She always did this for him when he worked overnight. But now she yanked with such a ferocity that he almost expected the words *The End* to flicker across the fabric.

Not long afterward, she left for work.

In bed, sleep eluded him. He lay on his back singularly focused on Majestic Hills. Staring at the ceiling, he began sketching a house surrounded by buxom trees and—despite his wife's pushback—designing a completely different world for him and Josephine.

On the rare weekend Langdon had off, the Blaques typically walked or Ubered to places. So, a few weeks later, he predicted that Josephine would be surprised when, in the late afternoon, he asked her to go for a drive. They hopped into their rebuilt maroon 1995 Land Cruiser that had belonged to his mother. Josephine kept asking where they were going, and he kept smiling obliquely, saying, "Wait for it. Just wait for it."

He watched her relax, shaking the strain from her neck as she breathed deeply. Maybe, he thought, she, too, needed a respite from the city. When the "Wobble" song blasted from the radio, they danced in their seats, her gyrating hips tooting toward him so that he could grope her ass, the way he did when they weren't buckled in. They felt in sync the entire ride, until about five miles from their exit, when an electronic Majestic Hills billboard loomed in the distance.

Josephine clicked off the radio. "Langdon July Blaque III, I hate being manipulated."

"Just see it, Josey, please." He placed his hand on her knee. She shifted her leg away.

He stared at her a beat too long, and the car rumbled across the rutted shoulder. Startled, she grabbed his forearm.

"There's a real estate agent, who—"

"A real esta—Lang, I thought you'd moved on from this nonsense."

Langdon hadn't brought it up again, but his Majestic Hills fever hadn't broken—as evidenced by the tattered brochure he now kept folded in his wallet. He had tried to calculate a new mortgage, in addition to the one currently on the condo. Josephine's salary was impressive, although she'd made a dent in her savings to pay the capital contribution required to make partner in the firm. His salary, however, was a pittance at this stage in his medical career.

He pulled over onto the shoulder and unbuckled his seat belt, facing her. He never did this on the highway, and Josephine glanced nervously at the semis and mammoth SUVs rumbling by, making the Land Cruiser shudder.

He told her about a child, a four-year-old boy he'd treated in the ER. Was it a month ago or two? It was all a blur now.

"The boy had a stray bullet lodged near his femoral artery," Langdon said, staring straight ahead. "At some point, as he'd been jostled from his home to the ambulance and eventually onto the trauma table, he'd lost the sock on his right foot. I noticed how clean his pajamas were, how his body had been lotioned, his hair cut and lined, and his toenails trimmed."

Langdon couldn't help thinking that the child's parents had taken such great care of him yet hadn't been able to protect him from the bullet that bored through their home.

"We got him ready for surgery, and I checked on him the next morning. A couple of days later, he went home."

Then, a week ago, Langdon had been hurrying out, trying to make the 5:45 a.m. train, when he passed triage bay six. He saw a woman leaving, her muffled wails burrowing into the chest of a man struggling mightily to keep her upright as they walked down the hall.

Langdon's stomach seized. He peeked into the bay.

"There he was," Langdon said. "That same little boy. A white sheet covered his body and was folded neatly under his chin. It looked like someone had tucked him in for the night. I still see his wispy eyebrows, uneven baby teeth, and perfectly lined fade. His chart said his cause of death was a thoracoabdominal GSW. A second bullet had ripped through his lower left lung, his stomach and bowels. He didn't have a chance."

Langdon said he felt then what he'd felt when he first encountered the child. That there was something sinister about his having cheated death the first time. Langdon had wondered then if it was only a matter of time before life would disappear *him*. And Langdon's inability to do anything about it inspired in him both anger and anguish, two no-count feelings he'd begun to view as indiscernible.

"I'm not so demoralized that I'm thinking about quitting my job," he said quietly. "And that isn't the first or last body of a child that I'll see on a trauma table."

He looked beyond Josephine to a picture-postcard red barn and silo in the middle of a cornfield.

"It's not just about the noise or caulking the windows," he said. "I can't breathe, Josey. I want a place where I can breathe. Sometimes it all feels like scavenging amid so much rubble."

She took his hand in both of hers. "Oh, Lang. I'm so, so sorry."

"I'm still that cat who goes all out for his patients. Who warns loved ones: 'Stay with your peeps when they're admitted, because they get far better care in the emergency room.' The higher-ups hate it when I say that." He looked in the rearview. "You talked about Minutemen and their AK-*whatevers*, but I see our young brothuhs killing one another. I think of that little boy and know there's no such thing as a stray bullet."

He shifted the Land Cruiser into Drive. But he didn't move.

"I can cancel with the agent. Or, we can look. You choose. Either way, it's fine."

He'd had her full attention the entire time, but now she nodded and turned away. She did not say a word. Not as Langdon steered them back onto the road or when the GPS announced, "In one mile, exit Goodenow." And not as they left the expressway, passing the New Pointe water tower and the old grain elevator, and crossed railroad tracks into the center of downtown.

"The Metro line that I take now goes straight out here. Your commute would be longer, but you could read your reports on the train."

Langdon pointed to several clothing boutiques, an antique shop, a creamery, and a VFW hall with a red *V*, a white *F*, and a blue *W* on its awning. Beyond the downtown, he showed her the charming post office, the empty football field, and the village hall, a nondescript building that doubled as police headquarters. He mentioned the bike lanes.

"They go on for miles," he said, watching her cut her eyes toward the shoulder.

The road opened, and they arrived at a three-way stop. A sign, One-Stop Gas, had an arrow pointing left.

"We're supposed to look for the Olympia Country Club." He reduced his speed. "Its golf course abuts Majestic Hills. The real estate lady told me the subdivision's entrance is hard to find." He leaned closer to the steering wheel, looking for an opening in the trees. "Like the Batcave."

"There it is," Josephine said, pointing.

He viewed her help as a gesture of goodwill, if not a full detente. He placed his hand on her knee, and she didn't move away.

Veering left into the woods, he passed under a half-built stone arch dressed in scaffolding. About a quarter of a mile beyond the opening was Willow Lane, and the first of the ten stately homes appeared, as though out of a pop-up book. Some of the houses peeked out from behind a few trees; others were fully exposed. Each had horseshoe driveways—like the photo on the advertisement. Because the landscaping hadn't yet been installed, the houses seemed unfinished, in transition. For Langdon, none of that mattered. He imagined emerald-green grass with sprinklers, children running through rainbows. He drove slowly, methodically, examining the old-time streetlamps and the identical stone-encased mailboxes, until he had passed five houses on the east side of the street and five on the west.

At the end of the cul-de-sac sat the Majestic Hills clubhouse, still under construction. The developer's trailer was parked out front, as was the real estate agent's idling car. As they neared, a Black woman got out and gestured for Langdon to park in front of her.

"A sistuh," Langdon said. "Her business card didn't have a photo. I've seen a lot that do."

Josephine shrugged. "Maybe she thought a photo would affect her sales."

Penny wore a blazer, despite the cold, with the inscription *Penny Larson Harmony Realty* on the breast panel. They made their introductions, and she handed them binders.

"This tells you all about our schools," she said. "They're some of the best in the nation. We have a substantial endowment from the Stanfield family. They're local and old money."

She started down the driveway toward the brown-brick house, and Langdon took Josephine's hand. He stopped midway to inhale the smell of pine and fireplace smoke. When Josephine inhaled too, he kissed her palm in gratitude.

Penny slowed, and when they caught up, she said, "Number five is my favorite."

"I'm sure you say that about all the houses." Langdon smiled, as they continued.

She shook her head. "I love number five because you wouldn't have anyone on the other side of you and you have a clear view of the pond. The morning mist." She made the blows-your-mind gesture with her hands. "The pond's not man-made. It's all natural. Just be super careful because it's quite mucky and deceptively deep. You guys swim?"

"We both do," Josephine said.

"I've seen people cannonballing off the dock," Penny said. "But I wouldn't do it."

When they were inside the house, she called their attention to the vaulted ceilings and large picture windows. In the kitchen, she ran her hand across the stainless steel and quartz and bamboo, citing their selling points: "sleek" and "state-of-the-art" and "eco-friendly." As she led them through room after room, she mentioned that New Pointe's United Methodist Church had once been a stop on the Underground Railroad, and was manned by Black

Abolitionists. Langdon and Josephine shared a quick glance that conveyed: *Bet ol' Penny doesn't regale her white prospects with such info.* Langdon listened to their echoey footsteps and sniffed the cinnamon plug-ins. This was the house. He could have curled up in a corner and stayed. He wanted to ask Josephine if she could imagine herself living there. He knew that, normally, she would have been full of questions—about plat maps, property values, and census data. But she was quiet, and he decided not to push it, grateful that she hadn't demanded he turn the car around. They were at the front door, about to leave, when Langdon asked Penny if he and Josephine could walk around the property.

"Absolutely. Take your time," Penny said. "I'll lock up and meet you by the cars."

As they tromped through dry leaves and twigs, he wished it were summer, that the trees weren't so skeletal and the sun wasn't waning. He stopped at an area staked off for the patio.

"We can have get-togethers right here," he said. "With Ken, Fat, and their badass boys."

Fatima was Josephine's best friend. The two had known each other since their first year at Howard Law. Langdon led his wife to the side of the house.

"Josey, you can plant that garden you always talk about." He stretched his arms out, attempting to graft a small dream onto a larger one. "We can truck in organic dirt and plant basil, rosemary, collards. You could snip, snip, snip, like they do on your cooking shows."

Her smile felt like an opening. When she looked past him, taking in the trees, Langdon felt the warmth of daylight, of possibility. He knew this wasn't over. Still, he walked up to her and threaded his hands around her waist through her open coat. She did not step away. An owl hooted. He pulled her closer, pressing his lips against hers, his tongue leveraging the space. As he led her back to the Land Cruiser, night was falling, the house slowly fading into the darkness.

"If you find yourselves in the neighborhood again," Penny said, opening her car door, "feel free to walk the property. Look in the windows. Admire the view."

Back in the Land Cruiser, Josephine rolled her eyes. "Black people walking through the woods on property we don't own," she said. "Sistuh's been out in *these* streets way too long."

They cracked up. It was a moment of solidarity, the two of them allies rather than adversaries. As Langdon left the subdivision, pulling out onto Goodenow, he felt as if a sliver of the trip to Majestic Hills had been salvaged. A sliver meant maybe a move was possible.

But as they neared the country club's entrance, a police car appeared, racing toward them. It passed their car, and Langdon watched in his rearview as it whipped around with a ravenous velocity, blue lights filling their mirrors. Langdon's thoughts swirled, and he began a calculus as autonomic as the quickening of his heartbeat. He sensed Josephine doing the same. But they were silent. He wasn't speeding. The license plate sticker and registration were current. He used to have one of his six Chicago marathon medals dangling from his rearview mirror, before he got stopped by a Chicago police officer and removed it. He kept his hospital ID—Dr. Langdon Blaque—in the cup holder. As if the word *Dr.* underneath his face on a plastic badge could render him bulletproof.

He'd once told his father that he felt guilty breaking out the ID. What about the brothers who hadn't gone to medical school?

"We do what's necessary to stay alive," his father had said. "So, use that shit."

Langdon clicked on his right-turn signal and pulled onto the shoulder. Time crawled, and he swallowed hard as the police car continued toward them. Only when it careened past, like a vulture zeroing in on prey but changing its mind, did Langdon loosen his grip on the steering wheel. He exhaled, his wedding band digging into his finger. He saw Josephine's chest expand, too. He returned to the road, and at the three-way stop they counted four cruisers surrounding a young man. His back was toward them, and they were blinded by a halo of headlights.

The ride home was mostly quiet, save for music neither would later remember. It wasn't until after they had parked in the condo's garage and boarded the elevator that Langdon turned to Josephine. "Any thoughts about Majestic—"

"I know you're going through something, Lang." Her voice sounded soothing, contrary to the way she jabbed the number twenty on the panel. "But let's find another option."

Sometimes Langdon's ears popped when the elevator shot up too fast, but the sensation he felt now was the allover ache of diving too deep underwater. They rode up in silence.

That night, they did not make love. They lay restless on the same memory foam mattress. They tugged on the same top sheet. But they did not truly sleep together.

CHAPTER TWO

eat your eggs, walter

Swann, Livingston, & Taylor occupied nearly the entire forty-second floor of a Michigan Avenue high-rise. The office had glass walls and large windows, allowing for stunning panoramic views of the lake and downtown. An upscale outplacement agency, it was designed for middle- to high-wage white-collar workers. Josephine had made partner when she was Josephine Taylor, and she'd opted not to change her name on the company logo even though, officially, she was Josephine Taylor Blaque. Her job was to set and implement the firm's goals as well as give legal advice to its corporate clients.

She entered her office and sat at her desk to text Fat. A civil rights attorney, Fat was on maternity leave with her fourth son and desperate for conversation that didn't involve chafed nipples or changing diapers.

morning girl. guess who rode out yesterday to see the lean-to Lang has the hots for

Seconds later, Fat's photo appeared, showing her caramel-colored skin, perfectly arched eyebrows, and natural hair with honey brown highlights that she'd pulled back into an Afro puff.

Before Josephine could say hello, she heard, "Never say never!" And Fat's signature sound, a crackle of laughter, followed.

Josephine acknowledged that the house was lovely. "We did, however, nearly get run off the road by the local police." Her voice pitched higher at the memory. "Even though they were *in pursuit* of somebody else."

"But nothing happened with you guys?" Fat asked, now totally serious.

"Nothing happened."

"Well, you're not going to like what I'm about to say." Fat's baby, Akeem, burped in the background, and she gushed—"Listen to you, sounding like a grown man!"—before returning her attention to her friend: "As much as I want you in the city, a few blocks from me, I think you should consider it."

"I'm considering." Josephine held her head in her hands. "He's really hurting, Fat. It's his job, mostly. Death—day in, day out."

"I'm so sorry," she said. "He'll pull through this. You both will. In the meantime, let's think about this strategically. You've already been talking about renting the condo to buy a larger unit in your building. Agree to go, with the proviso that you'll give him two years there. You might love it."

"I won't love it."

"You might. But, if you don't, you can sell that house and use the profit to buy a bigger unit in your building. I've been looking into New Pointe while mighty mouth here sleeps. Soon as I put him down for his nap, I'll send you what I've found."

Josephine could have done the research herself, but she hoped Langdon would come to his senses. Now she folded her hands atop her desk and sighed. *Shit's gettin' real.*

A few hours later, Josephine received an email with the subject line *Think compromise. For better or for worse.* Several links showed that Fat had scoured Drake County's databases on foreclosures, property transfers, delinquent property taxes, liens, property value reports. There was census data on New Pointe's demographics: Fat highlighted numbers showing that Blacks made up about ten percent of the population, while other people of color comprised five percent.

Hmm, Josephine thought. *Not bad for a hick town.*

Of particular interest was a documentary on YouTube from the mid-1990s. Josephine slid in her earbuds and opened the link on her desktop.

The voice-over began "New Pointe looks like any sleepy American hamlet" as the camera panned the area. "A volunteer fire department, a Rockwellian downtown, elite schools focusing on math and science. But New Pointe is in the headlines these days for its high school's pre-journalism program. Its students have pulled off quite a feat."

The camera held on New Pointe's Stanfield Academy, and the video cut to a classroom, where a Black woman sat behind her desk. "Lonnie Alexander" appeared on the screen.

"Generations of New Pointers have dined at The Plantation, a restaurant in town," Lonnie said. "Others have complained about the name, its historical context. But my students wrote powerful opinion pieces in the local newspaper explaining why the owners should change it." She smiled slyly at the camera. "It helped that the last of the old guard recently passed away and the younger owners have been more amenable to change. They've rechristened a former all-the-red-meat-you-can-eat buffet to The Plant—strictly vegetarian fare."

Josephine stopped the video and called up The Plant's web page. A photo showed a rustic building with bonsai-type landscaping. The menu laid out its "farm-to-table epicurean fare": a shakshuka with locally sourced organic eggs; avocado toast with chimichurri sauce; bread fermented in-house.

Dang, my mouth sho' is waterin'.

Langdon's keys jangled in the door just after midnight. He entered the bedroom, and Josephine turned on the light, making him watch the cued-up section of Lonnie in the video.

"So?" He yawned, emptying his pockets onto his nightstand. "A restaurant had a triggering name that was changed decades ago. And now it serves food right up your alley."

"Lang, it made me think about my dad." She sat up in bed, her legs folded under her. "The pain on his face when he talked about growing up in the Jim Crow South. Sundown towns. *The Green Book*. Things I've always been keenly aware of, but never felt so haunted by. Until now."

Her smile was uneasy, and Langdon sat on the bed beside her.

"What terrifies me these days is, if someone had a hankering to name a restaurant The Plantation, they'd do it in a heartbeat. And business would probably be booming." She placed her hand on his back. "Are you sure—I mean positively sure—this is the place for us?"

"No, I'm not positively sure," he said. "How can anyone be? But I do know you'd find this type of complicated history everywhere."

He reminded her of the day when they were in the lobby, observing the residents at their respective elevator banks. They'd realized that even their sixty-story building was somewhat segregated. The wealthiest people lived between the sixtieth and fortieth floors—and they were overwhelmingly white. The Asians and South Asians resided between the fortieth and twentieth floors. And who lived on twenty and below? Mostly, though not exclusively, Black and brown people.

"In our own little well-to-do ghetto." He moved his head from side to side, cracking his neck, and then knelt in front of her, taking her hand.

She eyed him suspiciously. "What? You proposing again?"

"Progress only means that the past recedes, but it doesn't disappear. And, I get that now, the past feels more present than ever. But we shouldn't be intimidated by it." He took a deep breath. "Only two Majestic Hills properties are left, Josey, so I called in sick today. I took twenty-five thousand dollars out of our savings, and I drove out to Majestic Hills to put down a deposit. All refundable. Just for them to hold it."

"You did what?!" A hot fury roiled through her, rocketing her to her feet. Tears burned the corners of her eyes. She smothered them.

Langdon stood, too. "I've got the paperwork to be preapproved for a mortgage. We've got two paths: one where we use the condo as collateral and one where we don't."

"You did this without me?" Josephine's voice quivered. "I know you're struggling. Believe me I do. But we *are* a team, right?"

He held up both hands, urging calm. "I only put down the money to buy time to persuade you that I really need this place, Josey. Nothing is final."

She exhaled, and it sounded as if an important seal had been broken.

He told her about driving back out to number five and meeting the next-door neighbor, Jackson, a blond guy with a receding hairline, originally from West Virginia. An avid beekeeper, he walked Langdon to the back of his property, to the boxes housing his bees.

"Really nice guy. Scrawny, no bigger than a minute. He owns a couple of elite bicycle shops and cycle studios. His wife is Asian American and a fitness expert—" He left the room and returned with his book bag. "He gave me this bottle of honey."

"Langdon." She paused to settle her spirit. "You fucking hate honey."

"I'm trying to tell you that I felt alive, Josey." He threw his arms up and began to pace. "Enlarged by the sky, the trees, the sound of the birds, and the quiet." He took her hand again, and she slid it away. "I found an open space, and I sat. I fell asleep. That's why I'm so late."

Josephine looked at her husband. She thought about the little boy who died in the emergency room, but she couldn't figure out how to say *You've got to move on,* without sounding insensitive. Once, Langdon had told her about a Black doctor, a friend and mentor, who counseled him on how to handle losing patients. He'd said, "To feel sad makes you human. To find some utility in that sadness will make you a better doctor. To wallow only makes you selfish."

As if reading Josephine's mind, Langdon looked at her and said, "I'm being selfish."

About moving? About the boy? About that $25,000? Hard to untangle. But yes, you are.

She wanted to tell him that he was not the only one who, whenever something bad happened at work, sought an escape. Clearly, nothing could trump a dead kid, but she had her issues too: the white client, a former C-suite exec, who pranced around the office cackling, "What do I care that they clipped me on my severance? My money is in prisons."

She walked over to the window, recalling her first night in the condo a decade and a half earlier, when Obama won the election. She'd been unpacking and sipping champagne while watching the Grant Park revelers on her television and outside her window. The city's skyline dazzled with tower windows spelling *U.S.A.* For a brief while, that Obama sky felt limitless, until it quickly hardened back into a ceiling. Now all she saw was a scattered dot matrix, like a punch card, illuminating very little.

"I didn't grow up the way you did," she said, still facing the window. "Big house, big yard on a big corner lot. We had two tiny bedrooms and one bathroom. Dad and I used the same bar of soap. He wanted me to have this condo as a leg up. For his—future grand-whatevers."

For decades Josephine's father had worked as a janitor and then head custodian at the University of Chicago Lab School, which allowed her to attend for free. Edward Taylor had formed a relationship with a professor who owned the unit, which was in foreclosure, part of the 2008 economic meltdown. Her father emptied out his 401(k) for a hefty down payment. He'd rented out the condo when she left for law school in D.C.

"I won't squander his gift by losing it." She turned back to the window. "He was seventy-four years old—seventy-four—and getting a first-time homeowner's subsidy."

"We don't have to sell it," Langdon said. "Maybe we can build on it. Or it can be seed money for something else."

Josephine twisted her wedding band—plain, white gold like Langdon's. She hadn't wanted a diamond. In that moment, she fought every impulse to rip it from her finger and fling it. Instead, when she turned to look at her husband, she saw the man she loved sitting on the foot of their bed, slightly hunched, staring grievously into his palms.

"Eat your eggs, Walter."

Lorraine Hansberry's *A Raisin in the Sun* was the first play they saw together. Josephine remembered being struck by the scene in which the husband tells his wife he's desperate to pursue his dreams, and she suggests that he satiate himself with his breakfast instead. For months, if Josephine or Langdon had a minor, unrealistic desire, they teased each other: "Eat your eggs, Walter." But this was not minor.

For the first time in their marriage, Josephine snatched his pillow off the bed, along with the throw on the storage bench, and pointed toward the bedroom door.

He accepted both, returning them to their original places.

"I'm not leaving, Josey. Not by inches. Not by degrees. I promised you. Remember?"

Damn Y chromosome.

But, yes. She remembered.

They'd met five years earlier in Ghana, outside Accra, at the Elmina slave castle. They had been on the same crowded tour bus, but she hadn't noticed him. She spent the three-hour ride gazing out the window, forehead pressed against the glass, relishing a totally unfamiliar world. She watched the tangle of people on the street, miles of men in loose-fitting sandals, with dusty, chapped heels and spindly calves, the women with their wares balancing ergonomically atop their regal headdresses. At the Strong Faith Business Center, other women sat beside makeshift stands hawking fruits and vegetables and, in one double-take instance, wooden coffins. One minute the bus was hurtling down the open road and the next inching through clots of traffic in lockstep with feral goats the size of puny dogs, as chickens ambled along the road.

The tour bus arrived at the coast. Josephine had fallen asleep. After everyone disembarked, the driver had to wake her. Langdon saw her descending the bus steps into the salty air. Her white shorts and halter accentuated her ebony complexion.

Their castle guide led them to an upstairs area where women had been held and raped. They toured a dungeon where men had been starved to death. Throughout the castle, she found herself stooping because of the low ceilings but also feeling so, so small. The walls held stains of mildew and algae. The stone and mortar floors still held centuries of blood. Finally, the tour guide led them to a damp room, pointing out a narrow gate, "The Door of No Return," through which human bodies had passed to board cargo ships to the so-called New World. Josephine examined the rusting thick metal bars and then looked outside at the sparse grass leading to sand, and farther still, the fishing skiffs thrown against the ocean's edge. Above it all, a grayish sky simmered, as it had for generations, like water being brought to a boil.

She began to cry. The handful of people still there were also sobbing, or on the verge of tears. Langdon approached her.

"This really fucks you up." His eyes were red-rimmed and swollen.

Startled, she studied him. Inhaled spicy cologne.

"I didn't realize how emotional this would be."

He patted his utility shorts and handed her a rumpled Kleenex.

"It's—it's not used," he said, a bit tongue-tied.

"Thank you." She smiled, wadding the tissue as she walked away.

He trailed her from a distance through the rest of the tour, and just before they returned to the bus, he saw her trying to take a selfie, the Atlantic behind her.

"I can do that for you." He extended his hand for her phone. He took several shots of her, giving him the opportunity to home in on her dark amber eyes and thick lips. Then he approached her, angling his face close to hers, photographing the two of them.

Well, that was presumptuous, she thought.

On the bus, they sat together. They both were staying at the Mövenpick Ambassador Hotel. He was in Ghana for a friend's wedding. She was vacationing alone, leaving in the morning.

At dinner, he told her that he'd grown up in the burbs and his parents had done well for themselves. Jules and Elise Blaque believed in travel, and by the time Langdon was sixteen, he had visited all fifty states and four continents. But this was his first time in Ghana.

She told him that her mother, the first Josephine, had died hours after she was born. For years, her father had tried to multiply himself to diminish the loss, despite knowing that there was no math, no mechanism to compensate for a child's never feeling her mother's embrace. Her father had called her J.T. since the first time he held her in his arms. He loved naming her after her mother, but he said that with her passing, his lips could no longer form her name. His death a month earlier had inspired Josephine's trip.

Later that night, Langdon texted his Ghanaian friend to say that he'd met a gorgeous lawyer:

At first I thought she was an African sistuh. Man, those cheekbones, those lips. She spoke and I was like, She ain't no African; she's Jenny from the block. AND WHAT ARE THE ODDS THAT SHE LIVES IN CHICAGO?

The next day, during a five-hour layover in Amsterdam, Josephine texted Fat: *Girl, I met an American at the slave castle. He gave me a tissue because I was blubbering. Then, at dinner, he stood to pull out my chair. Guys still do that? And, no, I didn't sleep with him. Truth? I kinda wanted to. He's not my type, though. A pretty-boy doctor, with those funny-colored eyes. Some women like that, I guess. Probably so full of himself. He's got beautiful feet though. Toes all even. Prettier than mine.*

Fat texted back: *Hold up. YOU were crying?*

It was a fair question. At her father's wake, the month before, Fat stood next to Josephine at the front of the chapel as she greeted family and friends with hugs and kisses and laughter. Tissues folded in her purse, Fat stood ready to console Josephine, but she did not cry. Not at the wake, nor during the funeral. When Josephine left the front pew and stepped elegantly up to the podium, she looked down at the poem she'd written for her father as a child and, rather than recite it, she began to sing it, serenading him. Josephine's voice grated, which somehow made her off-key rendition even more touching. As Fat passed tissues to the people seated around her, Josephine remained steadfast and composed.

A couple of weeks later, Josephine attended the funeral of one of her first clients, a successful Black man who'd maintained roots in a South Side storefront church. She found a seat in the back and was fine, until the man's son, playing a soprano saxophone, began a solo of "Come by Here, Good Lord." At the refrain, "Somebody needs you, Lord," the wail of the horn spirited through her, summoning the inextricable, inexhaustible grief she'd tried so hard to lock away. She burst into sobs. When a stranger in the row behind her patted her shoulder to console her, she knew she needed to get away—to begin to imagine an unimaginable life without her father.

Langdon and Josephine's second date was in Chicago. She wished her father had met him, this man who was earnest, bookish, slightly awkward. He loved his parents' music: Ray Charles, Nina Simone, Aretha Franklin, even Frank Sinatra. Langdon also, from time to time, seemed a bit nervous in her presence. Her father told her it was important to marry a man whose love for her was so immense, so deep that it rattled him, knocked him off his square.

After a year, Langdon got down on one knee and asked Josephine to marry him. She told him no, adding something he already knew: she wasn't good with compromise or sharing—he'd given her the key to his studio apartment months before she gave him the key to her condo. Because of her mother, she had abandonment issues. No, her mother hadn't *abandoned* her intentionally. But gone begets gone. Josephine didn't know how to argue or love without thinking it would end in a vanishing act.

After a few months, he tried a second time.

"I love you," he said, once again getting down on one knee. "And I want to be with you always—if you allow me. I promise."

Josephine had lived her life taking only the most calculated risks. "Always walking ahead of yourself," as her father often put it. By Langdon's second proposal, she said yes. She was ready to take a leap, which wasn't a big leap considering he was a great guy. But, more important, she believed he was a man who tried hard to keep his promises.

The Blaques had learned during lockdown that the condo wasn't big enough to hold resentments. Now, during the days following their blowup, it had never felt so small. They two-stepped around each other. Uncharacteristically, they barely touched, speaking only when necessary. A couple of times Langdon would be singing a song under his breath, and not long after, Josephine realized that she'd begun humming the same tune. It was as though they could only reach each other on an accidental frequency; neither seemed to know how to access on purpose.

Exactly one week later, Langdon asked Josephine to sit on the bed, and he joined her.

"I got the deposit back." He handed her a cashier's check for $25,000. "We don't have to move. I hate what this has done to us, Josey. I do. It's not worth it."

She considered the check she held. It was a good-faith gesture that he'd gotten the money back rather than merely offering to do so. She weighed the notion of compromise. He had spent four years in her space and only recently pushed against it. He also looked repentant and, most important, needed this move. So she swallowed her misgivings and every nagging instinct warning that leaving would be a horrible mistake.

"One year," she relented. Fat had suggested two, but Josephine tailored the idea to make it her own. "We move there for one year, rent the condo, and at the end of a year we reassess."

He read the worry on her face, placing his hands on her waist.

"Josey, we don't have to do this. I've made my peace with it."

"One. Year," she emphasized. "If it doesn't work, we'll take what we make off the sale of the house and return here. We'll buy a larger unit, providing there's one on the market."

"And," he said, smiling, "providing you want to have more bedrooms for spawns."

"But Lang, you can never exclude me from decisions like this again. Do you hear me?"

"I do."

Josephine laughed, her eyes welling.

"Whenever Daddy got a new sofa or chair, he bought a sheet to drape over it. For years, my ass never felt the original fabric of anything I sat on in our house. This condo is the one thing, the one place I really got to live in. The same man who tried to preserve our world provided me a new one. Lang, I can't lose it."

"We won't lose it." He gathered her in his arms. "I promise you, Josey. On my life."

CHAPTER THREE
here

The afternoon was warm for late April, close to eighty degrees. As Langdon and Josephine followed the moving truck through downtown New Pointe, they lowered their windows, inhaling the perfume of suburbia: freshly cut grass and fragrant, newly laid mulch. The town thrummed with residents entering stores where chalkboard easels offered everything from specialty teas to deli sandwiches to unique, hard-to-find books.

Beyond the downtown, the Blaques heard music, then felt its vibrations as they neared the farmers market. Cars lined both sides of the street, and signs invited families to return at dusk for the season's first Friday-night movie in the park.

Josephine began to fidget. She'd been rooting around in the condo's storage unit, and dust and cobwebs clung to her blue-jean shorts and black tank. She swatted at the fabric. When she began to strum the armrest, Langdon looked at her, a bit surprised.

"Nervous?" he asked.

"No." She shook her head for emphasis and then nodded instead. "Maybe, a little?"

"Thank you, Josey." He took her hand and kissed her palm. "I know we said a year here, but you can pull the plug at any time. Whatever happens, we'll be fine."

She had her doubts. Any move was a big deal, and the lawyer in her wondered now if she should have had her husband sign a sort of promissory note to return her life to her. She was also not sure they would be fine. During the run-up to the move, she'd confided in Fat that she and Langdon had been having "his and hers" bad dreams. Hers were painfully obvious: sprinting through Chicago's Union Station, watching the clock as she dashed from track to track trying to find the right train. But she always boarded the wrong one, heading in the wrong direction, leaving Langdon and her father on the platform as the doors closed.

Langdon didn't discuss his dreams, which were more like night terrors. His body had begun to twitch and jerk in his sleep, as if he were being riddled with bullets. Ordinarily, he slept so hard that it paralyzed him, and the only reason she never poked him to make sure he was breathing was that he still managed to snore to high heaven. Whenever she asked him what he'd dreamed, he'd smile and say he didn't remember. She didn't press.

At the subdivision, Langdon followed the moving truck under the now-completed stone arch. The words "Majestic Hills" had recently been soldered across the top. A garland of young white daffodils ringed hearty green bushes that would turn a deep crimson in the fall. Through the sunroof, Josephine saw flourishes of leaves, unflinching against the bluest sky. On Willow Lane, they craned their necks left and right, looking at the houses of people who on this day would officially become their neighbors. At the end of the cul-de-sac, they stopped as the moving truck backed into their driveway. Although neither Josephine nor Langdon said a word, they both felt the weight of arrival. *We are here*. He expelled a tremulous breath, and she inhaled one. It was a form of call-and-response to a day that they both—in their own distinct ways and with their own distinct motivations—had been preparing for. Langdon was alive to the moment. Josephine couldn't stop thinking about how they were moving from a high-rise—where neighbors rarely interacted beyond "Good morning" by the elevator or "Your package was left by my door"—to a subdivision where a meet and greet was already in the offing. Langdon had come out a few days before and found the invitation in the mailbox. Though the developer paid for it, one of the families was spearheading the event.

By noon, boxes filled most of the rooms in the house, and Langdon left to get lunch. Josephine stood on their front stoop as the moving truck lumbered down the driveway. She felt like she'd been dropped off on an island and was watching sunlight glint off the tail end of a plane that wouldn't return for months. She resisted the urge to wave. *Play nice, Josephine.*

She sat on the front step for a good fifteen minutes, staring at the driveway and thinking about her company's motto: "We are here to soften the landing." Was that even possible, anywhere? She was about to text Fat when a dog barked and started running up their driveway. The trees in the arc of the horseshoe obscured her view, but she heard the jingle of dog tags.

"No, Basil! No!"

Josephine was not afraid of dogs, but she stood, frantically searching for a large stick as the snarl of the beast running toward her bounced violently off the trees. When she finally saw the cute russet-colored dog, a man trailing it caught up and uncoiled a leash from his pocket, clicking it onto the dog's collar.

"I am so sorry!" The man was tall, with slightly graying golden hair and a square jaw. The kind of guy, Josephine thought, who could sit at the head of a conference room table and no one would question his competence or whether he belonged.

"He's got a nose like a bloodhound, and he's used to chasing rabbits over here. Won't happen again. I'm Christopher Thompson." He extended his hand, and Josephine shook it, introducing herself.

"My wife, Monica, and I live in number three," he said. "This is Basil. Your moving truck was leaving as we were heading out."

"Hi, Basil." Josephine stooped to pet him, and he lunged at her, barking loudly.

"Down, Basil. Got a lot of bass in his bark, but he's harmless."

"Is he a Lab?"

"With some husky mixed in. We got him as a rescue." Christopher shaded his eyes, taking in the house. "You've got a beaut there. Monica and I toured it, early on."

"How long have you been here?"

"A full month, today," he said, backing up. "Anyway, I won't keep you. There's a meet and greet tomorrow. Check your mailbox."

"We know, thanks."

When they were out of earshot, she FaceTimed Fat.

"We're here! This is here."

Josephine hurried midway down the driveway and flipped the camera view to show Fat the house and the soaring trees behind it, the rosebushes already in bloom and the lilies, with their white blossoms and pink-tinged centers.

Fat screamed. "Will you look at that? I don't think you'd landscaped the last time I saw it. Let me talk to Blaque."

"He went to get lunch. I'm all alone. Keep me company?"

Josephine held her phone in both hands, piloting it past the garage to show Fat the patio, the backyard, and the woods beyond them.

"Mr. Taylor would have been so dang proud!" Fat said.

"He would have, indeed." Josephine flipped the camera view to smile at Fat.

Josephine imagined her father entering the house, saying, *Point me to the latrine*. "The latrine" was what he called the bathroom. He would have referred to flushing as "pulling the chain." And when he got ready to leave, he would have told her he was stopping at the "filling station" to gas up before the long ride home.

Edward Taylor had fled Mississippi as a child, but it echoed throughout him his entire life.

Josephine was about to give Fat a tour of the inside of the house when she reached the front and saw Langdon in the driveway, unloading bags from the Leaf It to Us nursery.

"Your boy is back," Josephine told her. "And he's—Wait, he's coming toward me."

"Fat?" Langdon mouthed, forming a phone with his fingers.

Josephine turned her phone around, showing Fat's face.

"What up, Fathead!" he yelled.

"Once again: I don't appreciate being called Fathead. Girl, what do you see in him?"

Langdon wiped his hands on the back of his blue jeans and turned his baseball cap around. "Fatima, my wife will call you later. Right now, I've got to carry her across the threshold."

"Aww!" Fat swooned. "You so dang romantic."

"No, he's not!" Josephine ended the call, bracing as Langdon continued toward her. "It's corny, and you are not picking—"

"Oh, yes I am."

He scooped her up, and she dissolved into giggles as they entered the front door. When he put her down, he led her back out the same way, past the Land Cruiser to the side of the house.

"This is what took me so long." He pointed to chicken wire, flats of seedlings, and several bags of dirt. "We've got collards, kale, tomatoes, carrots, and beets, along with a bunch of herbs. I promised you a garden, and we'll do all this together."

"You're getting your pretty little hands dirty?" She patted his chest.

"Big hands." He looped his arm around her neck. "And, Josey, if this garden is fated to last only for one season, so be it. We'll be back in the city and—"

They were heading back to the front, nearing the Land Cruiser, when, without warning, a cloudburst unleashed sheets of rain. He grabbed her hand and sprinted to the car, trying the doors, but they were locked, with the keys still in the ignition. He hadn't opened the garage, so they ran to the front door only to find it locked, too. She leaned against solid oak. They laughed as water from the overhang's gutters sloshed around them. When Josephine wiped her face and cleavage, she followed his eyes to her wet T-shirt and his hands to her breasts as he traced her nipples with his thumbs, awakening all her nerve endings.

"The neighbors," she whispered.

"Girl, all these trees."

She stared at him, at the color in his cheeks and the ocean of sky in his eyes.

"I have an idea," she said.

This time she took his hand, and they bolted past the garage and across sodden grass and their future garden to a door on the side of the house. They stepped into the mudroom. Langdon lifted her T-shirt over her head and helped her out of her shorts. He pinned her against the wall as her entire being arched toward him. He drew back briefly to stare at her naked body as if she, like everything around them, were brand-new. She began to consider that a yearlong sojourn in Majestic Hills might not kill her after all.

"Remind me," he said, his voice raspy. "Takeout's in the car. Chinese."

"Oh, honey, I won't remember." As she unbuckled his belt and unzipped his pants, she thought about the dimple in the crown of his bald head, the beads of perspiration around it when he worked hard, the way it blushed.

She couldn't see it now. But maybe, in a few minutes?

His damp fingertips skimmed her ribs. Her thighs throbbed against his. She clawed at his wet shoulders. Then their breath aligned as their moans and grunts and cries began to flood every corner of the house like surround sound—stereophonic and all-encompassing.

It was early evening when they awakened on the pullout sofa. They had asked the movers to leave it in the family room, which was where they would sleep until the new bedroom furniture was delivered. Josephine's was old, and they wanted a new suite for this new chapter. Disoriented, she lifted her head a few inches from her pillow. She felt as if she were in a faraway time zone. Tremors of pleasure still coursed through her. She had to remember that she was not on the twentieth floor of the condo building which explained why, outside the window, squirrels catapulted from branch to branch and birds complained loudly. Langdon lay awake, staring out the window. She cuddled close to him, her leg lapping over his.

He kissed her forehead. "Day-um, girl."

It was not morning, but waking up there felt like a new day.

They got dressed and went for a quick ride around the town, trying to acclimate themselves, and wound up at the One-Stop for gas. A New Pointe police car was idling near the ice freezer, its speed gun trained on the road. Langdon pulled up to the pump and got out. Josephine went inside.

The convenience store was empty, but she heard raised voices coming from a back room and snatches of the conversation.

"Wade, listen to me." The woman pleaded something inaudible; then Josephine heard, "You're sixteen. Damn it, you can't live on your own."

Josephine inched closer to the back, near the water softener salt pellets and an ATM with an out-of-order sign.

"Mom," Wade said.

"Son, there's nothing for you to prove. This is about regret, and your father, and you on some insane mission to continue his work. But—"

"Somebody must be willing to work to change things. 'We shape our buildings, and afterward our buildings shape us.'"

Josephine heard an object thud against the wall.

"Winston Churchill also said," the woman yelled, "'a fanatic is someone who can't change his mind and won't change the subject!'"

Josephine moved, and salt pellets crunched to dust loudly underfoot. She froze.

"Not a fanatic, Mom. Just a young brother spitting truth. The geebies and Majestic Hills. Both of them—conceived and, as you once believed, built on a lie."

Josephine had no clue what the *geebies* were, but she certainly knew Majestic Hills.

A door slammed, and the woman shrieked. She flew out of the room, startled to see Josephine.

"Anybody tell you it's rude to eavesdrop?" She punched with the word *rude.*

Josephine recognized Lonnie Alexander immediately from the video Fat had sent. It had been a couple of decades since that interview, and Lonnie appeared only gently marked by time—face a tad fuller, her short, curly fade now a long, thick braid down her back. She'd seemed taller in the video and—Josephine realized this wasn't rational—nicer. She wondered what had happened that Lonnie had gone from being a distinguished teacher at a prestigious high school to working as a gas station cashier.

"I wasn't eavesdropping," Josephine lied. "I was only—"

"There are cameras." Lonnie pointed a lone finger to the ceiling and began walking to the checkout counter. "If you want a latte with some organic this or soy that, or stevia, I don't have it. I've got regular coffee, regular white sugar, and regular whole-fat white milk. Whole. Nothing skimmed or dumbed down to a percent."

Josephine spotted the candy aisle. She plucked three novelty chocolate bars she'd never heard of and trailed Lonnie to the checkout. Next to the counter, a stand holding Majestic Hills brochures, like the one Langdon first brought home, had been toppled, and most of the slick advertisements lay scattered across the floor.

"I can help." Josephine started to bend down.

"They will stay there until the jackass who knocked them over—" Lonnie stared at a video monitor on the counter and looked out the window. "Does that man belong to you?"

Josephine saw Langdon shaking the officer's hand. She nodded.

"I've seen him at the village hall." Lonnie began ringing up the candy. "Getting license plate stickers, permits. He sure can talk. Always holds up the line." She picked up a brochure, dropping it in the bag.

"Oh, I don't need one," Josephine said. "We just moved into a house there." She inadvertently rolled her eyes, a reflex she faithfully checked around Langdon.

"You're not a fan of the move, I take it." Lonnie leaned forward onto the counter, as if her customer had finally made herself interesting.

Josephine hesitated, scanning the headline of a framed news article on the wall behind the counter:

STANFIELD ACADEMY OPENS TO POMP AND CIRCUMSTANCE

"No, I'm very happy." *Which was true.* "I'm just going to miss our old place." *Also true.*

"I gave my husband a month when we moved here," Lonnie said. "That was over two decades ago." She stood up straight, immediately regretting having told her business to a stranger.

"But you guys are still here," Josephine said.

"Just me, now." Lonnie's voice maintained its edge, but grief radiated from her.

"I'm so sorry," Josephine said. Out the window, she saw Langdon parked closer to the front door. "I'm sure I'll be seeing you around."

Once again buttoned-up, Lonnie blurted, "Okay. Goodbye."

In the Land Cruiser, Josephine handed Langdon a candy bar.

"You chatting up the police now?" She stroked the back of his head.

"Nice guy," Langdon said. "Just letting him know Black folks in town. Letting him get to know our car, too."

Langdon drove away from the One-Stop, whistling. He never whistled. She didn't recognize the tune and simply attributed its jaunty timbre to his feeling jaunty. This made her heart swell for him.

She pulled out her phone, searched for "Geebies and New Pointe," and found nothing. She tried other spellings such as "G-e-e-b-e-e-s" and "J-e-e-b-e-e-s," and still nothing.

As they passed under the Majestic Hills arch, she wondered, *What did the young man mean, "built on a lie"?*

She looked over at her husband. His profile, his pursed lips, his jazzy meandering tune. She wasn't about to sour his evening by mentioning it to him. Instead, as they neared their new home, she snapped off a piece of his chocolate bar, which he'd placed in the cup holder.

First, she tasted sweetness and then a subtle bitterness she couldn't yet describe.

CHAPTER FOUR

the meet and greet

Bonnie and Bryce Fisher oversaw the meet and greet. Langdon had introduced himself to them during one of his solo trips out to Majestic Hills before the move. He'd spent his days off driving out for business with the Realtor, or the contractor, or the inspectors. Once, he drove out just to drive out, and he discovered a rustic little bookstore/coffeehouse, where he sat and read for hours.

He'd been leaving the subdivision one day when a red ball bounced in front of the Land Cruiser. Langdon hit his brakes. Three towheaded boys, triplets—Langdon guessed about five or six years old—ran to the edge of their driveway and stopped there. A curvy woman with deep dimples and a riot of raven curls and a man wearing shorts and sandals appeared seconds later, apologizing profusely to Langdon. They introduced themselves as Bonnie and Bryce and their sons as Harlow, Amos, and Issac.

Bonnie and Bryce were the type of people who never met a stranger. The same was often said about Langdon. When he told them that he and his wife had made an offer on number five, Bonnie clasped her hands in delight. The Fishers began to brief him on what they'd gleaned during their four months in Majestic Hills: the herons, wrens, and hummingbirds their backyard had hosted since the spring migration; the items that shouldn't be flushed—condoms, tampons—because they burn out septic pumps; the green generator, candles, batteries, and flashlights that should be purchased in case of a major storm. They recommended the One-Stop.

As Langdon watched the couple march their sons toward their house, he recalled his parents' story about the first time they drove out to what would become his childhood home. There was no For Sale sign on the lawn, and they asked the white neighbor, who was planting flowers, if the house next door was the one on the market. The man lied and said there were no houses available. But on this afternoon in New Pointe, Langdon had the opposite experience. He was under no delusion about what it meant to be a Black couple buying a house in a space that white folks considered safe and therefore sacred, how the Blaques' very existence might call that into question. But Bonnie and Bryce had made Langdon feel welcome. That went a long way toward making him feel at home.

So it didn't surprise him that the couple were in charge of the meet and greet. What had surprised him was his wife. When he'd told Josephine about it, with the caveat that they could sit it out if she preferred, she immediately replied, "No, let's go meet our neighbors."

The clubhouse was a gabled one-story cottage with a slate roof. Langdon and Josephine, each holding a bottle of wine, were leaving their driveway when an Asian American woman poked her head out of the clubhouse door.

"Well, you two are easy on the eyes." The woman smiled and held the door open as they entered. "I do a daily walk around the pond, and today of all days, I lost track of time." She wore capris, and silty watermarks encircled her ankles and bare feet.

"I'm Khai Chang-Kennedy. I live right next door to you. You're Josephine and Langdon." She pointed to each of them and tapped her chin. "Unless my husband said Joseph and Lana." Her squeaky laugh made Josephine giggle, which surprised Langdon. Josephine was not quick to warm to strangers. He felt a surge of happiness, interpreting her lightheartedness as a good sign for the afternoon, and maybe even for this new place.

"Jackson, my husband," Khai continued, "says I'm hard of listening."

"Are you?" Josephine grinned.

"Guilty." Khai pointed to Josephine's light blue flouncy sundress. "That blue is your color."

Khai led the way, maneuvering around a pool table and through a family room area that had a large screen television and a fireplace.

"You're the beekeeper's wife," Langdon said. "I met Jackson a few weeks ago. And, you're a fitness expert with, I think he said, more than a hundred thousand YouTube followers?"

"Again, guilty," Khai said. She turned to Josephine. "I've been thinking about"—she looked out a window that framed the water—"yoga on the pond. Still planning, though."

She opened French doors, and they walked out into a fog of barbecue smoke. Overhead, the speaker system softly pumped Billy Joel's "We Didn't Start the Fire." A long, rectangular table held an elegant spray of wildflowers, along with a charcuterie board and bottles of wine. Bonnie and Bryce's sons tossed a stick to what Langdon guessed was a chocolate Lab while running back and forth along the shimmery pond. In the distance, a red canoe was moored to a short dock. The scenery was indeed idyllic. As Langdon drank it all in, his face was full of magic and memories. He'd canoed as a child with his two brothers. Bryce reminded Langdon of his father—dealing with three unruly boys.

Khai pantomimed a throat slash to kill the music.

"Everyone!" she sang. "The Blaques are here, and they've brought wine!"

What followed was something loosely akin to a receiving line for Josephine and Langdon. They were the last family to buy into the subdivision, and the reception was the kind reserved for B-list dignitaries or aging rock stars, the kind that came with gifts. Two men in pastel-colored shorts and boat shoes—Langdon thought, *the uniform of suburbia*—brought over a small crate of specialty craft beers.

Langdon recognized Jackson right away. He offered a basket with still-warm honey, along with beeswax and candles. Bonnie and Bryce's three sons presented Josephine and Langdon with an oversize card made of construction paper, with the word *Welcome* written in chalk. When the boys grew bored, they pulled their father away and ran off to the dock. On the grass were groupings of gifts that the other families had received earlier.

"Were we supposed to bring something?" Josephine asked out the side of her mouth as neighbors mingled.

"No one told me. I swear." Langdon crossed his heart.

Josephine and Langdon were heading in the direction of the table when one of the boat shoes guys introduced himself as Marc Preston.

"I've seen your vintage Land Cruiser at the village hall," Marc said. "The FLEET FT license plate. You a runner?"

"I get by."

"He's pretending to be modest." Josephine touched his arm. "He's really good."

"We should run together sometime," Marc said. "If you don't think I'd be a drag."

"I'd like that," Langdon said.

Marc suggested that Langdon consider adding Mount Olive Cemetery to his route. Designed after Mount Auburn Cemetery in Cambridge, Massachusetts, Mount Olive had elegant gardens and landscaping, winding paths, and ponds with ornate stone bridges.

"I'm an architect, so stuff like that gets to me," Marc said. "The cemetery's design is a throwback to English aristocrats. It's about a mile north of the One-Stop. You know the One-Stop?"

"Absolutely." Langdon nodded. "Thanks, man."

"By the way," Marc yelled as he walked away. "Marc is short for Marco. I go by both."

Langdon and Josephine let out a simultaneous, "Hmmm." Marc was a white-presenting man, apparently with Hispanic ancestry, who could have easily passed, but was outing himself.

"Curveball," Langdon said, smiling at her.

But Josephine's focus had turned toward the dock. Bryce and his three sons were sitting there, appearing resplendently amphibious in their colorful life jackets as they climbed into the red canoe. The boys' gym shoes lay in a pile beside a couple of fishing poles and a tin of worms.

Now another man was angling toward them. He wore mirrored aviator sunglasses, and an unleashed dog trailed him.

"Josephine," the man said.

"Chris, right?" She smiled.

"Christopher," he corrected. "Chris was my father."

She introduced Christopher to Langdon and told him that they'd met the day before when his dog ran up their driveway.

Christopher patted the dog's head. "My B-man's a trespasser."

"B for Basil," Josephine explained to Langdon.

"Won't happen again. My wife—" Christopher gestured toward the table. "She's the one wearing the University of Chicago T-shirt, with her hand on her belly. We're expecting."

"Congratulations!" Josephine and Langdon said in unison.

Christopher turned to Langdon. "She's a doctor, too, a professor. Dr. J. Monica Johnson."

A doctor, too? Outside the hospital, Langdon typically avoided talking about what he did for a living. Of course, a quick Internet search gave him away every time. But he appreciated watching people's faces and demeanor change when they learned. He called it the Doctor Privilege Effect. Sometimes he could see them trying to remember what they had said or how they'd treated him before they knew.

"We had our real estate agent show us your house three times," Christopher continued. "I feel like I know it like the back of my hand. I don't want to sound like a creep."

Too late, Langdon thought.

"We couldn't decide between the stunning view of the pond or the extra square footage." He lifted his chin and smirked. "We got you by a good five hun'erd."

Langdon's eyebrows raised. *This fucking guy.* "It's all good, man. Who cares."

As Langdon was about to make his escape, a series of splashes redirected his attention to the pond. The red canoe had capsized about a hundred feet offshore. "No!" Bryce yelled. "No! No! No!" in rapid succession. He plunged from the canoe into the murky water as his three sons thrashed about, bobbing away from him.

Bonnie raced to the dock, her bohemian dress hiked up in both fists. Basil barked frantically. Langdon remembered Penny saying that the pond was natural and quite deep. Nothing to toy with. Within seconds, he flung his glasses onto the grass, yanked off his T-shirt, and kicked off his sandals. He sprinted to the dock and dove into the water. Although he knew the water must be cold, its bite didn't register, and he could feel someone else not far behind him as they both muscled their way to the canoe. He saw Bryce flip the canoe upright. He grabbed Issac by the scruff of his life jacket and hoisted him inside, and then Amos. But Harlow remained submerged.

Langdon took a deep breath, filling his lungs before diving below the surface. Without his glasses he could hardly see through the muck. In the water, Harlow's face appeared covered by a caul, and his blue eyes seemed afflicted with cataracts. His cheeks expanded as he held his breath. Langdon tugged on the child's life vest. He was tethered to something. What it was, exactly, wasn't obvious. He felt around and around, and as his hand skimmed the grab loop, used to carry the canoe and tie it to the dock, Bryce dove underwater trying desperately to free his son. Langdon tapped Bryce's shoulder and pointed to a small metal hook under the grab loop. A strap from Harlow's life jacket had snagged on it. Bryce freed the child, and Langdon pushed him to the surface. Langdon emerged himself as though blown from a whale spout. Marc was the person behind him, Langdon could see that now as Marc and Bryce helped the boy into the canoe.

As Langdon swam back to shore, he saw Josephine standing on

the water's edge. Once there, he lay on the grass, shivering and waterlogged, catching his breath. The music had stopped.

Josephine hurried over to him with a short stack of towels and sat down next to him, placing her hand on his thigh, the two engaging silently:

You okay?

I'm fine, really.

You sure?

Nothing to see here.

Langdon saw her carotid pulsing wildly. He noticed the mud streaking her feet and ankles, her hem wet from her having stood on the bank.

"I'm okay." He touched her knee. "I promise."

She nodded shakily. Changing the subject, she said, "You can thank Khai for the towels. The clubhouse has a swanky bathroom with a shower and a linen closet. It's impressive."

He sat up, flicking pond scum and sediment from his arms.

Other neighbors surrounded him, and when they too were certain he was fine, their attention turned to the dock, where Bryce and Marc were handing the boys over to Bonnie.

Before long, everyone who'd been in the pond appeared shipwrecked, sitting wet and muddy on the grass. Marc sat not far from Langdon, drying off as Bonnie wrapped the boys in towels, inspecting their scalps, torsos, arms, and legs.

"You're always fighting," Bryce spoke sharply, reprimanding Issac and Amos, pacing around them. "Little hellions!"

"Okay, okay," Bonnie said, her voice shaky. "We can talk about this later."

"I held my breath, Mama." Harlow beamed.

Bonnie teared up, kissing his forehead.

"I want to thank everyone for your kindness," Bryce said, looking around. "Our boys are little maniacs. I'm ashamed to say that this was not their first time tumbling into the water."

Bonnie's cheeks reddened from embarrassment, and she shook her head. "They're good boys. Rambunctious, is all."

No one announced it, but the party was officially over. In the distance, wind chimes sounded, and the pond now appeared perfectly still.

"And you had to be the hero!" Josephine said to Langdon, loud enough for the neighbors to hear. "What an attention hog." They laughed, and when Marc did too, she turned to him.

"I mean both of you."

A woman crouched beside Marc, who was wringing out his polo. She had auburn hair and wore large sunglasses and kitten heels. She handed Marc and Langdon each a glass of wine.

"I'm Danny Preston. Danielle if you want to be formal. In all the years this man and I have been together"—she stood, placing her hands on her hips—"he has never dived into a body of water fully dressed."

"I think you're a bad influence," Marc quipped to Langdon.

Danny started back toward the table. "That's why I like him already."

Marc smiled, resting back on his elbows.

"Nice meeting you, Danny," Langdon called after her. He appeared to be engaged, but he was distracted, eyeing Christopher, as dry as a bone in his aviator sunglasses, handing out bottles of water as if he were a first responder.

"A real top gun." Langdon had meant to say it to himself.

Marc laughed.

"So it's not just me, right?"

Maybe because he and Marc had undergone a sort of baptism by fire, their inhibitions were low.

"Christopher's not a bad dude," Marc offered. "Just a bit of a gasbag." He whacked the side of his head, unclogging his ears. "He's the SVP over his bank's empowerment zones division. You'll enjoy hearing him yammer on about what he's doing on behalf of Chicago's *beleaguered neighborhoods*."

Langdon knew the type, the dude who'd kill you with kindness and not think twice about the kill. The showman who'd smear mud on his legs to convince people he'd done more than merely hand out water.

Langdon was startled from his thoughts when he heard Josephine howling with laughter. He looked up to see her and Khai near the clubhouse, rinsing their legs with a garden hose, doubled over in merriment. He was still thrilled by the possibility that Josephine had found a friend in this new place. He watched as she composed herself, slipped into her sandals, and returned to his side.

"Ready, Blaque?"

"Guess it's time for me to go, Marc," Langdon said, standing. "When we married, we said I'd make all the hard decisions and she'd make the easy ones. Funny how in four years we haven't had any hard ones."

"Cue the laughter." Josephine lowered her voice, pretending to whisper to Marc. "For the record, he stole that line from his father."

Langdon walked barefoot, his sandals in his hand. Josephine swiped lingering foliage from his neck and arms as they entered their driveway.

"You jumped in the water," Josephine said slowly. "Apparently to save three little boys—hooligans, if we're to believe their father. Man, your God complex is real."

Her eyes widened, and she smiled. They had begun their after-party gossip session, which he knew Josephine loved, sometimes more than the party.

She looped her arm around his waist. "That Khai, I like her a lot."

"What was so funny?"

Josephine started to laugh. "I shouldn't tell you. You'll become conceited."

"Now you have to tell me."

"She said, 'I love my husband, so don't get me wrong. But I'd happily toss one of those cute little boys back into the water to see Langdon rip off his shirt again and run toward them.'"

Langdon smiled modestly and shook his head.

"Women think you're hot. Deal with it."

He showed her his wristwatch. "Good news and bad news," he said. "First, good thing my watch is indeed waterproof. But, the bad news is I missed the email about gifts. It invited neighbors to share their favorite items. I saw it now while I was checking this thing."

She lightly punched his arm. "So, the Black people are the only ones who didn't share?"

"Good thing I saved that kid. Worth far more than a gift."

Midway up their driveway, they saw their house brilliantly lit by the early evening sun. Although neither acknowledged it, both slowed to admire it. Their new home. Their new neighborhood. Their new neighbors.

"It's just day two, and I really don't want to press," he said. "But I'm wondering—"

"If we should unpack?" she asked.

"Yes." A knot tightened in his stomach.

When she smiled and nodded, he picked her up and swung her around.

"You smell like standing water. We should shower, and you can read to me on the sleeper." She held his hand and swung it. "Unless you wanna knock boots again? Bump uglies? Tickle wigglies?"

"That last one's not a thing." He laughed. "Mind if I go for a quick run first?"

"Nope. But hurry back or I'll start without you."

In the short time it took for Langdon to change into running clothes, the clubhouse had emptied. He passed under the arch and jogged in place, getting his bearings before running alongside speeding cars. At the three-way, he turned right, passing the One-Stop.

The cemetery's wrought iron gate framed the beauty of the grounds. And, with the sun beginning its descent, the white fluffs of the cottonwood trees shimmered like snow. Langdon marveled at the elaborate tombstones and modest markers, the small but ornate chapel, the whir of insects. He crested a short hill and was overwhelmed by the smell of lavender, entangled in it as if in a spiderweb. As he was heading back to the main gate, he saw the cashier from the One-Stop stooped in front of a large obelisk. He'd gone in for coffee a few times while gassing up, and she never said much. She was neither friendly nor unfriendly. But now she was sobbing so hard that, though she didn't see him, he felt his mere presence as an intrusion.

How many people had he seen weep like that? Writhing in pain in the hospital chapel or the waiting area. Their loss so raw you didn't dare touch them.

He walked quickly down a short lane, hoping not to be noticed, and resumed running. Now the fluff from the cottonwood trees looked more like ashes than snowflakes. The winding paths and the waning sunlight would make it impossible for him to ever again find the marker bathed in the cashier's tears.

CHAPTER FIVE
haunted and hunted

Josephine awakened on the sleeper sofa as the morning light poured in through the windows. She was more rested than she had been in a long time. It was their second morning in Majestic Hills. Langdon had left a note on the bed saying he'd turned on the heat to rid the house of its chill and had gone for another run. The family room had a built-in bookcase, and just as she was about to get up, she noticed his watch and phone on a shelf. He rarely ran without one or the other. Worry washed over her, but as quickly as it surfaced, she shook it off. She roamed the first floor and, in the powder room, lined the toilet seat with tissue paper before remembering it wasn't needed. *This is home*, she thought. Determined to embrace the possibilities of this new place, she got dressed and jumped into the Land Cruiser.

On Willow, she braked when she saw Khai standing by her mailbox.

Josephine lowered the passenger window. "Morning!"

"Hey, neighbor." Khai waved and leaned inside the car.

Behind her, Jackson wheeled a dolly laden with boxes over to a pickup.

"Quick question." Josephine looked down at her phone. "I'm foraging for groceries and, while I don't want to be *that* person, I'm wondering where I can get organic fruit and veggies."

"Lucky for you, I *am* that person," Khai said. "Martin's Gourmet Market. They've got a huge spread of organics, and they will squeeze the orange juice right in front of you. The store is a straight shot down Goodenow a few miles past the expressway."

"I'm there! Thank you."

"And there's the farmer's market. That's where we're headed." Khai twisted her mouth. "Between you and me, when you guys left yesterday, Danny was fangirling. Said you looked like Lupita Nyong'o. I said, 'No way. She's beautiful, but Josephine doesn't look like her.' I started to say 'And I don't look like Lucy Liu, either.'"

Josephine laughed. Khai's anti-model minority swagger was anti-establishment enough to make her interesting.

"Honey!" Jackson called out.

Josephine held back a smile. "Is he talking to you or the bees?"

"The little colonizers." Khai winked, backing away from the car.

Bee colonies. Josephine laughed to herself. After the meet and greet, she'd signed on to Instagram to follow Khai. A video showed her sitting alone at the table outside the clubhouse with a half-full wineglass.

"Just spent the afternoon with my beautiful new neighbors in my new 'hood,'" Khai said, clearly a bit tipsy. "You all know how I love music. There's an old blues cut that says, 'Everybody wants to go to heaven, but nobody wants to die.' Well, we've found heaven here. Can I say this place feels magical? No, I think the better word is *majestic*."

Now, as Josephine drove down Willow, she was becoming a believer.

Martin's was a sensory overload. Warmly lit and airy, its produce section smelled of citrus. Josephine got a bottle of freshly squeezed grapefruit juice and added blueberries and raspberries to her cart. Dinner was going to be a hearty stew of black-eyed peas and French lentils. She planned to roast a salmon filet for Langdon and stopped at the fish counter.

Back on the main road, Josephine saw a runner on her right, immediately recognizing the baseball cap, those shoulders, those calves, that kick. She looked into her rearview mirror to make sure no trucks were bearing down on her, then slowed to pull up beside him.

"Heeyyy, baby!" She drew the words out for the worst catcall ever. "Wanna ride?"

She loved Langdon's facial expression when he was surprised to see her. His eyes narrowed and his smile bloomed. "I think that would defeat the purpose of a run."

"Ooo-kay," she sing-songed. "I coulda rocked your world."

He laughed, and she sped off as he faded from her rearview. She couldn't wait to get home, to continue exploring and unpacking. Maybe they would take in a movie later.

She passed the country club and golf course, preparing for the subdivision's elusive entrance, when her heart lurched. She saw a group of white men dressed in orange baseball caps and orange windbreakers—a few in camouflage—holding rifles and standing around four pickup trucks. They were hunters, that was clear. But the image of a bunch of white guys lolling around with weaponry sent a chill through her.

She blew past the Majestic Hills entrance and pulled into the Leaf It to Us parking lot. Yes, she knew that people hunted in these types of towns. She didn't realize they would congregate practically in her backyard. She thought about turning the car around to catch up with Langdon and warn him about the hunters. But he would probably say she was overreacting.

The parking lot was full of customers filling their SUVs and trucks with large bags of dirt and mulch and flats of flowers. Josephine bit her bottom lip. *Think. Think. Think.*

There was precedent for this moment. About a year earlier, the morning after a rare shooting on the lakefront, Langdon was about to set out for his daily run, and she'd asked him not to go. What if some dude returned to the scene seeking retaliation? What if hardly any other brave soul came out and he was a lone target? He'd told her, in a gentle way, that he would be fine and wasn't going to be straitjacketed by fear. His or hers.

"Please, let me run in peace?" He'd kissed her forehead.

Or, rest in peace, she'd thought, and regretted it instantly. She recalled the heat emanating from his body—and he hadn't even begun to run yet.

Now she wished he'd taken his phone or watch.

She turned the ignition. By the time she reached Majestic Hills again, more pickups had joined the others, and more men, in their bloodthirsty orange, stood around, rifles slung over their shoulders. The group now included a few boys. Langdon religiously ran eight-minute miles, and according to the time on her phone, he would have been back by now had he come straight home. But he sometimes circled around and even retraced his steps to cover more ground.

He was nowhere in sight. She needed gas, so she turned right to go to the One-Stop, pulling up to the pump and heading inside.

Lonnie was behind the counter, and a young man sat cross-legged in a nearby aisle arranging jugs of antifreeze and coolant on a bottom shelf.

"Hello again." She offered her credit card.

"Hello, yourself," Lonnie said. She took the card but just held it. "Something wrong?"

Josephine had nothing even resembling a poker face. Her deep brown skin looked ashen.

"I have a question that may sound a little loony. There's a bunch of hunters near where I live. Should I be worried?"

The young man walked to the front of the store, his hands stuffed in the pockets of his blue jeans.

"My son, Wade," Lonnie said to Josephine.

He pulled his hand from his pocket for a lackluster wave.

Josephine noticed how much he looked like Lonnie, though he was a few shades lighter, with hair that was curlier and thicker, like an ermine helmet. He was about an inch shorter than Josephine, and his Crocs slides seemed too big even with his white ankle socks.

"My husband, as you know, is Black," Josephine said, staring down at her hands. "He went out for a run. To get home, he's got to pass a group of white men with rifles. They could be completely harmless, but I'm wondering: Should I be worried?"

Considering the question, Lonnie stared at a track along the counter. Josephine guessed it was where plexiglass had been removed after the pandemic.

"Before Majestic Hills was built," Lonnie said, "those woods were used for hunting and fishing. There's a shooting gallery and archery range over there, too. But now that your subdivision is private property, hunters only use the land south of Goodenow."

"They park out front because that's the entrance," Wade added.

Lonnie left the counter to pour a cup of coffee from the coffee station. When she handed it to Josephine, it struck her how different *this woman* was compared with the version she'd been a couple of nights before.

"I've been in town for decades with hardly a problem," Lonnie said. "Even though the town is overwhelmingly white, which I am not; and conservative, which I most certainly am not; and Christian, which I am only sometimes."

A loud crash came from the back. Everyone jumped. Lonnie mean-mugged Wade.

"Benny!" Wade yelled, hurrying toward him.

"Wasn't me," a boy's voice responded. "Swear to God!"

"What did your aunt say," Wade yelled again, "about swearing to God?"

Lonnie rolled her eyes but returned her attention to Josephine. "Those damn MAGA signs continue to sprout like crimson weeds on more than a few lawns belonging to people who surprised me." She looked out the window at the Land Cruiser and then back at Josephine. "You're shaking."

"I'm okay."

"Let me drive over there with you. I'm small but mighty." She smiled. "You can park your car near the ice freezer."

"Lang says I worry too much about him. Although I don't think he worries enough."

"Well, there may be truth to both." Lonnie picked up her cell phone. "Option two is that I call my friend Adam Daniels, the deputy police chief. Everyone calls him Deputy Adam. Want me to ask him to drive over?"

Josephine's neck tightened. *Do I really want to get the police involved? Might that escalate something that was nothing to begin with? Damn it. Black folks can't even be paranoid in peace.* "No." Josephine's voice petered. "I think I'll just go back home."

Lonnie returned her phone to the counter and touched Josephine's arm. "Suit yourself."

At the three-way, Josephine glanced at Langdon's ID in the cup holder. His smile—two front veneers, slightly off-center. She had to decide: turn left to go home and wait, or turn right to look for him and face the prospect of another argument. The driver behind her tapped his horn, and she veered left, following the road back to Majestic Hills. She heard a gunshot. A series of them. In the city, she never heard gunshots, just read about the carnage. Here, the killing fields were in your face. She passed the country club and golf course, preparing for the subdivision's entrance, when she saw three men in orange huddled around a man lying on the ground. Her chest cavity contracted as she realized that the man was Langdon. For a few surreal seconds she watched the wind kick his baseball cap out onto the road as if it were not his, but someone else's.

Is this the way I lose you? Is this how we end?

She sped up to pull onto the shoulder and leaped out of the car. "Langdon!" She clamped her hand over her mouth, seeing the blood on his right leg and forearm.

"Everything's all right," he shouted, lifting his head up. He was laughing.

Gunshots sounded in the near distance.

"It was my bad," he said. "I'm fine. I just stumbled."

Two of the men were helping him stand.

"Hey, neighbor," said one, serving as a crutch. His mirrored sunglasses reflected the sky. He smiled. "You know this gentleman?"

Josephine's heart drummed in her ears, and it took her a few seconds to discern the man's features. It was Christopher from two houses down. He had a rifle slung over his shoulder and a sheathed hunting knife clipped to his belt. His dog, Basil, chased down branches thrown by a couple of boys whom Josephine could make out only as flecks of orange behind a clump of trees. In her thirty-eight years, Josephine had never seen a rifle or any firearm up close. She'd never touched one. It looked slender but even more menacing than she imagined. She also had never seen freshly dead turkeys. A small mound was piled on the bed of a pickup, awaiting beheading.

"I guess I have to get used to running on gravel," Langdon said. "I wiped out, and these guys insisted on helping me."

Josephine examined the abraded skin on his knees.

"My ego got a bigger wallop."

"So why are you holding your arm like it's broken?" she asked, standing.

"It seemed like I should." He laughed, letting it fall slack. A dusting of fine pebbles clung to his forearm, but she saw no other wounds.

"These are my friends," Christopher said, gesturing to four men standing nearby. "A few venture capital and private equity guys." One wore American flag gloves and a cap with the words "Catch. Hunt. Kill." written in cursive. Another man with black tar under his eyes had chased down Langdon's baseball cap and was holding it.

"And, of course, you know Marc," Christopher said.

"Hey, Josephine!" Marc waved like a schoolboy. "I'll run with him from now on."

The men had earplugs dangling around their necks like jewelry. Every now and then they stuck their fingers in their ears at the sound of gun blasts that made Josephine jump.

"These guys," Langdon said. "They were worse than you when I fell." Josephine could tell that he was trying to sound upbeat. "All over me like I'm some damsel in distress. I begged them to leave a part of my dignity intact."

"He keeps refusing to let us drive him home," Marc said, adjusting a holster on his hip. "I think he'll be all right. But he would know better than me since he's the doc."

Langdon pulled away from the two men, and Josephine edged in beside her husband. "I've got him from here. Thank you."

"I invited them to come around for a beer," Langdon said as they walked to the Land Cruiser. "But they've got their own cooler."

Who cares about beer? she thought.

Josephine had calmed down, but she still felt the remnants of panic. Very little about the hunters being her neighbors sat any more right with her now than it had before. Sure, there's comfort in realizing that you know the armed white men. But there's also fear in the realization that the white men you know are armed.

She helped Langdon into the passenger seat. As she moved to close the door, he held her hand. "Everything really is fine."

Josephine nodded. She wanted to say *Lang, let's leave right now. Fuck unpacking. Let's just go.* But he might have reminded her that this was a fluke, totally his fault. And, although Langdon wasn't the type to go for the jugular in an argument, he might have felt justified in saying that maybe she was searching for an out, an opportunity to leave.

Shit happens everywhere. Including at his work.

Besides, she had now experienced the unthinkable: what it might feel like to lose him. And that was god-awful, canceling everything, including what she thought of all those men in their orange.

"They invited me to go deer hunting this fall." Langdon winced, fastening his seat belt.

"I hope you told them the Blaques may fish, but we don't hunt."

CHAPTER SIX

phantom parts

Just before ten p.m., Lonnie stood outside the One-Stop watching Wade ride his mountain bike in the direction of the trailer park, where he was living. Old Creek Road had only a handful of streetlights, and after a few minutes Lonnie had to stretch up on tiptoes to see his headlight beam and the reflectors on his helmet and book bag. Inside of which was a quart of milk, a small box of cereal, and a couple of cans of spinach and creamed corn that she had pleaded with Wade to take. Because he was on her Martin's Gourmet Market rewards account, Lonnie, unbeknownst to Wade, received email receipts every time he shopped. She knew that her sixteen-year-old had been feasting on a veritable array of doughnuts, hot dogs, and corn chips. She'd received receipts for boxes of tampons; four packages of Nix—probably for a burgeoning outbreak of head lice; a birthday cake and candles; and a sympathy card.

Lonnie wanted to pry, but she didn't dare. It was only a matter of time before her tech-savvy son would realize that his mother was surveilling him and he'd stop shopping at Martin's altogether. In the interim, Lonnie stocked the One-Stop with a few cans of healthier foods that she gave to Wade whenever a window presented itself. And, so that he wouldn't deplete his savings—his allowance plus money from several summers of caddying—she made sure that the One-Stop's shelves always had more than enough batteries, bandages, shampoo, conditioner, and mosquito repellent. She figured he could simply pocket them as needed. Although she had no idea whether Wade was sexually active, she no longer kept the boxes of condoms under lock and key. The last thing anybody needed was him knocking up some girl. She understood that she was aiding and abetting insanity, but work-arounds seemed her only option until she could persuade her softhearted, soft-in-the-head son to return home.

Lonnie squinted into the darkness. It had been a month since Wade moved out. A month since his three older siblings flew home for a failed intervention that left Wade sobbing but resolute about finishing his father's "humanitarian work." On this night, like so many others, Lonnie simply had to trust that Wade would make it to the trailer park without a driver sideswiping him. As if arriving there safely was any consolation. He might have been better off in a ditch.

"What a horrible thought," Lonnie muttered to herself.

Worse still, it wasn't like he could call her if he needed her. He refused his cell phone, describing it as a function of capitalistic greed and mind control. He left it on his nightstand and kept his mother wondering why he couldn't be the self-absorbed, selfie-obsessed teenager he used to be.

When she was certain she could no longer see him, she got into her pickup and drove to Goodenow Road. Rather than head directly home, she pulled onto the shoulder where the hunters had gathered hours earlier. The chain with the No Trespassing sign once again cordoned off a dirt trail freshly peppered with buckshot and shell casings that reflected the moonlight. Across the street, the entrance to Majestic Hills was illuminated by a lone streetlamp whose light could barely muster a shadow. Despite Wade's working her nerves all afternoon, she couldn't stop thinking about Josephine and her fears. The only weapon Lonnie ever owned was a razor her aunt had given her years ago with the directive to "slice any motherfucker who threatens you from asshole to appetite." Lonnie assumed that because her friend Deputy Adam hadn't entered the store with some juicy tale crackling from him like the static from his police radio, nothing remarkable had happened in New Pointe all day. But why would Josephine ask *her*, of all people, about the hunters? Lately, Lonnie felt painfully ill-equipped to give anyone advice. She wanted someone to advise her on managing the pain of her husband's sudden, inexplicable death, and her son whom she could neither console nor corral.

The only assurance Lonnie could have offered Josephine was that she, too, had loved a man who was headstrong, filled with wanderlust, and had his own ideas about the way he moved through the world. She, too, had believed that her time in New Pointe was only temporary. One month was what Geoffrey had asked of her. One month that turned into twenty-five years, a dizzying sweep of time that had felt like overnight.

Oh, the things Lonnie could warn Josephine about sacrifice.

Lonnie turned off her headlights and cut the engine. She was not supposed to even be in New Pointe. She and Geoffrey had planned to be living in downtown Chicago, dividing their time between there and New York. She'd hoped to finally make time for writing books and in-depth stories for national magazines. They would join the reverse migration of their friends, most of them Black, who had left the city to rear their children in the burbs but had returned recently as empty nesters. Now in their fifties, they still worked full-time and vacationed heartily, the women posting photos of their bikini-clad, Pelo-toned bodies and their overall Black-don't-crackness.

That was their plan. But Geoffrey was dead, and she missed his smile resting on the back of her neck every night before they fell asleep. And Wade—the only one of her children who used to sit next to her and read as she tried to write—now held her hostage.

She leaned her head on the headrest and stared through the sunroof at red airplane lights that flickered before being absorbed into the muted night.

Before Geoffrey, Lonnie had never dated a white guy, let alone imagined being wed to one. They met in the early 1990s at New York University. She was working on a master's degree in journalism. He was simultaneously completing an MBA and a master's degree in electrical engineering.

The first time she saw him was at a campus discussion she'd organized, and billed as "open and honest" about the white police officers who had recently been acquitted of brutalizing Rodney King. Despite final exams being underway, about a hundred students (almost evenly divided between Blacks and whites) gathered in a stadium-style lecture hall in the School of Communications. Geoffrey sat quietly in the top row. Lonnie stood behind a podium in the well of the room. The conversation bubbled around Geoffrey as a group of white students questioned why Rodney King had tried to elude police. It wasn't until someone asked why residents in tough communities didn't get as riled about Black-on-Black crime as they did about violent white police officers that Geoffrey stood to speak.

Tall and wiry, he was dressed in a wrinkled button-front and threadbare blue jeans. He wore eyeglasses that he nudged up the bridge of his nose, and although his thick brown hair was shaved close on the sides and back, a flop of loose curls mopped his brow. He was known around campus as the genius engineering student who often looked homeless—but whose family's name was chiseled into several NYU buildings.

Geoffrey first addressed the questioner: "There's a shitload of white-on-white crime. It's just that when white people commit crimes, race is irrelevant." He held up a copy of *The Inkster*, a free magazine about race and culture that Lonnie had started as part of her master's thesis. He turned to Lonnie: "I think your commentary here answers this question expertly. Alondra, is it?" he asked, checking the pronunciation of her byline.

"Lonnie is fine."

"Would you mind telling us what you wrote about our expectations and the police?"

He sat back down.

"I don't mind at all," she said. "We expect bad people to do bad things, no matter their race, but that shouldn't be the expectation of the police." She left the podium and walked toward the audience. "They're part of an institution that's one of the pillars of our society. If an officer diminishes his or her oath to serve and protect, it's not only the officer who's the bad apple, but the institution itself."

Geoffrey stood again. "Brilliant," he said. "Thank you."

When the discussion ended, students flocked to Lonnie, who was radiant in the glow of adulation. Geoffrey waited for the crowd to thin. When it didn't, he left through a side door.

Their paths didn't cross again for more than a year. He was walking through Washington Square Park with his lunch. His eyes widened when he spotted Lonnie seated on a bench, reading a book. He would later tell her that he'd read everything she'd written in *The Inkster*, from an examination of the crack cocaine epidemic to the power of RUN-D.M.C. When he saw her in that yellow dress, with her hair swept up in a bun and her large hoop earrings, his heart sputtered. He approached her, reminding her that he'd spoken at her Rodney King event.

"May I . . ." He pointed to the bench and sat before she answered.

Lonnie closed her book. "You're taking summer classes? Or are you a New Yorker?"

"I am definitely not a New Yorker."

He unwrapped a large sandwich and offered her half. She shook her head. The smell of pastrami reminded her of her father, Saturday afternoons, a trip to the deli, and jigsaw puzzles. She'd reserved pastrami for him alone.

"I grew up in a small town outside Chicago," he said. "I'm spending the summer working on a top secret engineering project." He lifted an eyebrow.

"Top secret, huh? Where?"

"It's in a triple-X movie theater in Times Square. The only thing I can reveal is that it's about ohms and amps and ooohs and ahhs." He lifted his chin. "Where are you from?"

So very weird and bawdy. She smiled to herself. She told him that she'd grown up on army bases in Hawaii, Germany, and France. When her father left the army, her family bought a home in Inkster, a Detroit suburb, hence her magazine's title. Her father was a whole-life insurance salesman, her mother a social worker. With them gone, her closest living relative was her Aunt Lydia, who owned an African art gallery in Washington Heights.

Geoffrey listened intently, but Lonnie could hardly speak for watching him eat. His forehead glistened as he tore through his sandwich, at the same time managing to shovel coleslaw into his mouth and glug lemonade.

Lonnie scrunched her face. This was not unlike witnessing a mauling.

"I'm sorry," he said. "You must think I'm a pig. Sometimes I'm so tunneled in on a project that I forget to eat, and my body doesn't register hunger until food is in front of me."

When Lonnie had to leave, Geoffrey took the receipt from buying his sandwich and split it in half. He penciled his telephone number on one piece and handed her the other.

"Can we keep in touch?" he ventured.

She wrote slowly. He was smart and kind of cute in a disheveled way. Still, she had no intention of calling someone who had no table manners. Besides, she was focused on her thesis and an internship at *The New York Times* following graduation.

A few days later he invited her to lunch at his favorite Village café. Before she could decline, he promised to "eat civilized." And he did. He invited her to dinner at Windows on the World, and dancing at the Palladium, where she learned that he had rhythm. They'd been seeing each other for about a month when, on their way to a Harlem night club, they detoured to her aunt's art gallery. Aunt Lydia always stood perfectly straight, wore colorful headdresses, and used a walking staff.

"Too vanilla," the old woman frothed to Lonnie as Geoffrey examined a Guinean virility statue with stumpy legs and a massive member. "He must have some good under-plunder."

"Auntie," Lonnie whispered. "We're not dating. We're certainly not having sex."

"Good." Aunt Lydia said. "And don't. He's *not* the one."

Too vanilla? Lonnie thought about being ten years old and eavesdropping as her mother and Aunt Lydia watched the 1977 Oscars. The women lost their minds when Eletha Finch, a Black woman, accepted the Best Actor award on behalf of her white husband, Peter Finch, who'd recently died. Aunt Lydia hooted and howled with pride as Eletha, dressed in a mink coat, recounted how her husband had said to her "Dah-ling" this and "Dah-ling" that. Lonnie didn't understand why Eletha mattered so much, especially since Lonnie's father was spending that same night working hard, visiting clients, and collecting insurance premiums.

Lonnie vowed that she would never even date a white man—as an allegiance to her father.

But she also hated being told *Don't*. Was it the power of suggestion that made her consider Geoffrey's "under-plunder" all night? She hadn't even thought about it until a few weeks before, when he'd read her essay on the Gulf War and placed both hands on her shoulders. Riveted, he looked her squarely in her eyes and said, "Your writing is gallant."

Gallant? Who says stuff like that? If he'd kissed her, as she thought he might, she would have let him, this wonderfully weird and kind man with an expansive mind.

At the nightclub, they sat side by side at a table, enjoying the comic onstage, when Geoffrey leaned over to say something to her. His lips brushed against her ear, and his breath tunneled through her, rousing a hunger she didn't realize was there. Several times, his knee pressed against hers. He touched her hand when he laughed. Ordinarily, he was a bit of a klutz, stepping on her heels when they exited a taxi or walked to their seats down an aisle, knocking over a glass of wine or water. But later that night in her three-room, university-owned apartment—where she'd never invited him before—he had the dexterity of a classical pianist or a pickpocket. As they made love, his touch was agile and adept, appropriately gentle or firm. His attention to detail sublime.

They graduated and had been officially dating for a year when, one morning while they were still in her bed, he asked her to marry him.

"I need my freedom," she said. "I want to travel wherever a story takes me and spend as much time as I need telling it. I want to write about real people and real issues most people don't think twice about." She thought aloud. "And I hate Crock-Pots."

"I hate them too," he said. "Whatever you want."

"Need," she corrected. She turned her back to him and looked out the window at the bricks of the fire station next door. "I want a really big life."

They married at City Hall without letting anyone know, including the Stanfield family lawyer who would have pressured Lonnie to sign a prenup. The newlyweds moved into her apartment and planned to stay there for the duration of her *Times* internship. Midway through, she learned that she'd been awarded a Fulbright to spend a year studying prisons in Finland. She'd applied on a whim, writing that she admired Finland's commitment to rehabilitating, not just warehousing inmates. Geoffrey was eager to join her. Growing up, he'd spent time there, as well as myriad other places his hippie parents dragged him off to: an ashram near Bangladesh, a village of yurts in Mongolia. Her editor at the *Times* planned to offer her a job when she returned stateside. Not yet as a foreign correspondent, which was her ultimate goal, but he believed she could be an outstanding one after a few years of paying dues.

Lonnie and Geoffrey were packed, a couple of days from moving across the Atlantic, when he received a phone call that his father had died. His mother had passed away years earlier, he had no siblings, and he'd always referred to his dad as his best friend. He wept torrents of gulping tears. It was the first time Lonnie had seen him cry.

Geoffrey asked her for a month—time to go home to talk to lawyers and sort through his father's estate, the family foundation, the will, trusts, bank accounts, board positions, investments. She agreed and called the Fulbright people to postpone their trip—for a month.

She'd held his hand in the back seat of the taxi as they arrived in New Pointe and made their way through town. He directed the driver to follow the white rail fence along the frontage of the Stanfield estate, down a private road winding through the woods. The house itself was white with a limestone base, and Lonnie was awed by how lovely it was, substantial but not at all ostentatious. Inside, Geoffrey carried their suitcases upstairs to a bedroom, and they agreed to unpack only what they needed.

But sifting through his father's affairs proved more daunting than they had imagined. Month after month, Lonnie postponed the fellowship, until four months in, she looked at the calendar and realized she couldn't remember her last period. She'd thought the minor weight gain had been from stress eating, but she was pregnant. The final deferment was for a year, after which she would never fulfill the terms of her fellowship.

After the first baby, a son, was born, she needed to get out of the house for a bit and began freelancing for *The New Pointe News*. She covered the village board meeting, where trustees approved plans for a new chicken processing plant, called the Grand Vistas, and an accompanying trailer park to house its migrant workers. On the property, the owners contracted to build a small church and a grocery store that sold Mexican goods. She wrote about the new subdivisions sprouting up around town and the wave of new residents. Within a decade, the population count on the "Welcome to New Pointe" sign had grown from one thousand to five thousand. She wrote about the conflicts between the old and the new residents, and the ordinances the village board passed to address the disputes. There were new fines for garage doors that needed painting, sagging gutters, and pockmarked driveways. At one meeting, a man in overalls with graying blond hair said that home repairs were nothing compared with the storm heading toward the town. Lonnie knew what he was inferring. For years, she had been one of a handful of Blacks in New Pointe. But its population boom also increased (albeit modestly) the numbers of its people of color.

By the time Lonnie and Geoffrey's third child, a second daughter, was born, Lonnie had gone back to school to become a certified teacher. She took a job as a creative writing/pre-journalism instructor at Stanfield Academy, Geoffrey's alma mater. In the thick of life, it seemed like a fine compromise, a stopover place until she could feed her heart.

Years later, she was in the attic picking around ballerina slippers, hockey sticks, baseball bats, and partially deflated basketballs when she found the book bag she'd planned to carry on the plane to Finland. Veiled in cobwebs and dust, it held a heavy, early-model Zenith laptop computer, several reporter's notebooks, a box of pens, a pocket dictionary, maps, a Finnish-English translation guide, several European plug converters, tape cassettes, and a recorder without its batteries—so they wouldn't corrode. All preserved like in a mudslide. Lonnie hurried downstairs with the recorder, inserted batteries, and pressed Play.

"Testing," her younger, soprano voice announced from the past. "Testing, testing." Seconds later, Geoffrey free-styled with his echoey Muhammad Ali impersonation. "My wife, Alondra Alexander, is the king of the world. The king of the world. The king of the world." And they'd collapsed into laughter.

For a long time, Lonnie had made peace with her choices—especially when she and Geoffrey seemed destined to grow old together. She chose to have babysitters rather than a series of nannies, and a part-time cook rather than a full-time one. They employed the cleaning and landscaping services the Stanfields had used for years. But when her children were of age, they had chores. They were not going to be spoiled, entitled brats. She chose to attend recitals and track meets and science fairs. And whenever Geoffrey gifted her a week or two at a summer writer's retreat, she chose to call home every night and, on a few occasions, fly home early even though Geoffrey tried to convince her he had everything under control.

Now, Lonnie questioned everything—her life with her husband and children. The career she cast aside. The grief counselor she and Wade had been seeing individually told them both that it was not uncommon to reassess one's life after the death of a loved one—to reflect on the paths taken and not taken.

We should have kept going to the counselor.

When headlights flooded Lonnie's rearview mirror, she scrambled for her keys, feeling around the seat and on the floor. She made sure her doors were locked as she shielded her eyes, trying to see around the glare in her side mirror. Someone got out of the car and started toward her. She unbuckled her seat belt and turned to try to see better. Then she relaxed. She would know those pigeon toes anywhere. Deputy Adam's feet always seemed to be in communion with each other as he walked, as if bargaining: *You let me by, and I'll let you by*.

He tapped on the window and spoke into his collar. "It's Lonnie Stanfield." He sounded chipper, as though they were reconnecting at a high school reunion.

Lonnie found her keys on the passenger seat. She turned on the ignition and rolled down the window. The clock on her dashboard showed just after midnight.

"Somebody reported an abandoned pickup outside Majestic Hills," Adam said. "You okay, Lonnie? You need me to trail you home?"

"Not at all," she said, trying to sound upbeat. "Just lost track of time."

"Janice asked me if you might want to spend the night with us again."

"That one night was enough. Tell her I'm grateful for the invitation."

"All righty." He looked at the road. "I drove through the trailer park. It's quiet there tonight."

"Excellent," she said dryly. "Good night, friend."

Adam tapped the pickup's roof twice. Soon he was pulling back onto Goodenow.

Lonnie felt for her phone. The home screen photo came from a *New York Times* profile of the Stanfield Foundation. She and Geoffrey were in their backyard pushing Eve, their second child, and Maddy, their third, on a swing set. Bradley, the firstborn, who was ten at the time, stood off to the side, looking bored. Wade was asleep in his baby carrier on Geoffrey's back.

Lonnie decided to return to the One-Stop. She had a cot in the back room. If Wade needed her, she'd be a hair closer to him than if she holed up in their big, empty house. Being next door to the cemetery also gave her a semblance of peace.

She knew that longtime New Pointe residents wondered why she was working at the One-Stop. The Stanfield family had owned the convenience store and its surrounding five acres for generations. The surly old man who'd managed the property since the 1970s had retired at the beginning of the year. Most longtime residents assumed that Lonnie was merely filling in until she hired his replacement. But as months passed, customers couldn't understand why she still stood behind the checkout counter. Parents who'd felt honored that she'd once taught their children at the high school now felt awkward waiting in line to purchase a container of ramen or a packet of batteries or a box of tampons from a Stanfield—even one by marriage. It was like queuing up for one of the royals to ladle a bowl of soup.

Lonnie U-turned, her high beams biting through a plume of fog over the Majestic Hills entrance. What would she tell Josephine about the hunters and New Pointe and the tug-of-war that is the unwinnable nature of time?

Lonnie would tell her to leave. She would say: *I have no doubt that Langdon loves you as much as Geoffrey loved me. But leave, Josephine, before your life is swallowed up by a crippling inertia: term papers and swimming lessons, longings and regrets. Leave before you have far more than you ever wanted, but not the one thing you truly needed. Leave before you are haunted by the past, and your dreams, once vital to who you were, are whittled away until all that remains are little more than phantom parts.*

CHAPTER SEVEN

"the doors are closing"

The wind blew fiercely beneath a speckled sky on the morning Langdon and Christopher and Monica, by sheer coincidence, pulled onto Willow at the same time. At the mouth of the cul-de-sac, while sitting at the stop sign, they tapped their horns and waved at each other before making a right turn onto Goodenow.

Langdon got caught by a red light and wound up pulling into the train station as Monica was leaving, having already dropped Christopher off. Langdon liked Monica. He often saw her in the yard as he was returning from a run. She always waved with both arms—like an SOS wave—and seemed so happy to be pregnant. He wondered whether Josephine would ever find her way there.

Langdon and Monica rolled down their windows.

"Morning, neighbor," she said. Her dark hair was pulled back into a ponytail, and her blue eyes appeared extra-large behind her thick glasses.

"How're you feeling?" he asked.

"I'm getting as big as a house and loving it."

"Good, good!"

"You should catch up with Christopher. Ride together."

"I'll look for him," Langdon lied.

Maybe it wasn't neighborly, but he preferred to ride alone. He couldn't bear listening to Christopher yap about his work for forty-five minutes.

Langdon had just parked in the lot when the high-pitched drone of the town's tornado siren sounded. He covered his ears. It was

Thursday morning, and he and Josephine had become accustomed to the low, groaning trill, followed by the text: *This is a test of the Drake County Severe Weather Emergency Broadcast System. This is only a test.*

As he pushed through the turnstile, he saw Christopher, his khakis the same color as his crossbody, standing farther down the platform. He, like everyone surrounding him, was enraptured by his cell phone. Langdon walked quickly in the opposite direction.

When the train pulled up, Langdon boarded a car near the rear and sat in a window seat by the bulkhead. Soon a tone sounded, an automated system announced, "The doors are closing," and the 10:50 express began to hiss and hum away from the station.

Langdon was on his way downtown to meet Ken, Fat's husband. Initially, they had been brought together by their wives, but the men had quickly learned that they genuinely enjoyed each other and forged their own bond. As the train made its way downtown, Langdon opened his phone and flipped through wedding photos from four years ago. One of his favorites was of Ken, a few inches shorter than Josephine even with locs coiled atop his head, walking Josephine down the aisle. When Langdon asked her to marry him, she'd told him that she would walk alone. She'd said it would be the happiest moment of her life, but also one of the hardest, without Edward Taylor there to do the honors. Langdon had held her and said, "Girl, I don't care how you get down that aisle. Just get to me."

The ceremony took place in the Hyde Park neighborhood church she'd grown up in but no longer attended regularly. When the Bridal song began, Langdon turned toward the rear doors expecting to see only Josephine. Instead, Ken stood beside her.

Later, Josephine explained that Ken had made a last-minute pitch, saying that she had men in her life who would step into any gap. He was one of them.

Langdon looked out the window. He was about to nod off when feedback screeched from the intercom system: "Up next, 55th Street, Chicago Sinai Medical Center."

It had been Langdon's stop when he lived in the condo. Now he mostly drove in to work. He was busy zipping his book bag when he looked up and saw that the electronic Majestic Hills advertisement, the catalyst for their odyssey, had been bashed in.

"The doors are closing," warned the automated voice.

As the train resumed, Langdon kept staring at the ad. He felt certain it had been defaced by someone who lusted after the life it presented. Lusted after it but found it utterly unattainable and was pissed off that it was being flaunted in front of him.

Nearing his stop, Langdon gathered his things and hustled down the aisle through the cars. He wanted to be closer to the escalator leading up to the Roosevelt Road exit. Midway, he saw the back of Christopher's head bobbing to a beat from his earbuds.

Langdon hurried past him, without looking back.

Café Cuz had been a favorite of Josephine and Langdon's when they lived in the condo. Its soul food menu had an impressive array of delicious vegetarian options. Langdon entered and immediately spotted Ken, his dreadlocks piled atop his head.

The two men embraced, and when they pulled away, Langdon patted Ken's button-front shirt, which strained against his midsection.

"Bruh, post-pregnancy pounds?"

"Man, go to hell." Ken threw his head back, his laughter pulsing through his throat. The sound was as startling as it was infectious, nearby patrons chuckling with him. Fat often joked that each of her sons entered the world with unbridled wails, courtesy of their father, that jolted them awake. Ken gestured for Langdon to sit.

"Y'all had enough of them burbs? You coming back to the city?"

It was a joke, and although Langdon immediately said no, his face revealed an uncertainty that he could tell Ken detected. Ken had a master's degree in counseling and saw patients in a small office nearby. Langdon never wanted to take advantage by monopolizing their conversations with his shit, but the men ordered their food, and Ken invited Langdon to unload.

So unload he did.

During the time he and Josephine had been in Majestic Hills, four more gunshot victims at the hospital had slipped through his grasp, two of them children: a boy who, according to the news, was so eager to start kindergarten the next school year that he left behind a book bag he'd begun methodically filling with supplies; and a girl who had been celebrating her sixth birthday. Her last breath was taken as she stood before her cake blowing out her candles. And Langdon still hadn't been able to forget the little well-kept boy with the missing sock.

He told Ken that he loved Majestic Hills so far. Still, he couldn't help wondering if being there made him a sellout. Living where he did, could he truly be an inspiration to some young lad living in shit conditions? Somebody with nothing to lose and was a senior citizen, an ol' G, if he makes it to twenty-five. And what was his responsibility to himself, his wife, and future children?

He told Ken about the hunters and how he'd felt when he saw them. This was something he hadn't even shared with Josephine, something he was now too embarrassed to tell her: He had tripped that day. He wiped out. But what happened was more complicated than that. He recalled running, getting closer and closer to a hostile-looking brood of men, hearing them yell "We got the boss" amid cheers and whoops, and the men patting one another on the back. "We got his ass." They were talking about the boss bird, the elusive dominant turkey. But at the time, Langdon had no clue. He remembered feeling freighted, weighed down by having to devise a strategy—in case they tried something. He recalled squaring his shoulders, preparing his body for a battle. And as he approached all that orange, his stomach knotted, his hamstrings locked, as if his body had morphed in preparation, becoming a monstrous thing.

Langdon talked far more than he'd intended, and Ken listened generously. He often said it was the least he could do considering the many late-night calls during which Josephine listened to Fat. Langdon would lie in bed as Fat's voice chirped nonstop from Josephine's earbuds. He would lean over and say, "Take a breath, Fathead." Or, according to Josephine, Ken would say drolly, "Common courtesy dictates you listen for a while." A few times Josephine fell asleep while on the phone, and Langdon removed one of her earbuds, placing it in his ear.

"Your girl's knocked out, Fat. Go to bed."

Now Langdon picked at his food with his fork. "There are days when I ask myself: Where do I belong? Where do I fit in this demonstration we call a city, a country."

"It's the reigning question of the day, bruh." Ken wiped his mouth with his napkin. "It ain't unusual to be experiencing buyers' remorse, or even a bit of Black guilt."

"Or feeling like a sellout?" Langdon studied the tin ceiling.

"All are understandable, especially with what you see day in and day out at the hospital. The desperation, the lack." Ken twisted his Alpha Phi Alpha pinkie ring. "You still seeing that therapist for what y'all called 'tuning up the circuitry?'"

"Yeah, he's the one who told me—"

"Oh, I remember: bruh said you got a savior complex, big as a muthafucka."

Langdon smiled, cupping his forehead. Ken gestured for the bill.

"I got this," Langdon said when the bill came. "Appreciate you, bruh."

"May as well go'on and settle in." Ken swiped crumbs from his shirt. "If you left right now, what type of return would you get on your investment? With your condo rented, where would you go? 'Cause y'all niggas can't live with us. Ain't no room in the inn." Ken laughed his big, hearty laugh. "Besides, Fatima tells me every time I look at her, she gets pregnant. So—"

"Maybe y'all need a television in your bedroom."

Langdon took the train back home and spent the remainder of his day off relaxing, playing video games. By early evening, the wind had given way to rain, and he picked Josephine up at the train station. They had dinner and made love.

They showered together, and Langdon stepped out first, toweling off. As Josephine remained in the bathroom, he went into the dark bedroom and stood by the slightly open window, watching the driving rain. A full moon, barely legible behind the clouds, hung low in the sky, elongating the shadows of the trees and making the patio glisten.

He heard the bells from a train entering the downtown station. It still amazed him that New Pointe was so quiet that on some nights the faint sound of syncopated ringing reached them from about a mile and a half away.

The way the house was constructed, Langdon could see the frosted glass of the bathroom window from the bedroom. The light was the only one on in the house, and when he heard the water shut off, he saw Josephine's naked silhouette. He grabbed his glasses from the nightstand, watching as her blurred figure bent over to dry her legs. He took in the curve of her breasts, the contour of her ass. It reminded him of peering through a keyhole in his childhood home, or through his telescope.

Lightning flashed, and Langdon gasped when he saw a figure standing on their property, just beyond the tree line. The person—who Langdon guessed was a man, by his shape and size—wore a yellow raincoat, the hood pulled over his head. He seemed to be looking up at the bathroom window. Although the light was still on, Josephine had moved away. Langdon started to root around on the floor for the pair of shorts he'd stepped out of. He felt for his cell phone to call the police. He had been meaning to install motion-detector lights over the patio, and now wished he had.

Thunder boomed, reverberating throughout the house. Outside, a dog barked, and Langdon looked up in time to see Basil bounding out of the woods, tags jingling, toward the man in the raincoat. Langdon knew then than the man was Christopher and watched him leash Basil.

It was entirely possible that Christopher never meant to be on the Blaques' property. In Majestic Hills, there were no fences separating the residents' expansive backyards—nothing at all acknowledging property lines. Basil could have taken off after God knows what—a squirrel, a rabbit, a chipmunk—and delivered them there. But trespassing wasn't the real issue. For Langdon, the question was whether Christopher had been checking out Josephine. Christopher was not among Langdon's favorite people, that was no secret. But it was nearly impossible to know whether he was also a voyeur, a Peeping Tom. Sheets of rain fell in the woods, refracting moonlight off the fog, distorting everything the way fun house mirrors do.

"Let's go," Christopher urged in a loud whisper. "C'mon, man."

But Basil didn't move. He sat on his haunches, hackles raised, panting.

CHAPTER EIGHT

shifty little vertebrates

Langdon had volunteered to spend Saturday morning helping Jackson cordon off an area of his property where he kept his beehives. The ground was still soaked from the torrent a couple of nights before, and a few spindly trees had uprooted. The men were in Jackson's yard, preparing to lay railroad ties, making it easier for him to mow grass and prune the underbrush back there.

From Josephine's point of view, they weren't working fast enough. Cocooned in her throw, she was sitting at the table on the patio, watching them heft yard implements onto a trailer attached to Jackson's John Deere. The clanking of metal against metal was disturbing her peace.

Her laptop sat atop the table, and she was supposed to be fine-tuning a presentation for a group of high-end human resources staffers in town next week for a convention. Instead, she was staring up at the sky. She did notice when Langdon started walking over to her. He wore the high-top Chuck Taylors she loved; they made him look like a cute, nerdy teen.

"Didn't you ask me to help you stay on task?" he asked.

They often partnered when one of them had homework. She encouraged him to transcribe patient notes, and she served as a sounding board when he had to testify in court to have parental rights terminated. For Josephine, her biggest challenge wasn't the work itself, but her procrastination.

"I'm getting there." She nodded toward her laptop.

He looked at the mostly blank document open on her screen.

"'Deluxe boutique career-transition services,'" he read. "'Full-time counselors. Research-based psychological assessments. Legal advice for negotiating packages.'" He cut his eyes at her. "This is exactly what you had last night."

"You jump right in. I mull. My ideas are percolating."

"If you want my help," he said, backing away, "you've got to help me help you."

"Thanks for nothing!" She watched him return to the clatter in Jackson's yard as seedpods helicoptered over their heads.

The morning reminded Josephine of Saturdays sitting on the grass as her father worked in their tiny backyard. They lived on the second floor of a two-flat building, and in exchange for cheaper rent, he did all sorts of chores. He told Josephine that if she were reading, she didn't have to work, so she used to sit on the grass with a book, any book, as he planted or raked or shoveled around her. When she drifted, staring at the sky or nothing in particular, he'd say, "You ready to help?" She'd snatch up her book to resume fake reading. The only time she really read was late at night when he called "Lights-out." There had been a billboard outside her childhood bedroom window, nowhere near as large as the Majestic Hills one on the expressway, but enough to illuminate the pages of her three favorite library books, *Beloved*, *Monsters*, and *Drown*.

Now Josephine looked over at the large oak beside the house. She'd taken to staring at it at night under the full moon while reading email. In the distance, she could barely see Langdon and Jackson making their way to the back of the property.

Indeed, the morning spoke to her. That was until she heard a hissing sound. Initially, she thought it was a sprinkler from a neighbor watering the grass. She looked over her shoulder, across several backyards. But when something slithered across her foot, she screamed—a harrowing, noise-canceling sound, scattering birds from atop the trees.

Langdon wheeled around and began running, as though a cord connecting them had retracted, commanding his body to hers. He barreled through the woods, arriving to find her crouched on the chaise part of the sectional, the area farthest from the table.

"What happened?!" Sheathed in sweat, he could hardly breathe. "Are you okay?"

"Snake!" She pointed a shaky finger at the galvanized tub she'd bought to hold ice and drinks for get-togethers. Her body squirmed on the sofa pillows.

He wiped his forehead on the back of his work gloves.

"It's probably a garter, and they're pretty harmless." He spied the thin culprit, about a foot long, slithering near the tub. "Yup, only a garter." He grabbed it.

"Well, it looked ginormous to me," she said. "And it made this awful hissing, spitting sound." Her attempt to mimic it sounded like a whistle.

He flung the snake as far as he could into the woods, watching its iridescent body wriggle through the air like the crack of a whip.

It was only when he turned to walk back that Josephine saw neighbors converging on their yard. Bonnie, Danny, then Jackson and Christopher. They each held their own makeshift weapons: a large branch, a trowel, a pickax. Only Christopher's stood out for its absurdity: *a butter knife? What, no steak knife*? Monica trailed him, carrying nothing.

"Thank you, neighbors." Langdon sounded like a game show host. "My wife saw a garter, a shifty little vertebrate, and I swooped in and saved the day. It's all good."

The neighbors laughed, lowering their weapons.

"I'm so embarrassed." Josephine stood. "Please, go back to your Saturday."

She appreciated everyone's words of encouragement: "We've all been there." "What are neighbors for?" "Even a tiny snake can look huge."

"Thank you," she said as she sat on the sectional. She pointed to Monica's maroon University of Chicago T-shirt. "I went to the lab school and used to wear that same outfit."

"The tee and these shorts, with the elastic," Monica said, "will be my uniform for the next few months."

Monica began to walk home across the yard, and Christopher followed.

"I have to get back, too," he said, waving the butter knife. "I make Monica breakfast every day. Helps with the morning sickness."

As he left, Josephine did a double take. She thought she glimpsed the outline of a gun stuck in the waistband of his shorts. He walked quickly, the distance increasing her uncertainty.

Khai was the last to arrive, a red sleep mask across her forehead. She squinted against the sunlight. "I am so hungover." She coiled into a ball on the sectional and slid her mask down over her eyes. "Everyone okay?"

As Josephine explained what happened, Danny approached the patio. Josephine was stunned by how different Danny looked. Ordinarily, her auburn bob and complexion were flawless. This morning, however, a baseball cap did nothing to hide the wispy strands fringing her forehead or the vengeful bald patches around its circumference. In the sunlight, her alabaster skin looked translucent and splotchy, revealing broken capillaries around her eyes.

"Josephine," Danny said. "I know exactly what it's like to be scared by an insignificant little fucker waiting for you to lower your guard."

"Thank you, Danny. It really did seem big," Josephine said.

Danny left, and Bonnie swept a few leaves off the sectional and sat beside Khai. As Josephine watched Danny walk away, Bonnie offered, "She has cancer." Bonnie's voice was resolute, as if to say *Nothing we can do.* "She's an interior designer, and she and Marc talked about it in a *House Beautiful* profile from ten years ago."

"Shit," Khai said drowsily, lifting her mask.

Although the women were not as exposed as Danny, Josephine realized how naked they were without their underwires and concealer. Bonnie's glasses magnified the crepey skin under her eyes. Khai's overnight face cream had hardened and flaked, making her skin appear scaly. Josephine hadn't had a pedicure in—she couldn't remember how long. Her unmoisturized feet looked like she'd been kicking flour.

"I had a stroke during my first semester of law school," Khai said. She extended her arm to reveal a marbling of old blood-draw scars. "Nobody's sure why. But afterward, I thought, Let me get on with my life. And, I will hate being a lawyer." She looked at Josephine. "No offense."

"None taken," Josephine said, placing her hand on Khai's knee reassuringly.

The women were quiet for a second, listening to the insects, the birds, the wind.

For Josephine, it felt good knowing that her neighbors had her back. In fact, it felt incredible. Her only concern, as she looked in the direction of Christopher and Monica's yard, was the neighbor who might have been strapped up.

"You know—" she said, looking at Bonnie, then Khai. "Um, well, never mind."

"No, what?" Khai prodded.

"It's Christopher—" Josephine said. "I'm not absolutely sure—but I think he had a gun tucked in the back of his shorts." To illustrate, she slipped her hand into the back of her cutoffs.

"So, the pretty boy came packing heat?" Khai said snidely.

"Talk about a shifty little vertebrate," Bonnie said. "I grew up around guns. Civil War antiques. My father's. I hated them then and now."

"I hear him next door sometimes." Khai lowered her voice, although no one else was around. "He hangs out in his garage with his hunting buds, laughing and glugging beers. Their pickups line his driveway, the mud flaps with the naked lady silhouettes and all those rifles peeking out of the truck beds."

"Bryce and I have been out walking and seen them, too. Out there smoking cigars." Bonnie slapped her thighs and stood. "Oh, well. Back to my little monsters. Juggle, juggle, toil and trouble."

The women left to resume their morning. Josephine thought about her gynecologist, a white woman with a scruffy bob who had asked her when they first met, "Are there guns in your house? Do you feel safe?" At first, Josephine wondered if she was being asked because she was Black. But the doctor explained that it was her protocol for all her patients and that the questions were a lifeline for victims of domestic violence. For years, at Josephine's annual exam, she preempted the question with, "We still don't own any guns, and I still feel safe."

Her answer would be far more complicated this year.

Josephine went inside to shower. By the time she returned to the patio, it was afternoon. Jackson was in his backyard, stepping out of the white jumper and hood that was his bee uniform.

"Is Lang with you?" she yelled over.

"Still out back," he said. "You've got a good man there."

"Yeah," she sang. "That's what he tells me."

She made her way through the woods to an area near the back of Jackson's property, where a florid display of wildflowers made the air thick with pollen. She stopped and stood behind an ash, marveling at Langdon, who was lying on the grass, almost swaddled in it. Jackson's beehives sat off to the side—the white boxes glimmering in the sunlight; the drone of the bees, like the hum in a monastery, providing a quiet comfort.

Langdon looked more content than he had in a long time.

Although the snake still made Josephine leery, she nestled her body next to his.

"I am so sorry about the fuss," she said.

"Girl, please." He nibbled her earlobe. "Snakes are scary." He put his arm around her, fondling the hem of her skort. "From behind?" he whispered.

"In public?" She giggled. "On somebody else's property? Man, respect the bees."

"Jackson said he's not coming back out here today." He pressed himself against her.

"Jackson said?" She sniffed him and fanned the air. "Besides, you are one loud Negro."

"I've been sweating in these fields for the man."

He laughed, and she felt relieved as the area around his solar plexus pulsed.

"Pheromones, baby," he said.

"No. Funk, baby." She turned around, gently pushing him away. "I need a haircut."

"Maybe I'll shave." He stroked his beard. "Time for my summer look."

"I hope you'll shower, too."

She plucked a burr from near his ear and leaned in for a quick kiss. But he cupped the back of her head, holding her as if she might slip away.

"I'll take you out tonight," he said. "How about dinner and dancing in the city?"

"I'd love that." She brushed her cheek against his face. "Goodbye, beard. I'll miss you."

CHAPTER NINE

county health department for the gvs

Lonnie was perched on a ladder when Josephine entered the One-Stop to ask about a barber. She took off her bike helmet and ran her hand across her tightly coiled curls.

"Any recommendations?"

Lonnie stepped down. "Not a salon?"

"Good God, no. A barber is so much cheaper, and I get to eavesdrop on the men and their conspiracy theories and misogyny. Invariably, somebody will ask me"—she deepened her voice—"Why yo' man allow you to wear yo' hair like that?' I just say, 'I don't ask him about his bald head, and he doesn't ask me about mine.'"

"I wore my hair short-short during undergrad," Lonnie said. "I always heard 'What's the matter? It won't grow?'" She twisted her braid. "I simply wanted a break from all the primping."

Josephine had been slightly self-conscious around Lonnie, whose tongue could crack like a leather strap. But since the incident with the hunters and witnessing Lonnie's softer side, she decided to lean in. "Ever wear your hair down? It's gorgeous."

Lonnie shook her head, touching her braid as if it were a foreign thing. "So why did you snip, snip, snip?" she asked.

Josephine was quiet for a second. "It was a spur-of-the-moment decision."

Ordinarily, she stopped the story there. To divulge anything more made her seem selfless when the absolute opposite was true. But once again, she leaned in.

"My best friend Fatima and I met in law school. After graduation, she found a job across the country. She came down with a violent cough, and tests showed a nodule on her thyroid."

Josephine told Lonnie that when an MRI and needle biopsy were inconclusive, Fat's doctor wanted her to repeat the biopsy, fearing it might be cancer. Fat was afraid to follow up, and she kept putting it off, even though Josephine pleaded with her.

"She told me, 'I don't want to lose my hair.' And I said, 'How about your fucking life?'"

Over the next couple of weeks, their fights were both epic and exhausting. When Fat still wouldn't budge, Josephine flew from New Jersey to Oakland, arriving at Fat's apartment wearing a skullcap despite the July heat. Josephine entered, saying, "You know I have to lay eyes on you." That was their saying when one was in trouble and "I'm fine" wasn't enough.

Josephine snatched off her hat and, to Fat's horror, revealed a point-of-no-return swath that Josephine had hacked down the middle of her long curls. Fat would later say that her best friend looked like Homey D. Clown. Josephine had started her big chop at home, so she wouldn't lose her nerve, and, for dramatic effect, finished the job in Fat's bathroom, standing over the face basin with her clippers. She promised to wear her hair as short as Fat's if it came to that.

Fat had another biopsy. The results were more definitive. She did not have cancer.

As Josephine spoke, she picked out a package of mints and tried to pay for it. Lonnie gestured for her to hand it over. She took a mint and returned the package to Josephine.

"On the house," Lonnie said, munching the candy. "A Black woman shaving her head for her best friend. That's a sisterhood thicker than blood."

Wade appeared from the back, carrying a box of motor oil. Lonnie turned to him.

"When this one was a baby, he would caress the scruff of my neck as he nursed."

"Really, Mom?" Wade faced Josephine. "I know a great barber if you want to trail me. But the owner is old and opens and closes on a whim." He picked up his bike helmet.

"No worries. At least I'll know where it is," Josephine said.

"You coming back, son?"

Josephine discerned an unfamiliar pleading in Lonnie's voice.

"Not today," Wade said, holding the door for Josephine. Once outside, he said, "She wouldn't have asked me that if you hadn't been here."

As Josephine and Wade rode their bikes along Old Creek Road, she made a mental note of landmarks: the cemetery, the historical society, an elementary school. Wade didn't stop until they reached an intersection a few minutes later where there was a strip mall. Most of its stores were shuttered, newspapers covering their windows. Only the barbershop, a liquor store, a coin laundromat, and a food pantry were in business. They parked in front of the barbershop. Its lights were out.

"I warned you," Wade said. "I'll ride back to the store with you if you want, but I need to stop home first." He patted his back pocket. "Forgot my wallet."

"I don't mind. It'll be good exercise," she said.

Initially, Josephine shadowed Wade, refusing to allow a teenager to outride her. But after the road meandered through the woods, she fell behind as they passed a rusting cell tower and an abandoned behemoth of a white building. Its windows were broken, and weeds overran its truck stalls. On the plant's façade was a weathered logo—Grand Vistas Chicken Farms, encircling a white cartoon bird with a freakishly wide wingspan. On a padlocked gate was a sign: To the Kill Line.

When the asphalt gave way to gravel, the air began to smell tinny. Josephine wondered where the hell Wade was taking her. She felt silly for having trusted him. She barely knew him, and—if she was being honest—he seemed like a bit of an oddball. Her pedaling slowed further. She stopped signaling. Coasting, she retrieved her cell phone from a sleeve under her seat.

"No service." Dread burrowed inside her.

Should I turn around? Could I find my way back to the main road?

She realized that no cars had passed for quite some time. Ahead, Wade had stopped and was straddling his bike.

When Josephine rode up, he said, "This is home."

An outpost of two porta-potties marked the entrance, their two stickers announcing County Health Department for the GVs and Neighborhood Watch. She nearly retched at the smell but took solace at the sound of children playing in the distance.

Wade began to walk his bike down a thicketed path. Josephine got off hers and followed him to an opening. She stopped abruptly. She had seen deprivation before, having visited Chicago's predominately Black public housing projects and hollowed-out, mostly white industrial towns outside the city. This, however, was equal opportunity squalor. A multiracial group of residents sat on cinder block stoops in front of decaying trailers, their children playing together in an open area ringed by dumpsters, a U-Haul truck on blocks, and an eighteen-wheeler. Josephine knew it had to have come from out of town because it had a Confederate flag on its front license plate.

On a mound near a stumpy concrete church—its steeple slightly off-center—two boys dressed only in hard-water-stained undershirts and tighty-whities tussled as a group of jeering older boys spurred them on. Wade hurried over and pulled them apart. One child scampered off, but the other remained in Wade's clutches. He had fair hair; pale, wishbone-shaped legs; and a broad chest. His eyeglasses were tilted sideways, with a lens missing. Although the boy was tall, he had a baby face, and Josephine guessed he was younger than his body suggested.

"Benny, man, go put on some clothes." Wade brushed off Benny's shirt, and his chubby cheeks shook. "What did I tell you?"

"My impulses don't control me?" Benny looked down at his bare feet and then at Josephine. "But they kinda do."

"Go." Wade half smiled, pointing to the only trailer with a pink propane tank.

Benny walked in an unhurried way for someone being outdoors in his drawers.

"Cute kid," Josephine said.

"He's been through a lot." Wade searched the patchy grass until he found Benny's lens. "He's only thirteen. Big for his age."

Benny returned, wearing a T-shirt, blue jeans, and ragged gym shoes. Wade led the boy to another nearby trailer. Josephine followed. Inside, Benny sat on an upholstered bench, and Wade opened a first-aid kit to tend to a cut under Benny's eye. Josephine noticed a bong sitting atop a dorm-room-size refrigerator. A small poster with an 800 number for the poison control hotline was tacked to the wood-paneled wall next to a piece of paper with an Amiri Baraka quote:

Since the rich eat more
than anybody else
It is reasonable to assume
that they are more full of shit

When Benny scratched his scalp vigorously, Wade bent over to examine the boy's hair. Josephine saw a slender book tucked into the back of Wade's pants. She recognized the book cover even though it only half peeked out over his belt. It was *Jesus and the Disinherited* by Howard Thurman, a Black theologian and civil rights leader who mentored and greatly influenced the Reverend Martin Luther King Jr. She'd read Thurman's work in a college class about the urban and rural poor. Other books and yellowed newspaper clippings cluttered the trailer.

Josephine recalled the fight that Wade and Lonnie had in the One-Stop. How Lonnie had said that a sixteen-year-old couldn't live on his own. It also occurred to Josephine that she'd misheard them.

Wade hadn't said the "geebies" was built on a lie. He'd said the "GVs"—the Grand Vistas.

"Why are you staying out here?" she asked him.

Wade stopped picking through Benny's hair.

"Why not here? They told me they needed fresh fruits and vegetables, and I helped build the garden. They said some of the kids needed tutoring—"

Benny raised his hand. "Like me."

"And I help tutor, which is how Benny and I met."

"Decent housing is a human right," Benny said, clearly parroting his tutor.

"Aren't you in school?" Josephine asked Wade.

He looked frustrated. Like she was asking too many inane questions.

"My parents homeschooled me, and I finished early. I've been accepted at Fisk, Princeton, and NYU, my parents' alma mater, but I'm taking a gap year."

He said that the Grand Vistas overflowed with empty trailers. If someone wanted his current quarters back, he'd move elsewhere.

Josephine looked confused. "I don't understand."

"I'm not sure you have to."

"Boy—" she started.

He exhaled. "My father helped unionize chicken plant workers. When it closed, he tried to find new owners, and when he couldn't, he started pitching in. I'm just doing the same."

Josephine still had questions, but Benny's stomach growled.

"Hungry?" Wade asked him.

Benny nodded, shoehorning himself into a small chair beside a built-in table that held a box of Lucky Charms. He folded his hands on top and watched greedily as Wade retrieved a bowl and utensils from a small cupboard and milk from the mini fridge. He sniffed inside the carton and placed everything in front of Benny.

While the boy ate, Josephine didn't know what to say. She certainly had more questions. Instead of asking them, she rummaged through her wallet and then turned her attention to Benny. "My husband wears glasses, too," she said. "And he's always breaking his."

She pulled out a miniature screwdriver and offered it to Benny.

"For when your lens pops out, and you have the screw. I realize they need more fixing today. But in the future."

Benny side-eyed her. "How much?"

The question caught her up short, and she was about to speak when Wade said, "It's a gift, Benny."

Surprise blossomed across the boy's face, and his nose reddened. "Thanks?" he shrugged, quickly returning to scarfing down his food, the color fading away.

Wade returned his attention to Josephine. "The Grand Vistas was built for Mexican chicken plant workers. At the time, the accommodations weren't so bad, the old-timers say, even with no gas lines and the water reeking of rotten eggs."

"How long ago?" Josephine asked.

"The plant opened in the early 1990s and closed about twenty years later, leaving hundreds of workers and their families behind. The trailers fell apart. There's mold everywhere. The wind blows in through electrical sockets that don't work. People share generators and cook on hot plates. Every day, county workers set three gallons of water on each front stoop."

"Just three gallons?" Josephine curled her lip.

Benny poured more cereal into his bowl and stirred. "I got Wade a birthday card," he blurted, his mouth juicy with milk. "But Wade didn't like the way I got it. So, he was like, 'Let's go pay for it.' And I was like, 'Let's pay for a chocolate birthday cake, too.'"

Wade mussed the boy's tangled hair. Despite their three-year age difference, Wade seemed so much older and Benny so much younger.

"I've been riding my bike all around New Pointe," Josephine said. "I don't remember even seeing this place on Google Maps."

Wade pulled a Drake County map from a shelf near the trailer's ceiling.

"Here's Majestic Hills." With his forefinger, he circled an area near the southwestern quadrant of the map and traced upward and to the right. "If they hadn't photoshopped in all these trees, the Grand Vistas would be here."

Josephine studied the map.

"We've been erased," Benny groaned.

"Right here," Wade said, pointing to the map. "There's an old horse trail that runs through the woods and ends between the golf course and Majestic Hills. It's not on the map, and hardly anybody knows it exists. It goes right behind your houses. There's always been a fence here in the Grand Vistas, cordoning off the path so residents couldn't access it."

Josephine couldn't help thinking that all she'd wanted was a Saturday-morning haircut. All this felt like way too much to process. She looked up from the map to glimpse sunlight creeping through the trailer's opaque windows. Afternoon had given way to early evening.

"I should be going," she said.

"I need to get some tape for Benny's glasses." Wade pulled a vest with reflectors from a hook. "Mind if I take you to the main road and you go the rest of the way alone?"

"Not at all." She said goodbye to Benny, but, absorbed in reading the cereal box, he didn't seem to hear her.

Once home, Josephine leaned her bike against the garage and paced around the Land Cruiser sitting in the driveway. She was exhausted and sweaty, her legs speckled with mud. She called Fat and spewed about the Grand Vistas. Its squalid conditions. Wade's idealism.

"Okay, take a breath," Fat said.

"I think . . ." Josephine stopped pacing. "I think Wade may have intentionally wanted me to see the Grand Vistas."

"You think he punked you?"

"Remember our trip to the Bahamas?" Josephine poked her sandal around in a bed of mulch. "We'd just landed and were heading to the resort when our taxi driver detoured off the main street. Said he was a local and knew a shortcut."

"He kept calling us rich Americans," Fat said. "But we were in-debt students on vacation after cobbling together credit card points."

"He drove us through that painfully poor area of the island," Josephine said. "Then he said he didn't expect white vacationers to care. But we should."

Josephine noticed that the Land Cruiser's body gleamed. She peeked inside and saw fresh vacuum lines on the floor mats. Langdon had taken it to the car wash.

"Crap, I've got to go," she said. "I forgot your boy wants to go dancing tonight."

"*A luta, continua*," Fat chimed.

Josephine turned to find Langdon standing in the driveway. He was clean-shaven, and his cleft, which Josephine sometimes forgot was there, was now fully exposed. He wore pressed dress pants and an open-collared shirt and held a bouquet of wildflowers upside down. Yellow petals gathered around his loafers.

"You stood me up, but that's cool." He smiled a fake smile that showed no teeth. "Makes me want to see this place that's so important. What's it called? The Grand Vistas?"

"Lang, I'm so sorry." Josephine rushed toward him. "The One-Stop's cashier, her son, led the way there, and I'd love to show it to you, but now it's getting dark, and I know I wouldn't be able to find it."

"In the morning, then." He shook his head. "I wish—I really, really wish—you'd explain something: Why must you confide in Fat *first* about every damned thing? Why am I always second?"

He didn't wait for an answer. He did make a point of going inside and slamming the door.

Josephine awoke early the next morning while Langdon slept soundly. Downstairs, she made a cup of tea and drank it on the patio, watching one squirrel chase another up and down several tree trunks. She wondered if the boy squirrel had said something stupid about the girl squirrel's best squirrel friend. With animals, it was difficult to divine whether they were about to fight or fuck. Just one day earlier, she'd been sitting at that very table, loving the backyard. Now, once again, she was homesick for those rare Sunday mornings she and Langdon shared in the condo, watching the sunrise over the lake. Their short walk to the diner, where they sat side by side devouring pancakes and quiche. *Eat your eggs, Walter* may have been hard for the husband to digest. But it was no picnic for the wife who merely wanted to say: *Negro, while you're doing well, why don't you let well-enough do you.* Hadn't they been doing well?

Josephine texted Langdon: *outside. ready when you are.*

He joined her a few minutes later. On their way to the Land Cruiser, he said, "I read about the Grand Vistas last night, mostly about high rates of asthma and cancer. The deaths of two little girls, infant twins, with melanomas got a lot of press because they were so tiny they could fit in a shoebox. The Drake County Health Department's web page shows that the overall health indices there are in the toilet. The property sits on oil buried from decommissioned electrical transformers and sludge dumped during the Pullman railroad car era."

"You've done your homework," Josephine said, sliding into the driver's seat. She was about to start the car when he placed his hand on her forearm.

"That was a cheap shot about Fat last night," he said. "Can you forgive me, or should we wage a fight that I can't win in a million years?"

"Fat is one of my two no-go zones, Lang." Josephine locked eyes with him. "I hope you know you're the other." She lowered all the windows, effectively changing the subject.

On Goodenow, the country club's marquee announced:

SPRING TOURNAMENT SUNDAY
1950S OLD FASHIONEDS, ARNOLD PALMERS,
MARTINIS SERVED

Throughout New Pointe, church bells tolled. It took Josephine a while—driving down dead-end roads and in circles—but she found the old chicken processing plant and then the porta-potties standing sentry. Soon, an off-key a cappella rendition of the hymn "Down to the River to Pray" hitched onto the breeze, lassoing them inside the trailer park. A gathering of mothers and fathers—more men than women—sang and swayed; a group of young men manned a barbecue pit; a couple of people yanked weeds from a garden and turned the soil; children flew kites. Animated by the people and the singing, the Grand Vistas didn't appear to Josephine as desolate as it had the day before.

Wade was working in the garden when he saw the Land Cruiser and ran over.

Langdon got out, extending his hand. "I've seen you from afar at the gas station, but we haven't officially met. I'm Langdon Blaque."

"I'm Wade Stanfi—" He paused mid-word.

Josephine's brows knitted, and she caught Langdon's doing the same.

"Call me Wade."

It was clear that Wade had stumbled somehow. The usually sure-footed kid looked momentarily rattled. But, having recovered, he spoke softly as a woman preached.

"The religious among us worship, and the secularists catch up on chores." Wade walked toward a garden, waving at Josephine and Langdon to follow. "If you come here and all you see is poverty, then you're not looking closely." He plucked a couple of large blueberries, like sapphires, from a thriving bush and ate them. "We had the dirt brought in because of the environmental problems. We grow dandelions, chamomile flowers, and sorrel for medicinal teas. There used to be a grocery store and restaurant for the workers, but it burned down, and we rely a lot on the garden." Wade walked the Blaques back to the Land Cruiser. "I'm doing a tutoring session in a few minutes. You're welcome to stay."

"I'm sorry, we can't," Langdon said. "I work tonight, but I'll come again."

Wade gave them a bag of blueberries from a nearby table. Inside the Land Cruiser, Langdon turned to Josephine: "You heard Stanfield too?"

"I did. You see the name around town, but I haven't thought twice about it."

"If they're Stanfields, why is Lonnie working at the One-Stop and her son living in a trailer park?"

At home, Langdon fixed sandwiches and brought them out to the patio, where Josephine had immediately sat down at the table with her laptop, searching for more information about the Stanfields. Initially, only pure nosiness inspired her. Was Lonnie a sidepiece? Was Wade a love child? Scratch that. The love child wouldn't get the spoils of the big family name.

The first search yielded the Stanfield Foundation website. It included information about scholarships, endowments, Stanfield Academy high school, an invitation-only black-tie gala, and an annual silent auction. A tranche of stories focused on Geoffrey Stanfield. He had been an angel investor in venture capital firms that supported socially responsible endeavors, and he'd given a highly regarded TED Talk, "Doing Well in Order to Do Good." He'd been in graduate school at NYU when he created a business, a translation service for U.N. delegates who frequented Times Square adult movie shops. They could don headsets and listen to the movies in their own language. That landed him on the cover of *Fortune*. National news profiles rarely failed to mention that Geoffrey was an unassuming philanthropist who married a Black woman and hoped to use his family's fortune for good. A *New York Times Magazine* piece included a photograph of Geoffrey and Lonnie in their backyard, accompanied by two daughters and two sons. According to the caption, Lonnie was Alondra Alexander-Stanfield, known primarily by her maiden name, Lonnie Alexander. In the story, she was described as a brilliant journalist who had won a Fulbright but sidelined her writing career to teach at Stanfield Academy. Josephine called up the video Fat had sent months ago. She realized she never finished watching it and cued it to where she left off.

"I try to instill in my students the idea that their voice matters, that there's power in their words. They are privileged to attend this school. My children are young, but my husband and I believe to whom much is given, much is expected. We hope they use their privilege to effect change."

Be careful what you wish for, Josephine thought.

The camera's shot widened to show Geoffrey Stanfield, holding two of their light-brown children, one in each arm. Josephine's heart sank as she recalled Lonnie saying that her husband had died. She found obituaries that ran in news outlets throughout the country and around the world, reading aloud to Langdon that Geoffrey died of cardiac arrest on a commuter train last October, while on his way from his New Pointe home to a meeting in Chicago.

"That sucks," Langdon said. "I saw Lonnie at the cemetery a few months ago, bawling her eyes out."

"Good Lord," Josephine said. "What she must be going through."

They were both quiet. In the distance, they could hear the murmurs and applause of the golf tournament underway at the country club.

"Yesterday, Wade told me there's a footpath behind our property line that runs to the Grand Vistas," said Josephine. "I want to see it."

They walked briskly through the woods to the edge of the trees, passing the area near Jackson's beehives. The footpath was part dirt and part gravel, stretching along a thatch of evergreens that lined an embankment overlooking the golf course. Across the fairway, women in large floppy hats and vintage dresses and men in gingham pants sipped cocktails.

The Blaques stared at each other. Now they knew what Wade knew. Here was a footpath, a horse trail, an artery like a twisted umbilical cord, connecting Majestic Hills to a wasteland slowly dying in the shadow of privilege.

CHAPTER TEN
the second clubhouse meeting

Josephine and Langdon told only two neighbors about the Grand Vistas. Josephine bumped into Khai at Martin's Gourmet Market and asked her, in a matter-of-fact way, if she knew anything about the trailer park. Khai responded that it was news to her. Langdon had begun running some mornings with Marc. When Langdon mentioned the Grand Vistas, Marc said that although he'd jogged for miles throughout the area, he'd never come across it.

After those brief encounters, word of the trailer park spread quickly in Majestic Hills. It seemed that many residents had googled the community and weren't thrilled with the results: police blotter items about petty misdemeanor breaking and entering, criminal trespass to property, disorderly conduct, possession of a controlled substance.

Josephine was riding her bike down Willow on her way home from the train when Khai, standing beside her mailbox, waved her down. Josephine stopped.

"That trailer park," Khai said. "It's got some people here low-grade freaking out."

"Some people?" Josephine asked. "How so? And are you among them?"

"No, not me. I couldn't care less. But some people are talking about wanting to know where exactly it is and having a meeting about it."

"Noted," Josephine said. "Thanks for telling me."

At home, Josephine hurried upstairs to the bathroom and changed into one of Langdon's T-shirts and a pair of his shorts. Langdon wasn't home, and she went downstairs to relax on the family room sofa. It had begun to rain. She closed her eyes briefly, and when she opened them, she saw someone in a hooded raincoat zip past the window. This was unusual. Neighbors drifted onto each other's property in the woods, but not on this side of the house, the side facing the pond. Josephine's body tensed, and she jumped up to look outside, seeing no one. She ran to the door leading to the garage and locked it. She had a habit of leaving the garage door up. She hurried to the living room window and saw the raincoat crossing the front yard, walking away from the house through the trees.

She ran outside. "Excuse me!" Josephine yelled.

"Excuse yourself, neighbor!" Khai turned, holding a wicker basket of vegetables. "Seeing you reminded me that you said I could steal from your garden!" She lifted the basket. "Cucumbers, radishes, and basil! Hope you don't mind?"

"Not—not at all!" Josephine stuttered.

Later that night, she and Langdon were in the bathroom brushing their teeth when she told him what happened. Although she'd expected that her neighbors might be on high alert, she hadn't realized she was. She felt like a hypocrite.

"When you grow up where I did," she said, "in a neighborhood where people say, 'don't go there,' solely based on rumor and innuendo, you feel like you should be more sensitive to that."

"Fear is a contaminant," Langdon said. He brushed his tongue and spat into the sink. "It's in the air, the groundwater. Even those of us who try to think rationally about these things aren't immune. You do your best and move on."

A couple of days later, an email arrived from the M&H Development Corporation, notifying residents about a meeting to be held at seven p.m. on June 28 in the clubhouse.

The night before the meeting, Josephine and Langdon were in bed, she sitting up working on her laptop, he lying on his back, his hands folded behind his head. He propped himself up on his elbows and peeked at her screen.

"Newbies?" he asked.

She nodded as she scrolled through the database the counselors had created, profiling the firm's latest crop of displaced workers they were helping to find employment.

"Okay, let 'er rip," Langdon said.

Technically, she wasn't supposed to do this—the confidentiality of it all—but she enjoyed sampling a montage of the more interesting profiles. She never mentioned names.

"There's the private school principal who speaks in platitudes." Josephine channeled her inner Julia Child and began reading from the principal's essay: "'You can either be a thermometer and reflect the environment or a thermostat and change it.'" She snickered. "We have a thirty-year newspaper veteran, an obituary writer who introduced himself lamenting, 'I thought I'd have a job forever.' That made me sad. Then there's a guy who said during orientation, 'The good thing about being out of work for three months and not wearing dress socks is that the hair on my ankles has grown back.'"

She laughed, but Langdon wasn't laughing. He wedged his head against her hip.

"There's no other way to say this." His voice sounded far away. "I've got to cover a shift tomorrow. I'm sorry, but I can't go with you to the meeting."

"No!" Josephine emitted a guttural sigh. "I've got to go to this thing by myself? Hang out with NIMBYs jazzed up about their property values, asking themselves whether they would have bought here if they'd known about a run-down trailer park down the way?"

"I promise you, Josey, I tried—"

"Not finished. People who, if I say, *maybe y'all should chill because the only police news near us is about teens shoplifting downtown or bashing in mailboxes*, some neighbors might not take *me* seriously because they'll assume that I've lived in challenged communities and have a higher tolerance for that than they have."

"I really tried to get out of it, babe. I swear." Langdon fluffed his pillow.

"You're serious?"

He nodded. "Make sure you tell them it's a trailer park. Not a prison or an asylum or a nuclear power plant."

He placed the pillow over his head, his signal for Josephine to turn out the light. But she ignored him. Instead, she used the moment as an entrée to ask a question she'd been tiptoeing around because it required finessing. She closed her laptop and tightened the drawstring of a pair of his scrubs that she'd cut into booty shorts.

"Do you have any regrets about moving here?" she asked.

"No." The pillow distorted his voice but she listened for a whiff of uncertainty.

Josephine's question really had nothing to do with the Grand Vistas and everything to do with Langdon's telling Ken that moving to Majestic Hills made him feel like a "sellout." Fat had come home as Ken was in the basement talking to Langdon on the speaker phone. The men were following up on their lunch conversation. Fat had sworn Josephine to secrecy, saying that she only eavesdropped because she believed Josephine should know about Langdon's uncertainty.

Maybe their house would be going on the market sooner rather than later.

That Langdon felt conflicted didn't surprise Josephine. The fear of straying from one's roots wasn't uncommon among people who'd managed a degree of success. She herself had felt it. Although Langdon had grown up privileged, his father, Langdon July "Jules" Blaque Jr., had come of age in a tough Chicago neighborhood. He often spoke about the importance of having a foot in two worlds: the one that forged him and the other one that gave him the freedom to forge himself. Jules made sure his sons partook of the best of both worlds.

As children, Langdon and his older brother spent several summers vacationing in a villa near Nice in a small town called Saint-Jean-Cap-Ferrat. Jules was on the board of directors of the company that owned the villa, one of an array of perks board members received. But Langdon and his brother, every summer, also spent a week with Jules's sister—their aunt—and her family. She lived in the modest Englewood neighborhood bungalow where Jules had grown up. There, the Blaque boys hung out with their cousins, running down the street to the corner store for Red Flaming Hots—which they did not get at home—and bingeing on their father's old Richard Pryor records and Eddie Murphy videos.

Now Langdon turned over a couple of times before once again propping himself on his elbows and turning toward Josephine.

"I needed a respite from the city," he said. "But I never wanted to fully insulate myself from the real world." He rubbed his leg against hers, finding her foot, their toes dovetailing. "I think that trailer park makes New Pointe less antiseptic, less pristine." He smiled mischievously. "I think it gives this quaint little town some soul."

Josephine hadn't been inside the clubhouse since the meet and greet, when the space appeared recreational. But now, for the meeting, the pool table had been wheeled off to the side, and about thirty people sat in folding chairs arranged in a semicircle around the fireplace. The room smelled faintly of cigars despite the No Smoking signs. Josephine sat in the first open seat she saw, in the middle row.

The woman at the center of it all, standing in front of the fireplace, was Penny Larson, whom Josephine hadn't seen since she showed them their house. Harmony Realty was a subsidiary of the M&H Development Corporation, and Penny was the builder's spokesperson.

She opened by asking if anyone had questions about the builder's warranty or foundation cracks or drainage issues, concerns that often cropped up in new developments. When no one had questions, Penny turned her attention to a perk the development company had just negotiated with the country club: a discount in membership fees for Majestic Hills residents.

A man in the back stood up. He was from the east side of Willow, and Josephine didn't know the homeowners there as well as she knew the residents on the west side.

"When are we going to get to the Grand Vistas?" he demanded.

"Of course," Penny said. "How about right now?"

She began to read notes from her phone. She told them that the Grand Vistas was in unincorporated New Pointe and under the jurisdiction of Drake County. That was important because when someone dialed 9-1-1, the county sheriff's deputies responded rather than New Pointe's police officers. New Pointe had been trying to annex the Grand Vistas for years. She said the forty-acre site included the chicken processing plant and, originally, two hundred trailers. As of June 2021, only about a quarter of them were fully inhabitable, with one hundred and seventy residents living there. The racial makeup was roughly forty percent Hispanic, forty percent white, and twenty percent Black. The median annual income: $12,100.

Josephine looked around the room. The residents were rapt.

"And the crime there?" Christopher asked.

Josephine turned and noticed him and Monica sitting in the row behind her.

"Minor, mostly misdemeanor stuff," Penny said. "Nothing to worry about. Majestic Hills is as safe as it is secluded."

"Secluded," Christopher repeated. "Okay, but we do get Jehovah's Witnesses literature in our mailbox at least once a week. And the Latter-day Saints ring our doorbell. Cleaning people come with their business cards, and so do lawn care workers."

Josephine sensed the tension slowly growing in the room. Neighbors looking around, trying to gauge whether anyone else was beginning to feel more vulnerable.

Then someone else suggested that the Department of Streets and Sanitation erect a No Outlet sign at the beginning of the subdivision so fewer cars would detour through Majestic Hills seeking a shortcut. Another resident said that maybe the black-and-yellow–striped entrance markers should be removed.

"I'm sure we all know where to turn in by now," he said.

"Maybe we don't need a stop sign either," another neighbor offered. "It's a big red flag. Without it, it's a natural stop. You look both ways and you jump on out there. It's not like it's a dangerous or busy intersection. Let people use their own judgment and good sense."

Josephine waved her hand. "Aren't we getting way ahead of ourselves?"

"I totally agree," Bryce seconded. "What we have right now is pretty safe."

Bryce was alone, and Josephine guessed that Bonnie had stayed home with their sons.

"It's an upside-down world when removing traffic signs is the answer to feeling safer," Josephine said.

"Otherwise," Bryce added, "we'll be talking about building a wall around us, or a moat."

There were no more questions or comments, but it was clear to Josephine that something in the room had shifted. As she looked around, she couldn't help but think, *Poor Penny*. She had one job that night: to ensure that Majestic Hills residents tucked themselves into their beds feeling safe, sound, and good about their investment.

Josephine wasn't sure that Penny had succeeded.

When the meeting ended, Penny said she and the developer would be available if anyone had any further questions or concerns.

Outside, Josephine stood at the foot of her driveway, watching neighbors walking into the darkness under spheres of light from their old-time streetlamps.

Overall, it had been a cordial meeting. Those who asked questions were polite. No one raised their voice. But Josephine felt unsettled.

Inside the house, it occurred to her that Lonnie had been a journalist. On a whim, she searched "Lonnie Alexander" and the "Grand Vistas," finding a profile of the trailer park written by Lonnie:

> ***Beyond the north woods, adjacent to land where a cornfield once ceded ground to a chicken processing plant, sits the Grand Vistas, a trailer park of rusting singlewides. Hemmed in by an expressway and a ravine, it's a community where garbage pickup lags, blown-out streetlights aren't replaced, and the effluence from the long-shuttered chicken plant still eddies and pools in the property's low-lying areas. In the Grand Vistas, the residents have little to lose or look forward to, which flies in the face of its name. It is, therefore, a development built on a lie.***

"Built on a lie," Josephine muttered.

She went outside and stood on the patio, staring toward the back of the property where a dome of light from the country club glowed beyond the trees. It struck her that Penny hadn't mentioned the footpath. Did she know about it? It had been the furthest thing from Josephine's mind during the meeting. Despite all the talk urging calm, she knew the footpath would have riled people. Wade had said it had been cordoned off on the Grand Vistas side.

But what the hell did a sixteen-year-old really know?

CHAPTER ELEVEN
red flags

New Pointe's downtown merchants grew accustomed to seeing Langdon and Marc jogging past idling delivery trucks and early-morning commuters. When the owner of Banned Books Only bookstore, a self-professed "old white hippie," told Langdon he enjoyed watching the two men run because they made him feel less pessimistic about the country's race relations, Langdon thought the man was merely blowing smoke. But when Marc heard something similar from a bubble tea shop owner and a florist, the men joked that they were doing their part to save the union.

They ran on a catch-as-catch-can basis. Langdon's work schedule was unpredictable. Marc traveled frequently. Langdon enjoyed running with him. They had developed a rhythm—calibrated strides that seemed to sync their breaths and maybe even their heartbeats until they were a singular machine. But Langdon did not like running with Christopher. He'd joined them only a few times, slowing them down and constantly pleading, "Wait up, guys."

On this morning, Christopher was droning on about his and Monica's Fourth of July party, which would start in a few hours, how he'd started storing up liquor at the beginning of the year. And he'd driven across the Indiana border to buy fireworks from the pyrotechnics store down the street from the gun shop he frequented.

"Each one posts signs recommending the other," he said. "That's synergy for you."

Langdon didn't respond. The problem was, Christopher *vexed* him. He'd heard two grandfatherly types in the emergency room using that word as they each explained to a police officer why one had smacked the other in the mouth. Both had swollen lips.

Langdon couldn't discern what vexed him more about Christopher: that he once coveted his house or currently seemed to covet his wife. Whenever Langdon looked out his bedroom window onto the backyard, he recalled that rainy night when Christopher stood in the woods. It was a moment that seemed to reconstitute itself repeatedly.

Langdon knew the exact tree. Since that night, he'd been drawn to it as if it were marked territory. He'd stood beside its flank, peering up at the frosted glass window through a fog of uncertainty.

The men ran through the downtown alongside lawn chairs lining the parade route and wooden barricades cordoning off traffic. The Bank of America clock alternately flashed 76 degrees and 11:15 a.m. Langdon had promised Josephine he'd return before noon to help marinade meats and prep veggies for their Fourth celebration, which would double as a housewarming. Fat, Ken, and their boys were coming, along with Langdon's parents and a host of other friends and family.

The men passed the village hall and police station. Just before the three-way, Marc said, "Last one home!" and they started to run full-out. As they neared the country club, they saw a bundle of red, white, and blue balloons bobbing near the Majestic Hills entrance. They reached the subdivision and stopped near the opening, sweaty and breathing hard. Langdon flipped his baseball cap around and leaned forward with his hands on his knees. Looking at his watch, he realized that he had some of his best run times when he ran with—or, more precisely, away from—Christopher. He turned toward the stop sign and, for the first time, noticed that the black-and-yellow-striped entrance markers had been removed. There had been two of them, like goalposts, one on either side of the entrance.

"What happened to the markers?"

"Oh, shit," said Marc. He walked toward the opening. "We discussed them at that meeting last week, the one the developer held."

"Josephine told me about it," Langdon said, nodding. "One of the many useless ideas bandied about."

"I guess the balloons are there because somebody wanted to make sure their guests didn't get lost trying to attend their little soiree."

Marc started walking, and Christopher followed, uncharacteristically quiet.

Langdon wondered why the man who had color commentary about every damned thing suddenly had nothing to say. He studied the area for a few minutes, then began walking home. He had hoped, or wanted to believe, that the anxiety about the Grand Vistas had been laid to rest or, at the very least, was dying down. He now realized he'd been naïve. Removing the entrance markers may have seemed inconsequential, but it spoke volumes about the budding fear taking root in Majestic Hills.

Along Willow, cars had begun to fill the driveways, and firecracker smoke already clung to the treetops. The American flag waved from several homes. When he and Josephine moved in, they had wondered what the bracket beside the front door was for. Now they knew. Theirs would always remain empty. They were not flag-waving people.

As he neared home, he saw the clubhouse decorated with festive bunting and, in his own driveway, his parents exiting their aging Jeep Grand Wagoneer. People often described them as a striking couple. Elise was tall, with graying, sandy-colored hair, fair skin, and green eyes. Langdon was the male version of her. Jules stood six-foot-three, an inch shaved from the height of his prime, with broad shoulders and brown skin that deepened against his short, cottony hair. They lived in a sprawling lakefront condo not far from Northwestern, where Elise worked as a chemistry professor.

When Langdon was a child, his family took long road trips every summer, he and his brothers sitting in the back seat of the Land Cruiser using the DRT formula (distance equals rate multiplied by time) to calculate arrival times and the miles remaining. They would watch their father gently palm their mother's head as she laughed and said, "You're messing up my do."

His father always glanced the rearview mirror. "Boys, what does that road sign say?"

The back seat chimed, "Stop a head" as they passed the Stop Ahead sign.

He longed to do that one day with his own child. To tell the same corny jokes. To relish in the same teachable moments.

Now he watched his father stretching out his back and staring at his sunburned left arm. Langdon had seen him adopt that posture countless times in their Evanston driveway at the end of their trips. It never failed to assure Langdon, more than anything, that he was home.

CHAPTER TWELVE

what to the slave . . .

As the Blaques' guests milled about the house and property, Josephine stood alone for a moment near the garden. Her heart was bursting at the sight of Langdon tussling in the grass with Fat and Ken's three older sons. Ken lay on a blanket not far away with the baby beside him.

Lang would be the happiest man in the world with a child.

There were children everywhere, climbing trees, doing cartwheels or backflips, chasing one another, flitting about. She caught herself laughing, resting her hand on her abdomen.

Elise sneaked up behind Josephine and hugged her around her waist. She squealed.

"It's only your mother-in-law," Elise said. "Look at you. Girlfriend, I'm loving those lilac shorts and that tank!" She danced over to Jules, who swung her around as they began to engage in the fancy footwork of Chicago Steppin'.

Langdon once told Josephine that he knew he'd fallen in love with her when he could tell her about his brother Nicky's death—the most devastating day of Langdon's life. He wanted her to know everything about himself, including how, as an undergrad, he'd broken down crying in a grocery store, holding a milk carton with an August 30 expiration date.

Josephine knew she could fall in love with Langdon the first time she saw him hug Elise. The way he slowly closed his eyes and rested his head on her shoulder, holding her tightly. His tenderness, his vulnerability, drew Josephine closer to him.

She appreciated that Elise never pressured them for a grandchild, but she wondered if it was because Elise didn't think it was her place, or if her losing a child had made motherhood a hard sell.

Josephine was watching Elise and Jules twirling around when Fat walked up next to her.

"That husband of yours has a paternal clock that's mad-thumping," she said.

Josephine smiled. "I'm aware."

"You stand next to him, and it's like sitting in traffic next to a boom car." She looked over her shoulder. "Come with me so I can show you something."

She grabbed Josephine's hand, and they fled into the woods, down the mulched path on Jackson's property. They wound up not far from the beehives, under the bough of a tree that had wild mushrooms adorning its base. Fat pulled a wine bottle from Akeem's sling.

"Thief!" Josephine laughed.

"Always be prepared," Fat said. "That's *my* motto. The Boy Scouts got that from *me*."

"Wait, you're nursing."

"Girl, I'll pump and dump. Our refrigerator and freezer are full of breast milk." She took a long swig from the bottle. "I may have backwashed."

Josephine reached for it. "God made dirt, and dirt don't hurt."

Beyond a small berm, Josephine watched Jackson and several men standing near his beehives. Each wore a jumpsuit that hadn't yet been pulled beyond their waists. Jackson was swinging the smoker he used to calm his bees. The tendrils of smoke reminded her of a priest in white vestments swinging his censer of burning incense over the pews.

"When I wanted to be a lawyer . . ." Josephine said. She drank and wiped her mouth on her wrist. "I saw myself in law school and in a courtroom. When I was thinking about getting married, it took me a minute, but I could see it. But having a baby? Fat, I try to imagine myself—"

"Stop." Fat held up both of her hands. "It is truly unimaginable—especially in the vision board way you lay out your life. So don't torture yourself."

In the distance, the music had cranked up, and the whooping and hollering accompanying dancing had begun.

"All I know is that before Mr. Taylor passed, you were all 'baby on board.' Now you're unsure. I get it. And I won't sugarcoat things. It's the hardest job you'll ever have. But I wouldn't trade any of my children." She snickered. "Maybe my oldest. But I just need you and Langdon to chop, chop with the S. M."

Someone overhearing might have thought Fat had said *S and M*. But she hadn't. The reference was from a story Josephine told Fat years ago about a woman her father dated while Josephine was nearing adolescence. He didn't bring many women around, but he enlisted this one—with her severe bottle-black hair and bun—to help explain things. She was so ancient she called Josephine's period her "courses"; having sex "having knowledge of"; and Josephine's vagina her "little smack madam." Hence, S. M.

"And the baby must be a girl," Fat pleaded. "I'm drowning in dicks, Josephine. Ken's got that good strong seed, but it's all for boys. They walk around the house naked, dicks swinging." She slapped her arm. "Y'all got these ghetto-ass mosquitoes."

"Let's get you back to the citronella candles."

Fat laced her fingers through Josephine's. "Whatever you decide, you know I'll love your child like my own."

Josephine's eyes widened. "But only if it's a girl?"

"No more boys allowed."

They were nearly out of the woods when Langdon rang a dinner bell to get everyone's attention. He was standing on the patio, Jules seated at the table behind him.

"I know those ribs are talking to y'all," Langdon said, laughing. "Can I have a moment?"

He waited as their guests coalesced around him on the grass.

"Welcome," he said. "First, a hearty thanks to my bride for preparing the food. Kale, cucumbers, and basil from her very own garden. That pesto is slammin'."

Standing in the crowd, Josephine curtsied.

"If you've celebrated with my family before, you know that every Fourth of July my father finds a way to orient us in what freedom and independence mean to Black folks. This year, he wants me to do it. He gave me instructions twenty minutes ago, so bear with me."

"It's your crib, son," Jules said from the table. "Heavy is the head."

The crowd applauded, and Langdon playfully shrugged.

"I grew up with Frederick Douglass's famous speech 'What to the Slave Is the Fourth of July?' For years, on the Fourth, we've read it, along with speeches from the likes of Sojourner Truth and Fannie Lou Hamer. But this past February, my parents decided to finally investigate our roots—the Blaque side of the family."

When a small gathering of people laughed over in Jackson and Khai's yard, Josephine watched as the crowd in her yard turned their attention next door.

Khai yelled, "So sorry!"

"It's cool," Langdon said. "Happy Fourth!"

He began by saying his parents started their research poring over old probate records at the Hinds County Courthouse in Jackson, Mississippi. Jules handed his son the archival box, and Langdon opened it. He held up a laminated bill of sale, a deed of manumission for his father's fifth-great grandmother, Luella, a woman born into slavery in 1817. She purchased her freedom in 1838, sixty-two years after the Declaration of Independence, twenty-five years before the Confederates surrendered in Vicksburg on July 4, 1863. The deed was witnessed by three people. Langdon began to read:

"'To all to whom this may be of import, understand that I, Hammerford Kaines, of Hinds County, in the State of Mississippi, do release from slavery, set free, liberate my Negress, Luella, 21 years old, who is of good stock and strong mental bearings, for the sum of $150."

The deed held Kaines's seal and described Luella as short of stature with welts of scars across her shoulders. A small diary said that as a child, she'd been a "foot warmer" who, on cold Mississippi nights, lay across the foot of the master's bed to keep his feet warm.

"How she got the money," Langdon said. "I don't know. Why she got the scars. I don't know that either. But I know she suffered. What kind of degenerate needs a child to warm his feet? Other documents say she chose the surname—Flowers. Luella Flowers. Her name on her death certificate was Luella Flowers Blackwell. We somehow became Blaque."

He looked down at the box and then up at Josephine.

"Years ago, my wife told me a July Fourth story about her father, whom I never got to meet because he'd passed away. I wish I had, though. Because I was forced to say a few words, I think it's only fair that she shares his story with you."

He waved her onto the patio. She pretended to pinch his bicep as he handed her the box as if it were a shared portal into both their pasts.

"Daddy grew up in a small Mississippi town, coming of age in the 1950s. He and his friends celebrated the Fourth by drinking from the park's "white's only" water fountain. They each would take a long, satisfying glug and then run. Of the three boys, my father was the most identifiable from afar because by thirteen, he was gangly and six feet tall. The police warned my grandparents that the next year, officers would no longer allow him to flout the rules. My grandmother immediately started preparing to move the family to Chicago. She couldn't trust that her son would heed the warning, and she didn't want a sip of water to cost him his life, the way lies about a wolf whistle had cost fourteen-year-old Emmett Till his."

Josephine gestured with the box.

"Historians used to say that if you're secure in your rights, you look to the Constitution if there's a threat to them. And for people still trying to make this country live up to its promise, they reference the Declaration of Independence. These days, both feel imperiled. We stand here celebrating, not because our union is perfect. It's far from it. But we still believe in our duty to strive to make it so."

The backyard filled with applause, Langdon joining in. But Josephine's attention returned to Khai's yard. She hadn't realized that Khai was listening until she saw her standing on a chair, clapping.

At dusk, the solar lanterns in the Blaques' yard began to glow weakly as Jules walked onto the patio. Elise, Fat, and Josephine were already seated at the table, Elise and Fat were hunched over a *People* magazine. Jules scoffed at them.

"Mr. Blaque, don't look at us in that tone of voice," Fat chided playfully.

"Wars, pestilence raging around the world," he said. "And y'all worried about 'Who Wore It Best.'"

"It's *better* not best." Elise sucked her teeth. "My husband can be so high-minded."

"Josephine, too," said Fat. "She should be standing over there with him."

Josephine flicked Fat's hand.

Fat's eleven-year-old, Malcolm, her oldest, was seated on the chaise portion of the sectional. Jules stood over him.

"Boy, unass my seat. It's got the best view."

"I'm in time-out," he muttered.

"So?" Jules said. "What's that got to do with me?"

"I'm trying to teach my son," Fat said, "not to slap his brother upside his head."

"Well, can't he learn that somewhere else?" Jules asked.

Jules and Malcolm turned to Fat, as if both were seeking permission. She jerked her head for Malcolm to move. Before the boy walked away, Jules placed his hand on his shoulder.

"Do not strike your brother," he said. "He's smaller than you now, but in a few years he might be bigger, and he'll remember all of this and decide to whup your—"

"J. B.!" Elise said.

"*Behind*," he emphasized to his wife, then turned to face Malcolm. "We good?"

Malcolm nodded and skulked off the patio. Jules sat alone for a while as Josephine left the table to engage with her other guests. She was in the yard, talking to one of Langdon's colleagues, when Jules called, "Hey, daughter-in-law!"

He was normally bold and brash, but as she got closer to him, she noticed that he looked terrified. His eyes were wide and cheeks sunken, his brown skin sallow.

"What the hell?" He stood on the edge of the patio, pointing to the woods on Jackson's property.

Marching down the mulched path were Jackson and his friends, ten men dressed in white jumpsuits and hoods, visible through the trees in frames, like in an old movie. They were walking single file through a shroud of firecracker smoke, railroad ties hoisted onto their shoulders.

"Our neighbor is a beekeeper." Josephine blinked to see better. "His friends are over there helping."

"They look like the KK—" Jules's voice trailed off.

"No. You've been thinking about your ancestor, and your imagination is—"

When Josephine looked again, she suddenly felt a sharp pang in her stomach. In the waning, shape-shifting light of the evening, clothing that once resembled hazmat suits had morphed into something she would never have imagined, something that momentarily appeared so menacing. Was it because one man in a beekeeper's suit was just that, but several of them formed a gang? Or had she been influenced by Jules's suggestion?

As the men stepped out of the woods into Jackson's yard, they looked like beekeepers again.

Fat and Ken were the last to leave, and after Josephine and Fat stalled for as long as they could, lingering in the driveway, they finally hugged and said good night. After Langdon went upstairs, Josephine headed to the One-Stop with a plate of barbecue chicken, greens, and potato salad for Lonnie.

Josephine arrived to see Lonnie sitting by the window, flipping through her cell phone. "You're out late," she said.

Josephine handed her the food.

"This is kind of you." Lonnie took the bag and placed it on the counter beside several other plates covered in foil or plastic wrap. Josephine felt unoriginal and a bit crestfallen.

Lonnie picked up a yellow gift bag. "This one's from your neighbor with the triplet boys. They spilled coffee down the aisle last week. She was so distraught. I told her, kids make messes and break things all the time." She crossed her arms over her chest. "Especially your heart."

"I've been meaning to ask—" Josephine hesitated. "How's Wade?"

"He told me that the barbershop was closed last week, and he showed you where he"—she made air quotes—"'lives.' I'm also guessing you met Benny, conjoined as they are."

Lonnie turned to watch Deputy Adam's police cruiser pulling up. Josephine turned too.

"Benny's a sweet kid. But my son is an ideologue, and he's in mourning." She took a breath. "He also told me he slipped up, and you guys probably know who we are."

"We do," Josephine said.

"You may have questions." Her tone turned a bit defiant. "But I'm not obligated to answer. I don't owe anybody an explanation."

Suddenly Josephine's heart began to race, and she felt lightheaded.

"I used to judge parents who couldn't control their children," Lonnie said, "and now—"

Josephine began to slump. She was standing a few feet away, next to the coffee station, and as she went down, she took a pyramid of K-Cups with her. Lonnie rushed to help her to the floor.

"I'm feeling faint," Josephine said. "I've only been nibbling all day. It's just hunger."

Lonnie hurried to the back room, returning with a cool, wet paper towel and a bottle of water. She twisted it open and handed it to Josephine. "You had your period lately?"

Josephine nodded as she sipped from the bottle and dabbed her forehead with the towel. "I'm sure I'm not pregnant."

"I was sure four times," Lonnie said, pulling her cell phone from the pocket of her khaki skirt and dialing. "Deputy Adam, come in here, please," she said into the phone. Outside, the police cruiser's brake lights flared. "Ms. Blaque isn't feeling well, and I don't want her behind the wheel. I'll drive her car, and you can trail us."

"No, I'm fine," Josephine said, slowly standing.

"You have no say in this matter." Lonnie walked down the closest aisle and brought back a pregnancy test, which had a bonus extra one. Handing it to Josephine, she said, "On the house."

After being dropped off, and assuring Lonnie that she was okay, Josephine walked through her bedroom, past Langdon, who was snoring. In the bathroom, she sat on the toilet. She hadn't taken too many pregnancy tests, because she'd always been so careful.

There was a time when she would flip through old photos of her mother, wondering what part of her would exist in her grandchild. Especially because Josephine looked so much like her father. Whenever someone said, "You and Langdon would make wonderful parents," she thought, *How can you be so sure?* Although she wasn't the kind of person who flocked toward the cooing baby in the room, she did believe that she'd throw herself in front of a speeding car to save a child. She just wasn't certain she was meant to be that child's mother.

She was so focused on the pregnancy test stick that she jumped when Langdon walked in.

"You think you might be . . ." His tone was measured, but she saw the hope in his eyes.

The timer on Josephine's cell phone chirped, and the stick showed a solitary, solid line. She breathed an audible sigh of relief and tossed the stick into the garbage.

"Your body's still acclimating to this new place," he said, turning to leave the bathroom.

"Lang." The last time the subject of children came up was when she was making an argument for not moving. "I do think about it, having a baby. I was just telling Fat—"

"I believe you do." He sounded dejected as he walked away. "It's been a long day."

She stood in front of the mirror above the face basin. Here was a man who, every time they walked down the street, almost tripped over his feet to position himself on the side of traffic. The first time he'd done it was in Ghana, when they went for an after-dinner stroll outside the hotel's fenced-in perimeter. She'd told him that he didn't have to keep maneuvering around her. He told her that most women appreciated that he was a gentleman.

Now she looked down at the garbage can as if that stick could say more than it already had. *Why are you afraid, Josephine? You know that man in there loves you.*

But even he, like iron, has a melting point.

CHAPTER THIRTEEN

a body in motion, a body at rest

At sunrise, a dense fog hung over the Grand Vistas, clinging to the tops of pine, ash, and cottonwood trees and sweeping across the trailers' disintegrating asphalt roofing. Benny stood on the road outside the trailer park, waiting for the summer school bus. It wasn't scheduled to come for nearly two hours, and Wade had told Benny it wasn't safe for him to be out alone at dawn. But Benny hated listening to his aunt talk in her sleep. That was the only time she not only looked like his mother, but sounded like her, too.

So there he stood, upwind of the porta-potties, his book bag strapped onto his back, standing starch straight as he stared off into the trees. The one time his aunt saw him out there, she told him that he resembled a little boy waiting to salute a casket. *Who'd want to do that?* Benny had thought.

The night before, Wade and Benny had sat in lawn chairs watching the Fourth of July sky thunder with color. Few streetlights had bulbs in the Grand Vistas, and Benny delighted in seeing everything lit up by something other than the moon or flames. When the fireworks were over, he and Wade had gone into Wade's trailer to continue reading Ralph Ellison's *Invisible Man.*

According to Benny's abysmal standardized test scores, the novel was leagues above the boy's reading level. But Wade believed he could handle it. Wade took his time with the more complicated passages and taught Benny the importance of looking up the definitions of words he didn't know. Benny told Wade he liked watching the pages "go down," marking their progress. What he didn't say aloud was that he loved when Wade told him he was smart. He loved that he didn't have to puff his chest with him.

Benny, an eighth grader, had to attend summer school before moving on to high school. In many cases, teachers recognized Benny's intellect—but they also said he talked too much in class and could hardly sit still. He fought at the slightest provocation and constantly needed to be disciplined. Wrote one teacher in an assessment for the school social worker: "Although Benjamin displays flashes of brilliance, he has a heart filled with chaos. He is not quick to anger, but when brought to his breaking point, he is prone to lashing out and there is no stopping this child who is no stranger to destruction."

Benny brought home a copy of the assessment, along with a letter remanding him to summer school to retake pre-physics and pre-algebra. He was supposed to give both correspondences to his aunt, his legal guardian. But since the school year ended, he'd been delivering documents to Wade. Although his aunt meant well, she worked long hours and prioritized opening bills over school stationery.

When Benny's mother was alive, he'd been her unofficial caretaker, spending night after night listening to her breathing—the sound of gears grinding. Administering dose after dose of medicine. Managing adverse reactions, such as when a new antibiotic sent her into what paramedics called "an altered mental state." She had lunged at Benny with a knife.

On the morning he couldn't wake her, he dialed 9-1-1. Then he used a broom and a footstool as a fulcrum to lift her gaunt body into the abandoned shopping cart she kept outside. She often used the cart as her walker. Benny was eleven, and if she'd waited a year to die, a growth spurt would have made him big enough to carry her over his shoulder. He knew the paramedics didn't always respond promptly, so he planned to push her to the nearest hospital, miles away. He hadn't realized how impractical that was, and that she had run out of time. To Wade's mind, Benny was in full command of physics—the idea of a body in motion, a body at rest. And when it came to algebra, the boy had already lived a life that required him to solve for so many unknowns—the elusive X, the probing Y—as he managed all the variables and vagaries of his day-to-day.

Not far from the porta-potties, a roadside memorial had been erected around that very shopping cart, and it had become rutted in mud. The cart, before it was removed, had been filled with teddy bears, balloons, grocery store flowers, and wooden crosses, including a painfully rudimentary one made from bed slats. There was a birthday card Benny had gotten from the drug store. He'd written, "Love u Mom. Hop to see you swoon."

A few months before his aunt came on the scene, a school social worker asked him to compose a one-page bio. It began, "I am an award of the state."

Benny was always the first child on the bus, and when it arrived that morning, he boarded and sat in his usual window seat in the rear. He never removed his book bag, so he sat pitched forward at an odd angle. But that didn't bother him as he took in the old chicken factory, the woods, the strip mall. On Old Creek Road, the bus passed the cemetery and the One-Stop, then turned left onto Goodenow. Benny saw two men jogging—one Black and the other white. He'd seen them from time to time since summer school began. The Black guy wore a baseball cap. The two men were always sweaty, running hard as the bus passed them. Benny extended his fist upward and pulled down in a way a kid would motion for a trucker to honk his horn.

But neither man saw Benny.

As he whirled around in his seat, his eyes laser focused on the men, he saw the Majestic Hills sign and watched them turn into the subdivision—a place beyond his view and, Benny somehow instinctively knew, his reach.

CHAPTER FOURTEEN

alums

Langdon arrived at the One-Stop as evening rush hour traffic was ending, and the canopy lights over the pumps were beaming on. While filling his tank, he saw Lonnie's truck parked on the side of the building where it normally sat. He looked over at the One-Stop's window to wave at her, but despite the Open sign on the door, she wasn't there. Two-week-old red, white, and blue balloons over the pumps from the Fourth had deflated, and he fought every urge to remove them, as the maintenance guy hadn't yet done so.

Langdon washed his windshield and threw away all evidence of the Frosty he'd bought on his way home. Josephine scowled at him when he ate fast food.

No harm, no scowl. He chortled to himself.

He and Josephine had cultivated their own relationship with Lonnie. Josephine stopped by for morning coffee on her way to the train during the week and on weekends when she wasn't heading downtown. He stopped by whenever he needed gas, which was often with the Land Cruiser. "I can't listen to you today, Lonnie," he'd joke. This, they both knew, was supposed to be ironic because Langdon always did most of the talking.

Now he looked at the window again, and still no Lonnie. Pure instinct drove him inside.

He pushed open the door and immediately saw her sitting on the floor in front of the checkout counter, crying, her back against the rows of Lifesavers, Orbit gum, and cigarette lighters.

He crouched beside her. She managed a smile.

"Tough day?" he asked.

"Really tough." She wiped her eyes with the heels of her hands. "I'm okay. Go home."

She wore a tailored navy blue business suit and black high heels. Her hair was cinched into a taut bun, and her makeup, flawless earlier in the day, now was smudged and smeared with streaks. He'd never seen her dressed up. For the first time, she looked like money.

"Maybe I can help." Langdon extended his hand for her to stand. She took it.

She walked behind the counter and handed him a diploma cover with Stanfield Academy on its face.

He opened it, expecting to see a diploma. Instead, there was a generic letter:

Dear Graduate,

If you have completed all necessary requirements, your diploma will be mailed in eight to ten weeks. Below is a QR code for students who want to join the alumni association.

Lonnie explained that Wade hadn't wanted to attend the ceremony. He was graduating two years early, and he'd been homeschooled and hardly knew his peers. His two best friends had moved away a year ago—months before his father died—and they wouldn't be attending.

Wade had told Lonnie that the ceremony was unimportant. He'd rather be in the garden pulling weeds in the GVs. Still, Lonnie had pleaded with him to reconsider.

She took the diploma cover from Langdon and held it.

"He finally agreed to attend," she said. "His siblings, Bradley, Maddy, and Eve, flew in. But you should have seen him. On his mortarboard, he scribbled, 'Free The Grand Vistas.' On his honors stole he wrote

'Decent Housing' on one panel and 'Is A Human Right' on the other." She strummed the counter. "He crossed the stage and stood for a minute facing the audience. A few people clapped, but most laughed."

"Screw the detractors," Langdon said. "Wade marches to the beat of his own drum."

"I'm often proud of that. I really am. But sometimes I just want to take that damn drum and bash it against the wall."

"So, homeschooled kids get to participate in the graduation?"

"Absolutely. He took gym and was part of the chess club at the school. He just did his academics at home. And we still had to meet the school's and state's requirements."

Lonnie said that weeks had passed since the graduation, and she thought she'd come to terms with it all. But earlier that day, Wade had come in, showing off the tassel he'd bought for Benny for when he completes summer school.

"There's no formal eighth-grade graduation. But I was like, 'Really, son, are you stupid? You give me a hard time about your own ceremony, but now you're celebrating someone else's?'" She loosened her bun. "We've got to start talking about college again. Will he take another gap year? When is he coming back home? I'm so tired of fighting—"

She squeezed her eyes shut, as if to stanch tears.

"My son is a smart but naïve kid who thinks he can plug every hole in the dam that's breaking in the GVs. In doing so, he gets to honor his father. But his mother be damned."

Langdon walked over to the coffee station. "I think you need a pick-me-up."

He poured a cup and handed it to her, pointing at her suit. "You certainly clean up well."

"I attended one of our annual meetings earlier today."

He assumed she was referring to a Stanfield Foundation meeting, where she was the president. But he didn't ask.

"Wade's sixteen," Langdon said. "He's just trying to flex. He'll come around."

“I keep saying he’s mourning, but that’s getting old.” She placed her hand on her forehead. “I don’t mean that. What an absolute shit show.”

Langdon was quiet, tugging on his bottom lip. Josephine always reminded him that he did that when he had to make a split-second decision to do or say something he doubted was the right thing.

“If this is any consolation,” Langdon said, “and I realize it may not be, but I gave my parents hell after my little brother died.”

He looked out the window, beyond the pumps, to the cornfield across the road, blanketed in darkness. Langdon was nine years old when they lost Nicky. But the hammer fell a few years later. He spent his freshman year of high school ditching classes and, for a while, intercepting truancy letters and emails, thanks to his parents using the same password for everything. He didn’t know what to do with himself. He couldn’t be in the house anymore. And yet, every time his parents talked about moving, that also tore him apart. He felt like he was simultaneously chasing a little boy’s ghost and running away from it. His older brother, Paul, had shared a room with Nicky. They didn’t have to, but Nicky never felt comfortable sleeping alone. And Paul had twin beds. Langdon didn’t want any part of their arrangement, because they were both slobs. His bedroom had been next to Nicky’s, and before he died, Nicky used to sneak into Langdon’s room in the middle of the night and sleep at the foot of his bed.

“After we lost him, I would go to sleep in my bed and sometimes wake up in his—curled up under his covers. I never remembered leaving my room.”

In his wallet was a photo of him and his brothers at the beach, in swim trunks, with their narrow bare chests and sandy-colored Afros. He considered showing Lonnie the photo. But he decided against it; sometimes he couldn’t bear to look at it, and this was one of those times.

“My parents cajoled and bartered,” he said. “But nothing worked. I was tuning out during therapy sessions or skipping them altogether. Self-medicating with weed.”

When he turned to Lonnie, her attention was all his.

"I'm sorry," she said.

"Yeah, me too."

"What turned things around for you?"

"I spent a night breaking car windows. I was about sixteen, like Wade. I got arrested, and my father wouldn't let my mother come get me. They fought and fought, and as I waited, I composed this essay in my head about being a troubled youth. About what that word tended to mean for young Black and brown men. How *troubled* was a shorthand people used to define us. But I wasn't the typical troubled Black kid. What they don't realize is that there's nothing typical about being troubled."

He began folding a napkin into something resembling a swan.

"In the end, I think I got lucky. I tiptoed around the abyss, but never completely fell into it. One day, I stopped fucking up. I was always a smart kid—academically. So I made up lost ground by attending summer school and taking heavy class loads."

Now Langdon doubted whether he should have said anything to Lonnie. He'd hoped that his falling back down into the pit of the past could have some utility for her. But what was the point? He changed, therefore Wade could, too? That was a bunch of bullshit. Langdon could make no guarantees. That was true even if Wade were living at home instead of in the Grand Vistas.

Langdon looked down an aisle. "I regret every moment my parents stayed up waiting for me or every time the school called for something I'd done wrong. And maybe Wade feels similarly. But he can't get out of his own way right now. I lost my little brother. Wade lost his father. When you lose someone at such a young age, you graduate into this awful club that absolutely nothing in your life has prepared you for. It rearranges your molecules."

Lonnie held the cup with both hands, the coffee shaking.

"It's okay," Langdon said. "I'm going to step outside for a second. All right?"

She nodded.

The air was humid and thick, with large bugs pinging the canopy lights. He called Josephine to tell her that Lonnie had had a rough day, and he didn't want her to drive home alone. Before long, Josephine was riding onto the property. She leaned her bike against the wall and entered the store. Langdon was having a hard time persuading Lonnie to allow them to help.

"We're taking you home," Josephine said to Lonnie. "Like you told me a couple of weeks ago, 'you have no say in this matter.' My husband will drive with you in your pickup. I'll follow."

On Goodenow, Lonnie pointed out directions until they reached a gate with a sensor that read the one on her windshield.

The floodlights painted the house whiter than it really was, making it appear luminous. Langdon watched Josephine tilt her face toward it as if it were something celestial.

"Nice crib," he said, helping Lonnie ascend the steps to the entrance.

"It's a roof," she said.

"Oh, it's way more than that," Josephine said.

Inside, Langdon eyed a grand piano and began gravitating toward it.

"Nope," Josephine said to Langdon. She turned to Lonnie. "He will sit there, and you won't be able to get rid of him."

In the family room, Lonnie plopped down on a sofa and patted the cushion next to her. Josephine sat. Langdon joined them a few minutes later, having rustled up a turkey sandwich and a glass of iced tea in the kitchen. Lonnie ate quickly and quietly, chasing the sandwich with a pill from a bottle on the cocktail table. Langdon sat in a nearby chair.

"Xanax," Lonnie said, shaking the bottle to show how full it was. "My doctor prescribed these damned things a month ago. This will only be my second."

She flung a throw around her shoulders and placed her feet on the table next to a framed photo of her older son in his cap and gown. Josephine slipped off Lonnie's shoes for her.

"These are super cute." Josephine's voice lilted as she examined a heel and peep toe.

"You want them?" Lonnie asked earnestly. "You can have them."

Langdon laughed. "Josey couldn't get half her foot in those little things."

Josephine tossed a sofa pillow at him.

"Wade's my only child who had head lice. He had to hug his kindergarten classmate—little patient zero—until her parents arrived."

Lonnie started to get drowsy, and she tucked the throw under her chin. "He's mad at me," she said. "He blames me for killing his father." Her voice coarsened, and she tamped down tears. "My husband's heart stopped for so long it cut off the oxygen to his—" She'd begun to drift, and she looked stumped, searching for the word.

"His brain," Josephine said, looking at Lonnie and then Langdon.

Lonnie nodded. "The doctor told us there was nothing left of him. My him. Wade's brother and sisters flew in to say goodbye. But Wade wanted us to wait. His father would still be hooked up to all those machines if Wade had anything to say about it. My child used that moment to start believing in miracles."

Lonnie laid her head on Josephine's shoulder.

"He's not in the Grand Vistas alone—Wade," she said, the Xanax talking now. "It's not a bad place—people think that. There are so many good people there. Still, my friend Deputy Adam has an officer drive by every night. I couldn't bear it if no one was watching him. Please don't tell—"

Her speech began to slur, and Langdon leaned closer, trying to hear better.

"Wade hates Majestic Hills. He and his father used to fish there, and he thinks the subdivision took that away from him—and not—" Her voice petered off.

"What was that?" Langdon asked.

"And not death."

CHAPTER FIFTEEN

nessun dorma

At the One-Stop, days later, Lonnie attempted to retreat into her former stoic, standoffish self with Josephine and Langdon. Saying things to them like "Let me know if I can help you." Josephine guessed she was embarrassed for having revealed more than she wanted to about her life. Josephine told her to get over herself.

"Everybody's got something. Everybody."

This worked—and a good thing, too, Josephine thought—because around that same time Lonnie had a bunch of tea to spill about the Blaques' neighbors, and Josephine delighted in hearing it. Lonnie told them that Marc and Danny came in one day and were about to pay for a couple of Red Bulls when his phone rang. They left the counter to stand next to the coffee station, both with an ear up to his phone. From what Lonnie could glean, they had just learned that a bankruptcy had been stricken from their credit report. They bounded out, leaving the Red Bulls behind. Lonnie told Josephine she'd wondered why they always paid with cash, something few people did nowadays.

Lonnie said that Bonnie was nice, but always in a hurry, late for something related to her sons. She'd recently bought all twelve copies of the *Vanity Fair* July issue. The cover heralded a feature on "America's Top 25 Documentary Filmmakers." She'd beamed as she plopped the stack on the counter. As she was about to leave, the pregnant lady came in, Dr. J. Monica Johnson. She too was courteous, which was notable because her husband, Christopher, rarely said please or thank you or good morning. Bonnie and Dr. J. Monica huddled by the coffee station for a few minutes, hugging and screaming. Lonnie overheard Bonnie explaining that her latest documentary, *Accidental Daughter of the Confederacy*, had been featured in the magazine. It chronicled Bonnie's life, growing up in Southern Illinois, ashamed of her Civil War reenactor father. Now, in his eighties, he dressed up as a Confederate soldier at the Abraham Lincoln Presidential Library and Museum. Dr. J. Monica had replied that the documentary reminded her of her dissertation, which had focused on Kentucky tobacco farmers who ferried their slaves across the Ohio River and Mason-Dixon Line so they could toil in the Illinois salt mines.

"She said that's how the local Stanfield family made their loot," Lonnie told Josephine. "She didn't know who I was, or that Geoffrey had told me the sordid details years ago."

With Josephine in the store, Lonnie called up Bonnie's documentary on her iPad. She'd only planned to watch the trailer, but she and Josephine wound up standing on either side of the counter for ninety minutes, engrossed in the film. At one point, a customer with Iowa license plates came in, saying that he'd honked, trying to get Lonnie's attention, but she was so unhelpful he wanted to complain to her manager.

"I'll make sure to tell her," Lonnie said.

Summer wore on, and Josephine and Lonnie's conversations turned to the relentless August rain. Water was everywhere, uprooting stately old trees, flooding cornfields, and washing out roads. In the condo, Josephine had always seen ominous storm clouds forming from a distance over the lake. But here the rain too often crept up on her, sneaky and unpredictable.

Early one morning, thunder that sounded like a sonic boom rumbled through Josephine, shaking her awake. She sat up straight and clawed at the bedcovers for Langdon until she remembered he'd worked an overnight shift. They had planned to spend their vacation week with his parents in the cottage they owned in Martha's Vineyard. But it had rained every day and after two flights were canceled, Josephine and Langdon decided to stay put and enjoy the inclement weather, their home, and each other.

She watched water cascade down the bedroom windows. Outside, the sky looked muddy, and the trees creaked against the wind. New Pointe's tornado siren began to blare, and Josephine's breath caught, even though the siren stopped shortly afterward. A text followed, saying there was no tornado sighting, just heavy rain. Although the siren had cried wolf all week, Josephine feared letting her guard down and being caught unaware.

"It'll pass," she muttered to herself. Her cell phone rang, and Langdon's face popped up.

"Hey, you," she said.

"You okay?" he said. "I'm on Goodenow, five minutes out."

"I'm not a baby." She was relieved to hear his voice.

"You're my baby. I'll stay on the phone with you."

"You so corny," she sang. "Are you tired?" She rose from bed and ran downstairs.

"No. I got good sleep in the on-call room. But I do have to pee so bad my teeth are floating."

She watched him pull into the driveway, saying, "You expect to kiss me with that mouth?"

Langdon showered, and he and Josephine shared a bowl of cereal, something Fat always called "sweet but disgusting." They decided to spend the day unplugged, so they powered down their phones and left them on the kitchen table. Upstairs, they stripped naked, and Langdon got into bed. Their goal was to binge on movies all day, venturing downstairs only for sustenance. Josephine went into the bathroom to brush her teeth and returned to the bed, pressing her pelvis against Langdon. She clicked on the television. Despite the "good sleep" he'd gotten in the on-call room, he was knocked out. She gawked at him—his veined eyelids, his freckles, his barely there ruddy-colored brows, his chin shadowed in stubble. Then he began to snore—drowning out the television, the rain, and everything except the pattering hail, which sounded like a jilted lover pelting the window with pebbles, vying for attention.

When Josephine awoke just after noon, the storm over Majestic Hills had not subsided, and the sky was still dark and gloomy.

Outside, a man yelled, "Fucking hell!"

Josephine hurried to the window. In the center of Monica and Christopher's lawn, a muddy oval was expanding, so stark against the surrounding greenery that it looked like a black hole. Christopher hopped around in the muck as if he'd stubbed his toe. Other neighbors formed a line, passing small pieces of furniture from the house to a tarp near the tree line. Josephine woke up Langdon.

"Christopher and Monica's house is flooding," she said. "We should help."

Langdon groaned. "Rock, paper, scissors," he said. "I win; we stay. You win; we go."

The Blaques arrived to the sound of Leon Bridges' "River" from Bonnie's playlist. The neighbors were working in what looked like a tar pit. Their drenched clothes pressed against their bodies. Mud caked bare legs or rain boots. Feet squelched in muck. The rain had paused, but droplets drizzled from leaves.

Christopher stood on the side of the house near a half-glass, half-wooden door. Inside, Josephine could see pieces of furniture, as well as an ornate cabinet holding several rifles, lining the hallway. She assumed the items had been brought up from the basement.

"What can we do?" Langdon said to Christopher, who looked frazzled.

His wet hair formed ringlets across his forehead like the calligraphy on an invitation to a garden party. His eyes were bloodshot. His soaked T-shirt stuck to his chest.

"What a nightmare. First thing in the morning I'm calling the developer."

Basil barked, sounding hoarse and angry.

"Poor bastard. He went out earlier and got stuck in the mud. I understand the feeling."

A large truck that had been vacuuming out the septic tank sat in the driveway. When the driver walked up in wading boots, smelling of excrement, Christopher said, "I've got to pay this guy."

He left Josephine and Langdon as Marc walked over. "Sure, come after we've done the heavy lifting."

"What happened?" Langdon asked.

Marc nodded toward the truck backing out of the driveway.

"Water's everywhere," he said. "In the septic system, in the basement." He lowered his voice. "A couple of lots here had wetlands on them. The developers told me that the Army Corps of Engineers made them re-create the wetlands in property that was adjacent to the subdivision before the developers could backfill to build the houses. If this was one of the wetlands, it may have drainage issues." He bounced gently, and his feet sank. "The ground here feels way too spongy. It may cost a small mint to fix."

"What about the rest of the properties?" Josephine asked.

"Drainage seems to be fine everywhere except here. Christopher drew the short straw."

Bryce yelled for Marc and Langdon to help him and Bonnie fold a tarp, which the four of them did, as if handling a giant bedspread. All the while, Bonnie belted lyrics from Brandi Carlile's "The Story."

On the patio, Danny was in full makeup, wigless, and wearing a baseball cap. Josephine walked up to her.

"Bonnie's got a great voice," Danny said, wicking rainwater from her cheeks as she stacked white buckets.

"She really does." Josephine began to help. "Were you bailing water, too?"

"No dear, these are for hunting," Danny said. "He uses these buckets to dress the animals he slaughters." She pulled a gutting knife from a bucket and examined it. "Just wait a couple of months until deer season. This yard will look like a crime scene."

A white wooden rocking chair, a white diaper changing table, and a white bassinet were the only items remaining in the yard on another tarp and covered in plastic. After each item was wiped down and placed back in the house, Monica looked relieved that none of the baby's furniture was damaged. Christopher brought out a cooler of beer and started passing bottles around.

"My fucking luck. Why do *I* always get the lemon?" Josephine noticed that he was looking directly at Monica when he said this, although he looked away, as if realizing the implication. "Thank you, neighbors."

"Oh, hush, you'd do the same for us," Bonnie said. She held up her cell phone. "Before we leave—how about a little dance?" She turned to Christopher. "You mind?"

"I'm not in a dancing mood." He wiped his face on his T-shirt. "But go right ahead."

Aretha Franklin's "Respect" filled the air, and the neighbors sashayed and twirled and stomped around in the wet grass. When the song ended, Langdon requested Aretha's "Nessun Dorma." Bonnie searched her phone.

"The 1998 Grammys," he said, his hands aloft as if he were about to direct an orchestra. "Luciano Pavarotti called in sick thirty minutes into the show, and Aretha was asked to fill in. She'd performed the aria at another event, but she hadn't practiced with this orchestra. *Nessun dorma* is Italian for 'none shall sleep.'"

Langdon nodded at Bonnie, and she pressed Play.

The orchestra opened with a melody that created a sense of urgency, the feeling of running—or even flight. As Aretha began to sing, the neighbors did not dance. A few swayed, like the trees behind them. But everyone was mostly still, eyes closed or staring at the ground.

"For her to sing such a challenging piece," Langdon said. "And on the fly, explained why she was royalty, the queen."

When the song ended, everyone applauded. If there were tears, the rain wiped them away. The neighbors lingered, as if to get their bearings. Marc held Danny around her waist. Christopher stood beside Monica, who rocked gently while rubbing his shoulder. Bryce held Bonnie from behind. Josephine lay her head on Langdon's shoulder and thought about the first time he played that version of "Nessun Dorma" for her. It was the night he'd told her about Nicky.

As they walked home, he looped his arm around her neck and kissed her nose.

"I fell asleep earlier," he said.

"I am aware." She placed her hand on his chest.

"And I'm about to make it up to you."

"Really?" She clapped lightly, enthusiastically.

"You have no idea what I'm about to do to you. It's 'bout to get real nasty, and quick."

"Oooo, I like you nasty."

"I'm thinking—should we start with a hot bath?"

They passed through the kitchen. Josephine stopped by the sink for a glass of water. Looking out onto the backyard, she took a sip, offering the glass to Langdon. He was standing behind her, about to kiss her neck, when she turned around.

"What—what if we have a lemon, too?" she asked. "You did get a land survey?"

Langdon's body froze. "Josey, why would you ask that?"

"I'm just wondering. You're the one who took care of that part."

"Is that how we do things? If it works, it's ours, but if it breaks, it's mine?"

"All I did was ask a question."

"Not a question, an accusation. You're suggesting I may have fucked something up, based on something Christopher, of all people, said."

"Okay, let's calm down."

"No, I'm calm." He left the kitchen for the family room and sat on the sofa, turning on the television.

"Langdon?" She trailed him and flopped down next to him.

"The guy's a dick and—" He leaned away from her. "I think he's got a thing for you."

"What? No, he doesn't."

"Josey! I never know if you're just daft about these things—"

"Daft? Damn, Lang. We're going there? I'm neither daft nor naïve, nor coy."

"Or maybe it's fake modesty? All—equally unbecoming."

She exhaled. "I'm not that person who assumes every man is flirting with her. And if he is flirting, Lang, who cares? I'm not doing anything wrong."

"I care," he said. "One rainy night—a few months ago—" He stopped. "Never mind."

"A rainy night? Go on."

"Nah. I'll wind up looking like a jealous lunatic."

He'd told her, early on in their dating, that he'd been with a woman who was so possessive that she secretly downloaded a tracking program on his phone. She would get upset if he joked with a female server at a restaurant or talked too long with someone at a dinner party. He'd vowed never to go through that again. Nor did he want to be the source of it.

"I know Christopher rankles you," Josephine said. "Him loving this house but choosing the bigger one." She elbowed him. "You guys and your square footage."

"Okay," he said, scratching his chin. "It's not that. And you know what? It's all good."

"I know his type, Lang. He's just another white guy who wants to rule the world."

Langdon picked up his Nintendo Switch and turned on a video game. “We can’t keep fighting like this.”

“No, we can’t.” She scooted closer to him. “Lang, you are my life. You know that, right?”

“I do.”

She adjusted herself on the sofa. “When we married, I remember one of the firm’s partners saying it was good that you worked odd hours. He said that couples who don’t see each other stay together longer. I told him I missed you when we were apart. I didn’t want to be that couple who’d rather work than be in each other’s company.”

He turned to her. “That’s not what I want either, Josey.”

They were quiet as he returned to his game, racing a car throughout a dangerous course, his speed building to 180 mph. His knee bounced, and his body twitched as the car mounted a steep hill. When it dipped into a treacherous curve, it ran aground and burst into flames.

Her breath caught and she smiled ruefully.

“See that?” He licked his lips and kissed her. “That will never be us.”

CHAPTER SIXTEEN

the great shit shoveler

The rain had mercilessly pummeled the Grand Vistas, and Wade's diatribes about the tony neighborhood of Majestic Hills intensified as he and several other young men pumped water and laid sandbags along two fetid retention ponds, one a microbial stew that now emitted a phosphorescent glow. They unclogged drainpipes and catch basins and helped relocate residents from trailers where water poured in through the windows or roofs or wood paneling. Majestic Hills didn't directly dump water onto the Grand Vistas, but Wade believed the difference in resources, the quality of housing and life between the two communities was so stark that the subdivision was an affront. As he shoveled excrement from around an older couple's septic tank, pushing whirlpools of human waste until his palms blistered, he might have spoken even more harshly about Majestic Hills, but he couldn't speak. Despite three bandanas covering his nose and mouth, he kept gagging from the stench.

For months, Wade had been telling everyone who would listen that affordable housing on land with proper drainage was a human right. Fresh fruits and vegetables, along with clean water and clean air, were human rights. Most of the teenagers had learned to tune out his complaints. In the same vein, Wade tuned them out when they said he talked like a white boy, or that his jeans, like the trailer park, were always flooding, or that he ate his weight in food. Weeks earlier, at a get-together for the community garden's first harvest, the boys had ridiculed him for the extra helpings of tomatoes and zucchini and cucumbers he piled on his soggy plate. One discerning young man guessed that Wade, then a mysterious newcomer, had known excess in another life and was unaccustomed to rationing.

The leader of the pack of boys could have demanded that Wade leave the Grand Vistas when he arrived. He'd confronted other squatters who had moved into unoccupied trailers, but he'd been awake on the night when Benny tried to push his mother in that shopping cart up the incline to the trailer park's entrance. After witnessing such a Sisyphean attempt, he could hardly look at Benny, let alone remove another person from Benny's life. The leader admired the way Wade cared for the boy, this child he'd only recently known. With time, he came to see that Wade was industrious, savvy, and one of the hardest workers he'd ever seen. Which was why, after watching Wade toil around that septic tank for a couple of days, the leader affectionately began calling him the Great Shit Shoveler. And because the leader referred to Wade that way, so did the other young men.

But not Benny. Benny was Wade's thirteen-year-old acolyte, and he deeply felt the strength of Wade's convictions in a way that no one else did. The deluge had inspired such robust anti–Majestic Hills commentary from Wade that Benny asked Wade to take him there when he finished shoveling. But Wade refused, and Benny set out to Majestic Hills alone, following the path he recalled Wade showing Josephine. Wade happened to see Benny riding into the woods dressed in the Superman T-shirt that had been his mother's. He'd told Wade that it was his favorite shirt because it felt like being wrapped in both a cape and a blanket. Wade thought of this now as he ran to his trailer to get his bike. But it wasn't there. He'd told the boys that they could borrow it when he wasn't using it. He'd created a log for names, as well as time-out and time-returned columns. But the sheet was filled with messages from Benny: "Benny was here." Or "Benny stopped by." Or "Benny hates albegra," which Wade corrected to "algebra." After searching up and down the rows of trailers, Wade found his bike behind the church.

The ground on the footpath was surprisingly compact, though water flowed along each side of it. Wade rode hard. He didn't want someone to mistake Benny as an adult trespassing on private property. In Majestic Hills, he found the boy walking through the trees, focusing on the backs of the subdivision's homes. A billowy fog hung low over the rooftops, giving the aura of being surrounded by mountains. It was early evening, and lights glowed warmly from picture windows. In one yard, a tarp lay over a muddy chasm.

Seeing Wade, Benny took off through the woods toward the house on the end, the closest to the pond and clubhouse. Wade followed, whispering loudly, "Benny! Hold up!"

Benny stopped under the bathroom window and leaned against the bricks, the way he'd seen cops do on television. Wade stood next to him. They heard water lapping and a man grunting, the sound growing louder and louder.

"Somebody's doing it," Benny whispered, giggling.

Wade pulled Benny's arm for him to leave, but he barely budged.

Wade did not know who lived in the house until the man's moaning crescendoed and a woman laughed. "Lang, I could have drowned. Water went up my nose."

Wade gestured for Benny to leave, and they retraced their steps back through the trees. Benny kept turning to see the houses, his face filled with awe. And yet Wade detected confusion. The boy looked like he was trying to solve an equation that was as abstract as it was concrete. Wade remembered the day he realized that *his* house was special. He was in the first grade, when his best friend visited and stood in the Stanfield driveway, looking up at the house. He'd called it a castle. Wade's friend lived in a very nice suburban split-level, but Benny lived in a run-down trailer. Wade knew that he'd had seen nice houses on television, but to stand next to one and peer into its windows—to smell the grass and clean air and know it was a mere bike ride away—was another matter.

"You okay, Benny?"

"Uh-huh," he muttered.

"You sure?" Wade placed his hand on Benny's shoulder.

Benny maneuvered away. "Let's just go."

The two rode back to the Grand Vistas, where Wade dropped him off at his trailer. They could see his aunt napping, a hair bonnet meringue smushed against an opaque window. Benny opened the door to the television blasting the five o'clock news and the local weatherman saying, "Finally, this low-pressure system is loosening its grip and moving off to the east."

Wade started toward his trailer but stopped. His body ached, and he was exhausted. He wondered how he'd even ridden to Majestic Hills and back. The fatigue wasn't only from several days of constant vigilance over the retention ponds, septic tanks, and septic field. The fatigue stemmed from the realization of the massive amount of work the Grand Vistas still demanded. The weather wasn't as cruel an adversary as the day-to-day. He sniffed his T-shirt and couldn't help thinking that hours after shoveling shit, the wretched smell still clung to his clothes and hair. He could take another shower, but the trickle of water in his trailer was pathetic. There was pressure bearing down on this place everywhere, except in the plumbing.

In the nearby trailers, people argued, someone laughed uncontrollably, and in the distance, coyotes howled, confused by the darkness. Wade didn't want to admit it, but he wanted to go home. Not to that trailer, but *home*. He wanted to get into his own shower. And dry off with his own towels. And sleep in his own bed. Just for one night. He remembered when he was thirteen years old, hiking with his parents from the rim of the Grand Canyon down to the Colorado River and back, a seventeen-mile trek with a nearly nine-thousand-foot change in elevation. He recalled the day clearly, how he wanted to give up every time they took a break. If Wade wasn't on his feet when their rest ended, Geoffrey Stanfield kept walking and called, "Catch up, or the coyotes will get you." Wade could see his mother slowing, constantly looking over her shoulder. But his parents didn't stop, and Wade was forced to will his body forward with every step. When the hike was over, he was rewarded with a sunset adorned by California condors with wingspans of nine feet soaring over the canyon. In the Grand Vistas, the geography was also complex, and the road forward was rocky, but unlike in the Grand Canyon, there was no brilliantly colorful endpoint.

Wade rode his bike to the One-Stop. He entered, seeing his mother behind the counter staring at her cell phone. She looked up, surprised to see him.

"Hey," he said. "You think it's okay if I come home for one night?" He was aware that he was handing her something destined to melt in her grasp.

"Son, you never have to ask me if you can come home."

"Thank you. Okay if I go on ahead?"

"You know the codes. Nothing has changed."

At the house, Wade went straight to his bedroom and to his bathroom, whose square footage rivaled that of a single-wide. He grabbed his clippers and leaned his head over the face basin, shearing tuffs of curly hair away until his scalp had what looked like crisscrossing vacuum lines. He trimmed his fingernails—under which fecal matter had begun to dry—with nail clippers rather than hacking at them with blunt scissors as he had been doing. When he removed his clothes, his full body occupied the mirror: his protruding ribs, his spine like a pearl necklace stretching from neck to waist. It was the first time in months he could see his entire body. The mirror in the trailer had mirror rot and showed only his head and neck. As he showered, dirt ran off him and down the drain. When he finished, he felt giddy, as though he had been standing beneath a waterfall. He tucked himself in his bed.

When he came downstairs to the kitchen for breakfast the next morning, he saw brochures and printouts of class catalogues from Fisk, NYU, and Princeton laid out on the table, surrounding an empty vase. Lonnie had left a note: "Time to choose." A few days earlier, before shoveling shit had chastened Wade, he might have ignored them. But now he inched closer to the table, flipping through the brochures.

The windows were open. He heard Lonnie outside, coming up the back steps. She wore a floppy hat, a T-shirt, and shorts. Her red rain boots were more muddy than wet, because the rain had stopped. She held black-eyed Susans.

"Morning, son."

She kicked off her boots and placed her flowers in the vase, gesturing for him to sit at the table. They were quiet, and he could feel her staring at his shaved head, his father's polo shirt.

"So." She clicked her tongue. "You know this can't go on much longer."

Fear swept across Wade's face. "Mom, I can't *not* help these people."

"Then let's make a deal."

Wade looked like he was overheating. His eyes welled with tears. But Lonnie was unequivocal.

"Accept my help," she said. "And once we've done the best we can do in the Grand Vistas, you come home and get ready for college next year."

He nodded slowly.

Lonnie beckoned for Wade to follow her into her home office, a high-ceilinged room with a wall of windows looking out onto a patio. It had an antique secretary, a plush sofa and two chairs, and a large, ornate oak table that served as her desk. On top were the telltale signs of the upcoming Stanfield Family Foundation's silent auction: formal invitations on the foundation's stationery, a legal pad color coded with names and needs.

When Wade was young, he'd fall asleep under Lonnie's desk, listening to his mother tapping on her laptop. His siblings screaming at one another. His father sneaking into the room, plopping down on the sofa, seeking refuge. Now the house was so quiet it seemed to him ransacked by absence and grief, divorced from time and memory.

Lonnie opened her computer, handing Wade a pen and a reporter's notebook.

"Trying to get people to care about the Grand Vistas has always been a long shot." She pointed to the sofa for him to sit. "Even your father knew that. But here we are."

She told Wade that the Grand Vistas was under the jurisdiction of Drake County, not New Pointe. He should send letters to county board members, describing the conditions in the trailer park, explaining to the powers that be why they should care.

Wade cocked his head. "Like, this week, I shoveled poop?"

Lonnie cringed. "That explains the smell last night. And, yes. Allow people to see and feel this place, to be present in your words."

When she advised him to engage in social media, he frowned.

"Them's the breaks," she said. "But that's how you'll get your message out."

Wade watched his mother print stories about how the county board had listened to plans to clean up the trailer park and replace it with affordable private and public housing. Years ago, a now-disbanded Grand Vistas tenant association had proposed Sears Roebuck–type homes, Levittown-style prefab communities, and tiny homes. In the end, the board pushed through New Pointe's plan to build Majestic Hills instead, prioritizing bringing in well-healed newcomers over doing right by low-income families already living within its zip code.

"They say the Grand Vistas project was postponed but delay sometimes is defeat."

Wade leafed through the material, looking overwhelmed. Lonnie searched her desk and handed Wade a business card.

"Josephine Blaque helps workers find jobs. Maybe she can be a resource. She and her husband have agreed to participate in this year's silent auction."

Lonnie turned her computer screen around so Wade could see it.

"Josephine emailed this to me, but it's a little LinkedIn, right?"

He began reading aloud: "'This hour-long lunch promises to counsel parents on how to enhance their child's college runway and career trajectory.'" He shook his head disapprovingly.

"I'll revisit it," Lonnie said. "This year, the proceeds are going to a domestic violence shelter. But next year—they'll go to the Grand Vistas. I promise." She adopted the lotus position in her chair. "One last thing: college campuses are a real wild card these days. But I want you to spend the next few years figuring out how to use your immense talents and that huge heart of yours to change the world. I'm glad you still believe you can." She placed her hand on Wade's cheek. "Don't forget your retainer. Your bottom teeth are shifting."

Later that evening, Wade returned to the Grand Vistas, walking his bike down the entrance. Steam rose from tall grass, and swarms of mosquitoes waged an attack. Although the toxic rotten eggs smell, which the rain had tamped down, had returned in full force, he chose to look up—at a yellow sequined moon, low-slung and unobscured by clouds. At Wade's trailer, Benny was seated on the steps next to his aunt. A wet T-shirt turban was wrapped around his head. Benny saw Wade and bolted toward him, clamping his arms around Wade's waist. Wade zeroed in on Benny's fresh black eye.

"I knew you'd come back, Wade. The guys said you'd had enough. But I said, 'Wade wouldn't leave without saying goodbye. I'm his best friend.'" He turned to his aunt. "Wade's other friends moved away. That's why I'm the best."

"You're a good friend," Wade said, patting the boy's back and waving at the aunt. "But explain something: How is it that I've only been gone twenty-four hours and you've gotten into a fight?"

"Only because there was nothing else to get into, Wade."

As Benny and his aunt walked back to their own trailer, Wade heard Benny whisper loudly, "Everybody says Wade's got that good hair." He removed the T-shirt from his head. "I think I need good hair and a haircut, too."

CHAPTER SEVENTEEN

aqua father

Josephine stood near the choir stand in Casa de Restauración. Although the church was indeed a house of God, she marveled at how the Grand Vistas chicken farm's logo, worn and fading, was everywhere in the sanctuary. Stenciled as artwork across the two entrance doors. Stamped on tattered Bible jackets and outdated Sunday bulletins. Affixed via stickers to the dusty candles and Communion wine flasks on the altar.

When Wade asked Josephine to participate, she'd said yes immediately. Finding jobs for lower-wage workers had always been as important to her as helping clients who commanded much higher salaries. But what had originally been billed as a job fair turned into a legal aid clinic after Wade, Benny, and other residents started going door-to-door handing out flyers. Many of the residents said they had jobs—although they sought better-paying ones—but no one had access to quality legal services.

Josephine had arrived early that Saturday afternoon to meet her outplacement firm's interns, a group of law students who would help with the clinic. The students had set up a table near the front of the church and were passing out questionnaires to assess needs, along with packets about the outplacement firm. The sanctuary was standing room only, but Josephine saw Wade and Benny making their way to her.

"'Sup, Miss Attorney Lady," Benny said, waving. He held a plate he'd brought from the potluck table in the back. The Grand Vistas neighbors provided food, along with babysitting services, as an enticement to get more people to come out.

"What's up yourself, Benny." She smiled and turned to Wade. "How long have people been here?"

"Some for a couple of hours."

Benny leaned against a lectern and thumped a long-dead mic.

"We do a lot of standing in line and waiting around," he said. "We're used to it." He extended his plate to her. "I can get you one. Or you can have some of mines."

"Mine," Wade gently corrected.

"No, but thank you," Josephine said to Benny. "It's time to begin."

She stood behind the lectern, Benny hovering nearby until Wade gestured for the boy to sit next to him in the choir stand.

"Hello, everyone. Can I have your attention?"

When no one quieted, Benny placed his plate on the grubby red carpeting, lumpy from warped floorboards underneath, and two-finger whistled.

Josephine clamped her hands over her ears.

"Okay," she said, looking at him and then into the crowd. "Thank you, Benny, and thank you all so very much for coming out." She held up a sample packet. "Here you'll find information about our firm, as well as the nonprofits and foundations we work with." She stepped away from the lectern. "Everyone should have a questionnaire. Share what you're comfortable with. I want to state clearly that we are not saviors. This type of work is baked into our company's bottom line. People like to say, you do well so you can do good. But it's also true that you do good so you can continue to do well. My colleagues and I have benefited from someone asking, 'What can I do for you?' And that's what we're asking you, now."

The sanctuary was quiet except for throats clearing or babies fussing. An older white man raised his hand. He was in a wheelchair parked on the end of a nearby pew. He said that his job at the chicken plant had been dispersing predator birds before they reached the chicken coops and grow-out house.

"I used to shoot them right out of the sky," he said. "Dirty little cannibals."

Josephine walked toward him.

"I don't mean to insult," he said. "I looked you up on the Internet. Your motto may be 'We are here to soften the landing,' but, ma'am, we don't know much about soft landings. For most of us, it's been one hard knock after another. Tuck and roll, I say. We're no easy bunch."

"That doesn't scare me," Josephine said. "So let us do what we do."

A thin woman who appeared to be in her fifties stood and introduced herself as Lilly. She explained that she had been four months pregnant years ago when she miscarried while working a twelve-hour shift on the skinner line.

"I received an extra $256 in my paycheck that month." Lilly shrugged. "I guess for my troubles. I like working at the old folks' home, but I want a job that has benefits like a 401K. So I can retire one day. Nobody I know ever retires." She started to sit but stopped. "And I'd like a job that will teach me how to work a forklift."

"I'm so very sorry for your loss." Josephine placed her hand over her heart. "Regarding the forklift—" She smiled. "We'll see what we can do."

A line formed in front of the table, and Wade and Benny continued to sit in the small choir area behind the lectern. Josephine hovered near the law students, prepared to assist if they had questions. Several tenants who'd lost items during the deluge were concerned about renters' insurance policies purchased from shoddy companies their landlord made them buy. Many of the companies had gone out of business. Other residents had questions about agents who had denied claims, referring them to the exclusions sections of their policies. Homeowners wanted to know how they would pay for the damage to their trailers and the loss of their belongings. But they also inquired about the county's responsibility regarding fixing new and old potholes, along with the land near their septic fields where water had pooled. There was another group who needed help getting their criminal records expunged. She counted twelve young men who had been seated in the very back row. They each had taken off their baseball cap when they entered the church. They were the last to line up to drop off their questionnaires. Josephine could hear snippets of their crimes—drug possession, unlawful possession of a firearm, aggravated assault.

The line was getting shorter, and residents were still scattered throughout the sanctuary when Josephine stood.

"Okay, last call, everyone," she announced. "Any more questions?"

There was silence.

"Please don't hesitate to get in line. We'll be wrapping up soon."

When Benny stood, his chair scuffed loudly against the wooden floor. Most eyes were on him as he walked along the wall toward the back of the sanctuary before turning and passing the young men in the last row. They snickered and pointed at his run-over gym shoes as he turned down the center aisle.

"Benny, man," one said, "you ain't got nothing—"

"Hey!" Josephine clapped one time. "If you can't be respectful, please leave."

She couldn't be one hundred percent sure, but she thought she recognized a few of the young men from her first afternoon in the Grand Vistas. The ones goading Benny to fight.

"Look at that walk," a voice whispered loudly, to more laughter.

Benny had begun to perspire, and he moved like a train lumbering up the side of a mountain as he joined the few remaining people in line. When he reached the table, he beckoned for Josephine to come toward him.

Josephine smiled at him, hoping it masked her fatigue. This was her day off. Langdon was working a double and wouldn't be home that night. All she wanted right now was to change clothes and spend the rest of her Saturday in front of the television.

This little boy, she thought. "Child, what is your question?"

"Miss Attorney Lady," he said, staring at the floor around the altar, at its old water-stained red carpeting, its fraying wool nap, like wild grass shoots, particularly noticeable at the lectern. "Do I have to be baptized to see my mother again? Someone said that I had to be, but I'm not—baptized in the blood. Mama meant to do it, but she got busy, then sick, then dead."

Benny told Josephine that there was a trapdoor beneath their feet. He bounced slightly, and she could feel the floorboards sink. She worried that they might fall through them.

He told her that years ago, on the first Sundays during spring and summer, the carpeting would be pulled back and the trapdoor lifted. Pastor Lucia would stand in the space, which was filled with water. Women and girls lined up in their white dresses, men and boys in their white pants and T-shirts. One by one, an usher led them up the step to the altar area, taking their towel before they stepped down into the minister's arms. He always recited the Lord's Prayer.

"Aqua Father, who art in heaven." Benny sounded as earnest as anyone Josephine had ever known. "Halloween thy name."

"Oh, Benny," she said.

She did not know how to answer him. She clutched a small stack of blank questionnaires close to her chest. In no universe was this a question she was expecting. She doubted whether this area beneath their feet would ever fill with water again. The church was in such disrepair. She imagined that there hadn't been a baptism there for a long time and that the plastic basin, as she'd seen in other churches, was cracked, allowing dirt and sediment to seep in, along with the creep of flora and fauna. She assumed that the plumbing no longer functioned.

"Benny . . ." she said again.

He sat near the lectern and crossed his legs.

In that moment, she thought about her own father. Wouldn't she tear back every floorboard with her bare hands if it meant seeing him again? Wouldn't Wade do the same to see his father? And Langdon his little brother?

"I don't really know how to answer," she said finally. "Is it okay if I tell you what I think?"

He nodded, still seated, running his hands across the carpeting.

"I think you are a fine young man, and whether you are baptized or not, you will always have your mother with you."

When Benny looked like he would sit there for a while longer, Josephine returned to the chair in the choir stand. She flipped through the questionnaires, resembling a teacher looking down at her lesson but also watching a student serving the worst kind of detention.

By the time Benny stood, most of the people had left the sanctuary. She saw Wade waiting for him by the back door and watched as they left together.

Before getting on her bike, Josephine checked her phone. There was an email about the upcoming Stanfield Family Foundation auction, which she would read later. She'd had enough work for the day. She opened a text from Khai:

Yoga in my yard tonight?

Hell to the yeah! Josephine responded.

At home, Josephine quickly changed clothes and walked next door to Khai's backyard patio with her yoga mat.

As the crickets made a fuss, the women sat facing each other, their bare feet touching. They were stretching, and the yawning height difference between them prevented them from clasping hands. As Khai leaned back and Josephine leaned forward, their outstretched arms only allowed them to reach. Just as they started to stand, a door slammed.

"It's not even her fault," Monica yelled from the house next door. "I happen to like her."

Josephine and Khai's attention turned to an open second-floor window and its billowy sheer white curtains.

"Honey, the neighbors," Christopher calmly urged.

"Fuck the neighbors!" Monica bellowed.

Khai flopped back on her yoga mat, tickled.

"You are *so* transparent," Monica said.

The way she said "so" reminded Josephine of a singer relying on her diaphragm to truly possess the note.

"I see it. Everyone sees it. It's humiliating when you're around her."

Josephine mouthed to Khai, *Who?*

"At the meet and greet," Monica continued, "you were practically salivating. And on the day of the deluge, her clothes were wet and clingy—"

"I was not sali—"

"You lose your mind around beautiful women of color. It's like a fetish," Monica said.

"I don't fetishize."

There was something inaudible, and Josephine leaned in to hear better. *Holy hell. They're talking about me.* She looked up at Khai. They were the only two women of color at the meet and greet. And Langdon had said he thought Christopher had a thing for her.

"Years ago, before our blind date," Monica huffed. "Kirk told you that I was a doctoral student in African American studies and that my name was *Jerusha.*"

Josephine and Khai locked eyes.

"So," Josephine whispered. "That's what the *J* in Dr. J. Monica Johnson stands for."

"And you assumed I was Black," Monica said.

"As would most people." Christopher's voice sounded droll.

Josephine guessed he'd uttered a familiar refrain in maybe a familiar argument.

"Monica," he pleaded. "Why are we having this conversation?"

No one spoke for so long that Josephine almost felt sorry for Christopher. Almost.

"A woman in my swimming class," she said, "was freaking out in the locker room this morning because she wanted to win lunch with Josephine. That silent auction and all. She was on her phone engaged in a spirited bidding war but finally lost to BankerGuy." Monica growled with frustration. "I'm guessing you're BankerGuy? Since that is your email. The guy who shelled out five thousand dollars for a lunch that—what did the description say?" She was quiet for a second. "Oh, here it is: 'Promises to counsel parents on how to enhance their child's college and career runway.'"

"First of all, it's the bank's money," Christopher said. "We're restructuring several branches. Closing some others. We're considering hiring Josephine's firm. We figured—"

"We?"

"*I* figured this would be an opportunity to get to know her. Gauge synergies. And second, I've never had an affair, Monica."

"Sometimes I wish you would. To get it out of your system!"

There was a long silence, and Josephine felt as if her ears were ringing. Literally.

"At the meet and greet," Khai whispered. "We were rinsing our legs with the hose beside the clubhouse. Your dress was hiked up. I remember looking up at the window and seeing him watching us—well, you. I never mentioned it because it didn't seem like a big deal."

"I should go." Josephine's head felt like it was about to explode. She didn't bother to roll up her mat. She dragged it across the grass to her house. Khai followed, trying not to trip over it. They reached the side of the house, looked at each other, and burst into laughter.

Khai's eyes were watering. "What are you thinking?"

Josephine felt gobsmacked. "I can imagine how Starbucks baristas look when they call the name *Jerusha* and she walks up? And what about job interviews." Her face turned serious. "Good Lord!" she said. "All of this is fucking bonkers, right? I don't know whether to laugh or throw up." She swallowed. "I think I just did, a little."

"Totally batshit crazy," Khai said. "He'll want to know if he should pick you up."

"Oh, stop."

"I'm also expecting a dozen roses. And, a mixtape."

"Please, stop."

"I bet he's trolling his playlist now." Khai waved as she walked back across the lawn.

Inside the foyer, Josephine pressed her palms against her cheeks. *Langdon was right.*

CHAPTER EIGHTEEN

a silent auction lunch

Josephine did not sleep well, and in the middle of the night she reached over to touch Langdon and remembered that he was at the hospital. Wide-awake, she read the Stanfield Foundation email she'd ignored earlier.

It confirmed that Christopher Thompson had been the highest bidder for an hour-long lunch with her. The date was to be determined by the two participants. The venue would be Stanfield Academy's outdoor dining terrace. It included a list of participants, but she recognized only Khai, who'd be teaching a yoga class for parents; Marc, who'd be chatting up budding architects and engineers; and Langdon, who'd have lunch with a group of science students and their families.

She opened the Stanfield Foundation's web page. The goal for the foundation's annual auction and dinner was to raise $1 million for the Drake County Women's Shelter. Auctioned items included donated artwork by award-winning artists as well as lunches with local and national celebrities, power brokers, and people who were experts in their field. A slew of corporate sponsors supported an invitational clay shoot and the Stanfield Family Golf Classic.

Josephine saw Christopher as one of those whatever-comes-up-comes-out kind of people. She worried that in the run-up to the lunch, he might say something stupid to Langdon, like: *I won your wife in an auction. Imagine that?* She worried even more that Langdon might punch him in the nose. This was a fraught situation that could easily ignite into an explosive one.

Langdon arrived home just before noon. Josephine heard the garage door lifting and then closing.

He was tired, but he clearly wanted to talk. Instead of going directly upstairs and taking a shower before bed, he sat at the table, leaning forward with his elbows on his knees, rubbing his hands together.

"I'm guessing you've checked your email," he said.

"Yes."

"You got BankerGuy for the auction."

"I know."

"Told you he's got a crush."

"I know that too . . ."

"Josey, to be clear, I'm not accusing you of anything." Langdon rode back in the chair. "One night, when it was raining, ol' Christopher was walking Basil and they wound up in our yard. You were in the bathroom, drying off from the shower, and I thought I saw him looking up at the bathroom window at you—your nude silhouette."

"Ick! What?" She squirmed. "Why didn't you say something?"

"I wasn't sure. It was raining, foggy and dark. Lightning flashed, and he seemed to be facing the window. Then it thundered, and he turned toward Basil, who was running to him."

"So there's reasonable doubt?"

"Yes, Your Honor." His smile seemed strained.

"Here's what I know with certainty, Lang: we agreed to do this for Lonnie. It's for an hour. It's at the high school. And it'll be good for the firm if I can bring in new business."

Langdon had taken off his shoes at the door, and now he removed his socks.

"I'm just telling you what I saw." He yawned and then stood to kiss her. "I don't want you to go. But I'd understand if you did."

On the day of the lunch, Josephine was on the train heading downtown for a quick meeting before returning, when Langdon texted her:

Hope you slept well. So, today's the big to-do.

He never used the word *to-do*. Josephine waited for more, but the typing bubbles disappeared and did not return. *So, today's the big to-do, good luck? Today's the big to-do, have fun? Today's the big to-do, and I want to hear every word and don't leave one thing out?* That last part was what Fat had said when Josephine told her about the lunch and what she and Khai had overheard. Josephine did not revel in being the subject (or object) of a married guy's crush, nor a married couple's fight. If there was something there, it wasn't about her, but rather about him. His own wife knew it.

She responded to Langdon with: *morning! will do my good deed for the day. looking forward to seeing you later.* She waited and waited, and finally the bubbles returned. He simply "liked" her text.

Josephine felt trapped between two storm fronts. One at home and the other gathering over lunch. She had dealt with creepy guys before: The ones at work who got a smidge too close as they whispered something, often work-related but not at all top secret. The handsy ones—even after Me Too—who weren't grope-the-ass-or-tit handsy but took liberties with a that-a-girl shoulder rub or a lingering handshake. Christopher was not a unicorn. She could handle him. Her bigger concern was Langdon. He'd told her flat out that he didn't want her to go. But, in the same breath, he'd given her absolution. Now she was having second thoughts about his sincerity.

Nearing noon, Josephine hurried up the gleaming white steps of Stanfield Academy's main building. It was just one of the venues hosting the auction lunches. Much of the summer had been rainy or brutally hot and muggy, but this day was stage-set, mid-70s, dry and sunny. Khai stood in the doorway waving like a madwoman. She wore a sheer shawl over her yoga tank and leggings, and her vaulted ponytail swung pendulously. She led Josephine inside to an atrium where they stopped behind a wide concrete column.

"Navy blue sleeveless." Khai traced Josephine's dress with her finger. "Nice and boring."

"And appropriate," Josephine said.

Khai nodded at a wall of windows showcasing a flagstone terrace. Christopher sat at a table for two set with a white tablecloth. Other auction participants milled about, getting food from buffet tables where the servers were dressed in white.

"My class ended early," Khai said. "I've been spying."

"Good God, woman." Josephine teasingly rolled her eyes. "Have you no shame?"

"He actually blew into his hand to sample his breath," she said. "He smoothed his cowlick and the front of his shirt. I think he even tugged on his zipper."

"Un-fucking-believable." Josephine chuckled as she hurried away.

Christopher stood when he saw her and shook her hand vigorously.

"Apologies for being late," she said.

"No, you're right on time."

Their table overlooked a ridgeline that dipped into a wooded area where there was a lagoon and a murmuring fountain. Josephine leaned over to see better.

"I can't imagine that the students here know how lucky they are," she said.

"When you grow up with this, it's your normal. I grew up on the rough side. You?"

"I would say it was very modest."

"People like us have to stick together." He pointed to the buffet. "Shall we?"

People like us? She couldn't imagine another scenario where he'd say that to her.

On his first business lunch, did he order only sides, not knowing what *à la carte* meant? Did the massive number of forks and knives stump him? Did someone mistake him for the host?

Christopher brought back braised pork with mango chutney. She chose a Caprese salad.

He asked her how her day was going. She replied that she was coming from a downtown meeting with the executives of a new Amazon fulfillment center. The meeting had gone well.

"I saw your bio on your company's About Our Team," he said. "I'm not stalking you." He laughed. She did not.

"My bank is hoping to work with Swann, Livingston, & Taylor for some belt-tightening. We want to offer fair severances."

He talked almost nonstop in a kind of nervous chatter. He said he was sensitive to downsizing and understood how it could ravage a person. When he was a boy, his father lost his job. The pink slip was a gutting knife. Sliced an inch off his father's height and maybe ten years off his life. What Christopher remembered most was that he'd gotten braces right before it happened and couldn't return to the orthodontist after his father was unemployed. He'd had studs on his teeth for a couple of years, until he took a steak knife and chiseled off the brackets along with tooth enamel, destroying his smile. He was thirteen years old. It was many years before he was able to afford porcelain caps, bringing back his confidence.

When the fountain gurgled, they both turned in time to see white geese skimming the lagoon.

Christopher told her that he felt at home with nature and in the woods—the vastness, the silence, the stillness. That was one of the things that had sold him on Majestic Hills. He'd grown up in Michigan's Upper Peninsula, associating orange with his FOID card, the beginning of hunting season, shooting woodcock, deer, and waterfowl. He loved the feel of the 20-gauge shotgun against his shoulder pocket. Once, he broke his forefinger and wanted to hunt so bad he pulled the trigger with his pinky.

Josephine listened, bracing for something suggestive or inappropriate. But there was nothing. No lewd comments. No innuendo. And, though she would never say that she felt comfortable riding her bike past his driveway, where the pickup trucks with the rifles seemed to propagate, it was no longer quite the same shock to her system. The way he talked about hunting now, at the very least, made her understand him a tad more.

"I appreciate your personal story about downsizing," she said at the end of the requisite hour. "As you can imagine, helping terminated workers is very important to us."

"I'm guessing business has been pretty good for you guys," he said.

"We've had strong second quarter earnings," she said, standing to leave. "Up nearly thirty percent compared with the same time frame last year. I fly out to Boston in the morning for work. We can connect early next week if you have more questions."

"One last thing," he said. "Did you know that the woman in the One-Stop oversees all this foundation stuff? The checkout lady's got deep—I mean seriously deep—pockets."

"Lonnie Stanfield," Josephine said. "We learned who she was a few months ago."

"Why's she working in a convenience store?"

"It's her store. Why did Warren Buffet drive an old car, or live in a modest house?"

Christopher offered Josephine a ride home, saying he had room in the minivan for her bike. She thanked him but declined.

By the time Josephine reached Willow, he was parked in front of his mailbox, reading from a manila packet. He looked up as she neared.

"Great lunch!" He waved the envelope. "Tell Langdon I have a proposition for him!"

"Will do!" She gave him a thumbs-up, something she never did.

As a type, Christopher was not unfamiliar to Josephine. The guy who had a beautiful wife, a child on the way, and a lovely home in suburbia. Who had a job that compensated him handsomely. Unlike his father, Christopher was a company man—dedicated, loyal to a fault, always willing to get his hands dirty. Restructuring, downsizing. Josephine was sure that he was now wondering when exactly had he downsized his ambitions. When had he ransomed his dreams? What life had he wanted before he landed this one?

He probably could hardly remember.

When Josephine arrived home, Langdon's back was to her; he was drilling something into the bricks near the front door. This was the beginning of a rare three consecutive days off for him. She hated that she was leaving town to woo a potential corporate client and would miss part of it.

Because of the noise, Langdon didn't hear her ride up, park her bike, and tiptoe behind him. She arrived as he was adding the last screw to a bronze plate inscribed *THE BLAQUES*.

He turned off the drill. She hugged him from behind, placing her chin on his shoulder. He smelled of metal but also lavender, a pile of which sat in the driveway.

"It's a gift from your father-in-law," he said, referring to the bronze plate. "We had one on our house growing up. And, to be clear, this doesn't nail our feet to the ground here. If we decide to leave, it'll come down as easily as it went up."

"Oh, it's fine." She cocked her head to the side. "I kinda like it."

He turned to face her. "So, how was lunch?"

"What lunch?" She joked, then got serious. "I don't know yet if we'll close a deal."

"And Christopher?"

"He was a complete gentleman."

"A complete gentleman?"

"From beginning to end."

"Really."

Then he looked past her, smiling in that awkward way of his that made everything beyond what he'd said indecipherable.

CHAPTER NINETEEN

a complete gentleman

Langdon had just returned home from taking Josephine to the airport. He stood in the living room watching Christopher cross Jackson and Khai's front yard. His stride was long and purposeful, and he had a large manila envelope tucked under his arm. Christopher had emailed Langdon a few minutes earlier, piggybacking on an email string Bonnie had sent inviting residents to join her for bird-watching and antiquing. He'd either hit Reply All by mistake or he intentionally wanted all the neighbors to know about his—according to the subject field—"Proposition for the Blaques." Christopher wrote that he had "a solution to our water woes."

Our.

Langdon was going to ignore it, but Christopher texted him, *Check your email, buddy*.

Buddy, my ass. Langdon rolled his eyes. He read the email and responded, saying that Christopher could come over to chat but for only ten minutes.

Langdon could feel his teeth grinding as he watched Christopher stop to talk to Jackson. In truth, Langdon had a totally free morning. With Josephine in Boston, he'd planned to unpack a couple of the remaining boxes in the basement. One was filled with his childhood comic books, and he knew he would feel awful if, God forbid, their basement flooded. Whatever he decided to do that day, he didn't want to spend a second more than necessary on Christopher and his "proposition."

Langdon looked at his Fitbit. He was giving Christopher ten minutes only and was about to start the timer when the doorbell rang.

"Morning, neighbor," Christopher said. "I'm here to make your day."

After vigorously wiping his shoes on the Blaques' doormat in a way that suggested something domesticated about him, he looked around as Langdon led him to the kitchen and outside to the patio.

"Beautiful home," Christopher said, sitting at the table. "We had our Realtor show this one to us twice—"

"I remember." Langdon's forehead vein was materializing. "Okay, man, what's up?"

"You recall that super rainy day?" Christopher unfolded a plat map from the envelope.

"Of course." Langdon nodded. He turned his baseball cap around so the bill didn't obstruct his view.

"My insurance company's fighting me on the payout, offering pennies. They're calling the storm a *force majeur*e."

"An act of God," Langdon said.

"Yes, and here are the options to alleviate my drainage problems." Christopher flattened the creases in the map. "There's an easement all the way in the back of our properties, and my contractor can run a drainage pipe from the house to back there. But frankly, that would cost me a ton. Or, the contractor can run a pipe from the house to the trench in front of all our properties, along Willow. That would be cheaper but still incredibly costly."

Langdon tapped his foot. Smarmy salesman Christopher was particularly unsavory.

"Here's my third option. I've already talked to Khai and Jackson, and they're on board if you guys agree. I can run a pipe from my house to the tree line, hook a right across Khai and Jackson's property, and continue here—"

He drew his finger across the tree line in front of him.

"Across my yard?" Langdon looked incredulous.

"Oh, you would never know the pipe is there. It would divert the water out to the pond, which is already designated for retention."

"I would be giving you an easement on my property," Langdon said.

"Only a technicality."

"You could dig up my property if the pipe clogged. Or, if the pipe burst, there could be water pooling over here."

"Never gonna happen." Christopher crossed his legs. "Think of it this way, if *you* ever have flooding problems, the infrastructure will already be in place—"

"But *we* don't have flooding problems."

"If you do—"

"*We* don't."

"But I do, and we're only talking about a sliver of land."

"It's never a good idea for a property owner to give up rights," Langdon said. "Not for any reason. But here's what I'll do: I'll talk to my lawyer and get back to you."

"Whoa," Christopher said, bearing a smile, but really baring his teeth. "We're getting lawyers involved?"

"Listen, man," Langdon said. "I'm sorry you're going through this. I truly am. But you come over here acting like this isn't a big deal when it would be a huge trench on my property. I'll talk to my lawyer, but in the meantime, I suggest you get more bids for the work. That way, you won't have to involve any of us."

"By lawyer, you mean Josephine?" Christopher baited, looking down his nose. "Your wife makes all the decisions?"

Langdon stood. "You should leave, man. Get off my property."

"You want me to grovel?"

"I don't give a shit."

For a few seconds, Christopher didn't move, staring instead at the tree line where he'd proposed the pipe. But then, as if spring-loaded, he leaped to his feet and gathered his things. He stomped across Jackson and Khai's backyard, stopping to fling one branch and then a second into the woods.

Langdon seethed. *A complete gentleman, my ass.*

Langdon hardly slept that night. By morning, he was still cranky as he drove to the airport to pick up Josephine. But his anger started to subside as he waited in the cell phone parking area, leaning against the Land Cruiser. He checked Reddit's *Am I the Asshole?* on his cell phone.

Josephine usually wrinkled her nose when he tried to read her a post he'd seen on this site, saying "Who cares what strangers think?" He hardly ever posted anything, but he enjoyed seeing those who were confident they weren't the asshole wind up getting roasted.

It left him feeling a lot better about his life choices.

However, last night, before going to bed, Langdon had posted *Should I give my neighbor an easement across my property to help him with his drainage problems?* He felt like he was in the right but was curious about whether others agreed.

The initial comments were overwhelmingly in Christopher's favor—until Langdon followed up, asking if it mattered that the homeowner with the request was white and the other was Black. Hundreds of Black people eagerly responded. They emphasized the historic implications of Blacks and stolen property, including through eminent domain. They mentioned Black Wall Street in Tulsa, farmland in Mississippi, and even urban renewal efforts from the 1960s and beyond. A few other commenters recognized the shift in the power dynamic, with a white man asking for access to a Black man's property. But a bunch of white people—and they identified themselves as such—said, in essence: The contractors were going to dig a trench and lay drainage tile and pipe. No one would ever know. Not everything is about race.

So much is, Langdon thought. *Whether it's obvious or not.*

His cell phone buzzed with a text from Josephine. He made his way to the terminal, committed to not allowing Christopher to ruin his evening with his wife. When she emerged from baggage claim, he grabbed her roller and lifted her lanyard over her head—the way he'd lifted her bridal veil. He kissed her.

When they lived in the condo, it took them about twenty minutes to get home from O'Hare in light traffic. But now they settled in for their hour-long trip to New Pointe. Josephine placed her hand on his forearm, and he placed his on her knee. She lay her head back on the headrest, emphasizing how happy she was to be home, saying that she might take Monday off so they could spend the day together.

Langdon had planned to wait for the proper entrée into the Christopher conversation. He really had. But he couldn't help himself.

"Your boy came over yesterday." He turned to meet her eyes.

"Who?" So much had transpired during the last twenty-four hours. "Oh, you mean Christopher? He's not *my* boy."

Langdon told her about Christopher trying to strong-arm him, his neck tightening just thinking about it.

"When I asked Christopher to leave, he sat on our patio for a second and didn't budge. I fought every impulse to knock the shit out of him." Under his breath he said, "That's your *complete gentleman*."

"Lang, I was only referring to the lunch when I called him that."

"Help me understand something. How could you even think that for one minute?"

"Well, you're the one who said yes to him coming over. Help me understand that."

He didn't respond. She didn't push. They were quiet for the rest of the ride home.

CHAPTER TWENTY

nothing but ribbons and rainbows

Word of the water rift spread fast in Majestic Hills. Most of the neighbors tried to understand both perspectives rather than take a side. The Blaques didn't want to relinquish a precious right-of-way to their property. The Thompson-Johnsons didn't want theirs flooding every time it rained. What even those who weren't privy to the situation saw clearly were the two flatbed trucks that parked in front of Christopher and Monica's driveway a couple of weeks after Christopher and Langdon had their falling-out. The trucks held earth-eating machines: an excavator, a trench digger, and a brush mower. By the end of the first day, a muddy chasm stretched from the backyard, alongside the house, and across the lawn to the front easement along Willow. Despite the workers diligently hosing down the area surrounding the trucks during the three days they were there, a sludgy trail followed them every evening as they left the subdivision. The muck forced residents pushing strollers or walking dogs to track mud everywhere, causing some to worry that the pristine beige bricks along Willow might be forever stained.

On the last day of the work, Josephine and Langdon left their driveway and saw Khai walking along the edge of her lot. Josephine reached over and tapped the horn. Khai waved. But Monica and Christopher were in their minivan, about to leave their driveway next door, and one of them returned the honk. Josephine and Langdon couldn't tell which one of them had done it, and whether the response was a gesture toward a truce or simply reflexive, like acknowledging a nod from a passing stranger.

Word of the rift did not stop in Majestic Hills, Josephine realized, when she entered the One-Stop and Lonnie, who had been sitting behind the counter staring into her laptop, nearly bum-rushed her.

"I thought Langdon was going to pummel your neighbor." Lonnie placed her hand on her hip. "The frat boy."

"Christopher and Langdon were here together?" Josephine's eyes crinkled.

"They most certainly were."

Josephine reasoned that Langdon hadn't told her because he'd had three overnight shifts in a row and they had been missing each other. But she worried that he, too, knew their mojo had been way off, and maybe he didn't want to chance yet another fight.

"They stood right there." Lonnie tapped her sandal to the floor in front of the newspaper rack. "Your neighbor acknowledged being an ass." She rolled her eyes. "But he extended his hand and apologized. And, get this, Langdon didn't shake it."

Lonnie threw her head back and clapped. "Such a powerful rebuke. I was like, okay, Mr. Blaque. I see you. Then frat boy said he thought doctors were supposed to be forgiving. Langdon said that if Christopher arrived in his emergency room, he'd treat him. No question. But Langdon wasn't ready for handshaking."

Lonnie walked back behind the counter. "They both looked combustible. But ol' Christopher turned tail and left."

"Wow," Josephine said, taking a few seconds to process it all. "His wife's baby shower is tomorrow."

"You going?"

"Yeah, the wife is fine. If she didn't want me there, she wouldn't have invited me. And Langdon says he doesn't care one way or the other."

Lonnie opened a pack of gum and handed Josephine a piece. It had become their thing: talking and munching their way through the One-Stop's gum, candy, and chips.

"When my kids were young, we joined the local chapter of Jack and Jill for the solidarity. Geoffrey loved when the parents got together for outings. We made lifelong friends. I remember couples talking about their strategies for suburban living."

"There are strategies for city living, too."

"True. But out here, my friends made sure their children were not overlooked for honors classes. Glee club, chess club, fencing, and lacrosse. Most of those kids just wanted to play basketball." She smiled wryly. "One woman, who looked quite young, told me that during her first visit to the pediatrician's office, she made sure to reveal her age—making it clear that she had not been a teenage mother. Another friend said that every year, when she talked to her child's teacher, she always mentioned her husband—to be clear she wasn't a single mother."

"It's so exhausting." Josephine sighed. "To always have to be either above suspicion or beyond reproach. At the same time, we have to be careful that we're not saying 'Hey, I'm different from other people who look like me.' *There but for the grace of God*, right? What about your experience *here*?"

"I've tried not to indulge in too many strategies, even when I was teaching," Lonnie said. "When people know me and the Stanfield name, things are a bit easier. But when they don't, like some of your neighbors, it can be the same old same old. You don't always know whether you're being slighted, or demeaned, or surveilled because you're Black or because the person is an ass, or whether it's some combination." Lonnie walked to the door and flipped over the Closed sign. "Because my children are different shades of brown, and because this world sees them as Black, Geoffrey and I tried hard to prepare them for what that entails."

Josephine gathered her things. "Unfortunately, it still entails a lot."

Josephine held a small canary-yellow box with a glittery gold bow as she walked down Willow. Khai stood at the end of her driveway holding two white bags, one in each hand, with shiny pink wrapping tissue spilling out. The pink matched her pleated miniskirt and blouse. She looked like a high school cheerleader holding pom-poms and waiting for the school bus. They began walking together to Danny's house, house number two, between Bonnie and Bryce's and Christopher and Monica's.

"Pretty box," Khai said. "Such a pity that there's only an expensive silver rattle inside, which the little girl will *never* play with." She held up her bags. "Nothing but ribbons and rainbows here. Two stuffed animals, a doll, and lots of candy."

"You do know she won't have teeth for a while?"

"The candy is for the parents, buzzkill."

As they passed Christopher and Monica's yard, they walked through a faint mist from sprinklers waving over a narrow swath of new grass.

"I've been meaning to ask." Josephine nodded toward the sprinklers. "When he wanted to run the pipe across your property, why did you guys agree so quickly?"

"We probably shouldn't have." Khai squinted into the sun. "But Jackson rolled over. If he were a sixteen-year-old girl, he'd be big pregnant."

In Danny's backyard, streamers dangled from tree branches. Wrought iron chairs formed a semicircle around another chair adorned with balloons. Of the women there, Bonnie was the standout. She stunned in a muted lime green A-line number whose hem fell above her knees. She was tending to two large tables: one for gifts, the other for food. Finger sandwiches, pickled veggies, and a handsomely decorated pink cake, inscribed:

It's a girl!
Due date: October 15th

"Wow, you look—fantastic," Josephine said to Bonnie as she hugged her.

"You're sure it's okay?" Bonnie whispered. She smoothed her hair, which, pulled up into a bun, hid the gray. She turned to look at her ass. "At least I think it fits."

Danny grabbed Bonnie by her waist, saying *"Trés chic!"* then sauntering away.

Although neither Josephine nor Bonnie said anything, they noticed that Danny no longer looked like a wax figure in the process of melting. She was tanned, with rosy color in her cheeks.

Monica tapped Josephine's shoulder. "I'm so happy you came," she said, grabbing Josephine's hands in hers. She squeezed gently.

"Of course. I'm happy to be here."

"I'm sorry about this whole mess with Christopher and the drainage. Our guys are such hotheads. What can we do?"

"We?" Josephine's eyes widened. "Monica, this isn't an equivalency. Christopher started this with an unreasonable request. I'm here because I have no beef with you, and I'd like to be neighborly, but I'd never push Langdon on this."

Danny snuck up behind Monica to slip a pink hat with purple bows over her head, unknowingly dousing the tension of the moment.

"Now you have to take the seat of honor," Danny said.

As she was led away, Monica mouthed, "Sorry" to Josephine, who shook her head in that *no worries* way.

Monica sat, and they all took their seats. There were games and prizes, food and cake, and Monica opened her gifts to gasps of delight. She gave a special thank-you to Danny, whose gift was decorating the nursery, and passed around photos of the room with its stark white crib, white rocking chair, and white changing table, all offset by a beautiful accent wall with a vibrantly colored silk tapestry that Danny had hand-sewn.

"Can I say something?" Monica rubbed her abdomen. "I'd been trying to get pregnant for years—two miscarriages, two failed IVF attempts. The baby is fine. But sometimes I feel like I don't deserve to be this happy. Like something bad's going to happen."

"That's understandable," Bonnie said. "And it's normal. My advice: always trust your gut and check in with your OB-GYN if anything, anything at all, feels off."

"I agree," Josephine blurted, fully aware that she wasn't the expert there. Still, all eyes were on her. "Our prayers are with you."

Our prayers are what? She had no idea where that came from.

It was midafternoon when the women began gathering their belongings to leave. Bonnie rolled out her sons' vintage Radio Flyer so that she could walk Monica next door with her gifts. Khai left to go swimming. Josephine was about to head out when Danny waved at her.

"Mind staying for a minute?" she asked.

She led Josephine inside to the kitchen table, where they sat. Danny folded her hands. Josephine noticed her nubby-bitten nails. When they first met, she'd taken Danny for the standing-appointment manicure type.

"I'm going to cut to the chase," Danny said. "Marc's not good with making new friends. Most men aren't. But when he and Langdon run together, Marc bounds in, excited about how hard they ran or what they discussed, and how he can't wait to do it again."

"Langdon's fond of Marc, too," Josephine said. "He keeps meaning to get over here to see a dressmaker's dummy. An exact replica of your grandmother's body? Something about anatomy, physiology, blah, blah, blah."

"So deliciously weird!" Danny lifted an eyebrow. "Come with me."

Josephine followed her down a hall with framed *House Beautiful* and *Architectural Digest* covers. One hailed Danny as "Interior Design's New It-Girl." The other called Marc "Architecture's Gritty New Cuban-American Phenom."

Danny pointed to the word *gritty*.

"He would have preferred the word *gifted*," she said. "But what can you do?"

In the sewing room, standing beside an open suitcase of Butterick patterns, was the dressmaker's dummy. Jaundiced, with dangling threads like sutures, the figure had swatches of linen, silk, and gingham affixed to its bodice with rusty straight pins.

"In the 1950s," Danny said, "some higher-end seamstress shops wrapped women in a thermoplastic material to create these forms. And voilà—Nana's slim shoulders, thirty-eight Ds, and rotund belly."

She patted the form's midsection.

"Twelve children. No multiples. That was never going to be my lot even without the cancer." She palmed her breasts. "I did get two perky new tits, though. Two new tits with areolas and nipples sewn on like appliqués." She faced Josephine. "Seriously, though, about this mess between Langdon and Christopher—"

"Oh, that's so unimportant," Josephine said.

"I want you to know: I love Monica, but I'm Team Langdon." She gestured like an umpire calling a base runner safe. "I've said no more chemo, which means my prognosis is dire. I look okay now because my body is weaning from the drugs. But that won't last." She stiffened her back, strengthening her resolve. "I'm just hoping our husbands will remain friends. Sometimes men get lost in stuff that doesn't matter."

"Danny, I'm so sorry."

"Will you make sure? Nudge them from time to time if they need it?"

"Of course."

Danny gave Josephine a quick tour of the house. She clearly bowed before the gods of symmetry, finesse, and clean lines. She said she'd studied to be an artist but took up interior design to pay the bills. They had five bedrooms, and aside from the primary and guest bedrooms, the others were used for sewing, painting, and sculpting creations for clients.

Josephine walked home with a lump in her throat. She admired Danny's bravery—her decision to control her own destiny. It was not lost on Josephine that she'd just heard an end-of-life story at a beginning-of-life event. She realized that she, Danny, and Monica, each nearing forty, were standing at three very different crossroads.

In her mid-twenties, Josephine had considered freezing her eggs. She'd made one visit to Chicago's top-rated fertility clinic and tacked its business card onto her kitchen corkboard, where it remained buried under receipts and coupons and her favorite takeout menus. She'd told Langdon that freezing her eggs had once been top of mind because she knew nothing about her mother's gynecological history. When was her first period? Did she, like Josephine, have fibroids, which could make conceiving difficult? And menopause? Totally unanswerable. As Josephine packed for Majestic Hills, she'd cleared the corkboard and uncovered the card, almost totally pristine, as if the idea itself had been frozen and was still viable. Only it wasn't. Now beyond her optimal egg-freezing years, she tossed it out—still uncertain about whether motherhood was for her.

She was keenly aware that her own birth was an end-of-life story at a beginning-of-life event. Arriving home, she wasn't sure if she was welling up about Danny's story or her own.

CHAPTER TWENTY-ONE

a fickle memory

Geoffrey Stanfield, a licensed pilot, owned a 1963 Cessna Skyhawk that he'd purchased from the Chicago Aerial Survey Company. His father had built a hangar and a runway on five acres toward the rear of the Stanfield property. Lonnie hated when Geoffrey flew, especially when he took Wade up with him. So he rarely did either. But on those radiant blue-sky afternoons when father and son climbed into the cockpit and strapped on their headsets, they took off, soaring over New Pointe, high above the property that would become Majestic Hills, the area that was already the Grand Vistas, and all the open land—the woods, the cornfields, the wild prairie—in between. Geoffrey would tell Wade to take measure of every part of the carpeted expanse below.

"Remember the shape of the pond," Geoffrey said, his voice stuttering into Wade's headset over the roar of the engine. "Remember the way the tall grass bows and the trees shimmy." He pointed out the window, the plane's shadow rippling over a wheat field. "As the song tells us—'amber waves of grain.'"

Wade admired the way his father always made even the mundane, the inconsequential seem so significant and relevant.

"Land has a fickle memory, son. You must map it out in yours because one day what you see below might all be gone."

Now Wade stood in a poorly lit, windowless room in the Drake County Courthouse. The smell of mildew competed with that of disinfectant. It had been a month since the night he slept at home after the deluge. He had taken his mother's advice and started an Instagram, and now he had a few hundred followers. He'd spent most of his time on the platform posting about the county board's upcoming meetings and urging his followers to contact their representatives. The board met monthly, and the first agenda item for its September meeting was the Grand Vistas.

At the front of the room, on an elevated stage, was a wooden table with seats for the twenty board members. A handful of people were in the audience, including a homeless man fortressed by bags, a reporter looking at his phone, and Benny. A week before, during a town hall with a congresswoman whose district included Drake County, the room had been packed with residents demanding to know what the hell she was doing down there in Washington.

Wade was perusing a series of photographs that had been blown up and placed on easels throughout the room. There were aerial shots of Majestic Hills, the Olympia Country Club, Leaf It to Us, the One-Stop, and the cemetery. In one photo, Wade zeroed in on a downed tree near the pond. He thought about the afternoon he'd spent sitting on a tree trunk while smoking his first joint with his pal Gil. Not far from that site was a bluff, where he was supposed to have been tutoring Maya Johnson, a year his senior. Instead, they had lain in the grass cavorting, grinding their bodies into the undergrowth, her hands kneading and tongue probing his previously unprospected areas.

Other enlarged aerial photos showed the shuttered chicken factory and the Grand Vistas property, with its labyrinth of single-wides strewn about like the bleached bones of a carcass. For the first time, Wade realized that American flags adorned almost every trailer, the ones standing upright as well as the ones nearly flattened like metal cans. There were even several Pride flags he'd never noticed before. He inhaled deeply at the scope of things.

At 6:45 p.m. Wade sat next to Benny, watching the board members enter. He was focused on the door, looking for his mother, who had promised to attend.

"She'll be here," Benny said without looking up. Officially a high school freshman, he was bent over his algebra homework. "I'm not worried."

Wade pointed to the page. "Remember rise over run. This will be the slope—"

"I'm rising and running, and where is it getting me?"

"Okay, we don't have to do this algebraically. We need only determine how high we went up, and how far over we must go."

Benny looked lost.

"We'll figure it out at home."

"Hallelujah!" Just as Benny slammed his textbook shut, he looked up. "There she is."

Lonnie was rushing in. Wade breathed a sigh of relief and waved at her.

She found a seat across the aisle, a few rows behind him and Benny. It reminded Wade of when his parents took him and his friends to a movie. Geoffrey and Lonnie would sit all the way in the top row, and Wade would turn around to look at them, feeling independent but also reassured by their presence. He knew they always shared a box of Junior Mints, and halfway through, no matter the movie, his mother fell asleep, her head on his father's shoulder.

When the board members and paltry audience stood, facing the flag, Wade noticed how seriously Benny took the Pledge of Allegiance, how straight the boy's back was as he firmly placed his hand over his heart. They sat for the invocation and the roll call. After Benny picked at a weeping crimson pimple on his neck, he pulled Wade's sleeve.

"What?"

"Never mind." Benny folded his arms over his chest. "This is so boring."

A woman walked up to the podium. Fooling with Benny, Wade had missed her name, but he did hear that she was a demographer the county had hired for the sole purpose of taking stock of the Grand Vistas. She said a survey of the trailer park found that its residents lived under some of the most blighted conditions in the county.

No shit, Wade thought.

"My recommendations are on page thirty-six," she said. "They include shuttering the Grand Vistas—"

"Shuttering it?!" Wade blurted.

The interruption startled the speaker.

"With the goal," she continued, "of making sure the residents are treated fairly."

"Thank you," said the county board's chief executive.

He added that the board had just learned that the Majestic Hills developers were close to closing on the purchase of the Grand Vistas property from the company that used to own the chicken plant. The developers planned to clear the trailers to build luxury housing. New Pointe was updating its proposal to the county to annex the land.

Wade stood. "What does that mean?" He squinted, searching for clarity.

The chief county board executive slammed down his gavel, which startled Benny, who had been drifting off. But he rustled himself onto his feet.

Lonnie moved to the seat beside Wade. He saw her in his periphery.

"Young man, you're not on the agenda," the chief executive said. "We have not yet opened the floor for questions or comments."

"Sir, the Grand Vistas is a community." Nerves made Wade's voice shaky at first, but he settled himself. "Yes, some people there fight sometimes, but they also look out for one another. They sweep and shovel each other's doorsteps and bring by casseroles when someone dies or gets married. Some families have known one another for generations, going back to when the chicken plant made them feel hopeful. It's the only home they know. You can't just take that away from them!"

"Young man—" the chief began.

"Sir, you guys promised improvements there, but all the money went to Majestic Hills instead." Wade lowered his head in frustration.

"Everything's been built up around these people, but they keep getting overlooked. Have you seen how bad the potholes are out there? A school bus driver who lives in the GVs told me he hadn't tackled roads that bad since he drove a Humvee in Iraq."

Had this been a New Pointe village board meeting, members might have recognized Wade and tolerated him because of his family name. They definitely would have known Lonnie. But at the county level, neither made an immediate impression.

"Young man." The county executive banged his gavel again. "We're merely making recommendations. A final vote, thus a final decision, won't come until our December meeting."

"It's not fair." Wade's voice trembled. "To pull the rug out from under them."

Two short but muscular county sheriff's deputies stood by the door. The chief executive looked over at them. Wade felt Benny pull Wade's shirttail as a warning.

"Young man?" the county executive said, clearly wanting to move to the next agenda item. Wade continued to stand, staring at the empty seat in front of him.

"Son," Lonnie said in a low voice.

But Wade didn't look at her. He had spent four months in the Grand Vistas, shoveling shit, tutoring Benny, stressing her out. To what end? Had he even made a sliver of a difference? Maybe his siblings, with their reproachful FaceTime faces, had been right to call him selfish.

"Young man, we've been patient."

"The Grand Vistas residents have been patient," Wade said. "You're a bunch of overpaid, lard-asses who don't care about any-fucking-body but yourselves."

Benny looked stunned. Wade knew it had nothing to do with the threat of him losing his home, a salient point the boy missed. It was because Benny had never heard Wade say such things.

Benny saw the chief executive flick a finger toward the deputies. He nudged Wade. Lonnie placed her hand on his back and scooted to the edge of her seat.

The two men, one unholstering plastic handcuffs, started toward Wade. He stared them down until they were halfway there.

"I don't need to be restrained," he said. "We're leaving."

The room was quiet as Lonnie, Benny, and Wade crossed the center aisle with the microphone and the area in front of the homeless man and his bags. The reporter followed behind them. "Care to give me your name and age?"

Lonnie and Geoffrey had for years drilled into Wade that he should say "no comment" if he were ever approached by the media. But now, to the reporter, he said, "Wade X. And, long live the Grand Vistas!"

Lonnie, Wade, and Benny boarded the elevator.

"I didn't know you cursed," Benny whispered loudly. He pointed to his chest. "I say shit and goddamnit when I stub my toe—"

"That's enough, Benny," Wade said. "I shouldn't have used those words."

Their attention turned to Lonnie, as though they both had forgotten she was there.

She suppressed a smile. "I didn't hear a thing."

Outside, Lonnie offered them a ride back to the Grand Vistas, but Wade asked if they could take the bus. He was teaching Benny how to use public transportation. It wasn't yet completely dark and the ride wasn't very long.

As they waited, Wade said, "I shouldn't have lost my temper." His eyes were apologetic.

"I know," Lonnie said calmly. "You have to keep your composure. Getting kicked out won't help your cause. So, what do we do—"

"We breathe deeply and count to ten?" Benny offered.

"Yes, Benny," Lonnie said, patting his shoulder. "But I was going to ask Wade, *what do we do next*?"

Wade thought for a second. "I'm going to start by writing letters," he said. "As you recommended."

"Fantastic," she said.

Several buses arrived, but not the one that would get them close to the trailer park. Even with the right bus, they still would have to walk half a mile.

"There's something else," Lonnie said. "The chief executive said a formal vote on closing the Grand Vistas won't come until December. But, son, I'm sorry to say that it's my experience that a backroom deal has probably already been struck."

"A deal?" Wade asked.

"A decision has already been made. These public officials go through the motions, but it's often pure theater."

"Mom, I—we—still have to try."

"Write something, and I'm happy to take a look." Lonnie saw their bus coming and nodded toward it. She hugged Wade and mussed Benny's hair. "Text me when you're back in the GVs. We'll talk tomorrow."

Over the next week, Lonnie helped Wade craft letters and emails to officials they believed could help. They created boilerplate information that included a brief history of the Grand Vistas. But Lonnie also instructed Wade to research each official's background and legislative record so that they could tailor opening paragraphs and explain why the Grand Vistas merited their support. As mother and son waited for responses—the days and then weeks ticking past—she encouraged him to write an editorial for *The New Pointe News*.

When an editor quickly agreed to publish it, Wade was ecstatic. On the day he'd been told it would run, he stayed up until midnight, refreshing his screen. He'd been so hopeful that this was the breakthrough he needed.

But then he read it.

He had originally written that after the chicken plant abandoned the area, the Grand Vistas' grocery store was shuttered, and most residents now visited a food pantry. Even an on-site clinic that had once provided contraception and children's vaccines had closed. Those details were distilled down to "When the chicken plant left, so did its resources." Wade had written, "Residents are either under- or over-policed. All systems that serve and protect a community have broken down." That was stricken and replaced with "personal and institutional failures abound."

The only untouched paragraph was the final one, which Lonnie had added. It quoted Dr. Martin Luther King Jr. from his 1961 commencement address at Lincoln University in Pennsylvania. The speech had been delivered eight years before America landed on the moon, King contrasting man's technological expertise and his moral aptitude: "Our jet planes have compressed into minutes distances that once took days," King had said. "Through our scientific genius we have made of this world a neighborhood; now through our moral and ethical commitment we must make of it a brotherhood. We must all learn to live together as brothers, or we will all perish together as fools."

Wade was angry. He texted his mother, asking if he could come home for the afternoon. She'd already texted him that she'd seen the editorial and was disappointed by it.

She immediately responded: *Of course, son. You never have to ask.*

CHAPTER TWENTY-TWO

run!

After Monica's baby shower, Josephine had told Langdon that Danny had ended her chemo treatments. From then on, Langdon made sure to invite Marc on a run even more frequently. For the next several weeks, they ran and ran. Whenever Langdon asked about Danny, Marc would only say that she was fighting or that she was a bruiser or scrappy. He never asked Langdon for doctorly advice or complained.

On a bright late September morning, they were completing a run when Marc took off his pullover, turned to Langdon, and surprised him, saying, "I'll tell you something few people know." And without mincing words, he added, "I went to prison."

Langdon slowed and nearly stopped. "Man, get the fuck out of here."

"Seriously. A minimum-security facility. One year, three days, and about five hours."

"What for?"

"I beat the crap out of this guy. He didn't deserve it."

"And you did it because?"

"He was ragging on my wife. She'd finished a bout of chemo and was bald and thin. He mocked her, and I snapped."

Not much shocked Langdon anymore, but he was taken aback.

"At the trial, I pleaded guilty to second-degree assault," Marc continued. "I was ordered to pay restitution to my victim, along with his medical bills. I was fired from my firm and radioactive for a while. Danny and I had to file for bankruptcy."

"That's a lot, man."

"Those were some dark days, brother . . . I bet you're wondering why I'm telling you this."

"It crossed my mind."

"Today is the seven-year anniversary of the day I left prison. And—I shit you not—on this same day last year, an architect friend in Michigan told me about Majestic Hills." Marc was running faster as they turned into the subdivision—as though his thoughts about his second chance had given him a second wind. They reached the base of Marc's driveway.

"You never know a person," he said. "Hope this doesn't lower your opinion of me."

"Nah, it's always been low." Langdon snickered. "Really, really low."

He was about to continue home when he and Marc saw Christopher's minivan racing out of his driveway. Inside, Monica was in the passenger seat, head thrown back, panting.

Christopher, laser-focused on the road, sped past them.

A couple of weeks later, Langdon headed out for a solo jog. The falling leaves colored Willow a bright crimson, burnished orange, and sunny yellow. It was below freezing, and he wore a skullcap, gloves, and a hoodie that still smelled of smoke from a backyard bonfire. He pulled his collar over his beard. As he passed Christopher and Monica's house, he noticed that the cardboard stork proclaiming, "It's a Girl," next to their mailbox had been removed.

Langdon arrived at the Mount Olive Cemetery and turned in. He studied the growing number of pumpkins adorning the gravesites, the gourds and the cornstalks and a few headstones draped in cottony webs.

God, how Nicky loved this time of year.

Nicky had only seven Halloweens, only seven costumes. For his first Halloween, he was four months old, and Jules had dressed him in a pumpkin onesie. For his last one, he'd planned to be Quailman. He'd just turned seven, Langdon was nine, and Paul was twelve. That summer, they were in their backyard. Paul was swatting baseballs against the brick wall of the garage. Nicky wanted a turn at bat, and when Paul refused, Nicky ran in front of the wall as Paul was swinging. The ball slammed into Nicky's chest, his legs buckled, and he fell to the ground.

"Stop playing, boy!" Paul said, standing over him, still holding his bat.

Langdon, who'd been sitting under their massive oak, ran over to them. Nicky was lying face up. Paul was on his knees, trying to shake Nicky awake.

"Stop playing," Paul mumbled. Then he screamed, "Help, Mom! I need help!"

When their mother didn't come fast enough, Paul tried to lift Nicky. When he couldn't do it, he began to drag his brother by his collar. Nicky's spindly arms were by his side, and his hands, palms down, bumped against the grass as if he were playing a piano tune.

In the emergency room, after the official death pronouncement, Jules and Elise were doubled over, unable to stop Paul when he took off running, head flung back, zigzagging down a long hall awash in fluorescent light. Langdon did not run, but both boys had suffered the same amputation. That Jules could hardly chase after Paul only amplified the father's grief. When they returned, Langdon looked at his brother—the curve of his shoulders, the absence in his eyes—and knew that he, too, was gone.

Langdon left the cemetery near Majestic Hills and ran and ran, checking his breath, his pulse. The air was chilled, the sky was the color of slate, with a squall line hovering over the eastern horizon. As much as he tried, as hard as he ran, he couldn't shake loose the memory of his brother. His stride, which had been strong, became wobbly, and he was like a car motoring down a road on a flat. Still, he kept pounding, willing his body forward.

On the morning that would be the last time Christopher ever ran with Langdon and Marc, no one knew it was the last time. The air smelled of a coming rain, odd for November, and the sky was an ominous seafoam green.

"Morning," Marc said, coming down his driveway.

Langdon started to jog in place. "I was in the city yesterday, walking to the train, and I thought, Why can't you architects design a building where pigeons don't shit all over the place?"

"It would be easier to potty train them," Marc said. "Speaking of potty training, guess who's joining us?"

Langdon stood still and looked over at Christopher's house. "I fucking hate running with him."

"Maybe cut the guy some slack." Marc placed his hand on Langdon's shoulder. "New baby. His in-laws are in town. He says he hasn't had a full night's sleep in three weeks."

"What do I care?" Langdon looked at his watch. It was just after five a.m. "So where is he?"

"In my powder room." Marc frowned. "Taking a dump. He lives right next door. How is it that his damn bowels weren't signaling to him before he left his own house?"

They waited. When Langdon looked at his watch again, they were ten minutes behind. He looked down the driveway, and the door to Marc's house opened. Christopher began walking toward them. As he got closer, Langdon could see that he was wearing black socks. This ticked Langdon off even more because Christopher had teased Langdon about his, saying the socks made Langdon look nerdy.

"Incoming," Langdon said to Marc.

"Woosh," Christopher said when he reached them. He rubbed his gut. "I did some damage to your bathroom, friend."

Langdon started running, Marc followed behind him, and Christopher uttered his signature, "Wait up, guys."

"This fucking guy," Langdon said to Marc.

When Christopher caught up, he said, "Let's mix it up and try some unfamiliar terrain. I want to show you this place Monica and I discovered driving around one day to quiet the little one."

"How is little Moni?" Marc asked.

It had been Christopher's idea to name the baby Monica after her mother. Monica balked initially, but after Christopher said he absolutely loved the name, she agreed.

Once outside the cul-de-sac, Christopher turned left instead of right. They never ran in this direction. Later, Langdon would wonder why they even followed Christopher. What drove them that morning?

The three men passed Leaf It to Us and the Stanfield's property, continuing until they reached Granger Road, where they headed north. At an unnamed gravel road, they turned left again, heading west to where there were no leaves because the trees were all dead. Langdon guessed that they were not far from the southern edge of the Grand Vistas. They kept running, and Christopher brought their attention to a 1950s-style Texaco gas station and repair shop, the entrance nearly covered in a trellis of dead tree limbs. The gas pumps had big, circular heads. A rusty shell of a pickup sat in the garage. A sign read Auto Wash $1.50.

"This is something you don't see anymore," Christopher said. "Am I right?"

They slowed but did not stop.

"And for good reason," Langdon said. "It should be demolished."

"It's vintage," Christopher said. "Our parents' stomping grounds."

"Not mine," Langdon snapped.

They pressed forward, running side by side, with Marc in the middle, or single file. The few cars that were on the road that morning inched into the eastbound lane, giving the men a wider berth—while kicking up gravel.

They were following a sloped area when they saw the headlights of a souped-up old Chevrolet Impala. It pulled around them and slowed until its brake lights flared. Two young men, teenagers, one Black and the other white, jumped out, followed by another Black guy, who looked a bit older. Each wore high-top sneakers and oversize jackets. The older one brandished a gun. Another white guy remained behind the steering wheel, his arm propped out of the window. Langdon, Marc, and Christopher held up their hands.

An absurd thought occurred to Langdon: In movies, there was often a white criminal to balance a Black one. It was politically correct, but the weight of being Black and male and a perceived criminal tipped the scale.

"Nice wedding bands," said the guy with the gun. "Y'all know what time it is."

Langdon's stomach spasmed, his rib cage feeling set afire.

About a month earlier, a gangbanger had been lying face down on the trauma table, a bullet having grazed his right butt cheek. Langdon was dressing the wound and listening to the guy recount a *National Geographic* episode he'd seen about African elephants. Patients often did that—tried to show that they were smart. Gangbangers were no different.

"These elephants," the banger had said. "The young shorties lost they mind because poachers had separated them from the herd. And the elephants were tearing shit up. Marauding."

"Marauding, huh?" Langdon had asked. He hated metaphors with Black men as animals, and this one was no exception.

"Yeah. Check this out: somebody realized these shorties hadn't been socialized by the OGs. They didn't care about right or wrong. You feel me?"

"I feel you," Langdon said. "Why you out there bangin' and getting shot in the ass if you're smart enough to make a connection like that?" He'd finished bandaging the boy's wound and walked over to look him in the eye. "Why are you both poacher and marauder?"

The teen looked at Langdon pensively and smirked. "It's eat or be eaten. You feel me?"

Now the guy with the gun waved it in a circular motion. "Y'all live around here?"

"No," Langdon said quickly, fearing they might be kidnapped and driven home to be robbed. "We're from out of town, getting in a run, and—"

"Nah, I think y'all live around here."

Langdon wondered why he'd felt compelled to speak first. Because he and the young man were Black?

"Look," Marc said. "We don't have anything of value, nothing in our pockets." He patted himself down. "We don't know anything, like what you guys look like. Nothing happened here. Why don't you let us be on our way?"

We have nothing of value except our lives, Langdon thought.

The teens seemed to consider it. But they had to defer to the leader, who said, "Be on your way? Shut the fuck up, white boy."

Langdon realized that until now, he'd felt free running with Marc. It had felt like being surrounded by a force field. He knew he'd been running on Marc's privilege—a white-presenting man's ability to move freely in so many vaunted spaces, including the outdoors. He wouldn't have admitted this to Josephine—because she worried—but he had run for much of his life wholly aware of what it meant to be a Black man in motion outside the context of a sports arena. Averting his eyes to avoid looking into the windows of houses or cars. Worrying about trucks slowing down or speeding up, nearly sideswiping him, or about someone hurling beer bottles out of a car window or shouting slurs, or a Karen simply having a bad day. Even the lakefront trail in the city, at times, felt fraught.

"We ain't got all day? Y'all must have something on you."

Until that encounter with the thugs, Langdon had run alongside Marc feeling unencumbered, relieved of the weight of worry and fear. Both dragged on forward motion, speed, and the spirit. He resented Christopher for redirecting them.

"Who got the debit card?" the leader said. "Apple Pay on your cell phone? Five-hundred-dollar daily limits times three."

The Black teen offered, "Maybe we should let the nigga go."

Bile rose in Langdon's throat. "C'mon, man." He looked at the car, the mottled red and yellow leaves stuck to the back window. "We don't have a thing. You can go on about your business."

"Hell, nah!" the leader yelled, losing patience. "All skin-folk ain't kinfolk. So, some motherfuckin'-body's got to give up something."

The leader guy had taken a step toward Langdon when they heard a crack of thunder. The autumn sky, which had been teasing all morning, suddenly unleashed a torrent of rain. The thugs yanked their hoods over their heads. A shower of pea-size hail began to pelt them. Still, Langdon kept his hands raised.

"Fuck!" the gun-toting thug cried out. "Y'all lucky." He pulled his hood down further over his forehead and ran back to the car, jumping into the front passenger seat. The teens followed, piling into the back.

Langdon, Marc, and Christopher did not speak or move until the Impala pulled away, fishtailing as the driver gunned the engine. Then the three men hightailed it through a cornfield of downed stalks and into the woods, running flat out before sheltering beside a tree. Marc dialed 9-1-1, and as he spoke, Langdon noticed a gash above Marc's left knee, though he had no clue how he got it. Soaking wet and cold, they broke into a run again. At one point they crossed the footpath that connected Majestic Hills to the Grand Vistas. The path looked so different from the section that Langdon had seen, it didn't occur to him that they could take it south, back to the subdivision. So they kept running west.

It wasn't until they saw a ridgeline and a mausoleum that they knew where they were. Langdon had never been so happy to see headstones. Midway through Mount Olive, they saw blue lights hovering over Old Creek Road. As they got closer, the Impala came into view. It was in a shallow ditch, surrounded by police cruisers. A thug was in the back seat of three of the vehicles. A sheriff's deputy was tromping through the field across the road with the handcuffed leader who'd wielded the gun.

“That’s him!” shouted Christopher.

Langdon and Marc exchanged a quick glance. He’d been mute during the entire ordeal.

“They were going to rob us,” Christopher said. “And God knows what else.”

An officer motioned for Christopher to stay back.

“Fucking lowlifes,” Christopher yelled, jabbing the air.

“They’re from out of state,” the officer said.

Now Langdon homed in on the Missouri license plate in the rear window.

“They were on I-57 when they got off to gas up. Left without paying,” the officer continued. “We’ve been looking for them for the last thirty minutes.”

“He had a firearm,” Christopher said, as if he’d just remembered. “He could have killed us.” He raised his voice, intending to be heard through the rolled-up windows.

Langdon, Marc, and Christopher were each quickly questioned by the officers and asked to come to the police station later for more paperwork.

Marc and Langdon started to head home. “You coming?” Marc asked Christopher, who continued to yell at the officers, gesturing wildly.

“I’ve got to go,” Langdon said to Marc. “You can wait if you want.”

Marc joined him. “He’s so full of shit.”

“Nope. He took care of that in your bathroom,” Langdon said.

Opening the front door, Langdon began rehearsing in his head how to tell Josephine what happened. *Don’t freak out* was the first thing that came to mind. But he realized that no matter what he said, of course, she was going to lose it. Who wouldn’t? He certainly would have if it had happened to her.

He ran upstairs, hearing the shower.

"Hey," he said, entering the bathroom.

"Hey, you." She wiped steam from the shower door so she could see him.

Shampoo ran down the curve of her back. He removed his clothes and glasses and joined her. Her eyes were closed, and she smiled. *That smile*, he thought. He held her around her waist.

"Everything's okay," he said. "But something happened this morning during our run. These guys tried to rob us. They've been arrested, but they had a gun. I'm fine."

Her body flinched. Langdon could see her midsection fold in on itself. She wiped shampoo from her eyes and cupped his face in her hands. She blinked, trying to see him clearly.

"It's okay." He pulled her closer. "It was an isolated incident. Everything's fine."

As they held each other, he could feel her heart thumping wildly against his. She stepped out of the shower, and he followed. "I can hardly breathe, Lang." She wrapped a towel around her.

"It's okay." He placed his hands on her shoulders. "I know this is scary, but it's over. Look at me, I'm right here. It's okay."

"Stop saying it's okay. I think—I've been thinking we should leave this place. Sell now, not later."

He pulled away. "Josey, can you not overreact?" *That was unfair.* While her reaction was genuine, he also knew she was savvy about finding loopholes.

"Overreact? Are you kidding me?" She wiped her face with the towel as if she were fighting with it. Her bottom lip trembled. "You could have been shot and killed. My husband could have—"

"Nothing happened."

"Oh, something happened. Running in the middle of nowhere."

"They weren't even from around here." Langdon chewed on his tongue. "The police said it was a one-off type thing. Shit happens."

"Shit happens?!"

"Listen, if you want to leave, let's leave. But let's not pretend this is the reason."

"You think this is about me plotting to move rather than about my husband almost getting shot? The man whose heartbeat I actually enjoy feeling against mine?" She handed him the wet towel. Her shoulders were shaking. "Okay, Blaque—whatever." She left the bathroom.

"Josey, I didn't mean—"

"Nope, not now."

CHAPTER TWENTY-THREE

broken windows

On the 7:45 a.m. train an hour later, Josephine settled into her window seat and called Fat to tell her about the near robbery. She cupped her hand over her phone, trying to whisper while simultaneously trying not to rant. She was tired of New Pointe and Majestic Hills. Tired of the train ride. She had been worried about those hunters, but had been totally blindsided by a different group of predators. She felt like a fool for letting her guard down. That was the way of this place. It lulled you, tricked you into believing you could breathe and just be. And that's when it bit you, right in the ass. Josephine could hear her voice cracking, feel her eyes stinging. She looked out the window and, because it was early morning, could see only a ghost of her reflection, a likeness that was and was not her.

She talked and talked, letting it all out, and by the time she reached her Michigan Avenue office tower, Fat was standing on the sidewalk in front of the revolving doors. She wore her glasses, not even having taken time to put in her contacts. Her navy peacoat clashed with her baggy pink joggers and red rain boots.

Josephine fell into her friend's arms. They latched on to each other through several deep exhales.

"The security guard"—Fat nodded toward the front desk—"wouldn't let me in. You think he mistook me for a sex worker?" She palmed her breasts. "The humongous boobs and all."

She laughed, and Josephine laughed, fighting back tears. "The building's not open yet, and you do not look like a sex worker."

"Where can we talk?" Fat asked. "You know I had to lay eyes on you."

Upstairs, only a handful of workers, mostly executive assistants, had arrived. Josephine dropped her things off in her office and led Fat around several cubicles to the one room without glass walls, where she knew they could have some privacy.

"We can talk in here." She opened the door to what was, in essence, a massive closet.

The room was a time capsule. For years it had served as a reminder of the firm's longevity as a high-end agency. It offered every amenity, including attire for the casually dressed client who happened to be in the office when a prospective employer said, "Can you come over right now?"

Josephine sat on a leather bench, and Fat eased in beside her, holding her hand, but looking around the room.

"Tell me what's going on," Fat said.

"Would you believe Lang had the nerve to say, 'Let's not overreact.' As if he couldn't have been shot." Josephine's leg bounced. "Sometimes it feels like—as soon as I'm getting used to that place, something happens and blows it all to hell."

"And what about the fight?" Fat stood, removed her rain boots, and stepped into a pair of 1970s slingbacks. She returned to Josephine's side.

"It's the way we fight. The way we retreat and avoid each other afterward." Josephine's eyes narrowed. "How do we survive this? What do you and Ken do?"

"After our really big fights?" Fat said. "Nine months later, bam. So I guess we've had four." She walked over to an old rotary pay phone on the wall and poked its coin return. "I know Blaque. You both will get through this. He's got a great wife. You've got me."

"Who's got my boyfriend?" Josephine asked. "You clearly left the house fast."

"He's with the new babysitter. Fourth child, and you're like: 'References? Not necessary. And that blunt behind your ear—can I hit that?'"

She slumped back onto the bench, admiring the shoes.

"Oh, please. Your background checks are like those in the White House."

"I like these steppers," Fat said. "They're a little boring, but I can pimp 'em out."

"I see the vision." Josephine laced her fingers through Fat's. "They're yours."

After Fat left, Josephine sat at her desk staring at the framed selfie Langdon took of them in Ghana: she looking at the camera, he looking at her, so smitten even though they had just met. She stared at the photo, studying her husband's former self. At the time, he had hair, albeit wispy around the crown. Now, with his clean-shaven head, his go-to dinner party joke was "I wasn't bald when I met Josey. You draw your own conclusion."

Cue the laughter.

In the days leading up to Thanksgiving, a cloud of fear and anxiety had descended on Majestic Hills. Maybe the unease could be felt throughout New Pointe, perhaps across the downtown and along the corridor closest to the expressway. But Josephine recognized it most in the subdivision, where, more and more, she saw clusters of residents gathering on Willow. Neighbors who had been out walking their dogs or checking their mailboxes stopped to huddle.

She was at work when she opened a message Christopher had sent to all the neighbors, mentioning that he'd moved at least one of his handguns from a basement cabinet to a lockbox he now stored under his bed.

I've also contacted this great company called American Home Security. He hyperlinked the website. *They install state-of-the-art alarm systems, with high-tech video cameras and ultrasensitive volumetric motion detectors. I asked if they would give Majestic Hills a group rate, and they will. So, call today.*

That Saturday, American Home Security vans were parked in several driveways. Josephine and Langdon saw the vans and, out of curiosity, visited the company's website.

"Should we consider it?" Josephine asked, hedging, not wanting to reignite their argument over the matter.

She knew that Langdon was still recovering from the ordeal. He'd been having nightmares. A couple of nights before, he'd woken her up, kicking and gasping for air. Later, he told her that in his dream, when the bad guy said, "Let the nigga go," he ran away. But he stopped when he heard two gunshots and turned in time to see Marc and Christopher toppling over.

Now Langdon looked up from his computer screen. "Josey, I don't want to live in fear, or under surveillance."

They scrolled through page after page of plum reviews from customers who were "extremely satisfied" or "absolutely elated" or "overjoyed to have such peace of mind." One review stood out: "Why should someone from a shithole country or a shithole neighborhood be allowed to take a crap on my little slice of heaven? American Home Security (and the Second Amendment) is all the protection you'll need."

Josephine and Langdon looked at each other.

"Well, I feel safer," she said sarcastically. "You?"

"American Home Security . . ." Langdon sounded like a radio announcer. "You pay for the equipment. We happily throw in the illusion of safety for free."

On the night before the holiday, Josephine was driving home from Martin's when she saw Danny and Khai standing by Danny's mailbox. She pulled up beside them. Even with Danny bundled up in her winter coat, there was no denying how thin she'd gotten.

"We should form a united front to get our guys to take a break from running," Danny said.

"I don't know about Marc," Josephine said, "but that's not going to happen with Lang."

"What can you do?" Danny sighed. "Monica says Christopher's decided not to run."

Punk ass, Josephine thought.

Danny threw up her hands. "I'm cold and going inside. Happy Thanksgiving!"

Khai ran over to the Land Cruiser's passenger side and jumped in. "Can I get a ride?"

Josephine drove a few yards and turned into Khai's driveway.

"Her cancer's raging," Khai said in a near whisper.

Josephine's expression turned solemn. "I suspected as much."

She waited for Khai to get out, but Khai leaned the seat back and got comfortable. She glanced at the box of wine on the back seat.

"Are you hosting your in-laws tomorrow?"

"They spend Thanksgiving in New York with their oldest," Josephine said. "So, it'll be my family—a group of cousins who run the gamut from college-educated to, well—" She looked at Khai. "Put it this way: I have one ne'er-do-well cousin. Every year, we've got to stow away our loose change container. He spends the afternoon buttonholing Langdon, trying to get him to look at his bumps and boils and prescribe him some antibiotics."

Khai laughed, reaching for the door handle. "Everyone has a relative like that. Have a great holiday, neighbor."

As Josephine pulled out of the driveway, she immediately regretted telling Khai about her cousin. Yes, every family had one or two. And yes, she really liked Khai and felt comfortable with her—maybe too comfortable. Still, Josephine made it a habit to try not to denigrate a Black person in front of a non-Black person. Every group had their stereotypes, and Josephine never wanted to aid and abet in validating them.

The next day, the Blaques' guests began arriving at two p.m. Josephine had initially called for a five o'clock arrival, but relatives complained on the family text string that the drive to "Majesty Hills"—as several erroneously and intentionally wrote—was too far. They didn't want to be caught in the boonies after nightfall. They had compromised on a 3:30 arrival, but Langdon was now running up the stairs yelling, "Josey! Josey!"

She was lying across the bed in the shorts and tank top she'd slept in, reading and reveling in the calm before the storm.

"They're here," he said, entering the room and looking down at his watch. She wondered if he was checking the time or his blood pressure—considering some of her family members.

She got up, and he followed her to the bedroom across the hall. They peeped around the curtains like spies. Sure enough, a caravan of cars was idling in the driveway a whole hour and a half early. She headed back to their bed.

"Get dressed," Langdon said. "I'll go down and greet them."

"You will do no such thing," she said. "We set a time, and those Negroes decided to do something else. They're all in collusion."

She had catered much of the dinner. The only thing she had to do was bake a couple of sides: her decadent five-star macaroni and cheese and a broccoli casserole. She had already assembled them, and they only needed to be placed in the oven.

Josephine had invited Wade to come get food for anyone in the Grand Vistas who didn't have a holiday meal. She'd been careful in the way she offered, for Wade could get testy about handouts. She was pleasantly surprised when he agreed to stop by.

"Baby, it's cold outside," Langdon said to her now. "Like the song." He got in bed and scooted next to her. It was his attempt to say *we are not in battle right now because we have a common enemy*. It had been a couple of weeks since the attempted robbery. They were not on solid ground, but neither were they sinking.

"Let's savor our last few minutes of sanity, shall we?" she said. "Then I'll take a quick shower and get dressed."

"Cool—" He lowered his chin and looked at her. "J.T."

She clucked her tongue and smiled. Today was the one time of year when she would be surrounded by people who called her J.T. Not Josephine. Not Josey. Not Attorney Taylor. Or, as Benny referred to her, Miss Attorney Lady. *J.T.* was what her father called her, which meant she was in the presence of people who knew and loved Edward Taylor.

By the time Josephine made her way downstairs, all twenty guests had arrived and were in the driveway. She opened the door, holding the collar of her sleeveless shirt against the chill. Her family had a way of raising her blood pressure and temperature and she wanted to keep cool. She waved everyone inside. Among the cousins was seventy-year-old Kathleen, who played on a seniors' pickleball team. She entered the foyer and squealed with delight, looking around.

Claudine, a sixty-something, was always impeccably dressed. She was known for lowering cutlery into her lap before dining, and wiping it off, which she did in restaurants and banquet halls. Josephine had long moved past taking offense.

"When are you going to stop wearing your hair like a dude's?" asked Claudine, contorting her mouth.

"I love her hair this way," Langdon said, taking Claudine's coat.

"Hmph. You're just an enabler."

Cousin Tony, whom everyone called Lemon Pepper because he always sprinkled it on his food, entered with his wife, Lily, and his customary brown paper bag.

"Here you go, J.T," he said to Josephine, gifting her what she knew were two jars of pickled pig's feet. "Nice spread."

Lily shook her head. "I told his ass nobody who wants to live eats that shit anymore."

As Langdon helped her with her coat, Tony said, "Well, I guess we don't have to worry about parking this year."

With that, Langdon and Josephine exchanged a glance. This was the same man who, every year on the Monday after Thanksgiving, placed a solitary parking ticket—which he'd gotten from having "forgotten" to pay the meter downtown—in the mail to them without a note or return address so they could pay it, which they did.

When it was time to eat, the family gathered in the kitchen and held hands for the prayer. The house was quiet for a few minutes as everyone took their inaugural bites, and then it was loud again, filled with raucous laughter.

After dinner, some of the relatives coalesced around the television in the family room to watch football. Others gathered in the kitchen, looking at albums of old photos that Josephine had spread out for viewing. Another group played bid whist.

The doorbell rang, and Josephine welcomed Wade and Benny. Behind them, their bikes, both with small trailers attached, were parked in the driveway between cars. Wade presented Josephine with a bouquet of autumn flowers, which she guessed had been Lonnie's idea. Josephine had invited Lonnie to dinner, too, but her other children were in town, and she was celebrating with them.

Josephine introduced the teens to her relatives, and they wound up spending nearly an hour chatting with her fifteen-year-old cousin. At different intervals, she passed them as they debated over the video games *Metal Gear Solid Δ: Snake Eater* and *Black Myth: Wukong*.

When Wade tried to explain why these games were so popular—the characters, their backstories, the fights—Josephine said, "Please stop, you're hurting my ears."

She walked away thinking that, for the first time, Wade looked like any ordinary, geeky teenager. Not someone trying to move heaven and earth in a trailer park. She had never seen him like this, so unburdened, so at home with himself. She almost didn't recognize him. Benny also appeared different. He was seated beside Wade and Josephine's young cousin, shifting his focus from a cluster of men in the living room singing and reviving old dance moves to the laughter from the women playing cards. From where Benny sat, he couldn't see the women, but his body leaned toward them like a pea shoot stretching toward the sun. Wade and Benny stayed far longer than Wade had initially intended.

It was nearly dark, and the streetlamps beamed on as Josephine and Langdon helped load aluminum pans of food onto Wade's trailer. There was sliced turkey and dressing, macaroni and cheese, candied yams, and vegetables that Langdon joked were stewed in so much pork fat they'd jumped food groups. Wade tied two tarps over it all, and he and Benny navigated their bikes around the guests' cars.

Josephine spent the next few minutes feeling good about the day, the gathering. As she mingled with her family, she felt that something had clicked with Wade. Baby steps, she told herself. Her young cousin lived in the city and attended a prestigious public high school. Josephine couldn't help imagining reasons to connect the three boys again: A movie at the AMC River East. A visit to a museum. A stroll along the lakefront.

Caught up in her imaginings, she happened to pass the living room window as a police car, lights swirling, was turning in front of the clubhouse, heading back the other way. She walked outside into the cold in her sandals and sleeveless shirt. All along Willow, cars, SUVs, and pickups lined the street, overflow from driveways. Josephine spotted the two police cars pulled up next to Wade and Benny. Wade's bike was overturned, and food had spilled onto the street. She ran toward them as fast as she could.

Josephine placed her body in front of the teens. "Somebody tell me what's going on."

One of the officers and Wade spoke at the same time.

Josephine held up her hands and pointed to Wade. "You first."

"I didn't hook the trailer up to the bike correctly." The carefree teen from a few minutes ago had vanished. "We were hurrying so the food wouldn't get cold, and the trailer overturned and rolled."

"Food just exploded everywhere," Benny said.

Shivering, Josephine folded her arms across her torso and turned to the officers. "You guys are here for a spill?"

"We got a call that two men were going through mailboxes, and we were nearby, passing through."

Wade rolled his eyes. "Yeah, right. Passing through."

Josephine turned to Wade. "Something else I should know?"

"Nah, it's all good."

"Miss," the officer said.

"Attorney Blaque," she said.

"We weren't going into anybody's mailbox," Wade said. "We were cleaning candied yams off it."

Josephine smelled the food as she saw it splattered around the base of the stone.

"Miss Attorney Lady," Benny said. "We were cleaning up. Swear to God."

"They are children," Josephine said to the officer. "Not men. Not intruders."

"I see that now, ma'am. We're both new to the force, and we're still—"

"Children," Josephine insisted. "I don't care how new you are—"

"I'm not a child," Wade grumbled, the cold turning his cheeks and nose red.

"Me neither," Benny said, staring at Wade.

"Okay, why don't we calm down," Josephine said. She turned to the officers. "I live down the street. I'll run home and get something to help clean up."

She happened to glance beyond the mailbox and realized that they were in front of Christopher and Monica's house. They also had an audience. She could see people she assumed were guests standing in the bay window, watching.

CHAPTER TWENTY-FOUR
boy

Every time Josephine passed Christopher and Monica's mailbox, she inhaled the memory of candied yams and the great evening before the spill. After she'd returned to the house to get her coat, Langdon had left with her to help clean up. She, Langdon, Benny, and Wade had worked as Wade lectured her about calling him a child.

She explained that she'd said what was necessary, dealing with officers whose hands hovered over their holsters. But Wade said she'd belittled him. When she denied it, he raised his voice. "Okay, whatever!"

Langdon stopped cleaning. "Boy, watch your tone. She was trying to help, okay? End of story."

But it wasn't. Days afterward, when Josephine and Wade crossed paths at the One-Stop, he barely said hello. When she drove to the Grand Vistas to drop off a few items of clothing and notions from her firm's time capsule closet, he stood at the entrance and politely accepted the box. He mumbled only "Thank you" and began walking toward the trailers.

"What is your problem?" Josephine asked.

He kept going.

"Wade!"

He stopped and returned to her. He stood quietly, searching for the right words.

"There's a book," he said. "*A Lesson Before Dying*." He struggled to hold the heavy box.

"Put it down." She spoke softly.

He sneered at her as if this too was burdensome. But he lowered it onto dormant grass.

"Let's talk," she said. "You and me. I know the book."

"Oh, you do?"

"White defense attorney has a Black client on trial for murder. His defense is that the guy is as dumb as a hog and not smart enough to have committed the crime." She looked over at kids chasing one another near the trailer park's entrance. "His godmother knows he's going to be sentenced to death. But she wants him to leave this earth knowing he's a man, not an animal." Josephine took a breath. "Wade, I did not call you a hog. I said you were a child."

"For a Black man, is there a difference?"

"Good Lord. Wade."

"Is it better to lose your life or your dignity? I expect that from them. But not from you."

"Boy, you are blowing this way out of proportion. You're sixteen. Legally, you are a child."

He looked up at the sky and shook his head before picking up the box again, shuffling away like a weighed-down old man.

Wade was sullen for days, for weeks. The only thing that seemed to lift his spirits was the toy giveaway that the Grand Vistas residents organized every year. This was his first time experiencing the event, and he threw himself into helping, the way he did with most things. Benny's excitement about it was palpable. He had a growing wish list of items that he kept revising.

In the One-Stop, Josephine was browsing through a *Chicago Tribune* when she heard Wade finalizing Benny's list at the counter.

"A new cell phone?" Wade was incredulous. "Man, what you need is a scientific calculator, so you can give back mine."

Benny looked insulted. "I can do math in my head, like you, Wade."

"Uh . . . Benny." Wade laughed. "No you can't."

"Bet money! Test me, right now."

Josephine smiled. It was clear that Benny admired Wade and wanted to be like him, and that Wade took his role as a big brother figure seriously. Wade's smile was somewhat asymmetrical, but it stood out that day because it was rare, suggesting that maybe he believed the world wasn't as much of a shit show after all. For a moment, it eclipsed his sullenness and highlighted how handsome he was, and how much he looked like Lonnie.

But that would prove short-lived. On the morning of the toy giveaway, the Saturday before Christmas, *The New Pointe News* posted a story about the Drake County board's vote to allow New Pointe to annex county land needed for the Majestic Hills expansion. Lonnie had told Josephine and Langdon about Wade and Benny attending that board meeting months earlier. The gist of today's news was simply that Majestic Hills could go forward with its plans to build into infinity—more stately houses so far north that it would mean razing the Grand Vistas rather than shoring it up.

The comments section of the story overflowed with residents saying good riddance, bring on the relocation stipends. Only a handful of neighbors vowed to fight.

"And here we arrive bearing toys," Josephine said as she and Langdon passed the porta-potties and entered the trailer park.

"It's a dick move on the board's part, but not surprising," Langdon said. "Urban renewal, suburban renewal, rural renewal. One and the same if you're poor and the ones being gentrified."

"So true," she said.

He pulled in as Bonnie and Bryce were unloading elegantly wrapped gifts from their Prius. Langdon had told Bryce about the event, and he and Bonnie had arranged boxes for toy donations in the corners of their sons' classrooms and in the Majestic Hills clubhouse. Bonnie had told Josephine that her stash included stuffed animals, dolls of every hue, and a couple of LEGO sets.

"Good grief," Josephine said to Langdon, pointing to the area where the vegetable garden had been. "Look at that."

Three tables overflowed with presents that were arranged with large placards regarding age appropriateness. A well-contained bonfire and a coffee station were a few yards away.

"Lang, I didn't wrap anything. I've only been collecting stuff." She rolled down the window. "Hey, Bonnie. You wouldn't happen to have more wrapping paper, would you?"

Langdon sighed. "My wife, the Grinch."

"I've got beaucoup gift bags." Bonnie reached into her back seat, handing Josephine a small stack, along with red and green tissue paper. "I'm guessing you guys heard the news about this place?"

"We did," Josephine said.

"Merry fuck you Christmas, right?" Bonnie joined Bryce, who was sipping coffee and warming his hands near the bonfire.

Josephine began to put items in the bags and stuff them with tissue. Langdon wrinkled his face.

"You're not doing it right," he said, nodding at the tissue paper. "You've got to fluff, fluff, fluff." He pantomimed fluffing, a sweep of the hand akin to tossing rose petals into the air.

She chuckled. "Well, okay then."

He got out, joining Bonnie and Bryce. But she remained in the car, placing gifts in bags. She stopped to look at the children gathering near the toys, laughing and shaking boxes. But there was no Wade.

Josephine did spot Lilly, who was wearing her new Amazon skullcap. Josephine had been excited when a staffer told her that Lilly had been hired to drive a forklift at a fulfillment center, just as she'd hoped.

As Josephine scanned the crowd, she saw little evidence that anyone was distraught about having to uproot. Still, as a homeowner in Majestic Hills, she felt like she was the enemy. That she and Langdon were in this in-between space, where they tried to have a foot in both worlds, toggling between "them" and "us," pretending they didn't have to choose.

She wouldn't say any of this to Langdon. She still wasn't supposed to know that he'd been having similar conversations with Ken. Why hadn't she and Lang been talking to each other? Was it too much for him, the husband, to say to her, the wife, maybe this move was a mistake? Maybe they should have stayed in the condo, which was not at all perfect. Yet, at twenty stories up, she still felt far more grounded there than here.

Her mind was racing, and she was utterly frustrated by it all. "Oh, fuck me!"

"Mama!"

Josephine looked out the window at a little boy pointing at her. Despite the cold, she hadn't rolled it back up after talking to Bonnie.

"That lady said a bad word."

His mother heard it, too. She scowled at Josephine before spiriting her child away.

Josephine finished the gift bags and got out of the car, handing the packages to Langdon, who divided them among the tables. She rubbed her mittened hands together, and he brought her a cup of coffee, wrapping his arm around her.

"Have you seen Wade?" she asked, looking around.

"That's odd." He shook his head. "We'll take a look when this is over."

"Hello! Hello!" Lilly waited for everyone to settle down. "This is our tenth year organizing this toy drive!" The crowd applauded. "And it's bigger and better than ever. Let's give away some Christmas gifts!"

The residents assembled around the tables. First the parents with very small children came up, and next preadolescents and teens. Josephine saw Benny in line with his aunt, inching toward the front. When it was their turn, she could see Benny negotiating, going back and forth with the woman passing out gifts, until he had four, one more than the other teens.

When all the gifts had been distributed, Josephine and Langdon joined Bryce and Bonnie and a few other adults who were chatting around the bonfire.

"Well, we came," Josephine said. "We saw. We did that thang."

"We're about to leave, too," Bonnie said. "Don't forget about tonight."

The holiday dinner. Bonnie had reserved a private room at The Plant for the five families on the west side of Willow. Langdon and Josephine waited for their neighbors to drive off. As they started walking toward the maze that was the trailers, she worried aloud about Wade.

Langdon followed her. "I'm sure he's fine, Josey."

Although she had been in the trailer park several times, she hadn't been to Wade's trailer since her first visit there. She wasn't sure she could remember where it was, but she felt compelled to try. She saw Benny camped out on the steps of a trailer that had a doorless entrance.

"Hey, Ben!" she said, trying to sound upbeat.

"Hey, Miss Attorney Lady. Hey Dr. Langdon. Sooo—" He dragged out the word and nibbled on the top of his yellow highlighter. "Fun fact: I prefer Benny."

"So sorry, *Benny*." Josephine would have laughed if she hadn't been so concerned. "Where's Wade?"

He returned to marking up the Martin's Gourmet circular balancing on his lap. Beside him were his gifts.

"I saw him this morning." He tapped his temple, thinking. "Maybe it was yesterday morning."

"What you got there?" Langdon asked, nodding at the circular.

"Wade gave me this yesterday." Benny fanned out the pages. "He told me to check off everything I want for Christmas dinner. My aunt and me normally leave town, but we're staying this year. Beef Wellington." He pointed to each item, nearly drooling. "Braised lamb shanks, Honey-glazed ham."

Josephine leaned in closer. Benny had drawn a star by nearly every item on each page.

"Do you have any idea where Wade might be?"

"He was mad about the news. Kicking stuff around in his trailer." Benny folded the circular. "He's still mad about the men, too. From Thanksgiving."

"The officers?" Josephine asked.

"No. Three men came out of the house right after his bike trailer tipped over. Before the officers. They came out when we were cleaning up the food. They were like—" He spoke nasally. "'Son, you made a great big mess here.' Wade said, 'We're cleaning it up.' But he looked back toward the house, and I looked back toward the house too, and there was this guy standing under a light with a rifle slung across his back, like he was going hunting. And Wade said, 'Why he got that rifle?' The man said, 'Son, don't worry about him. You two lost?' And Wade said, 'No.' The man said, 'Where you boys from?' And Wade said, 'Boys?' And that man said, 'Okay, son, don't be so sensitive. It's not like that.' I hate that word—*sensitive*. The school counselors call me sensitive. And the fellas here say I'm *soft*. Like those two words don't mean the same. Wade says people called him soft and sensitive too. Before he was homeschooled. Anyway, the man by the mailbox said, 'Clean it up good. You better hope everything looks brand-new. You hear me, son?' I said to myself: How could we do all that? But Wade told the man, 'I hear you.' The three of them walked back up the driveway, and they were laughing, and I heard somebody say, 'Baby Huey.' Like I haven't heard that before. But as Wade always said, my impulses don't control me. Wade kept cleaning. And I thought about it: I told him, screw—I mean, forget that. If those men were going to act that way, we should leave it. But Wade said, 'We made a mess, so we should clean it up.' I said, 'There are messes all over the place. What's one more?' And then the police came."

Langdon and Josephine looked at each other.

"Benny," Langdon said. "Can you take us to Wade's trailer?"

"Now?" Benny asked.

"Yes, now," Josephine said.

"Okay," he groaned.

He walked swiftly down an aisle of trailers, passing his own and slapping the pig-pink propane tank. He turned right and then right again, walking straight for a bit before extending his hand as if to say *There it is. Now can I return to my work?*

Langdon knocked and banged on the door. Josephine tried the door handle. It wouldn't move.

"Credit card, please," Benny said matter-of-factly to Langdon.

"I guess," Langdon said, retrieving his wallet. "We're breaking and entering now, too?"

Benny took the card and jimmied the lock.

"Wade?" Langdon called out, pushing open the door. "We're coming in."

Inside, they saw the kitchen nook and the bong and a herbarium. On the wall, two sheets of paper were taped together. Josephine assumed the writing was in Wade's hand:

"Sometimes you have to deal Devilishly
with drowning men in order to swim them to shore"
Gwendolyn Brooks

Next to it, written in block lettering and shaded in pencil was:

"I AM DELIBERATE
AND AFRAID OF NOTHING"
Audre Lorde

And . . .

"The only alternative to anarchy
is to wreak havoc"
Wade X

"Wade X?" Langdon whispered to Josephine. "What, he's a revolutionary now?" Langdon peeked into the bathroom. "You don't want to go in there."

Josephine's brows knitted. Langdon shook his head. In the tiny bedroom, a pallet lay on the floor.

"Guys," Benny said. "He's not home."

"You're absolutely right," Josephine responded, hoping her level tone disguised a nagging instinct that something was terribly wrong.

"Let's go to the One-Stop," Langdon said.

The three of them walked to the Land Cruiser.

"Okay, bye." Benny didn't wait for a response. He ran back toward the trailers.

"Christopher," Langdon said as they drove out of the Grand Vistas. "That fucking guy."

"Someone standing in the background with a gun?" Josephine replayed the night in her memory. "He wasn't there when I got there. I had no idea."

"The dude's hyped up. All that bluster is nothing but fear. He or somebody saw something *suspicious* going on in front of his house. I get that. But even when he realized it was just two kids cleaning up, he still had to put on a show. In-fucking-sufferable."

Josephine shook her head. "My question is: What happens when your neighbors are all strapped up and you aren't?"

"Let's hope we never find out."

At the One-Stop, Lonnie was locking up. A Closed sign hung on the door, and red sleeves covered the gas nozzles. She'd finally hired a replacement who would start at the beginning of the year. Langdon pulled up to the door and rolled down Josephine's window.

"We saw the story about the Grand Vista's closing. We were wondering how Wade's doing," he said to Lonnie.

Josephine knew that Langdon didn't want to sound alarmist by saying, *We haven't seen your son. Have you?*"

"He came home early this morning," she said. "He's angry and hurt. We both are. But we're going to ring in the new year in London with his sister and her wife. He's already agreed, and I've made the reservations." She threw her hands up. "There was this cute little Indian restaurant that his father loved. It'll do us good to get away and put all this behind us. I think he's looking forward to the new year, too."

Langdon pulled out of the One-Stop. He and Josephine both stared at the road in front of them. There was no need to say aloud how each of them desperately hoped Lonnie was right.

CHAPTER TWENTY-FIVE

reason and faith

Earlier that morning, Wade had been sitting in his trailer on his pallet, having hardly slept all night. By sunrise, he felt he had to get out of the Grand Vistas. He wasn't interested in the toy giveaway or being around people who were engaging in superficial holiday measures centered on assuaging guilt and making themselves feel like they had done something meaningful. He filled his backpack, the large one he used for hiking, with his books and most important items. The Grand Vistas' days were numbered, his time there ending. He went home, had breakfast with Lonnie, and then fell asleep. He awakened with a powerful desire to visit his father's gravesite, where he hadn't been since the burial. This was his second holiday season without his father, and it felt as impossible to get through as the first.

He pedaled standing up much of the way to Mount Olive. Passing under the cemetery's wrought iron gate, he remembered, as if it were yesterday, the path the funeral procession took. How the limousine circled around a grove of oak trees and over a short hill. He remembered how the birds sang, the way the sunlight glinted off the metal on the markers and headstones.

On the day Geoffrey died, he'd been running late for the 10:20 a.m. heading to downtown Chicago. Wade was in the thick of a sprawling calculus problem that Geoffrey had created for him as part of a math test. Wade barely said goodbye.

"Don't worry, buddy," Geoffrey had said. "You've got this."

Wade lay his bike on the grass and walked over to his father's gravesite. There was a Stanfield mausoleum, where Geoffrey's parents and grandparents lay, but Geoffrey had wanted to be buried out in the open.

Wade fell to his knees before the headstone, tracing the epigraph with his fingers.

GEOFFREY JOSEPH LESLIE STANFIELD
"In the woods, we return to reason and faith."
Ralph Waldo Emerson

Wade sat, crossed his legs, and finished the quote: "There I feel that nothing can befall me in life—no disgrace, no calamity (leaving me my eyes), which nature cannot repair."

He remembered the day when he and his father were driving past the cemetery and Geoffrey said, "How many dead people you think are over there?"

Wade started to count, trying to extrapolate to come up with an approximation.

But Geoffrey interrupted him: "They're all dead, son."

His father flashed a sly smile, and Wade's face filled with glee.

Now he began to sob so hard he felt as if his insides were boiling over and he might throw up. It had been just over a year since his father's death. Wade felt naïve, ashamed that he'd believed he could change anything and make any kind of difference. All this was inevitable. The lie about improving housing in the Grand Vistas. Building Majestic Hills instead. At some point, the trailers would be moved, and only their faint outlines would remain.

In the spring, large drainage pipes would line old roads, potholes would get fixed, the pollution would be dealt with until both air and water were pristine. Things that were impossible when they would help poor people suddenly became possible for the rich.

With Wade's defeat came the relief of having nothing left to lose. He composed himself and rode across the cemetery to the footpath. The wind dried his tears. Grit blew onto his lashes.

In Majestic Hills, he traipsed through the woods to the pond, sitting with his back against a tree. He pulled his hood over his head, hugging his knees.

He was looking across the water at lawn care workers bagging the last of the season's leaves near the clubhouse when he heard twigs crunching underfoot.

Benny was running toward him.

"Shit," Wade said under his breath, wiping his eyes and nose on his coat sleeve.

"Hey, Wade." Benny scooched in beside Wade and hugged his knees, too. He stared at him, out of breath. "You okay? You look flustrated."

"Flustered or frustrated, Benny. One or the other. Why're you here?"

"Looking for you," he said. "You missed the toy giveaway. Everybody was like, 'Where's Wade?' 'Have you seen Wade?'" He swallowed. "And I was like, 'How should I know, haven't seen him.' Then I thought about you and the footpath and fishing. So I came here."

Wade was quiet. The men across the pond were returning their equipment to their trucks. They didn't seem to notice him and Benny, or maybe they didn't care. His eyes began to water again. He tried to stop it. Without looking at Benny, he knew the boy's eyes were watering, too. For Benny, tears were as contagious as a yawn.

"I hate this place, too, Wade," Benny muttered. "These houses destroyed everything. And the people in them only think of themselves. Sometimes my auntie says, 'You only think of yourself.' Like when I don't turn off the lights, or I eat the last cookie or forget to flush."

"I'm sorry, Benny." Wade bowed his head in a solemn, deferential way.

Benny looked incredulous. "For what, Wade?"

"I failed you. You're losing your home, your community."

"Auntie says that with her savings and the money or vouchers or something coming from the developers, we can have a brand-new life." Benny dusted snow off a tangle of tree roots. "She said it won't be brand, brand-new, but new enough. We can get a house where frogs don't climb up through the floorboards and you can see the sky only when you want to. She says we're going to Nashville for the holiday, and we'll figure things out when we get there. I told her that I want to live near you, Wade, in a nice house like one of these." He jutted his chin toward the houses. "But not in Majestic Hills."

"All that sounds really great." Wade sniffled and turned to Benny. "You are indeed one of my best friends. But do you mind if I sit alone for a while?"

"Are you going to be okay?"

"I—I'll be fine." Wade's body shivered.

"Okay, Wade." Benny placed his hand on Wade's shoulder. "Just remember to breathe in through your nose and out through your mouth."

Wade nodded. Breathing was what adults had always urged both of them to do during a meltdown. But instructing someone to breathe when he felt strangled, or felt like he had a knee on his neck, seemed to Wade pointless and lame. He watched Benny head back through the woods, looking over his shoulder several times before offering one last wave goodbye.

Then he disappeared beyond the tree line.

CHAPTER TWENTY-SIX

kiss! kiss! kiss!

There was a kind of caravan later that evening as the residents of Majestic Hills left their driveways on their way to The Plant. Langdon pulled out behind Khai and Jackson, who were following Marc and Danny. Everyone slowed at the place where the stop sign used to be and then drove the couple of miles to the restaurant.

Langdon hopped out of the Land Cruiser to open the door for Josephine. He never wore a winter coat over his dark green velvet blazer, which he said amped up his holiday cool, so he raised his collar. On their first Christmas together, she'd joked that the green velvet made him look like John Legend. On their second Christmas, he'd gifted her the dress she was wearing—short, off-the-shoulder, and cranberry red. As he extended his hand to her, he saw Christopher drive up to The Plant's front door to allow Monica to hurry inside with little Moni. He parked and opened the automatic side door.

"Check out the B Man," Christopher said, directing everyone's attention to Basil in the back seat, sporting reindeer antlers.

A few neighbors stopped by, and Basil barked and wagged his tail, until Christopher left to join Monica. In the group chat, he'd told everyone that his family would attend long enough to say hi, but they would take their meal to go. The baby wasn't ready for prime time yet.

The way Christopher had dealt with Benny and Wade gnawed at Langdon. Christopher was a coward and an asshole, and the fact that he'd implicitly threatened them only deepened Langdon's disdain.

Still, he didn't want to take it out on Monica and the baby. He walked up to her and leaned in to see the little one.

"Could she be any cuter?" he asked.

"Oh, she's looking more like her dad every day. I hope I'm in there somewhere."

God, I hope you are, too, Langdon thought as he said, "She really is beautiful."

Everyone was fawning over the baby. Everyone except Josephine.

As was customary, she leaned in and cooed "So cute" and then scampered off. This time it was with Khai. She worked the baby scene the way she worked parties, breezing through the bloat, glad-handing, and avoiding small talk.

Despite Langdon's irritation with Christopher and, if he were honest, Josephine too—albeit to a lesser extent—Langdon decided to make the best of the evening.

At the table, he joined the conversation as neighbors discussed the Majestic Hills expansion and the closing of the Grand Vistas, asking, "Should we be worried?" and "What do you think it all means?" and "How will it affect our bottom line?"

"You know, guys," Langdon said. "I think we'll just have to wait and see."

Bryce clinked his glass and said, "Everyone. Let's take a picture before Christopher and Monica leave."

He snapped his cell phone into its tripod and asked the neighbors to form a semicircle around the fireplace. Monica spied mistletoe over Langdon and Josephine, and pointed to it, chanting, "Kiss! Kiss! Kiss!" And all the neighbors chimed in with "Kiss! Kiss! Kiss."

Langdon puckered up, planting his lips on Josephine's cheek as she smiled wistfully, her eyes cast toward the ceiling.

But the mighty groundswell continued—"Kiss! Kiss! Kiss!"—until he finally said, "Okay, Blaque, let's do this." He took her in his arms, dipping her and kissing her passionately to whistles and whoops and applause.

All of it proved too much for little Moni, who began to squirm and howl as Christopher and Monica said their goodbyes.

There were a few hours of dancing and laughing and laying out New Year's resolutions. When the party was over, Josephine, still vibing on good tidings and cheer, jumped into Khai's car. Jackson and Langdon rode back together.

The moon was bulbous and bright, and yet, by the time they reached the country club, they could see blue light levitating over Majestic Hills.

"What the hell is that?" Jackson pointed.

Langdon leaned forward to see better. "I don't know."

On Willow, four police cruisers, their lights swirling, were parked on the street in front of Christopher and Monica's house. Other police cars sat in their driveway. Neighbors who hadn't attended the festivities gathered nearby, some wearing heavy coats over pajamas.

Khai pulled into her driveway, and Langdon followed. The four got out and stood in Khai and Jackson's yard, their attention focused on the house next door. They watched as officers hurried up the driveway, shining their flashlights inside the garage and around the outside of the house. They could see the beams of other officers already inside, up on the second floor.

Christopher appeared in the driveway with Deputy Adam, Lonnie's friend. His arms windmilling, Christopher spoke so loud they heard every word.

"I'll tell you again," he said. "The baby was crying. We took the long way home so she could settle down. We had pulled into the garage, and my wife was unbuckling the baby's car seat, when Basil started to lose his fucking mind, barking and flicking off those stupid antlers."

Langdon was listening so intently he barely felt Josephine draping a blanket around his shoulders—they'd always kept it in the Land Cruiser. He hadn't even noticed that she'd stepped away.

Christopher told the officer that Monica had gotten out of the minivan with their takeout and he'd gathered up the baby. When he pulled the seat up for Basil, the dog stormed out of the minivan to the door leading into the house. He barked furiously, and they worried that he would wake little Moni. But the second Monica turned the knob, she felt a gush of cold air. Basil shot inside. Christopher and Monica entered to a horrific sight: their house had been vandalized.

"Fucking lowlife!" Christopher yelled.

Before Josephine, Langdon, Khai, and Jackson could hear what Christopher said next, an officer approached their group.

"Who're the homeowners here?" he asked.

"We are." Khai waved her hand between herself and Jackson.

"You have cameras on the side of your house. Were they engaged?"

Khai nodded.

He said it appeared that Christopher and Monica's house was the only one vandalized, but they were asking other residents who had been at the party to check their homes, too. Josephine and Langdon found nothing disturbed or out of place, nor did Khai and Jackson. By the time they returned from inspecting their property, large snowflakes had begun to fall, and officers who had fanned out in the woods to search for the culprit were returning, their flashlights sabering through the frost.

The officers assembled in the garage, and a few minutes later, Deputy Adam walked with Christopher to the side of the house, pointing to the back. The deputy tried to speak low, Langdon guessed, to be professional and maintain Christopher's privacy. But every time Christopher interrupted, he was loud. And what Langdon, Josephine, Khai, and Jackson gleaned was that although the police had combed the house and the property, no one had any more answers than when they started. Nothing was missing. Christopher and Monica's flat-screens, laptops, iron sconces, candleholders were all accounted for—although busted up. A credit card and a checkbook that had sat atop a desk in plain view were still there. The second floor was untouched. But the first floor was ravaged, including their Christmas tree.

Christopher insisted that he couldn't think of anyone who was angry enough at him or his wife to pull off such a crime of passion.

"So far," he said to the deputy, "all you know is that the lowlife entered and left the house through our side door. Which is painfully obvious, given the shattered glass." Christopher brushed his hair back. "Your guys saw tracks in the woods and rutted earth left *maybe* by a bike? The person who did this was *maybe* a drifter. Or *maybe* it was some teens."

Deputy Adam seemed used to absorbing rage. He continued to scribble in his notepad in a way that appeared to Langdon merely perfunctory.

"He opened our refrigerator," Christopher went on. "Pulled out bottles of my wife's breast milk. Splattered them across the floor. Who does that? We had a beautiful Scotch pine in the family room. He trashed my family's ornaments, passed down through generations, stole candy canes right off the branches. Who the fuck does that—" Christopher's voice cracked.

"It's awful that this happened to your family," Deputy Adam said.

"I don't need your sympathy!" Christopher yelled. "I need you to find who did this!"

"My guess is that it was a one-off. A horrible one-off. But we can't be sure." He flipped a page in his notepad. "Your alarm system—brand-new?"

Christopher nodded. He kicked the snow.

"But it wasn't engaged?"

"We have a new baby! We were hurrying out to that stupid Christmas party!"

He threw his hands up and stalked off toward the house.

Adam followed, joining the officers still assembled in the garage. When they began to head to their patrol cars and leave, the neighbors on the street returned to their homes.

"We're going to bed," Jackson said, extending his hand to Khai.

"We are, too," Josephine said, wiping tiny ice crystals from Langdon's beard.

In the Land Cruiser, Langdon sat at the base of the driveway before pulling onto Willow. One police car remained in Christopher and Monica's driveway. Another was parked on the street near their mailbox. Langdon blew into his hands, warming them.

"Are you thinking what I'm thinking?" he said. A chill ran through him.

"I am if you're wondering: Could this have been Wade?"

CHAPTER TWENTY-SEVEN

the footpath

Historically, the New Pointe Police Department had very little to do. Officers in their cruisers often parked downtown, fattening the town's coffers by clocking an impressive number of motorists who had overlooked the business district's twenty-five-miles-per-hour speed limit. Other than that, patrolmen spent their time chasing shoplifting teens, following up on minor domestic squabbles, and redirecting traffic for anything from natural disasters to the Fourth of July fireworks celebration. Every now and then, New Pointe's officers worked closely with county deputies if something happened in The Grand Vistas. But for the longest time, New Pointe had been one of those sleepy, bucolic little towns people liked to call "quaint." Now, in the span of about a month, it had two major incidents: a near robbery and a huge vandalism case.

During Adam's two decades on the force, he hadn't experienced anything like it.

The morning after the vandalism, he arrived at the station before dawn. He sat at his desk with its nameplate "Wade Adam Daniels, Deputy Police Chief" and placed his coffee mug next to the framed studio portrait of himself, his wife, Janice, and his two stepdaughters. He was waiting for the sun to come up so that he and his team could return to the footpath behind Majestic Hills. He hoped new evidence might reveal itself in daylight. Patrolmen had interviewed many of the Majestic Hills residents. No one recalled hearing the home invasion, let alone seeing anyone connected to it.

His phone rang. The dispatcher had a call from a resident of Majestic Hills.

The wall clock showed just after six a.m. "Send it through," he said.

The man introduced himself as Marc Preston.

"My wife and I are hosting our neighbors, the family whose house was vandalized."

"Yes, how can I help?"

Marc said that he'd forgotten something during the commotion the night before. Earlier in the day, he'd been out walking when he saw a man sitting on the far side of the pond. His back was against a tree, and at one point he was pitching rocks into the water. Plunk. Plunk. Plunk. Marc told Adam that the only reason he'd seen the stranger was because he stopped to get a card from one of the Leaf It to Us workers who'd been blowing leaves from around the clubhouse.

"Can you describe the man?" Adam asked.

"A brown man," Marc said. "He was so far away, though. Maybe he was brown? There were shadows falling through the trees. You can check with the lawn care workers. Maybe they saw something." A baby began to wail in the background. "I did see him leave, though. Walked right through the woods behind the Blaques' house and beyond the trees."

"If you think of anything else—"

"I'll reach out," Marc said.

Behind the trees was the footpath. Adam knew it well.

As he sat at his desk, he thought about the days when he and his childhood best friend, Geoffrey Stanfield, used to walk along it, slogging through the woods to get there, often trying to dislodge buckshot from the trees along the path. For years, the Stanfields owned horses, and Adam and Geoffrey rode Giselle and Lenny, moseying like cowboys out for a stroll. That was long before Majestic Hills and the Grand Vistas. Geoffrey loved telling the story of meeting

Adam in the third grade and watching him run with those pigeon toes of his, his shoulders hunched, as though two orderlies had him snatched up by each arm.

On the footpath, the boys had talked about a business they concocted, selling brooms. Years later, when they were men, he and Geoffrey walked the path, and Geoffrey told him about the woman he'd met in grad school and how he'd planned to marry her. Later, Lonnie and Geoffrey would name their fourth child after him. Instead of Wade Adam, he would be Wade Alexander. He would have been Wade Adam, but Lonnie wanted one child to have her maiden name.

Now Adam couldn't remember the last time he and Geoffrey had been on the footpath together before he died.

The sun had come up. Adam slipped on his coat and duck boots and picked up his coffee. As he drove through his once-sleepy town, he thought about how Majestic Hills was no longer a things-like-that-don't-happen-here neighborhood. He pondered what that did to the residents' collective psyche. How it warped their sense of safety and self. Adam worried about the anxiety and desperation that often ensued from a person's desire for protection. Even if it meant moving to a different five-thousand-square foot, two-story piece of fiction.

At the three-way, Adam saw Langdon and Marc running in the direction of the One-Stop. He tapped his horn, and they simultaneously lifted gloved hands. Adam liked seeing them run together. The two men had developed a rhythm. They seemed to push each other, match each other's stride.

Adam continued on to Majestic Hills, joining his officers on the footpath. He told one to ride over to Leaf It to Us to find the workers who had been at the clubhouse the morning before.

The remaining officers scoured the footpath, following bicycle tread marks that swerved away from and tapered into snowdrifts. Two parallel tracks showed a round trip, originating at the Grand Vistas and crisscrossing each other in the darkness. Officers found a couple of candy canes and golf balls.

Adam was poised to ring Marc's doorbell when he saw Marc walking up his driveway, returning from his run. Adam asked Marc to show him where he saw the brown man. At the pond, Marc led him to the tree and Adam took a small branch, brushing aside decomposing leaves that were covered in frost. But he found nothing of note.

Because of the holidays, it took three days to locate and interview each of the eight lawn care workers and then to find the one who had been so enamored by the way the steam rose over the pond that morning, the way light danced across the water, that he had snapped a photo.

The worker texted the photo to the officer, who forwarded it to Adam.

The mist and the distance made for a picturesque composite of the pond, but the man in the image was out of focus and barely in view. Adam pinched the photo to enlarge it, but that only added to the distortion. He then held the photo at arm's length.

He gasped. The person looked like Wade. Once, Adam had gone fishing with Geoffrey and Wade, and when the two men caught fish and Wade hadn't, he sat on the water's edge with almost exactly the same dispirited posture and slumped shoulders as the man in the photo.

Adam hurried to his cruiser and drove to the Grand Vistas. As he entered, two U-Haul trucks were off to the side, waiting for him to pass so they could leave.

Since the news about the trailer park's closing, it had begun to look even more like a ghost town. And though it wasn't unusual for folks to leave during the holidays, this felt different. The development company had offered residents what it called generous housing vouchers and sliding scale stipends, the amounts decreasing the longer it took for people to leave. Now, many trailers were empty, and the wind slapped doors against their frames.

Adam knocked several times on Wade's door. He didn't answer.

The door was unlocked, and when Adam entered, he saw that Wade's clothes and books and posters were gone. Even his bong.

Months ago, Wade had asked Adam not to tell his mother about that. What was Adam supposed to do? Reveal to his best friend's widow that her son had been hotboxing?

He hadn't said anything.

Now, his walkie-talkie crackled, and he heard, "Sir?"

"Yep, go 'head."

"Sir, we have a young man here who says he wants to confess to the vandalism in Majestic Hills."

Adam's heart plummeted. "He give his name?"

"Yes. He says it's Wade Stanfield."

CHAPTER TWENTY-EIGHT
detention

Wade's decision to turn himself in had not come easily. Three days after the vandalism he had called Benny on his aunt's cell phone to check up on him. Benny picked up immediately.

"Wade, you know what I'm getting for Christmas? I found the stash before they wrapped everything."

Wade could feel Benny's excitement. "I don't think you're supposed to know," he said.

"Well, I do. I got two sweaters, three pairs of socks, and some other clothes stuff and—" He allowed a dramatic pause. "A brand-new cell phone."

"And? Something else?" Wade asked.

"That algebra calculator," he said with far less enthusiasm.

Wade knew about the calculator because he'd bought it and given it to Benny's aunt.

"Sounds like you racked up. Did you like riding the Greyhound to Nashville?"

"Nah. I liked *arriving* better. And I'll like leaving, too. We always come back after a few days so Auntie can get ready for work."

"What have you been doing?"

"I've been—"

Wade heard a screen door slam in the background.

"There you are, Benny." The voice belonged to a young child. "I want another one."

"Hold on, Wade," Benny said. He had a habit of hitting the Speaker button when he meant to hit Mute, which he did now.

"Another what?" Benny asked.

"A candy cane," the child said.

"Candy cane! Candy cane! Candy cane!" Benny yelled. "Stop begging. I'm all out."

"You ate them all?" The child started to cry.

"Benny?" Wade's voice came over the speaker. "Should I phone you later?"

Benny didn't answer, and the call abruptly ended.

Wade didn't think much of it until he was scrolling through the *New Pointe News* site, and a headline caught his eye: "Majestic Hills Vandal Still At Large." The story said that the perpetrator was believed to have come from the nearby trailer park, the Grand Vistas. New Pointe's Deputy Police Chief W. Adam Daniels would not confirm that, but he was quoted as saying that the person, or persons, of interest appeared to have entered the subdivision via a little-used footpath behind the property. A footpath that would now be monitored closely. The story ended with a quote from the Majestic Hills homeowner whose house was vandalized.

"We have a brand-new baby," said the Chicago bank executive, who asked not to be identified. "The intruder savaged our home. He trashed bottles of my wife's breast milk and stole all the candy canes off our Christmas tree. Every one of them. What kind of lowlife breaks into someone's home and steals candy?"

Wade sat straight up. *The footpath? Candy canes?* Had Benny vandalized that Majestic Hills home? It could have been someone else, he told himself. But he couldn't imagine Benny covering his tracks too well. He also couldn't imagine the boy in juvenile detention or foster care. He had no idea where Benny would land. Such was the precarious nature of his life. Wade tried calling Benny's aunt's phone several times, but it only rang and rang. Then he got a recording apologizing for the number being out of service. Why was it out of service? Maybe the aunt just wanted a new start. He had no idea. But he was certain that it would only be a matter of time before the police figured out that the vandal was Benny.

This, too, was part of Wade's reasoning: the Stanfield family had a fleet of attorneys whom Lonnie called for all manner of things. Most important, his family had the money to fight. What did Benny have?

At the New Pointe jail, Wade entered booking and processing. When Adam arrived, he waited until Wade was alone in a cell.

Adam sat next to him. "I am searching my brain, Wade, trying hard to square this circle. This doesn't sound like you."

Wade looked at the floor. "I did it," he said. "I did everything."

"Were you in Majestic Hills last Saturday, sitting near the pond?"

"Yes."

"I can believe that. You and your dad used to go there. But this is extremely serious."

Wade was silent.

"This could brand you for life," Adam said. "Whatever promising future you had—all of it—could disappear."

Wade swallowed hard but remained quiet.

"I've been trying to reach your mother."

"What the fuck, Uncle Adam?" He stood. "She's in the city with some friends from out of town."

"You have a detention hearing in the morning," Adam said. "She should know."

Wade looked down at the concrete floor.

"This isn't a joke, son. Whatever you're doing, damn it, stop it right now."

CHAPTER TWENTY-NINE

a brown man

Josephine and Langdon steeled themselves as they walked through lightly falling snow down their driveway to the clubhouse. They were the ones who first made Majestic Hills residents aware of the Grand Vistas and, months later, its Christmas toy drive. They anticipated they might be blamed—rightly or wrongly—for the vandalism.

"I sympathize with Christopher and Monica," Langdon said. "I really do. But he's the last person whose house should have been broken into."

"Just horrible," Josephine said, pulling up the hood on her coat.

"With him, you want to say, *Shit happens. Vile shit happens to all of us. Don't be such an entitled white guy.*"

Inside the clubhouse, the pool table was rolled off to the side, and three rows of chairs faced the fireplace, the same configuration as the previous meeting held there. Langdon estimated that there were about forty people seated in chairs, on the sofas—a few standing. Marc and Danny were in the front row. They waved hello.

Only two empty seats remained—in front of Christopher.

"Guess we drew the short stick," Langdon muttered as Josephine led them down the row.

She draped her coat over the back of her chair. "What happened to your family was just awful," she said to Christopher.

"I appreciate that," he said, standing and extending his hand to Langdon.

The last time he attempted to shake Langdon's hand was at the One-Stop, right after he'd tried to cajole Langdon into draining water across his property. Langdon had refused the handshake. Now he'd be the dick if he didn't follow through.

"Hey, man." He clasped Christopher's hand. "Let's hope the police have some answers."

"Thank you. I want to get to the bottom of this."

Langdon waved at Bonnie and Bryce, a few seats down the row, and Khai and Jackson, who were all the way at the end.

At exactly seven p.m., three uniformed officers stood at the front of the room.

"Good evening, everyone," said the one in the middle. "I'm First Patrolman Dave Bennett. I'd like to acknowledge others here in attendance."

He introduced the two officers, along with two village board members and a state legislator who was in town, rather than in Springfield, for the holidays. They were seated in the front row. The goal was to send the message that Majestic Hills was important. So were its residents.

So was its expansion.

Officer Bennett continued. "I'm sorry about the circumstances that have brought us here tonight. But—"

Christopher leaped to his feet. "Wait! Where's that Deputy Adams guy?"

"Mr. Thompson, Deputy Police Chief *Adam* Daniels couldn't make it tonight."

"What? Something more important came up?"

"Sir, I assure you, he's fully committed to this case. Earlier today—I was going to get to this later—someone turned himself in for the vandalism."

Langdon leaned forward on his elbows and glanced at Josephine. Wade was still front and center in both of their minds.

Officer Bennett continued. "Deputy Adam is going through the proper protocols for the investigation—"

"So you got the guy? That's fantastic." Christopher clapped. "Was it a drifter as he thought? And what's there to investigate? Dude turned himself in. Yay for the home team?"

"We have to follow procedure," Officer Bennett said. "We will let you know more when we can, I guarantee you. But let's focus on tonight's meeting: the investigation, what we can divulge, and the ways to help each of you regain your sense of safety." He removed his hat and placed it on a seat. "Mr. Thompson. First, tell us how you and your family are doing."

Christopher tucked in his shirt and sat. "We may be feeling better if this suspect thing pans out. But our lives are in disarray."

He said that little Moni and Monica were staying out East with her parents. They would return when the renovation was complete. The contractor told him that the damage appeared worse than it was.

"Luckily, my insurance company is putting me up in a rental in town so that I can oversee the construction. It houses Basil and me fine." Basil lay near the fireplace. His ears perked up when he heard his name. "I just want the bastard locked up."

Officer Bennett regained the floor.

"Thank you, Mr. Thompson. Now, let's talk about the investigation. As I mentioned, a person of interest turned himself in today. But we're still working hard on this case. Someone here in Majestic Hills said that on the afternoon of the vandalism, he saw a man sitting on the other side of the pond."

"That was me," Marc said, raising a finger. "I saw him."

Christopher stood again. "I heard it was a *brown* man."

"Yes," Officer Bennett said.

"Don't you think that's important? 'A *brown* man?' Don't be afraid to say it—"

"I'm not afraid, Mr. Thompson."

"We're trying to get to the truth, right?" Christopher sat back down. "A brown man."

The officer continued. "Whether the person—"

"Whatever the man's race," Josephine interrupted, facing Christopher, "we don't know that he was the one who vandalized your home. But we do know that as soon as someone says Black or brown or white or Asian or Hispanic or Arab, our minds become supercomputers and we start browsing every file we've created on skin color or ethnicity. We focus on the bad stuff and delete everything else offering balance and perspective."

"If he's brown, he's brown," Christopher said.

"But if he's brown and not the vandal, you're only stoking fear."

"Let's settle down," the officer said. "Whether the person who's in custody is the perpetrator, that's what we're working hard to determine. I can't stress enough that crime in New Pointe is low—as evidenced by every statistic we have. The most activity we get in the area is in the Grand Vistas. And that's still relatively modest, even though it's not in our jurisdiction."

He unfolded a map with Majestic Hills and the footpath. The two other officers held it up.

"Most people don't know about this connection," Bennett said, pointing to the trail. "If you follow it, you see that it links Majestic Hills and the Grand Vistas. During our investigation we found fresh tire tracks showing that someone rode a bike from the trailer park to here and back. There, we had to cut down bramble and brush to get through. So I'm guessing that most residents don't know it exists and don't use it."

"A footpath?" Christopher said.

Langdon imagined the gears shifting in his brain.

"To the Grand Vistas?"

Langdon and Josephine exchanged glances: *Here we go.*

Christopher was silent for a moment. He tapped the backs of Langdon's and Josephine's chairs. "You guys had that fundraising drive for them? You spearheaded it?"

"Yes." Langdon rose to face him. "We helped out. Many families did."

"I'm sorry this happened to you," Josephine said, standing too. "But we don't know that the perpetrator came from the Grand Vistas.

The fact is, the person could have come from anywhere, and any one of our houses could have been broken into."

"But yours wasn't, right?" Christopher asked.

"What are you implying?" Langdon said. A sudden heat prickled the back of his neck.

"I'm stating the facts."

Josephine looked earnest. "But we don't know *all* the facts. That's why there's still an investigation—"

"I'm all for philanthropy and altruism," Christopher continued. "But you two made us vulnerable. Some people you can't help." He turned toward Bonnie. "I was bilked out of a hundred bucks for the Grand Vistas."

"Fifty." Bonnie bristled, slowly enunciating the word and turning toward him. "You gave fifty dollars. And, if I recall, you got your bank to match the donation."

"Now I wish I hadn't given a dime."

Josephine started to sit, but she stopped. "About making people vulnerable, Christopher: last month, when you, Marc, and my husband were running, you suggested a different route, and you guys nearly got robbed at gunpoint. One could argue that *you* made *them* vulnerable."

"That was different," he said. "I didn't know—"

"Exactly. How does anybody know—until they do?"

Langdon and Josephine sat. The neighbors started to murmur.

Officer Bennett gestured with the folded map. "Okay, let's not lose focus here. And let's try not to place blame. This investigation is ongoing, and we're working hard to find the culprits. In the meantime, some of you asked about measures you can take to be safe and to ward off intruders. Officer Dabney will speak to that."

Officer Bennett stepped aside.

"There are some relatively simple things you can do," Officer Dabney said. "For example, if you have an alarm, please turn it on."

Christopher breathed out extravagantly.

"Create a text string, especially for emergencies," the officer continued. "When Marc saw the man by the water, he could have texted something like 'Does anyone know the guy who's sitting by the pond?' Maybe someone could have identified early on whether he was a threat."

Across the room, heads nodded.

"You know the saying 'If you see something, say something.'"

"But what about the footpath?" Christopher asked. "That seems to be our biggest vulnerability."

Danny raised her hand. Although Langdon always asked about her when he and Marc ran together, Langdon hadn't seen her in a while. She looked frail, even though Marc always insisted that she was a formidable fighter.

"We could have a blue light surveillance camera installed back there," she said, pitching a shoulder forward in a half shrug. "A blue light camera is in your face and easily seen."

"But aren't those for bad neighborhoods?" asked someone from the back row. "Is that what we're trying to project?"

Christopher raised his hand. "Marc and I have been talking about purchasing a police scanner."

"Whoa." Marc swiveled around. "No—you mentioned that to me, and I said I didn't know how helpful it would be."

Langdon saw Bonnie lean forward to get his attention, and they rolled their eyes.

"As I said," Officer Bennett interjected, "crime is very low here. There's no need for a police scanner."

When Langdon didn't think it was possible for the ideas to get more outlandish, a couple of neighbors recommended that someone start a running list of the residents' license plate numbers and the makes and models of their vehicles, so they could detect suspicious ones. Another neighbor suggested speed bumps along Willow.

"What?" Bryce threw his hands up. "To slow getaway cars? Never mind that the vandal might not have arrived via Willow."

Undeterred, the same neighbors suggested building a small outpost and hiring a twenty-four-hour security service to sit in it when they weren't patrolling the area.

"You know," Marc said, "the developer considered making this a gated community with a wrought iron fence around the property."

Langdon stood again. "What about adding razor wire and a guard tower with a sniper?"

Eyes focused on him.

"Oh, is that too—wait for it—over the top, for the brown man?"

"You know me, brother," Marc said.

"Which is why I expect more from you," Langdon said. "But let's talk about what it means to be a brown man in beautiful Majestic Hills. To be working in your yard when the new UPS guy tells you he can't leave your package with you because he has to leave it with the homeowner. You say, I *am* the homeowner, and he looks skeptical or dumbfounded, hard to read, for a good long minute before he finally entrusts you with your package. Then there's the Saturday afternoon when your doorbell rings and you open the door to find a woman and her daughter selling Girl Scout cookies. The woman literally flinches when she sees you. She thinks it isn't noticeable. But it absolutely is."

Josephine touched his hand. He hadn't mentioned either incident to her.

"I grew up with strangers thinking that my family didn't live in my childhood home," he said, looking out the window. "You form calluses."

Marc scratched his head. "So are you saying I shouldn't have said a brown man?"

"Of course, you had to tell the police that," Langdon said. "But you went back and told this guy, Mr. Gunslinger here." He spoke directly to Christopher. "You taunted two of my Thanksgiving guests. One of the teens' bike trailer tipped over in front of your house, spilling food. Maybe at first you didn't know they were cleaning up. But when you realized it, you still had to give them shit while one of your rifle-toting bros waited in the wings."

Christopher placed his hand on his forehead. "We were just joshing with them," he said. "No big deal. We also may have been a little overserved."

"You mean *drunk*?" Langdon looked at him over his glasses. "Why don't you say the word, Chris. Drunk. Don't be afraid to say it. We're getting to the truth, right? Isn't that what you just told my wife?" Grown-ass bullies."

"Who's the victim here?" Christopher yelled. For the first time all evening, Basil began to pace. "I'm the one whose house was destroyed." He thumped his chest. "Me. I'm the one!"

The room was quiet enough to hear sleet pelting the window. Normal for that time of year. But then rare claps of thunder and flashes of lightning joined in.

Bonnie stood. "I've been thinking about the meet and greet," she said. "Our sons spilling out of our canoe and how everyone leaped into action. We barely knew one another back then." She smiled at Josephine. "And what about the morning with the big, scary snake?"

Josephine wriggled a bit at the memory.

Bonnie turned to Christopher. "And that afternoon when your house flooded and we all gathered in your yard to help. We had a moment, right? Several, before all of this? We shouldn't let it divide us."

Christopher scoffed. But others nodded.

"She's absolutely right," Officer Bennett said. "The bad guys win if that happens. That's one of two major things I want you to take away from tonight. The other is that you should feel free to contact us immediately if you think of anything else from that day. No tip is too small."

Josephine raised her hand. "Have you gotten many tips?"

"Quite a few," he said.

"Would you give us a sample?"

"One person recalled that a neighbor may have invited a few

family members for Thanksgiving dinner who were dicey." He added air quotes around *dicey*. "The person suggested they might have been casing the subdivision. I don't know how true that is, but it fits into the 'nothing is too big or too small' category."

Josephine gasped. It was barely audible, but Langdon heard it and then watched her look down the row of chairs. He couldn't tell who held her gaze.

"You okay, Blaque?" he whispered.

She didn't respond. She flashed a brittle smile and stood, squaring her shoulders. She did not speak for what seemed to be an excruciating ten seconds, fifteen, thirty. She kept staring toward the fireplace. Langdon placed his hand on the back of her thigh.

Almost inaudibly, she said, "Khai."

Langdon looked down the row at Khai, who stood, staring into her palms. Sniveling, she met Josephine's eyes. Her cheeks reddening. Her mouth moving. But nothing coming out.

As calmly as she could muster, Josephine said, "No one in my family is responsible for any of this, Khai. And I deeply, deeply resent your suggesting it."

"Josephine, all I was saying was . . . Josephine, this has no reflection on you . . . Jo—"

"Khai." Josephine grabbed her coat. "Go to hell."

CHAPTER THIRTY

the lowlife, the intruder, that bastard

By daybreak, snow covered the Chicago area's roads and expressways, making them nearly impassable. After the clubhouse meeting, Langdon had taken the train into work, but he was stranded the next morning. News reports said that Metro's switching mechanisms had frozen, and trains were either crawling along or stuck.

Josephine decided to work from home. She was in the kitchen, still in her pajamas and sipping ginger tea, when her phone rang. She ignored it. It wasn't yet nine a.m., and she'd already received five texts from Khai. Josephine not only refused to respond, she refused to even read them. She was hurt, but mostly she was furious at herself for believing she could speak freely to Khai. Angry that she'd been seduced by the idea that she could have a Fat facsimile next door, a friend, an ally. And, Khai's "Josephine" this and "Josephine" that, the night before, reminded her of what her father used to say when she did something wrong and tried to "Daddy" him to death: "Little girl, you can't rinse your mouth out with my name."

When the phone rang again, Josephine picked it up to tell Khai to stop calling. But it was Lonnie. "Josephine, I need a huge favor."

Desperation filled her voice.

"Absolutely, how can I help?" Josephine lowered her cup to the table.

"My son." Her voice quaked. "Wade's been arrested."

"Oh, Lonnie."

"His detention hearing is this morning," she continued. "Because the roads are so bad, my attorneys can't get there in time. I spent a rare night near the Wisconsin border visiting some friends who were in town for the holidays and a spa day. And—"

She sounded breathless, as if she were in free fall. "I hate to ask, but is there any—any way you can stand in?"

"Of course." Josephine was already walking upstairs. "Text me all the details. I have to ask: Does Wade have any priors?"

"None." She began to cry. "I should have been there—"

"Stop it," Josephine said. "You didn't know. And you deserve some time to yourself."

In the Land Cruiser, Josephine struggled to get out of their driveway, which hadn't been cleared. Willow was better, but it was still snowing, and New Pointe's plows couldn't keep up.

She was turning toward the arch when she hit an icy spot and the car began to glide off the road. She screamed, gripping the steering wheel as she hit a snowbank.

Marc had just left his driveway and was a few yards behind her. He drove up next to her and rolled down his passenger-side window.

"You okay?"

Josephine nodded, catching her breath.

"Don't worry," he said. "I got you."

As he pulled in front of her, Christopher was arriving at the subdivision. He too pulled over and joined Marc behind the Land Cruiser.

"Put it in four-wheel drive and give it some gas," Marc yelled. "Slowly. Gently."

The tires spun as the two men pushed and rocked the Land Cruiser. Josephine watched them in her side mirrors as snow flew into their faces and their feet slid behind them. Finally, the Land Cruiser got traction and she was able to pull back onto the street.

Josephine rolled down the window. "Thank you both so much."

"No problem," Marc said, dusting snow from his coat and blue jeans.

"It's what neighbors do," Christopher said with a hint of snark.

Anger replaced Josephine's fear. "Thank you, but I know exactly what neighbors do."

The detention hearing took place in a small courtroom in the police station. When Josephine entered, the gallery was empty, but the clerk and bailiff stood near the judge's bench, which was flanked by an Illinois flag and a U.S. flag. The prosecutor, a white man in his fifties, sat at a table, poring over papers. She introduced herself to him. He told her his name was Terry Penn.

"How'd you make it here with this snow?" Josephine asked.

"Most of us live in town," Terry said. "One bad storm years ago, I got here on a snowmobile."

She took a seat at the table across from him and busied herself by looking over her scant notes. She hadn't represented anyone in a while, and she didn't want to muck things up.

A side door opened, and a police officer escorted Wade into the courtroom. He wore an Army green jail jumpsuit and plastic green slide sandals with white socks. His eyes appeared heavy and empty.

"Your lawyer couldn't make it because of this snowstorm," she told him. "Your mom is away, and she asked me to—"

"She shouldn't have," Wade snarled.

"Listen, you must let me do all the talking. When it's time, you stand here quietly. You understand?"

Wade stared off beyond Josephine's shoulder.

"Hey," she said. "Look at me. I need to know that you understand."

He nodded.

"I will enter a plea of not guilty."

"But I did—"

"Quiet. Your plea will be not guilty because that's the way we do things."

He inhaled, his chest fluttering like a wounded bird.

She pointed to some documents on the table. "This is the police report. I've got to skim it super fast."

She knitted her fingers over her forehead and began reading. Several things stood out to her. Seeing the destruction, Christopher had brought up a shotgun, which lay on the floor by the front door. He'd presented his FOID and concealed carry cards to the arriving officers. He'd referred to the vandal as "the lowlife," "the intruder," and "that bastard," saying that he'd tracked mud throughout the first floor of his home and bashed in windows and walls and appliances. He'd used Christopher's hunting knife to viciously slice the sofa's upholstery. But he left untouched a stack of new baby onesies that were folded there.

Josephine finished reading, and Judge Celeste Coles entered shortly afterward. Everyone stood. The clerk handed the judge a file, and she looked at it and then at Wade.

"Are you Defendant Wade Alexander Stanfield?"

Josephine answered, "Defense Attorney Josephine Blaque, Your Honor, on behalf of Wade Alexander Stanfield."

"What?" Came an outburst from the back.

All eyes turned toward the rear of the courtroom. The gallery had four rows of seating with an aisle down the middle. Josephine saw Christopher in the last row. She thought, *Damn it.* The betrayal on his face was unmistakable in the scathing look he gave her.

"Sir," the judge said to Christopher. "Will we have to remove you?"

"I apologize, Your Honor. But it's my house that was destroyed."

"Will you need to be removed?"

"No, Your Honor."

The judge returned to looking at the file.

"Mr. Stanfield," Judge Coles said, "you are charged with two crimes: one count of residential burglary and one count of criminal damage to property."

The judge read from papers in front of her.

"On count one, the state alleges that on December 20, you knowingly entered the dwelling of Christopher Thompson and Dr. J. Monica Johnson at 25 Willow Lane in New Pointe, Illinois. You did so without authority and remained within the residence with the intent to commit a felony. On count two, the state alleges that you entered the same house and damaged property, the value of which exceeded one hundred thousand dollars. If you're found guilty of both or either of these offenses, your sentence could range from probation to up to four years in the state's Department of Juvenile Justice. Do you understand the charges and possible consequences?"

"We do, Your Honor," Josephine said. "My client pleads not guilty to both. We're asking that he be released under his mother's supervision."

The judge turned to the prosecutor. "Attorney Penn?"

"Good morning, Your Honor," he said, standing. "We're asking that he be detained."

"Attorney Blaque, have you anything to add?"

Josephine laced her fingers behind her back. "My client is sixteen years old, and he's from a well-known, distinguished family. He's a brilliant student who's already been accepted at three universities. His family would be here today, Your Honor, if not for the snowstorm. We can guarantee that he will not flee."

"Thank you, Attorney Blaque," the judge said. "Attorney Penn?"

"Thank you, Your Honor. I have photos of Mr. Thompson and Dr. Johnson's home I'd like to submit into evidence. The property damage we're talking about here was devastating and senseless. No one deserves to return home to something like this." He shuffled manila folders. "We believe Mr. Stanfield should be detained. The Thompson-Johnson family doesn't yet know the total amount of damage incurred, but, so far, the cost for repairs is estimated upward of one hundred thousand dollars. This fits the Class 2 felony destruction of property threshold. Lastly, Mr. Stanfield confessed, Your Honor."

"Attorney Blaque?" the judge said.

"Your Honor, my client has no priors. I do not know the details of said 'confession,' but I can tell you that he's a bright teenager who understands the gravity of the charges he's facing. He poses no threat to society and should be released to his mother who, as I mentioned, would be here, but she's stuck in traffic because of the storm."

"I want to say something," Wade said, staring at the floor.

"Wade—" Josephine said out of the corner of her mouth.

Adam was standing near the empty jury box, and he slowly shook his head.

"Mr. Stanfield, I suggest you refrain from speaking," the judge said. "Do we understand each other?"

"Yes, Your Honor."

"Wade," she said. "I'm releasing you only into the custody of your mother. When she arrives here in New Pointe, you may leave. Your next status hearing will be in February. The clerk will provide the exact date."

Christopher stood. "So he just gets to walk out when his Mommy comes?"

"Order!" the judge admonished.

"Did you see those photos? Did you see what he did to my house?"

"Mr. Thompson," the judge said, "in the criminal justice system, there's a process. We have begun it, and we must go through it. Do not make me regret not removing you earlier."

A police officer led Wade back to the jail to wait. Josephine watched until the door closed. Christopher approached her.

"You and I are neighbors." Christopher showed her the road salt from the Land Cruiser still on his coat. "And you take that—that delinquent's side over mine and Monica's?"

"He's a sixteen-year-old who's still mourning the loss of his father—"

Christopher stomped his foot. "I lost my father last year, too."

Josephine took a breath. "I know you want justice."

What she wanted to say was that justice didn't have to mean that another misguided young Black man had to grow up behind bars because he made a huge, nonviolent mistake. But she knew Christopher wouldn't hear her. Instead, she said, "I sincerely believe he did not do this. If I didn't, I wouldn't be here."

"He confessed!" Christopher shook his head. "I hope he rots."

Josephine took a step closer to him and met his eyes. "Have you ever made a horrible mistake, Christopher? Have you ever done something you later regretted? I pray to God that your beautiful little girl—"

"Don't you bring my daughter into this."

"I pray to God that she's never in a position where she's the one in need of a second chance."

CHAPTER THIRTY-ONE

strange fruit

The roads didn't fully open until evening. Lonnie inched her way back to New Pointe, checking in often with Josephine. By the time Lonnie arrived at the police station, it was too late for Wade to be processed to leave, and he refused to see her. She phoned Josephine.

"Go home," Josephine told Lonnie. "I'll meet you there in the morning."

"I can't leave until I see him," she said.

"You can't stay there, Lonnie. You've got to be exhausted. Please, go home."

She was quiet for a long time. "Fine."

But when Josephine entered the police station the next morning, she saw Lonnie sitting in the waiting area, her head flopped forward, asleep. She'd clearly been there all night, and she looked disheveled despite a cute new haircut she'd gotten during her day at the spa with her friends.

Josephine didn't want to disturb her, so she checked in and went right to the legal visiting area, a bright room that had a table with two chairs across from each other and a plastic floor plant. Early in her career she had spent a year as a public defender, a real torture chamber of a job. As she waited for Wade, she admired how clean this room was, a far cry from what she'd experienced in Chicago: the sickening smells, the walls scrawled with epithets, and the legions of men and boys whose lives had been constricted and diminished by one holding cell after another.

Josephine was looking out a narrow window when a police officer escorted Wade into the room. He was wearing the same Army green jail jumpsuit he'd had on the day before. He sat at the table. The officer stood outside the door.

"Your mother's telling me you won't see her," Josephine said. "She's been sitting in the waiting area all night. What's that about?"

"I can't right now," he mumbled.

"I don't even know what that means. Or why you'd agree to see me and not your mother. That woman busted her ass to get here, and you're refusing to see her? I'm off this case. You've got attorneys up the wazoo on their way."

"I got a lot going on in my head, and I'd prefer not to be lectured."

Josephine pressed down on the table. "Your ideas, Wade, your pursuits and goals are noble, but this is not the way to go about it."

"You don't have to pretend to care about me." The vertical veins under his eyes were protruding. "Invoice my mom. She'll take care of you."

"You're being an ass."

Outside, the snow had begun to come down hard again. Wade looked over at the window.

"You and your husband are just as bad," he said, turning back to Josephine. "You parachute in and parachute out. Pretend to make a difference, then go home to your cozy lives."

"That's not fair. You think you're the only person who has looked at the world, been pained or disillusioned by it, and wanted to change things? Langdon had his own run-in with the law when he was a teen. He got arrested for busting up car windows."

"What's that got to do with me?" he asked bluntly.

"Lang had been in mourning, with no idea what to do with his pain," she said. "So he tore shit up. It drove his parents crazy."

Josephine had a sense that Wade was now listening closely. Even though he wouldn't look at her, he sat up straighter.

"During one of Lang's hearings, he addressed the court, talking about how he was a troubled and at-risk youth. I found the transcript of what he said, and I've read it many times, because he was eloquent." She began to recite:

"'I am a troubled youth, Your Honor. But I am not your typical troubled youth, because I come from a family of means. I live in a nice house, on a nice street in a community that affords me every leg up. But, Your Honor, I am still an at-risk youth. I am at risk of losing faith in so many institutions. I am at risk of losing my humanity, in part because I am highly visible but woefully unseen. I am a young man who's on the verge of salting his fields because they only bear strange fruit.'"

She told Wade that the last line came from his parents' love of Billie Holiday's music.

"They played it on Saturday mornings." Josephine smiled. "I think Langdon told me that story because he was trying to mack." She stared at him. "You know, show his street cred, flirt?"

"I know what *mack* means," Wade mumbled. "And I know Billie Holiday, too."

"Okay, Smarty Pants. It took a while, but Lang figured things out."

"And you think I can?"

"I don't know, Wade." She leaned toward him again. "I hope so. But if you don't allow your mother to see you, I won't come back. Ever. You hear me?" She took a breath, trying a different tactic. "You should see her hair. She's got this cute haircut. Big chop. Shoulder-length and wavy. She needs to see you."

Wade's eyes welled with tears.

"I know she's mad at me." He began to sob uncontrollably. "I know she hates me. I was just telling her that I was going to college in the fall. I can't do anything right."

Josephine held both of his hands. "The police don't believe you did this."

He pulled away from her. "You mean Uncle Adam?"

"I don't believe you did it, either. Once I saw those photos of the destruction, I knew."

"I'm responsible, though."

"It's a hunch, but I think you're protecting that little white boy, Benny."

"Why does he have to be 'that little white boy'?" His tone was strident.

"Because you're in here and he isn't. Don't mess with me, Wade. This is your life." She adjusted herself in the seat. "Who are you protecting?"

"No one," he said. "I did it. It was all me."

"Okay," Josephine said. She picked up her book bag. "You have thirty minutes, maybe a full hour left of this nonsense. But you can't stay here. I hope you know that."

Josephine left the room and walked down a long hall to Lonnie, who stood when she saw her coming.

"How is he?"

"He's hanging in there. He hasn't devised an exit strategy yet. He knows he's hurting you, and that breaks his heart."

They sat for an hour, talking about Wade, and about what, for Lonnie, had been a wonderful day with her friends until Adam called about Wade's arrest. Just as Josephine opened her mouth to say she needed to go home and that Lonnie should do the same, Lonnie nudged Josephine's arm. Wade was walking toward them, wearing the blue jeans and peacoat he'd arrived in.

Lonnie stood, but she didn't move. He walked up to her and began to cry again.

"I'm so sorry, Mom. I'm so, so sorry."

Josephine was standing back watching them when Adam hurried out of an office.

"Can I talk to you for a second?" he asked her.

"A quick second, I hope," Josephine said. "I seriously need to leave."

"Yes, super quick. Come with me. Attorney Penn happens to be in the building, and there's something I need to show both of you at the same time."

"But I'll be handing off this case soon."

"That's okay. Right now, you're still one of the attorneys of record, and you're here."

They walked down a short corridor and through a series of glass doors that he held open for her. They entered a room with a projection screen and a laptop at the head of the table. Christopher sat with his hands folded. The prosecutor was seated next to him.

This was, Josephine predicted, not going to be quick.

She sat across from both men.

"Hey, neighbor," he said sarcastically. "Long time no see."

"Hello, Christopher," Josephine said. She took out her cell phone to take notes.

"It's early and it's already been a long day," Terry said. "What do you have, Adam?"

He sat at the computer, tapping away. When the screen lit up, they each turned toward it.

"We thought we'd accounted for all the security cameras on the west side of Willow. We knew that Marc and Danny Preston, in the house next door and directly south of you"—he looked at Christopher—"have a camera facing their patio and the woods. We looked at it and saw nothing of note."

He flashed a few images across the screen from the Prestons' camera.

"Your family has a camera, but the entire alarm system wasn't on. We even looked at the video from your next-door neighbors to the north of you." Adam turned pages in his notebook. "That's Khai and Jackson Kennedy. They have a camera that gave us a great view of your side door."

The screen showed the suspect entering and leaving the house.

"He's clutching a bat," Deputy Adam said. "He's got on that ski mask, and there aren't many, if any, distinguishable features. He's covered well. I'll admit we'd been a bit stumped. Yesterday, after Wade's hearing, I walked the footpath again, wondering what we missed. I walked and walked, and when I sat down, I saw a small electrical box beside Mr. Kennedy's beehives. It was peeking out from a snowdrift. I asked him what it was for." Adam typed on the laptop. "He has cameras back there to check on his bees. Fussy beekeepers, right?"

"Why didn't he say something before?" Christopher asked.

"He said the system hadn't been working. It turns out that it wasn't connecting to his cell phone correctly, but it had been recording since it was installed. All of that to say: we have better footage of the person who vandalized the house."

Christopher turned his chair so that it faced the projection screen.

"Here's the shot again from the camera on Jackson's house of the vandal entering your side door."

The footage showed someone in a puffer coat and ski mask at 6:59 p.m.

"Ten minutes later," Adam said, "we see him exiting the house, running toward the woods."

Christopher huffed. "All that destruction in ten minutes?"

"It doesn't take long when you're wielding a bat," Adam said. "Now I'm going to show you the footage from the camera near the beehives."

Everyone leaned forward, staring at the blank screen.

"We were lucky we had a full moon reflecting off the snow that night. Both gave us some pretty good lighting," Adam said. "Also, the picture is in color—as opposed to being black-and-white and grainy."

He started the video. They watched the suspect running toward the beehives.

"Here's the money shot," Adam said. "The guy stops, tucks the bat under his arm, and lifts his mask to, of all things, munch on a candy cane." Adam pauses the video and walks to the screen with a pointer. "Here we see his cheek and nose and mouth. The blond curls. The bottom rim of his eyeglasses." He turned back to the table. "This is not Wade Stanfield. Whoever it is, he's a doofus. He didn't have to lift his mask to eat."

Josephine and Terry rose to be closer to the image.

She thought it looked like Benny. But she wasn't sure. She examined the black puffer coat and recalled her first time visiting Majestic Hills, seeing a young man leaning over the hood of the police car.

"In light of this," Josephine said. "I believe the charges against my client should be dropped."

"Maybe those charges," Terry said. "But your client now faces obstruction of justice."

"C'mon, man," Josephine said.

Christopher joined them. "This means the bastard is still roaming around. But how do we know that the rich kid didn't have a sidekick?"

"That's a great question," Adam said. "We only found one set of footprints in and around your house. We've painstakingly examined the camera footage from both your neighbors, and we don't see a second person. That's not to say the suspect wasn't acting on someone else's orders. But he appears to have been a lone wolf."

"So how do you find him?" Christopher kneaded the back of his neck.

"We've been in the Grand Vistas every day, conducting interviews," Adam said. "Keep in mind: a few residents left for the holidays. But many are leaving for good. The developers are clearing it out."

"So what now?" Christopher asked. "There's nothing you can do?"

"We're still working extremely hard on this case," Adam said.

"I recommend that you guys find this redneck white trash kid. I will protect my family. If he decides to break into my house again, he won't walk out."

CHAPTER THIRTY-TWO

a pig-pink propane tank

Wade and Lonnie left the police station without having heard the latest development about the video. Because the weather had changed dramatically since Wade entered jail two days before, his gym shoes proved no match for the compacted snow on the sidewalks, and his peacoat offered little warmth against the stinging wind.

The temperature on the car dashboard showed twenty degrees.

"Mom," he said. "I need to go to the Grand Vistas one last time."

Lonnie's shoulders slumped, and she placed her forehead on the steering wheel. "Wade, I can't keep doing this."

"I'm sorry, Mom. I'm so sorry about all of this. But please, I need to go there before everybody leaves and there's nothing left."

Wade needed to see Benny. He hoped Benny would be back from Nashville by now. Wade needed to talk to him about what happened and explain that what he did was horrific and wrong. He wanted to assure Benny that he would never tell a soul, and that Benny should never tell either. Not even his aunt.

Lonnie's pickup inched along Goodenow. Tow trucks were rescuing several vehicles that had slid off the road into snowdrifts.

Lonnie signaled to turn left at the three-way. She passed the One-Stop, the cemetery.

"I can't imagine that the roads have been plowed anywhere near the Grand Vistas."

"When we get there, I'll get out and walk if I have to," he said.

"You are working every nerve I have."

Wade stared ahead. At the road leading to the Grand Vistas, snowplows had done a fine job opening the street. It took a second to spot the entrance, because the porta-potties had been trucked away. In their place were a couple of backhoes that had begun digging into the trees and brush. It had been less than a week since Wade was last there, but the change was dizzying.

Lonnie parked and followed Wade to Benny's trailer. He felt disoriented because the pig-pink propane tank was gone.

When he knocked, there was no answer. He peeked into the window, but it was too opaque. When he tried the door latch, it opened. The smell of methylated spirits engulfed him. Most of Benny's and his aunt's belongings were gone. The table in the kitchen nook was empty except for a stack of old Powerball tickets. A small television with a rabbit ears antenna sat on the floor in a corner, wrapped in its cord.

Wade stood near the bathroom and called Benny's aunt's number again. He hadn't tried it since turning himself in to the police. He got the same recording.

"They're not coming back," Wade said, leaving the trailer. "Benny must not have known."

Inside the pickup, he stared into his lap and fought back tears. Lonnie placed her hand on his shoulder, allowing it to linger.

"I thought I could make a difference here," he said.

"You did make a difference." She tilted his chin forward. "Hold your head up, son. You tried, and you cared. Most people don't. I am exceedingly proud of you. Your father . . ." Her voice began to break. "He would be so proud of you. I believe Benny's aunt will do her best to create a better life for him."

Her phone beeped, and when she started the ignition, there was a message from Adam.

Call me. I have great news about Wade's case.

"But now we have to move on, okay?" she said.

He nodded.

As she turned the car around, Wade saw discarded items in the area that used to be the garden. The corrugated skirts of trailers, wooden planks that had formed front stoops. A wheelchair ramp. An old cigarette machine lying on its side.

And there it was, the pig-pink propane tank, belly-up amid it all.

CHAPTER THIRTY-THREE

mr. charlie

Over the last few days Josephine had been feeling out of sorts. She blamed her restlessness or malaise, or whatever it was, on the tumult surrounding the home invasion and Wade's arrest. Both had been black holes that had absorbed too much of her time and brain energy.

On the night before Christmas, when she arrived home after finalizing the paperwork regarding Wade, Langdon met her at the garage door.

"I have a surprise for you," he said.

He placed his hand over her eyes, leading her into the family room. He removed his hand, and standing next to the fireplace was the artificial white Charlie Brown tree she'd inherited from her father's room at his senior care facility. She and Langdon had planned to purchase a new tree from the tree farm Bonnie suggested, but they got too busy and ran out of time.

"You've been a little down lately," he said. "So I pulled out the big dawg."

The tree was about five feet tall, wide-hipped and swaybacked and garishly decorated with ornaments dangling from limbs that were twisted or duct-taped together. It had not fared well over the years. Still, in the condo, Langdon and Josephine always joked that their Christmas tree was no shrinking violet.

Ordinarily she would have loved such a kind gesture. But now her eyes welled with tears at how pathetic it looked in such a grand space.

Worry filled Langdon's face. "What's the matter, Blaque?"

"Thank you." She managed an overcompensating smile. "I'm just really tired."

She went up to bed.

They canceled holiday plans with his family and had a quiet Christmas and New Year's Eve at home. She spent a couple of days driving into the city to swim in the condo building's indoor pool. And, oddly, she wanted to run. Josephine was not a runner. Swann, Livingston, & Taylor closed for the holidays, and she missed not being buried under a mountain of work. She told Langdon she'd felt like she was off her game ever since her falling-out with Christopher. She knew he viewed her as a traitor, but she wondered if the other neighbors felt the same.

She found herself obsessing over that—and she rarely obsessed. And, although she didn't want to admit it, she missed Khai.

"Don't worry," Langdon said on a night just after the new year. "Everybody's off their game. What happened to Christopher and Monica threw us all off—"

"I have no regrets about representing Wade," she said, trying not to sound defensive.

"I wasn't suggesting that you should. Besides, Marc mentioned that Christopher and Monica are happy with their renovations and may stay a while longer rather than sell."

"Oh, goodie." She sighed.

"To some degree, they may be trying to put this behind them," he said.

The Blaques' one-year anniversary in Majestic Hills was just over three months away, and they each knew they would have to decide soon whether to stay or leave.

But neither dared broach the topic—until the day Langdon was leafing through a stack of mail and found a letter from their tenants in the condo.

Josephine was seated at the kitchen table, staring out the window at the woods. Langdon joined her.

"'Dear Josephine and Langdon,'" he read. "'Happy New Year. This is just a quick note to let you know how much we've loved your place and want to renew for another year. It's astounding how time has flown by. We enjoy walking to our research labs along the lakefront. On the weekends, we've visited South Side museums and eaten at the amazing restaurants. I've found a bakery with the best baklava and lahem b'ajeen that transports me back to my native Lebanon. Audrey found a café on Michigan Avenue that reminds her of her favorite Parisian brasserie. And watching the sunrise over the lake every morning is a gift. Our visas have been renewed (seems like a rarity these days), and we would love to extend our lease for another year. Please let us know your thoughts. Audrey and Nabil.'"

"Given all that's transpired," Josephine said, "I've assumed our days here were numbered."

"We should at least talk about this, Josey. No matter the outcome, we should decide together."

"I don't feel like fighting, Lang."

"It doesn't have to be a fight. Let's ride, if that's what you want. Hat up."

"What I really want is *us* back, Lang. I don't think we can get that here. I miss you. I miss us. This place has asked too much of us, and I'm not sure what it's given in return."

"We'll be fine," Langdon said. "We still have us."

When Fat began burning up Josephine's phone, asking her to lunch, Josephine knew that Langdon had orchestrated it all. He wanted Fat to help Josephine with an unease that even she didn't fully understand.

As Josephine and Fat dined, Fat cut right to the chase.

"Come on back to the city where it's not safe, but at least nobody's delusional about it." Fat rubbed the top of Josephine's hand. "What we city dwellers have in our favor is the law of large numbers. Out there, you guys are crabs in a barrel."

"I don't think that's how the law of large numbers works." Josephine took a forkful of her salad and inhaled a stuttering breath.

"Oh, Blaque. What's the matter?" Fat stood and went over to her. "Whatever it is, we'll make everything all right."

"I feel—" Josephine sniffled. "Well, my father used to say, 'like I don't know my ass from a hole in the ground.' I'm tired all the time. I've got awful brain fog."

Fat returned to her seat. The expression on her face slowly changed as she stared into the remains of Josephine's baby arugula, as if consulting tea leaves.

"Ohhhhh, my God," she said in a loud whisper. She stood but sat back down. "Ohhhh, my Jesus!"

"What?" Josephine's forehead furrowed.

"When was your last period?" Fat believed she'd solved a riddle.

"Girl, your liquor is talking." Josephine nodded at Fat's empty wineglass. But she thought and thought, swallowing hard. "Oh, God. Maybe early October?"

"November, December—" Fat cheerily ticked the months off on her fingers. "January." She squealed. "We are pregnant. I'm sure of it."

Josephine told Fat that she was supposed to have her quarterly Depo shot around Labor Day, right after Monica's baby shower. She remembered now because her gynecologist, pregnant with her second child, had made a joke about her due date being Labor Day. She had told Josephine that she would be on maternity leave.

"I totally blanked on making the appointment. Now I remember getting a reminder call. But I blanked on that too. I go every three months, and I normally make the appointments ahead of time, but I guess with the move and all the other stuff going on—" Josephine stared into her plate. "Since I've been getting the injection, my periods have been erratic. So that wasn't odd."

Fat could hardly contain herself. "What are you thinking?"

"I'm thinking: Is this really happening? If so, can I do this? I think I'm happy. I know I'm scared. I have so many questions. For one: Does this mean we stay in Majestic Hills?"

"But first . . ."

"I know, I know. First I need to find out. But I've never felt this way in my life."

Lunch ran longer than Josephine expected and by the time the train arrived in New Pointe, it was late afternoon. At home, she dropped her coat and book bag at the door. She jogged up the stairs to the bathroom, pulling the pregnancy test from the back of the vanity drawer. It was the second of two from the package Lonnie had given her that night on the Fourth. She peed on the stick, placed it on a paper towel on the counter, and set the timer on her phone. For the next five minutes she stared at the stick. She paced around it. She looked out the window at a bank of orange-tinged clouds skimming the horizon.

She waited and waited until, like magic, she saw the two distinct solid red lines. She felt faint. Not pass-out faint. But like she was floating. She tried to call Langdon but only got his voicemail. She texted him to call her immediately. She had great news. Great? Yes, great news. She wanted to tell Fat, but she knew she couldn't tell anyone before telling Langdon.

She needed fresh air. Langdon's birthday was in a few weeks—and their anniversary shortly afterward—and she considered surprising him with the news on one of those dates. But who was she kidding? She couldn't sit on this. She pulled on one of Langdon's sweatshirts, yanking the hood over her head. She loved that she could smell him on it. She stepped into her snow boots and tucked in her earbuds, belting out "Pink + White" by Frank Ocean to calm her nerves.

Josephine stood out on the patio, but she was too antsy to sit—even on the stoop. She made her way to the pond and stared for a while at the water and bobbing chunks of ice. Then she circled back between her house and Jackson and Khai's, on her way to the rear of the property. She hadn't been there in weeks, and she needed to walk.

The light from the setting sun filtered through the trees, casting the late afternoon in a fiery glow. The backdrop recalled the evening when her father-in-law thought that Jackson and his friends, in their white hoods and jumpsuits, looked like the KKK. She couldn't wait to tell Langdon's parents about the baby.

As she walked, she felt so much joy, then so much fear, then utter disbelief at the thought of a little one.

What she did not realize was that she had been drifting across property lines. Instead of walking due west, she was walking southwest, her music blasting through her earbuds, her head bobbing to the beat as she sang.

Just then she heard a gunshot blast. She had become somewhat accustomed to the sound because of the weekend hunters.

But this was not the weekend. And the sound was too close.

Too loud.

She heard a second gunshot and then felt pain on her upper arm near her shoulder. A burning, searing pain that somehow simultaneously made her arm feel numb and on fire.

She ducked, falling to her knees onto the snow and yanking out her earbuds.

"What the fuck?"

CHAPTER THIRTY-FOUR

have you ever . . .

Josephine saw Marc sprinting toward her first. Christopher was a blur, running clumsily behind him, as though his legs were shackled. What was clear, however, was the rifle slung over his shoulder.

"Get away from me!" She started kicking at them both. Her breath trembled.

Backing up, Marc slammed into a tree. "I'm here to help, Josephine. Look at me. I'm dialing nine one one." To the dispatcher, he said, "I'm reporting shots fired in Majestic Hills." He paused. "I don't know." Another pause. "Please, just come."

Marc placed his hand over his phone. "Your sleeve," he said to Josephine.

It was nearly dark, and with the last vestiges of sunlight she could see a rip in the fabric and then blood.

"I didn't mean to—" Christopher pleaded. "I didn't."

He turned, and she glimpsed a handgun, in addition to the rifle, tucked into the back of his pants.

"I didn't know it was you. I thought—"

"Are you shot?" Marc asked Josephine.

She didn't answer. His lips continued to move, but she could not fully make out what he was saying. He sounded muffled, as though she were underwater trying to listen to him.

"I think it nicked you," he said.

Christopher's eyes were wild. "Shit. Oh, shit! Shit, shit! I'm so sorry." Spittle lined his mouth. "I didn't mean it." He began to ramble—semi-coherently—about being home alone and looking out the nursery window and seeing what he thought was a prowler.

A tall, thin man.

A tall, thin brown man.

A tall, thin brown man in a hoodie and blue jeans walking toward the pond, circling back, and walking in the woods, away from the houses.

"I thought," he said, turning to Marc and then to Josephine, "What if this guy has stolen something or vandalized somebody else's property?" I ran to my cabinet and—I only intended to volley a warning shot up in the air. I promise you. I only meant to scare him off."

Josephine remembered listening to him talk about hunting. She knew now that what Christopher sniffed was an animal, prey. What he'd said he had a nose for in the woods. For him, the hunt fed a desire as primal and piquant as the taste of blood. She knew that when he'd lifted the rifle to look out the scope, he'd seen a dark-skinned profile—someone who was strutting and bobbing his head and *trespassing*.

Christopher was wheezing, hyperventilating.

"Pull it together," Marc told him, saying under his breath, "Goddamn George Zimmerman."

"Marc." Josephine beckoned him closer. "Lang can't know that he shot at me."

Marc's expression changed. They both watched Christopher heave and begin to retch.

Josephine pulled Marc closer to her.

"Langdon can't know, because he will throttle that man—or worse." She looked toward Christopher. "There's already bad blood between them. Lang will rip him apart and spend the rest of his life in prison. Do you understand? A man shot at his pregnant wife . . ."

"Pregnant?" Marc mouthed.

"I just found out," Josephine said, touching her abdomen. "You'd better act surprised when he tells you. I don't want him in prison. I want him with me." She held her hand over the rip in her sleeve as if to conceal it. "I have to go in the house and get rid of this thing."

She started to stand and Marc helped her. She looked him squarely in his eyes.

"What happened is this: I heard one shot. Only one. It scared me, and I fell. And that explains the scratch on my arm. I tripped and fell."

She recalled what she'd said to Christopher in the courtroom after the bond hearing: "Have you ever made a horrible mistake? Have you ever done something you later regretted?"

"Marc, you get Christopher onboard," she said, racing through the snow to the house.

Inside, she took off the hoodie and threw it in the back of a closet. The wound resembled a rug burn. She placed a bandage over it and put on her sweater and coat.

She watched through the window at Marc helping Christopher compose himself.

When the ambulance pulled into her driveway, followed shortly afterward by three police cars, Josephine told the officers that she was fine, but the gunshot blast had made her fall. Because she was pregnant, she wanted to make sure the baby was okay.

She overheard Christopher telling another officer that he had seen what he believed to be a prowler.

"Given what happened to my house, I've been on high alert. I fired up into the air."

"Which you know is illegal here," the officer said.

"I know," Christopher said.

"Where are your weapons now, sir?"

"Back there on my patio."

The officer read Christopher his rights, handcuffed him, and placed him in a police car.

CHAPTER THIRTY-FIVE

this just felt sullied

The sun had set when Langdon turned onto Willow. He saw the lights from the first responders immediately and sped toward them. As he pulled into his driveway behind a patrol car, he saw Josephine inside the ambulance, a paramedic strapping her into a gurney. Marc stood by the door, and Josephine was laughing. Still, Langdon hurried to her.

"I'm fine," Josephine said to Langdon preemptively. "Marc, tell my husband everything's okay."

"She's fine," Marc said. "I'll give you two a moment."

Langdon jumped into the seat next to the gurney. He placed his hand on the side of Josephine's face. "What is going on?" He pulled out his wallet and showed the paramedic his hospital ID.

"I work in the emergency room at Chicago Sinai. Please tell me her vitals."

The woman looked at the ID. "They're excellent, Dr. Blaque." She handed him a clipboard.

Josephine covered it with her hand. He moved her hand away.

"The only reason I'm in this contraption is because I have something to tell you." She turned to the paramedic. "Give us two seconds?"

"Just two, because we're about to get going," the woman said.

Josephine looked at Langdon. "We're having a baby."

"A baby?" For a second, it was as if the words transported him somewhere nicer than the back of an ambulance. "You're pregnant?"

"I think that's how it works." Josephine strummed her chin. "I took a tumble, and out of an 'abundance of caution,' as they say, I'm going to get an ultrasound. But, to be clear, it was like a slow-motion fall, and I'm sure any child of ours is already tough and—"

"You're happy about this?"

"Enormously happy, plus super, super scared."

He bent over and kissed her lips, her cheek, and the corner of her eye. When he brushed her left arm to hug her, she grimaced.

"What's the matter?" he said, touching her more gently.

"Just a flesh wound. Totally superficial."

He didn't believe her. "What happened, Josey?"

"I was walking in the woods, and a gun went off—our neighbor shot a gun in the air—and it startled me, and I tripped. But see? All is well. I'm fine."

"Our neighbor? Christopher?"

"Yes. I had on one of your hoodies, and I was walking in the woods. He thought I was a vandal or something, and he fired a warning shot up in the air. The noise threw me off-balance."

The paramedic returned, telling Langdon that he could follow them to Lutheran General, but he couldn't keep up with them.

"No speeding. No running red lights," she said.

"I know the drill."

Langdon hurried to the Land Cruiser. But he saw Christopher in the back seat of the patrol car. He was leaning forward, which Langdon assumed meant he was handcuffed.

Josephine fell in the woods? That didn't make sense.

Thinking about a baby, their baby, took his breath away. He always knew that if they had a daughter, Josephine would lobby for the name Fatima, or Nicole Fatima. But a boy—maybe Nicholas? He hadn't yet reconciled whether he could name a son Nicky. Now he felt, God willing, he'd have to work that out soon.

But first things first: Josephine fell in the woods. Their neighbor believed she was a prowler. He got his gun and fired up into the sky. It still didn't make sense. Langdon's father often said, "There's the good version of a story, and the real version."

He would bet his life that this was not the real version.

As Langdon reached Goodenow, the ambulance transporting his pregnant wife pulled away. Its lights glowed in the distance until they disappeared. He was sure they'd keep her overnight. Her age made her pregnancy high-risk.

For years, when he fantasized about the moment that he learned Josephine was pregnant, he had envisioned being overcome by a singular, solitary emotion: unadulterated joy. A moment when his whole world shifted and his heart ached with happiness.

But this. This was not that. This just felt sullied.

And it was all Christopher's fault.

CHAPTER THIRTY-SIX

the dark side

Langdon spent the night on the sofa in the hospital room. He hardly closed his eyes. As Josephine slept, he couldn't stop staring at the ultrasound photo. Fourteen weeks pregnant. *Hey, you*, he thought, holding the photo. He wanted desperately to call his parents to tell them about the baby. But he'd have to explain why Josephine was in the hospital. He wasn't ready for that. Hell, he didn't really know himself. He certainly had his suspicions. He could hardly keep his eyes off the bandage on her arm.

When Langdon was in medical school, he'd met a Black doctor who encouraged him to spend a year or two in Chicago's Cook County Hospital or a rural clinic in the South or in the Rust Belt.

"It's the volume, man," he'd said. "You'll be so much quicker at identifying diseases that present in unusual ways, not to mention the people who lie—lie right to your face and lie even more fervently to themselves."

Langdon had seen myriad gunshot wounds. The ones that looked like circular clusters of pomegranate seeds. The ones shaped like small birds, with blood crusted and haloed around them. The ones that looked like pale, fleshy morning glories. The horrible ones that resembled contorted, open ruby-red mouths in the middle of a scream. A grazing was different. They were what one might imagine. Skid marks on the ground or contrails in the sky that varied in shape and depth, width and length.

He'd thought about this the night before, when the doctor came in to see Josephine's arm.

"I hear you had a fall?" she'd said to Josephine.

"I am so embarrassed," Josephine responded.

"Can I take a look?"

"Langdon, honey." She rarely called him *honey*. "Can you go get me some water? I'm so thirsty."

"Absolutely." He nodded. "But first I want to take a look, too."

The doctor removed the bandage. "Hmm, it's not so bad," she said.

And it wasn't, Langdon thought. *For a bullet wound.*

He placed the ultrasound photo on the sofa and left the hospital room to call Lonnie. Her hands were still full with Wade, but he needed a favor.

"That New Pointe police officer you're friends with," he said. "Can you call him? A neighbor was arrested last night. I'm wondering if you can find out the charges. His name is Christopher Thompson."

"I'm well aware of Christopher," Lonnie said. "No need for Adam. It'll be public record and online. I used to do this all the time when I covered the police beat. It's easier now."

Langdon paced the corridor, at the end of which was a large window. He walked down to it and looked outside at yet another wooded area. He was no longer enamored with trees.

His phone rang.

"What's up, Lonnie?"

"Your neighbor has been charged with disorderly conduct. It says he shot into the air to fend off what he thought was an intruder. But it was actually—what the hell—Josephine Blaque?"

"Yeah. I'm pretty lit up about it," he said. "She's fine. But she spent the night in the hospital as a precaution. We're still here."

"Why is she in the hospital if she's fine?"

Langdon took a breath. "Okay. You can't say anything, but she'd just found out she was pregnant—"

"You're having a baby? Oh, that makes me so, so happy!"

"Well, Josephine says she tripped because the gun blast frightened her. She wanted to make sure the baby's okay. And he or she is."

"Despite my youngest recently losing his mind, I still view parenthood as magical."

"It is pretty wonderful, isn't it?" Langdon said. "But then this happened. This fucking guy gave her such a hard time about defending Wade. And he gets off with a disorderly? I can't let this go. Can I?"

"Here's the thing. New Pointe has an ordinance that says shooting into the air in a residential area is illegal. Your neighbor could have been charged with reckless discharge of a firearm, but he's a good ol' boy, and somebody, maybe his lawyer, probably said, 'Oh, he didn't mean it. Even though he's a hunter and certainly knows better, he's been jittery because somebody tore up his house. Can't we let this slide?'"

Langdon walked back down the hall, looking in on Josephine through the door's glass window. "What if—and this is only a hypothetical: What if he'd shot *at* her?"

"Well, your lawyer will tell you that's vastly different territory. Whether he hit her or not, that would be aggravated discharge of a firearm. It's a Class one felony. And that's between four to fifteen years in prison. But that, too, is probationable with the right attorney. Why do you ask? Is there something more to the story?"

"I can't say right now, Lonnie. But thank you. I've got to get back to her."

Langdon opened the door to find Josephine snoring lightly. He lay next to her, placing his hand on her abdomen. She jumped lightly, covering his hand with hers. She fell off again, and he couldn't help wondering: If his suspicions were correct, how could she possibly sleep?

At home, they sat on the sofa in the family room making the requisite phone calls about the pregnancy. The first, which was on the speaker, was to his parents. Elise screamed at the news, and Jules cried.

To Elise, Jules said, "Get your things together, we're driving down."

"Honey, we can't just pop in," she replied. "They may have something to do."

Jules returned to the phone. "Y'all got something to do?"

"Not at all. Yay!" Josephine said, her head on Langdon's shoulder. "Please come!"

Langdon laughed. It was the first time he'd done so all day, the first time he wasn't distracted by the acid roiling in his stomach. "You're welcome to come, Dad."

"We're on our way," Jules said. "We'll bring ice cream."

In the background, as Jules was hanging up, they heard Elise ask, "Why ice cream?"

"Because that's what you do—"

Next, Josephine used her phone to FaceTime Fat. She, Ken, and the boys were in their car. Fat screamed, not letting on that she'd correctly guessed the day before.

"You guys are no longer enviable," Ken said. "Welcome to the dark side."

"It's not dark," Fat said. She lowered her voice. "Well, it is a little. I'll call you later."

This was what Langdon had envisioned. All of this. The excitement surrounding a new child. The overflow of affection and joy.

Just as he'd started to lower his guard, the doorbell rang. Several neighbors assembled in the driveway: Marc and Danny, offering flowers; Bonnie and Bryce, presenting a casserole and two cloth bags of groceries; Khai and Jackson, holding a wicker basket and gift bags. The Majestic Hills residents knew only what Marc had told them: that Christopher had thought Josephine was an intruder and lobbed a warning shot.

"Wow!" Langdon placed his hand over his heart. "Thank you all so much."

Despite all this, he knew that he and his wife needed to have a conversation about what really happened.

Soon.

CHAPTER THIRTY-SEVEN
troubled

Over the next few days, Josephine had trouble sleeping. The lie needled her. She understood her reason for telling it, and she truly believed she'd done the right thing. Still, she had never told Langdon a lie this big, this consequential. She felt enormous pangs of guilt. As each day passed, she fully expected the lie to become impossible to bear or correct.

The afternoon they'd left the hospital was the first time she'd seen him walking in the woods, trying to parse out what happened. She knew how his mind worked. He was wondering *How did my wife fall and hurt her arm?* She'd watched Langdon from their bedroom window, trudging back and forth along the southern edge of their property. There was no way he could see beyond Khai and Jackson's backyard to Monica and Christopher's, but he was looking in that direction.

As the days passed, she'd watched him from the kitchen window and from the patio. Stooping, as if he were lining up a golf shot. Kneeling as if he were about to pray. Before the home invasion and the shooting, he would have simply walked unencumbered through the woods to get to Christopher's yard. But no one did that anymore—pretended there were no boundaries. That there were no consequences for taking liberties.

Josephine wondered if Langdon had gone over to Marc's property. Now, there—that's where he might have been able to see something: The path she had taken. The tree she tried to hide behind. Maybe Marc could have even been Langdon's tour guide. Although Josephine knew she'd had to confide in Marc, she hated doing so. He was Langdon's buddy, his running partner. Not hers. Why did she believe he owed her anything—especially his allegiance or silence?

And what if there was video from the cameras on Marc's house or Christopher's?

She decided that she had to tell Langdon. But she wasn't sure how—or even when.

A week after the shooting, Josephine sat in on a court appearance for Wade. Although she was no longer involved in Wade's case, she wanted to support him for his obstruction of justice hearing. And it was a welcome distraction. She still hadn't told Langdon the truth.

She entered the courtroom as the proceedings started and slid in behind Lonnie, placing her hand on Lonnie's shoulder. Lonnie stood quickly to hug her.

Judge Coles was already on the bench, talking to the attorneys. When they returned to their seats, she said, "Wade, because of this new evidence, the residential burglary and criminal damage to property charges against you have been dropped. However, because you lied to the police, you now face an obstruction of justice charge." She nodded to the prosecutor. "Attorney Penn?"

"We are willing to waive that in exchange for supervision and one hundred hours of community service."

"Your Honor," the defense said, "may I have a minute with my client?"

"You may."

Lonnie leaned forward and huddled with the attorney and Wade. Josephine heard her say, "Take it. Don't even think twice. You told me that you wished you could fix things. Take it, and you'll be finished before you go away this fall."

Wade nodded to his mother and the attorney.

"Your Honor," the attorney said. "My client will agree to supervision and one hundred expungeable hours of community service."

"Very good," the judge said. "Attorney Penn?"

"That's fine, Your Honor."

"Thank you, Ms. Stanfield," the judge said, grateful for Lonnie's input. The judge turned to Wade. "I hope you can use this as a learning experience and never be in this position again. It's beyond me why you landed here in the first place."

Josephine was about to stand to leave when Wade said, "I would like to explain, Your Honor."

What the hell? Josephine thought.

Wade's attorney looked at him, then said to the judge, "Your Honor, we're not prepared for this." He turned to Wade, urging him to be quiet, but the teen pushed back.

"Your Honor, my client insists on speaking, against the advice of his counsel," said his attorney.

"I would like to explain," Wade said again. He turned to his mother and Josephine. "I won't hang myself."

Wade faced the judge. "I am a troubled youth, Your Honor."

Little thief. Josephine smiled, recalling telling Wade about Langdon's run-in with the law as a teenager.

"But I am not your typical troubled youth. As you know, I come from a family of great means. I did not vandalize Mr. Thompson's Majestic Hills home. I sincerely apologize for lying. I did so because I believed that if the culprit did indeed come from the Grand Vistas, I would have a much better chance waging a fight in the criminal justice system.

"Lastly, Your Honor, there are many of us who can imagine what Mr. Thompson felt as he entered a house that had been turned upside-down. We can feel the horror of that type of destruction. The subtext is, if you work hard, you deserve a decent place to live . . . that we have what we have because we did most things right. And that people who live in trailer parks or public housing have what they have because they failed in some way. One of our greatest deficiencies is that far too few of us can relate to or understand a person whose life has delivered him to a moment when he believes his only recourse is to wreak devastation—to be that storm."

Wade sat. The judge remained quiet for a second. The only other people in the courtroom aside from the attorneys, Josephine, and Lonnie were the court reporter, the clerk, the bailiff, and Deputy Adam. They, too, were quiet. Josephine wished that Christopher had attended. It may not have made any difference, but she felt Wade deserved a much larger audience.

"Wade," the judge said, "you are certainly an eloquent and bright young man. Your attorney wrote that you'll be attending college in the fall. And you plan to find your place in social justice work?"

"Yes, ma'am," he said. "I mean, Your Honor."

"Godspeed, Wade. I wish you well."

Wade left the courtroom with Adam. Lonnie turned to Josephine and rolled her eyes.

"Really?" Lonnie said. "I swear that boy is trying to kill me. But I am not giving him the pleasure." Her face turned serious. "I want to thank you again, Josephine, for pinch-hitting. You could have said no, but—"

"I'm having a baby," Josephine blurted, pointing to her midsection. "When I found out, you were one of the first people I wanted to tell."

Josephine briefly considered confiding in Lonnie about what really happened during the shooting. But that was out of the question. What happened was too deeply personal, and if she told anyone, she'd have to tell Langdon first.

"A baby . . ." Lonnie sang. She rose and sat next to Josephine, hugging her. "You look happy? A far cry from that night on the Fourth."

Josephine nodded. "You gave me a gift—that test. It was a twofer, and that's how I found out about this." Josephine's expression turned urgent. "You have any advice?"

"Me? Advice?" Lonnie waved her hand around the courtroom. "Case in point? My children said that I favored Wade because he was the last and he looks more like me than the others. Of course I believe

I treated each of them according to their needs. What can I tell you?" She held up her hands. "All I know for sure is that I'm moving on. I feel myself pulling away from the house, the property, New Pointe. After all these years, I'm finally leaving and letting go. Wade is bypassing Princeton and NYU to attend Fisk University."

"In Nashville, where Benny is," Josephine said.

"Who knows where that child is by now. My son thinks he'll one day run into him. As if time and people stand still. What are the odds? Anyway, once Wade leaves, I'm moving to New York to write. We have a brownstone there."

Lonnie flipped through her cell phone as she spoke.

"A friend has invited me to dinner and dancing. Monroe Stevenson is a past president of the National Association of Black Journalists, and a former conquest. He was a couple of years behind me at NYU. Back then, he used to sell incense on the street corner, wearing a burgundy leather jacket. Sexy as hell."

Lonnie held up her phone to show Josephine a photo of a dark, brown-skinned man with a gray goatee.

"He's divorced now and living in New York. Writes for *The Atlantic*."

"So handsome," Josephine said. "I'm loving that smile."

"Probably old and broke down." Lonnie laughed but quickly got serious. "I do have advice about child-rearing." She turned, facing Josephine squarely. "It goes so fast, Josephine. People say that. One minute they're on your hands and the next they're on your heart. But you won't believe it because the beginning is so exhausting. Sometimes it will help that you have a partner in this; sometimes it won't. Children learn fast how to divide and conquer. But you and Langdon are a good team."

Josephine's smile turned tepid, and she thought, *If you only knew.*

Lonnie nudged her shoulder.

"You *are* a *great* team, and you're so lucky," she said. "I miss Geoffrey so much, sometimes I feel like I'm losing my mind. The pain is yesterday, today, and tomorrow. Wade and I were in that house—

his grief and mine, two great beasts circling each other. We could hear each other's sobs, yet we couldn't console each other."

Josephine detected a sense of urgency about Lonnie. As if she were trying to cram into this moment everything she'd wanted to say over the last several months.

"When Wade left for the Grand Vistas—and I haven't said this to anyone else—a part of me was relieved. You see why I shouldn't give advice? I made sure he was safe, but for the first two days I could cry and allow the anguish to pour out of me. I had nothing left to give. And there was comfort in being selfish."

Josephine took Lonnie's hands in hers. "Will you sell the house?"

"I've begun the process of transforming it and the surrounding acres into the Stanfield Institute. It's something Geoffrey and I planned to do. We wanted innovators in journalism, STEM, and the arts to come together and share ideas. Try to make this world fairer. And, of course, it will include a writer's retreat, with cute little cottages scattered throughout the property. It will be open most of the year for programming. The only exception will be in December, when, I'm hoping, the entire brood will converge on the house for the holidays. I want you and Langdon to know that you and your family are always welcome to join us—regardless of whether you stay in town."

Josephine wiped her eyes. "You'd better accept that Monroe guy's invitation."

"Hell, yeah, I'm accepting."

The two women dapped each other.

"And it's my hope that every time I walk through Washington Square Park, I'll begin to believe that the city that gave me my first great love might offer up . . . another."

CHAPTER THIRTY-EIGHT
we should talk

As Langdon approached Majestic Hills, a clap of thunder distracted him, and the Land Cruiser veered off the road a bit. He regained control as he passed the country club. Above-freezing temperatures in recent days had melted much of the snow. Only a few mounds of ice remained atop the saturated ground.

Before turning into the subdivision, he glanced across the street at the hunting area. He'd had a rare, quiet night in the emergency room, and he'd had time to think about what couples shared and what they kept from each other. People tended to want to know the exact moment a marriage dissolved—an affair, a financial dispute, drugs, or alcohol. Sometimes it was not a cataclysmic event, but a series of minor deceptions, quiet compromises, seemingly inconsequential deceits.

He was angry. It had been ten days—yes, he was counting—since the shooting, and Josephine still had not told him the truth about it. As he entered their driveway, he said over and over to himself, "Can we talk? We should talk."

Once home, he sat at the kitchen table, waiting until it was time to pick her up from the train station. He looked out the window at the rain and over his shoulder at the clock. He understood that having this conversation would mean risking the ache of knowing. A part of him appreciated the uncertainty—the minute possibility that he was wrong.

At eight p.m., he picked her up, standing outside the turnstile with his umbrella. She gave him her classic hug and kiss. "Happy Friday night," she said.

When they arrived home, she took off her coat and patted her midsection.

"Nothing seems to fit," she said, grabbing a bottle of water from the refrigerator. "I'm running upstairs to change into stretch pants. Hope you're still up for a movie."

He placed his hand on her arm. "Can we talk?"

She tipped her head forward. "Is everything okay?"

Langdon knew it was Josephine's tell when she was scared or nervous. He motioned for her to sit at the table, and he sat across from her. "Do you trust me, Josey?"

"Of course. Where is this going?"

"Ever since I took out that money for the deposit—"

"We got beyond that, Lang."

"Yes," he said, nodding. "But I think something has broken in us—"

"Broken?"

"There was a crack that's been deepening and widening."

She looked scared, but not confused. He could see her breath fluttering in her throat.

He swallowed. "Why didn't you tell me Christopher shot at you—and please, please don't lie to me, Josey."

Outside, the rain splashed against the window and poured into the gutters. He heard the attempts the house made to push back against the wind.

"I didn't want you to lose your temper, and maybe"—she took a sip of water—"hurt that man."

"You thought I was incapable of restraint?"

"Lang, I ran the film in my head. I saw you beating the shit out of him. I imagined you getting arrested. I know how you feel about him."

"Yeah, he's a condescending, grade A douche. But how I feel about him is irrelevant. When have I ever shown you that I was capable of violence? Maybe this is about something in *your* character, Josey. Not mine."

His hands were folded on the table, and she placed hers on the table, too, around her bottle of water.

"I'm always afraid of losing you," she said. "When you're in the emergency room, or running, or—"

"You can't live in fear, and neither can I."

"We all live in fear." She sighed. "They fear us. We fear them. And sometimes we fear us and them." She peered down into her lap. "I deeply, deeply apologize."

He believed she was sincere, but that alone didn't seem sufficient.

"Josey, every day, all kinds of people look at me and think I lack self-control, assume I'm violent. All kinds of people think they know me. But my own wife?"

He got up and walked over to the door to the patio. Flashes of lightning illuminated puddles in the backyard.

"I'm a grown-ass man, and you have to trust that I'm smart enough not to go to prison. At the same time, a man aimed his gun at my wife—my pregnant wife—cocked it, and pulled the trigger. And you chose not to tell me? It makes me wonder what else you've tried to save me from. How do you think that makes me feel?"

"Awful, and I'm truly sorry. I've been trying to find a way to tell you—"

"You've been trying to find a way—to tell me that he shot at you?" His raised voice surprised her as he walked back to the table and sat. "He was on his high horse about Wade when he thought Wade had busted up his shit. Then, at his first opportunity, he shot at a person he thought was a Black man. And he only got a fucking disorderly!"

"I know this is bad," she said, her palms pressing down on the table.

"I hired an attorney. We've got a meeting with the police chief on Monday."

Josephine opened her mouth, and for the longest time, no words came out.

"They need to know the truth. I want the charges elevated to aggravated discharge of a firearm."

"Langdon, honey, I lied to the police. That's obstruction of justice. What I just went through with Wade."

"Nobody's going to accuse you of obstruction of justice."

"Lang." Josephine touched his hand, and he gently pulled it away.

"You were pissed off at me about that twenty-five thousand dollars." He pointed to her wedding band. "I remember you twisting your ring. Scared the living shit out of me."

Her face fell slack, and she placed her hand atop his. Again, he pulled it away.

"You said you doubted whether you could trust me," he said. "And never did I lie to you. Not once. So why shouldn't I doubt *you* right now? Why shouldn't I be twisting *my* ring right now?"

"I should have told you, Lang. I made a mistake. And as the days passed, I didn't know how to disentangle myself from it. I'm so, so sorry. But I'll ask you what you asked me: Can you ever forgive me?"

His fingers formed a steeple. He tapped the tips of his forefingers together. "I don't know."

"What? Okay. This is huge. I know that. I get it. It's awful. I fucked up royally, but Langdon, we can fix it. It's not irreparable."

He got up again and pushed the chair under the table.

"When we were first dating, I stood behind you and said 'Fall back.'" He stretched out his arms. "Do you remember that?"

She nodded.

"I said 'Don't even think about it, just let go. I will catch you. I promise you.' And what happened?"

"I—I couldn't do it."

"I said this is a classic trust experiment. And you couldn't do it. But you know what I knew, down to my marrow? If Fat—and I love her—but if she asked you, you wouldn't have to think about it. Does she know Christopher shot at you?"

"No. No. The only person who knows, other than Christopher, is Marc. He was there when it happened, and I asked him not to tell you."

His jaw clenched. "This gets better and better."

"Langdon." She grabbed his hand.

"He shot at my wife. I'm sorry—my pregnant wife—and you decided to protect me because I'm this animal who lacks so much self-control that you couldn't tell me."

She was biting her fingernails, a childhood habit she'd given up years ago. He'd never seen her do this.

He left the kitchen, went into the family room. and turned on a video game. He played for twenty minutes and lifted himself to see Josephine still seated at the table. There was a blind spot when looking into the kitchen from the family room, but he could see her reflection in the glass doors. He played for another thirty minutes, and she was still sitting there, her hands clasped on top of the table. When he finished the game, it occurred to him that he'd read studies in which sitting for long periods affected an expecting mother's mental health and her endocrine system. He thought about the way babies experienced trauma in utero, how some kids could be marked before they were born.

He stood up one more time to see her, but she was gone.

CHAPTER THIRTY-NINE

mea culpable

The tornado began as a brooding, whimpering wind that built slowly as it moved across the property that had been the Grand Vistas and south over the acres of cornfields now designated for the Majestic Hills expansion. It reached the subdivision and cherry-picked its way through the woods, uprooting trees here and there, tossing them about at will.

All night, Langdon had struggled to sleep. He was downstairs chugging orange juice from a carton—knowing Josephine would have chided him for doing so—when he looked out the window. To his astonishment, the ground was convulsing, trees careening toward the house. For a second he felt like he was in a dream, until the entire house shook and he heard wood sundering and windows shattering. Dropping the carton, he rushed back upstairs.

A night-light in the hall made dust particles glimmer as they floated out of the room.

He stepped over glass and sticky, rain-slicked leaves to get to their bed. Tree limbs fanned out over it, along with a blanket of insulation and buckled drywall. The sky was a vivid palette of black, and he could see his breath in the air.

"Josey!" He started clawing through the debris on the bed, splintered wood slicing him across his right eyebrow and arms. "Josey!"

"Lang!" Her voice came from the bathroom, sounding shaky. "Lang!"

He ran to the door. "I'm here, Josey." He twisted the knob, but the door didn't move.

"There's a tree blocking it," she said, sounding far away.

A cold breeze blew across his bare feet.

"It came in through the window—" Her voice was cracking. "Like someone threw a javelin, and now the branches are splayed against the door."

"Can you break off the smaller ones?" He blinked to clear grit from his eyes.

"I have to get on my knees to try to get closer," she said.

All he could hear was scratching and thudding, each sound terrifying.

"Lang." She was by the door. "It's wedged in tight. And it's huge."

"Let me try." He hoped to sound calm, but fear penetrated him. "I'm right here."

From the bedroom, the door looked as though he could simply push it open.

"Move out of the way," he said.

He imagined her backing up quickly, cradling her abdomen. She'd become so protective of the baby.

"I'm away!"

He led with his shoulder, transforming his body into a battering ram. Wires dangled like tentacles over his head. She squealed every time he connected. The frame creaked, but the door didn't budge.

He had done this once before, when his brothers messed up his normally neat bedroom and locked him out of it. He was eight years old, crying and flailing his little body against the door's seemingly impenetrable surface. And this time, like the last, he kicked with his bare feet and pounded with his fists, again and again.

Finally, he stopped. The door hadn't moved.

"Lang," Josephine yelled. "This isn't working, is it?"

"Josey, I—"

The wind hissed and howled, and the house shuddered again.

"I've got to get something to tear this door down."

"No! No! No!"

He looked down to see her fingers, flecked with dirt, reaching out under the door.

"Please, don't leave me, Lang."

"Josey, I've got to try another way," he said. He bent to touch her fingers.

"Lang!"

"I promise! Listen to me, okay? I promise. I'll be right back."

He ran down the hall, but for the first time, he had no plan. Langdon July Blaque III always had a plan. The house was eerily dark, and he felt like he was staring down a shaft. Something had begun to smolder. He remembered Jackson recommending that he purchase an array of tools. Now he wished he'd gotten every one of them.

In the kitchen, in the light of the moon, he whirled around, searching. Maybe he could pry the door apart instead of trying to burst through it. What he needed was something akin to a wrecking ball, which was exactly the way his heart felt pounding in his chest. As he was about to run into the garage, he thought about the fire extinguisher under the sink. He grabbed it, ran back upstairs, and began to swing it against the door.

For the longest time, the door seemed unwilling, unable to relent. Tree limbs snapped overhead, and pieces of flashing whizzed by.

"Please, God," he said. He glanced up at the sky. "Please."

Langdon heard a crack, and he kept swinging until one panel of wood gave way, then another. He threw the fire extinguisher down and wrenched the door apart with his hands.

"C'mon, Josey!" He was so happy, he felt lightheaded.

He pushed his glasses up the bridge of his nose. But as he helped pull Josephine across the threshold, the house seemed to sway. He helped her stand. "Hurry," he said, taking her hand. They ran down the stairs and out the door to the driveway.

They stood there, he in his undershirt and boxers, she in his oversize Morehouse T-shirt. The wind calmed, allowing them a clearer view. The toppled trees. Their neighbors' belongings strewn about. The rain had hammered the ground so furiously that the softened asphalt began to devour their mailbox and massive slabs of concrete in their driveway. The area looked like it existed in an alternate dimension—a place with no laws governing gravity or motion, mass or time.

There had been no warning. Even the town's bad weather detection system had colluded and fallen mute. So sensitive was it to the subtlest atmospheric disturbances that it sometimes gave off a full-throated holler during a particularly spirited thunderstorm. But nothing that night.

Josephine and Langdon were surveying the damage when they heard an explosion. They had no idea where it came from. When trees started upending behind them, they ran, joining their neighbors as they funneled into the clubhouse.

Langdon helped Josephine to a corner of the main room, which was cast in a pale yellow light. The French doors clattered, and in the distance, the sirens blended into the background. Langdon had a ludicrous thought about all the fundraising robocalls he'd ignored from the local fraternal order of police and the volunteer firefighters. Now he wished he'd donated to both. He dragged two chairs against a wall and unfolded a throw from the back of a sofa, draping it around Josephine's shoulders. He touched her abdomen.

"You have any pain?" He peeled foliage from her shins.

"Not at all." Her teeth chattered. "But you're bleeding." She traced his brow with her thumb.

"I'm okay." He felt around her neck, along her arms. She let out a shallow cry when he touched her spine. He removed the throw and lifted her T-shirt. He winced.

"That bad?" she asked.

Twigs had lashed and gouged her back. He knew she was in shock and would feel the onslaught of pain later. The photo of his ancestor from the Fourth of July immediately came to mind. That rendering showing the scars across her shoulders.

"You'll need a few stitches," he said, hoping to downplay the severity of it.

He knelt and saw surface scratches on her calves and bare feet. He placed his hand on her abdomen again, then lay his head on it.

"I'm fine," she said, beginning to cry. "I'm fine. I am fine."

At first he appeared to be listening for the baby, but he began to breathe hard, and he could feel his own heart pounding against her lap. He held her so tight it almost hurt.

He, too, began to cry.

For a few seconds they felt alone in a space teeming with people. And for a few seconds they lost themselves—until Bonnie called out, "We need some help here!"

Bryce hobbled in, leaning on Bonnie and barely able to put weight on his left foot.

"Go," Josephine said to Langdon, nodding toward Bryce. "Go, do you."

A handful of neighbors had had the presence of mind to grab their cell phones, and Langdon glanced around as they moved throughout the clubhouse holding them up—near windows that were quickly fogging—searching for bars and reception.

"Did you hear that explosion?" Bryce said, panting as Langdon wrapped his ankle in torn sections of a towel.

"Probably a gas line," said Marc, staring at his phone. To no one in particular, he added, "Danny and I used to track storms on the Weather Channel."

Langdon was finishing wrapping Bryce's ankle when Christopher burst in, holding little Moni, with Monica right behind him. The baby's body was limp and a shocking gray-blue. She wore only a diaper. Monica and Christopher were sobbing. Monica's hands were bleeding and muddy. Christopher's face and arms were slashed. Their nightclothes were in tatters. Christopher hurried over to Langdon.

"Please, can you—" He thrust his daughter at Langdon as if she were a sacrifice.

Langdon took the baby and rushed over to the pool table. The residents standing around scattered to allow him through.

"I felt it," Monica cried. She held both hands over her neck as though she were about to choke herself. "There's something lodged in her throat, but, oh God, I think I pushed it down farther. Oh, God! Oh, God!"

Langdon quickly made sure there was no head or chest or abdominal injury. He opened little Moni's mouth and placed his ear against it. When he heard nothing, he sat her up on the pool table. She resembled a dirt-stained, waterlogged doll with articulated limbs full of welts. He placed his hand on the front of her neck, holding her head up.

With the flat of his other hand, he slapped her against her back.

The room was still enough to hear the thwack and the gasps of the residents. The clap of a heavy hand against a baby's back. They recoiled, as if they could feel it.

"I was digging through—" Christopher started. "Lightning flashed, and Monica saw Moni's bassinet in a tree. I climbed—"

"Quiet." Langdon placed his ear against the baby's chest.

He flipped her upside down, propping his leg against the pool table, supporting her neck and head on his lap. He gave her five thwacks to her back, aiming downward.

One. Two. Three. Four. Five.

"Can you, can you do that thing with the pen?" Monica said, rocking, her hands clasped in prayer. "Where you blow into her neck?"

"Quiet," Langdon said. He knew he was losing time.

C'mon, Langdon. C'mon, God.

He sat the baby upright again and stuck his finger in her mouth to try to feel what Monica felt, hoping he could pluck it out. When he couldn't, he lay her flat on her back on the table and tried the

Heimlich. Three quick thrusts between her little ribs. He was about to begin CPR, when he saw a slight lump in her throat. He hoped that something had dislodged just enough to make a difference.

He turned her upside down again. Thwack. Thwack. Thwack.

This time, a small, smooth landscaping rock flew from her mouth.

Almost instantly she began to cry and turn pink. Smiling, Langdon held her up again, and she peed, her diaper overflowing onto the pool table and him. He laughed, and everybody cheered quietly so that they wouldn't upset her.

He handed her to Monica, who rocked her back and forth, sobbing.

Josephine placed her hand on Langdon's back. An aftershock moved through him, his body shivering. He turned around to hold her, burying his face in her neck. He thought about the little boy with the missing sock. The child who had been on the trauma table months ago. The one who had been shot and eluded danger the first time only to succumb the second time.

The thing he regretted about that night, the thing he never said aloud, was that he left as the staff was lining up along the hall outside the bay to honor the boy. Langdon had felt like he'd failed him and didn't deserve to stand there. He knew he did the best he could when he first treated him. What child gets shot twice? Had he prayed for the boy?

It all felt so unfair, so random.

Jackson asked if anyone knew the time. Someone yelled, "Almost four thirty!"

Who cares? Langdon thought. Right now, in this moment, time was a useless, inconsequential thing. The sky, for one, offered no hint of daybreak. People were still in shock—having run for their lives and become homeless and lost their belongings. They were trying to digest it all. Who dared contemplate the next few minutes, or hours, or days? Yes, they were in the clubhouse, which was standing ostensibly only because of the hopscotch nature of the storm. But in their heads, they were still climbing through the wreckage, waking up into a nightmare. What use was there for the here and now when the not-so-distant past still played on a loop?

"You should sit," Josephine said, leading Langdon over to two empty chairs by the window. He collapsed onto one.

They were there only for a few minutes when Khai approached warily. She was wringing her hands, looking like she was seconds from turning away. But she stayed.

"After the shooting," she said, "I wanted to stop by alone, without the big crowd, but—"

"It's okay," Josephine said. "Thank you."

Khai was groping for words, just as she had the last time they sat in this room together.

"I—I'm so sorry, Josephine." Khai stared at her open palms. Her sleep mask dangled from her wrist. "You considered me your friend. And I didn't honor that. Mea culpable."

Mea culpable? Langdon thought. He saw Josephine roll her eyes. He expected that, but not what followed. Tears.

"See?" Josephine wagged her finger. "That's what I liked about you, Khai. The quick wit. That renegade spirit."

"I'm so sorry—"

"No, please." Josephine placed her hand over her mouth, but it was no match for what had burst open inside her, every emotion rushing to the fore.

"What we'd all been told—" Josephine said. "If we can live together, or work side by side. If we can get to know one another. It always feels like an experiment, you know?"

Across the room, little Moni cried but quickly settled down.

"Langdon's parents will probably insist that we stay with them until our tenants move out," Josephine said. "But when I think about this entire experience, our time together, it all breaks my heart."

Khai crouched beside Josephine. "When I told the police about the Thanksgiving family member, I never said it was *your* family member, Josephine."

"You didn't have to," Langdon said.

"Initially, I didn't want to move here," Josephine continued. "But I began to really like it, in no small part because of you. Now I think about the cost of putting down stakes. It makes me wonder: Where does my family fit?" She placed her hands on her abdomen. "And what about this little one?"

"You're having a baby?" Khai asked.

Josephine smiled, nodding. Langdon rubbed her shoulder. Her face turned solemn again.

"I wonder—can I keep this baby safe and healthy? Can I keep him or her hopeful? How do I make this child whole?" She turned to Langdon. "I've been trying to figure out where we could go that's best for the baby. Should we stay in the city? Try another suburb? It feels like *pick your poison*." Josephine took a breath. "My father thought his daughter, with her fancy schools and fancy job—he thought all this would give me more agency than he had. And it did. But to what end, you know? So much of it feels like such a waste."

"No, not a waste." Khai shook her head. "Not a waste. I'm hoping one day we—"

"Maybe." Josephine wiped her nose on her T-shirt and sat up straight. "There's so much to sort through right now." She had nothing more to say, and neither did Khai.

When the silence between them grew too uncomfortable, Khai said, "Congratulations, you two. I really, really mean that."

As Khai returned to Jackson across the room, Langdon saw Danny making her way toward the restroom. Her nightgown hung like loose skin, and a blanket lay heavily on her shoulders. She held on to the wall with each step, appearing so unsteady that Langdon caught up with her. She wore a turban, and when it slipped off her bald head, he helped slide it back on.

"I've got to pee," Danny said. "Marc went to get me water. I hear the bathrooms are a mess."

Langdon helped her inside, stepping back to give her privacy but standing close enough in case she called out. He saw Marc returning with the water and not finding Danny. He looked panicked as he scanned the room.

"She's in here!" Langdon waved at him, and he hurried over.

"Thank you, man." Marc's eyes filled with relief.

Danny left the bathroom, grabbing Langdon's arm instead of Marc's.

"He thinks I can't do anything by myself," she said to Langdon. "With your help, we showed him." She turned to her husband. "Be a dear and give us a few minutes?"

He nodded and left again.

"When I first saw him," Danny said, "I thought, what a beautiful man. I got to know him, and I loved the way his brain lit up about stuff way over my head. Steel beams and concrete foundations. The mathematics behind skyscrapers. Then I learned how much he loved running. How it unburdened his soul."

Langdon led her back to where she'd been sitting, almost directly across the room from Josephine. In front of her, Bonnie's sons were now asleep on the pool table. Bonnie stood over them.

"Do you remember what you thought when you first saw your wife?" Danny asked. "What you liked about her before you loved her? Do you remember your beginning? I promise you, at the end, that's all you'll think about. It will consume you."

Langdon was sure that Danny knew about the shooting. Spouses did that—shared secrets. He watched Bonnie sit beside Josephine. They were talking, but he couldn't hear them. He saw Bonnie place her hand on Josephine's abdomen and hug her.

"Do you remember?" Danny asked Langdon. "Because it is the only thing that will matter. More than all your squabbles and the ways you disappointed each other. More than the number of times you had to say I'm sorry. Or I forgive you."

As Bonnie returned to her boys, Marc approached Josephine, twisting open a bottle of water. He handed it to her and adjusted the blanket over her shoulders. He sat next to her to talk, and before long, she glanced at her midsection and then over at Langdon, pointing at him. She placed her hand over her heart.

"What did you like about her before you loved her? You remember?"

Eyes fixed on Josephine, Langdon answered silently. *Everything.*

By seven o'clock, the whir of rotors drew the neighbors to the window. A helicopter hovered over the pond, its searchlights trawling the water. The sky over Majestic Hills was becoming a perfect post-tornado blue. The roar of chain saws and woodchippers had replaced the wail of sirens, and the red and blue lights of first responders fought with the glaring sun.

Despite the devastation, the injuries were relatively minor.

Earthmoving machinery made Willow passable as the blond bricks were shunted off to the side, and what remained was a dirt and gravel road that no longer curved. The residents watched a short bus slowly making its way down Willow to the clubhouse. Cell phones were back online, and Langdon used Marc's mobile to call his parents and text Fat. He assured them that he and Josephine seemed okay and they were heading to the emergency room to check on the baby.

At the hospital, Josephine was set up in a bay and given an ultrasound while Langdon looked on, holding her hand. The lacerations on her back were tended to and bandaged. His shoulder was x-rayed, and although it wasn't broken, it was badly bruised and would need icing. He changed into a pair of scrubs and slip-resistant hospital socks. A doctor stitched the cut above his eyebrow.

Josephine was sound asleep as he tried his watch. The screen was shattered, but it still worked. He swiped gingerly through the local news feed, stumbling upon a video of Marc, Christopher, and him outside the clubhouse, waving at the helicopter. At the mouth of the subdivision was a staging area where there were ambulances, fire trucks, utility vans, county sheriff and village police cruisers. A graphic, along with a short story, showed the original aerial shot of Majestic Hills—the one used in the marketing campaign—and a new image of the subdivision from that morning. It allowed viewers to toggle left and right to compare the before and after.

The story said that Majestic Hills had borne the brunt of the storm.

Josephine had begun to stir when a nurse peeked in. "You have a bunch of people in the waiting area who are getting restless," she said, looking at a sheet of paper. "Several people with the last name Taylor. Lonnie Stanfield and her son. Elise and Jules Blaque." The nurse side-eyed Langdon. "Good grief, your mother could never deny you."

Langdon wiped his glasses on his shirt. "Maybe she should get a DNA test."

"Cue the laughter," Josephine said, placing her hand against his cheek.

"There's another couple," the nurse continued. "The man is kind and respectful. But his wife, Good Lord. Surly! She needs to be sedated."

Josephine and Langdon smiled at each other.

The nurse looked at Josephine. "She says she's your sister. Someone named—*Fat*?"

EPILOGUE

all that could be salvaged

As soon as Langdon pulled the rental car into the subdivision, he and Josephine saw three long white tents, under which were three long white tables holding what looked like the remnants of an archaeological dig. Their neighbors sifted through the items.

The Federal Emergency Management Agency's update said that the storm's debris field was about a mile and a half wide, and residents' belongings had been recovered along Old Creek Road, in the cemetery, and in the country club, as well as in backyards near and far. The items had been dropped off at the police station and the village hall. By Monday morning, three days after the storm, workers from the town and the local Red Cross had assembled the bulk of the things near the Majestic Hills arch.

This was not at all accounting for what remained buried beneath the houses.

For Josephine and Langdon, the goal of the day was to determine all that could be salvaged. They wanted photos, of course. Those of Langdon, Paul, and Nicky—as young boys. Those of Edward Taylor and Josephine. They wanted their framed diplomas and their favorite books and their laptops—and all their important documents. And, the Land Cruiser.

It wasn't lost on the Blaques that their marriage might be balancing atop the heap. In the middle of the tornado, having skirted death, they had forgiven each other and recommitted themselves to their vows. However, over the last forty-eight hours, they each quietly obsessed over the argument that had preceded the storm. Neither said a word about it. But they knew that the past had a way of resurfacing, bubbling up through fissures in the oddest of moments, and they wondered if they could bear and survive it all.

Rental cars and vans lined a berm near the arch. Langdon pulled up beside them. Loose stones had been carted off to the side, and the mangled metal part had twisted in half, separating the words *Majestic* and *Hills*.

Josephine and Langdon got out and stood, unsure which table to tackle first.

The hulking mounds seemed so daunting. To have your life on display, mixing and matching with the belongings of people with whom you've lived side by side.

One text from FEMA had warned residents to expect the unexpected.

When Langdon placed his hand in the pocket of his new jacket, he felt his to-do list. An asterisk was beside a two p.m. meeting at the police station with Deputy Adam. As far as Langdon was concerned, no matter what came up, he would keep that appointment.

The couple bided their time at the mouth of the subdivision. They knew that at some point they must turn the corner; they must take stock of the ruins, wrest meaning from what used to be their home, what briefly had been their community.

"Ready, Blaque?" Langdon asked, and held out his palm.

"Ready, Blaque." Josephine nodded, taking his hand.

Together, they walked in the direction of the rubble.

ACKNOWLEDGMENTS

Any author is fortunate to have *one* editor who believes in her, as well as in her work; who is patient, yet relentless in the pursuit of the story; and who is expert in helping to mold it. I am incredibly fortunate to have had *two* brilliant editors: Marysue Rucci and Anne Speyer. Your editorial prowess is unparalleled and not only enabled me to realize my vision for *Majestic Hills* but also exceed my wildest dreams. A hearty and heartfelt thank-you to you both.

Ayesha Pande, you are an exceptional literary agent and a true advocate. I'm grateful that you championed this project from the very beginning and guided me as I found my footing along the way. You will never know what your hard work and support have meant to me.

A huge thank you to Scribner's copyediting and production teams, as well as its publicity, marketing and sales staff whose members worked tirelessly to give this novel the absolute best launch possible.

My deepest thanks to author extraordinaire Christine Pride, my esteemed editor for *Three Girls from Bronzeville*, for encouraging me to pursue this project when it was little more than a musing, and for sharing your invaluable insights.

I'm grateful to Beth Kujawski and Jordan Miller for assisting me in honing early, raw drafts of the manuscript and allowing me to spitball and brainstorm ideas.

I so appreciate the men of the Chicago-based Visible Man Review (VMR), a group of professional Black and brown brothers who love reading and meet regularly to talk about books, their families, life, and work. Several members read an early draft of my manuscript and convened virtually on the night before Thanksgiving, 2024, to discuss my pages. VMR founder Alex Breland sent me the transcript of their conversation. The insights of Breland, Cameron Barnes, Eric Flatt, Marcus Thomas, and Gessel Berry—my real-life cousin—were outstanding and illuminating.

Thank you to Mikal Ramadan, a retired emergency department physician, for sharing your vast medical expertise. And, thank you to physician Constance Shabazz for your stories about your work providing healthcare to residents in beleaguered communities.

I'm grateful to Kathy Bankhead, a former assistant state's attorney, who answered all my questions about courtroom procedures and pertinent Illinois statutes and codes.

I owe a massive debt of gratitude to dear friends and colleagues who supported me in so many ways, from providing incredibly constructive criticism about my pages to offering kind and encouraging gestures. Thank you to Jeanne Miller, Paul Miller, Jamila Minnicks, Dawn Palmer, Gil Palmer, Dahleen Glanton, Gracie Lawson-Borders, Marcia Lythcott, Daniel Greene, Ruby Mendenhall, Verleane Williams, Susan Keaton, David Trice, Colette Mann, Alicia Stewart, Debra Trice, Janina Edwards, Christopher Thornton, Lee Whack, David Sylvester, and my family in Chicago and Memphis. I'm truly humbled by your generosity.

A huge thank you to my daughter, Hannah, who remains the great big light in my life. You are beautiful, inside and out, and so smart, so witty, so funny, and so, so charming. I love your stories.

Lastly, I dedicated this book to my mom because she's my confidante, my rock, my port in the storm. Her unwavering belief in me knows no boundaries or measure. If I said, "Mom, I'm building a rocket ship and traveling to the moon," she'd say, "Okay, be careful and call me when you get home."

Thank you, Mom. You are my lodestar. With you, I am always home.

ABOUT THE AUTHOR

Dawn Turner's memoir, *Three Girls from Bronzeville,* won the inaugural Pattis Family Foundation Chicago Book Award and a National Association of Black Journalists Book Award. Turner has held fellowships at Harvard University, the University of Chicago, and the Maynard Institute for Journalism Education. She lives in Chicago.